DARK CRIMES

DARK CRIMES

GREAT NOIR FICTION FROM THE '40s TO THE '90s

FIRST ANNUAL EDITION
EDITED WITH AN INTRODUCTION BY
ED GORMAN

Carroll & Graf Publishers, Inc.
New York

To the Gold Medal writers:
John D. MacDonald, Evan Hunter, Charles Williams, Harry Whittington, Peter Rabe, Gil Brewer, Donald Hamilton, Edward S. Aarons, Bernard Mara, Bruno Fischer, Robert Edmond Alter, Robert Colby, David Goodis, Wade Miller, John McPartland, William Campbell Gault, Vin Packer, Malcolm Braly, John Trinian, Richard S. Prather, Dan J. Marlowe, Stephen Marlowe, Marvin Albert, Lionel White, Day Keene, Richard Jessup, Fletcher Flora, Clifton Adams, Dan Cushman, William Ard, and Theodore Pratt.

Contents

Acknowledgments

For permission to reprint the stories and novels in this anthology, grateful acknowledgment is made to:

"While She Was Out" by Edward Bryant, copyright © 1988 by Edward Bryant. Originally published in *Pulphouse*. Reprinted by permission of the author.

"On the Sidewalk Bleeding" by Evan Hunter was originally published in *Happy New Year, Herbie and Other Stories,* copyright © 1957 by Evan Hunter. Copyright renewed 1985 by Evan Hunter. Reprinted by permission of the author.

"The Seventh Grave" by Vann Anson Lister, copyright © 1986 by TZ Publications, Inc. First appeared in *Night Cry,* Summer 1986, as "Seven Graves for Sinbad." Reprinted by permission of the author.

"Hot Eyes, Cold Eyes" by Lawrence Block, copyright © 1978 by Lawrence Block. Reprinted by permission of the author.

"Souls Burning" by Bill Pronzini, copyright © 1991 by Bill Pronzini. Reprinted by permission of the author.

"A Handgun for Protection" by John Lutz, copyright © 1974 by Renown Publications, Inc. Reprinted by permission of the author.

"The Crooked Way" by Loren D. Estleman, copyright © 1988 by Loren D. Estleman. Reprinted by permission of the author.

"Exit" by Andrew Vachss, copyright © 1989 by Andrew Vachss. Reprinted by permission of the author.

"Deathman" by Ed Gorman, copyright © 1991 by Ed Gorman.

Introduction to Gil Brewer by Bill Pronzini, copyright © 1989 by Bill Pronzini. Reprinted by permission of the author.

10 ACKNOWLEDGMENTS

The Red Scarf by Gil Brewer, copyright © 1958 by Gil Brewer. Reprinted by permission of the author and the author's agents, Scott Meredith Literary Agency, Inc., 845 Third Avenue, New York, New York 10022.

"But You'll Never Follow Me" by Karl Edward Wagner, copyright © 1990 by Karl Edward Wagner. Originally published in *Borderlands*. Reprinted by permission of the author.

"The Tunnel of Love" by Robert Bloch, copyright © 1948. Copyright renewed 1976 by Robert Bloch. Originally published as "Hell Is My Legacy" in *New Detective*. Reprinted by permission of the author.

"Tony" by William Relling, copyright © 1980 by Dugent Publishing, Inc. Copyright re-assigned to William Relling. Reprinted by permission of the author.

"By the Hair of the Head" by Joe R. Lansdale, copyright © 1983 by Joe R. Lansdale. Reprinted by permission of the author.

"Red Light" by Max Allan Collins, copyright © 1984 by Max Allan Collins. Reprinted by permission of the author.

"Taking the Night Train" by Thomas F. Monteleone, copyright © 1981 by Thomas F. Monteleone. Reprinted by permission of the author.

"Stoner" by William F. Nolan, copyright © 1988 by TZ Publications, Inc. Reprinted by permission of the author.

Introduction to Peter Rabe by Bill Crider, copyright © 1990 by Bill Crider. Reprinted by permission of the author.

Anatomy of a Killer by Peter Rabe, copyright © 1960 by Peter Rabe. Copyright renewed 1988 by Peter Rabe. Reprinted by permission of the author's agent, Max Gartenberg.

"Night-Walker" by Robert J. Randisi, copyright © 1978 by Robert J. Randisi. Reprinted by permission of the author.

"Dust to Dust" by Marcia Muller, copyright © 1982 by Marcia Muller. Reprinted by permission of the author.

"Faces" by F. Paul Wilson, copyright © 1988 by F. Paul Wilson. Originally published in *Night Visions VI, Dark Harvest*. Reprinted by permission of the author.

Introduction

With the Jim Thompson revival dazzling a good part of the crime fiction industry, I thought that now would be an appropriate time to collect some other noteworthy examples of the modern *noir* story.

Sure, Thompson was good, but he was hardly alone in what he attempted to do, and—my opinion only—I don't think he was even the best, despite the ludicrous claims made by some trendy critics.

Thompson came out of a specific historical period, the Depression, that also informed the work of such other worthy writers as Charles Williams, Cornell Woolrich, and David Goodis. Then there was that generation that came of age during World War II, Peter Rabe and Gil Brewer and John D. MacDonald among them. These men were certainly as good as Thompson. Following them were writers fashioned by the upheavals of the sixties and seventies and others just now coming of age in the nineties.

All these writers, and many others (including such wonderful women writers as Dorothy B. Hughes and Helen Neilsen) contributed to the development of *noir* as a spiritual influence on the modern crime story.

Similar work was being done in motion pictures, as well, with such diverse directors as Alfred Hitchcock, Nicholas Ray, Orson Welles, Ida Lupino, Anthony Mann, Rudolph Mate, and Edgar G. Ulmer enriching the genre even more.

European intellectuals, particularly the existentialists and especially the French, have long been interested in this particularly American expression. They find it helpful in explaining their own philosophy that even in despair there can be dignity, even in defeat there can be spiritual triumph. Flawed as the end may be (two good acts and a final, bad act!) Nicholas Ray's film *On*

Dangerous Ground is an especially moving example of what I'm talking about.

Dark Crimes is an attempt to show the scope of *noir,* from its origins in the Depression to its use by today's writers. Of special note are the two full-length novels, *The Red Scarf* by Gil Brewer and *Anatomy of a Killer* by Peter Rabe. Both men were shaped by World War II and found a different America on their return. Their disillusionment is evident in their novels.

I hope you find my selections both entertaining and instructive. You'll find a part of the modern world here, certainly a dark side, but also, I think, a thoughtful and vital side. The heroes of those old Gold Medal novels that both enlivened and sustained *noir* in the United States had their own style of wisdom and honor.

—Ed Gorman

While She Was Out

by Edward Bryant

Edward Bryant has won many awards in science fiction. In recent years, he's begun working successfully in the horror field as well. His story here set a new standard for the modern crime story. It is, without doubt, a real classic.

First published in 1988

It was what her husband said then that was the last straw.

"Christ," muttered Kenneth disgustedly from the family room. He grasped a Bud longneck in one red-knuckled hand, the cable remote tight in the other. This was the time of night when he generally fell into the largest number of stereotypes. "I swear to God you're on the rag three weeks out of every month. PMS, my ass."

Della Myers deliberately bit down on what she wanted to answer. P*X*MS, she thought. That's what the twins' teacher had called it last week over coffee after the parent-teacher conference Kenneth had skipped. Pre-holiday syndrome. It took a genuine effort not to pick up the cordless Northwestern Bell phone and brain Kenneth with one savage, cathartic swipe. "I'm going out."

"So?" said her husband. "This is Thursday. Can't be the auto mechanics made simple for wusses. Self defense?" He shook his head. "That's every other Tuesday. Something new, honey? Maybe a therapy group?"

"I'm going to Southeast Plaza. I need to pick up some things."

"Get the extra-absorbent ones," said her husband. He grinned and thumbed up the volume. ESPN was bringing in wide shots of something that looked vaguely like group tennis from some sweaty-looking third-world country.

"Wrapping paper," she said. "I'm getting some gift-wrap and ribbon." Were there fourth-world countries? she wondered. Would they accept political refugees from America? "Will you put the twins to bed by nine?"

"Stallone's on HBO at nine," Kenneth said. "I'll bag 'em out by half-past eight."

"Fine." She didn't argue.

"I'll give them a good bedtime story." He paused. "The Princess and the Pea."

"Fine." Della shrugged on her long down-filled coat. Any more, she did her best not to swallow the bait. "I told them they could each have a chocolate chip cookie with their milk."

"Christ, Della. Why the hell don't we just adopt the dentist? Maybe give him an automatic monthly debit from the checking account?"

"One cookie apiece," she said, implacable.

Kenneth shrugged, apparently resigned.

She picked up the keys to the Subaru. "I won't be long."

"Just be back by breakfast."

Della stared at him. What if I don't come back at all? She had actually said that once. Kenneth had smiled and asked whether she was going to run away with the gypsies, or maybe go off to join some pirates. It had been a temptation to say yes, dammit, yes, I'm going. But there were the twins. Della suspected pirates didn't take along their children. "Don't worry," she said. I've got nowhere else to go. But she didn't say that aloud.

Della turned and went upstairs to the twins' room to tell them good night. Naturally they both wanted to go with her to the mall. Each was afraid she wasn't going to get the hottest item in the Christmas doll department—the Little BeeDee Birth Defect Baby. There had been a run on the BeeDees, but Della had shopped for the twins early. "Daddy's going to tell you a story," she promised. The pair wasn't impressed.

"I want to see Santa," Terri said, with dogged, five-year-old insistence.

"You both saw Santa. Remember?"

"I forgot some things. An' I want to tell him again about BeeDee."

"Me, too," said Tammi. With Tammi, it was always "me too."

"Maybe this weekend," said Della.

"Will Daddy remember our cookies?" said Terri.

Before she exited the front door, Della took the chocolate chip cookies from the kitchen closet and set the sack on the stairstep where Kenneth could not fail to stumble over it.

"So long," she called.

"Bring me back something great from the mall," he said. His only other response was to heighten the crowd noise from Upper Zambo-somewhere-or-other.

Sleety snow was falling, the accumulation beginning to freeze on the streets. Della was glad she had the Subaru. So far this winter, she hadn't needed to use the four-wheel drive, but tonight the reality of having it reassured her.

Southeast Plaza was a mess. This close to Christmas, the normally spacious parking lots were jammed. Della took a chance and circled the row of spaces nearest to the mall entrances. If she were lucky, she'd be able to react instantly to someone's backup lights and snaffle a parking place within five seconds of its being vacated. That didn't happen. She cruised the second row, the third. Then—There! She reacted without thinking, seeing the vacant spot just beyond a metallic blue van. She swung the Subaru to the left.

And stamped down hard on the brake.

Some moron had parked an enormous barge of an ancient Plymouth so that it overlapped two diagonal spaces.

The Subaru slid to a stop with its nose about half an inch from the Plymouth's dinosaurian bumper. In the midst of her shock and sudden anger, Della saw the chrome was pocked with rust. The Subaru's headlights reflected back at her.

She said something unpleasant, the kind of language she usually only thought in dark silence. Then she backed her car out of the truncated space and resumed the search for parking. What Della eventually found was a free space on the extreme perimeter of the lot. She resigned herself to trudging a quarter mile through the slush. She hadn't worn boots. The icy water crept into her flats, soaked her toes.

"Shit," she said. "Shit shit shit."

Her shortest-distance-between-two-points course took her past the Plymouth hogging the two parking spots. Della stopped a moment, contemplating the darkened behemoth. It was a dirty gold with the remnants of a vinyl roof peeling away like the flaking of a scabrous scalp. In the glare of the mercury vapor lamp, she could see that the rocker panels were riddled with rust holes. Odd. So much corrosion didn't happen in the dry Colorado air. She glanced curiously at the rear license plate. It was obscured with dirty snow.

She stared at the huge old car and realized she was getting angry. Not just irritated. Real, honest-to-god, hardcore pissed off. What kind of imbeciles would take up two parking spaces on a rotten night just two weeks before Christmas?

Ones that drove a vintage, not-terribly-kept-up Plymouth, obviously.

Without even thinking about what she was doing, Della took out the spiral notebook from her handbag. She flipped to the blank page past tomorrow's grocery list and uncapped the fine-tip marker (it was supposed to write across anything—in this snow, it had *better*) and scrawled a message:

DEAR JERK, IT'S GREAT YOU COULD USE UP TWO PARKING SPACES ON A NIGHT LIKE THIS. EVER HEAR OF THE JOY OF SHARING?

She paused, considering; then appended:

—A CONCERNED FRIEND

Della folded the paper as many times as she could, to protect it from the wet, then slipped it under the driver's-side wiper blade.

It wouldn't do any good—she was sure this was the sort of driver who ordinarily would have parked illegally in the handicapped zone—but it made her feel better. Della walked on to the mall entrance and realized she was smiling.

She bought some rolls of foil wrapping paper for the adult gifts—assuming she actually gave Kenneth anything she'd bought for him—and an ample supply of Strawberry Shortcake pattern for the twins' presents. Della decided to splurge—she realized she was getting tired—and selected a package of pre-tied ribbon bows rather than simply taking a roll. She also bought a package of tampons.

Della wandered the mall for a little while, checking out the shoe stores, looking for something on sale in deep blue, a pair she could wear after Kenneth's office party for staff and spouses. What she *really* wanted were some new boots. Time enough for those after the holiday when the prices went down. Nothing appealed to her. Della knew she should be shopping for Kenneth's family in Nebraska. She couldn't wait forever to mail off their packages.

The hell with it. Della realized she was simply delaying returning home. Maybe she *did* need a therapy group, she thought. There was no relish to the thought of spending another night sleeping beside Kenneth, listening to the snoring that was interrupted only by the grinding of teeth. She thought that the sound of Kenneth's jaws moving against one another must be like hearing a speeded-up recording of continental drift.

She looked at her watch. A little after nine. No use waiting any longer. She did up the front of her coat and joined the flow of shoppers out into the snow.

Della realized, as she passed the rusted old Plymouth, that something wasn't the same. *What's wrong with this picture?* It was the note. It wasn't there. Probably it had slipped out from under the wiper blade with the wind and the water. Maybe the flimsy notebook paper had simply dissolved.

She no longer felt like writing another note. She dismissed the irritating lumber barge from her reality and walked on to her car.

Della let the Subaru warm up for thirty seconds (the consumer auto mechanics class had told her not to let the engine idle for the long minutes she had once believed necessary) and then slipped the shift into reverse.

The passenger compartment flooded with light.

She glanced into the rearview mirror and looked quickly away. A bright, glaring eye had stared back. Another quivered in the side mirror.

"Jesus Christ," she said under her breath. "The crazies are out tonight." She hit the clutch with one foot, the brake with the other, and waited for the car behind her to remove itself. Nothing happened. The headlights in the mirror flicked to bright. "Dammit." Della left the Subaru in neutral and got out of the car.

She shaded her eyes and squinted. The front of the car behind hers looked familiar. It was the gold Plymouth.

Two unseen car-doors clicked open and chunked shut again.

The lights abruptly went out and Della blinked, her eyes trying to adjust to the dim mercury vapor illumination from the pole a few car-lengths away.

She felt a cold thrill of unease in her belly and turned back toward the car.

"I've got a gun," said a voice. "Really." It sounded male and young. "I'll aim at your snatch first."

Someone else giggled, high and shrill.

Della froze in place. This couldn't be happening. It absolutely could not.

Her eyes were adjusting, the glare-phantoms drifting out to the limit of her peripheral vision and vanishing. She saw three figures in front of her, then a fourth. She didn't see a gun.

"Just what do you think you're doing?" she said.

"Not doing *nothin'*, yet." That, she saw, was the black one. He stood to the left of the white kid who had claimed to have a gun. The pair was bracketed by a boy who looked Chinese or Vietnamese and a young man with dark, Hispanic good looks. All four looked to be in their late teens or very early twenties. Four young men. Four ethnic groups represented. Della repressed a giggle she thought might be the first step toward hysteria.

"So what are you guys? Working on your merit badge in tolerance? Maybe selling magazine subscriptions?" Della immediately regretted saying that. Her husband was always riding her for smarting off.

"Funny lady," said the Hispanic. "We just happen to get along." He glanced to his left. "You laughing, Huey?"

The black shook his head. "Too cold. I'm shiverin' out here. I didn't bring no clothes for this."

"Easy way to fix that, man," said the white boy. To Della, he said, "Vinh, Tomas, Huey, me, we all got similar interests, you know?"

"Listen—" Della started to say.

"Chuckie," said the black Della now assumed was Huey, "Let's us just shag out of here, okay?"

"*Chuckie?*" said Della.

"Shut up!" said Chuckie. To Huey, he said, "Look, we came up here for a vacation, right? The word is fun." He said to Della, "Listen, we were having a good time until we saw you stick the note under the wiper." His eyes glistened in the vapor-lamp glow. "I don't like getting any static from some 'burb-bitch just 'cause she's on the rag."

"For God's sake," said Della disgustedly. She decided he didn't really have a gun. "Screw off!" The exhaust vapor from the Subaru spiraled up around her. "I'm leaving, boys."

"Any trouble here, Miss?" said a new voice. Everyone looked. It was one of the mall rent-a-cops, bulky in his fur trimmed jacket and Russian-styled cap. His hand lay casually across the unsnapped holster flap at his hip.

"Not if these underage creeps move their barge so I can back out," said Della.

"How about it, guys?" said the rent-a-cop.

Now there *was* a gun, a dark pistol, in Chuckie's hand, and he pointed it at the rent-a-cop's face. "Naw," Chuckie said. "This was gonna be a vacation, but what the heck. No witnesses, I reckon."

"For God's sake," said the rent-a-cop, starting to back away.

Chuckie grinned and glanced aside at his friends. "Remember the security guy at the mall in Tucson?" To Della, he said, "Most of these rent-a-pig companies don't give their guys any ammo. Liability laws and all that shit. Too bad." He lifted the gun purposefully.

The rent-a-cop went for his pistol anyway. Chuckie shot him in the face. Red pulp sprayed out the back of his skull and stained the slush as the man's body flopped back and forth, spasming.

"For chrissake," said Chuckie in exasperation. "Enough already. Relax, man." He leaned over his victim and deliberately aimed and fired, aimed and fired. The second shot entered the rent-a-cop's left eye. The third shattered his teeth.

Della's eyes recorded everything as though she were a movie camera. Everything was moving in slow motion and she was numb. She tried to make things speed up. Without thinking about the decision, she spun and made for her car door. She knew it was hopeless.

"Chuckie!"

"So? Where's she gonna go? We got her blocked. I'll just put one through her windshield and we can go out and pick up a couple of sixpacks, maybe hit the late show at some other mall."

Della heard him fire one more time. Nothing tore through the back of her skull. He was still blowing apart the rent-a-cop's head.

She slammed into the Subaru's driver seat and punched the door-lock switch, for all the good that would do. Della hit the four-wheel-drive switch. *That* was what Chuckie hadn't thought about. She jammed the gearshift into first, gunned the engine, and popped the clutch. The Subaru barely protested as the front tires clawed and bounced over the six-inch concrete row barrier. The barrier screeched along the underside of the frame. Then the rear wheels were over and the Subaru fishtailed momentarily.

Don't over-correct, she thought. It was a prayer.

The Subaru straightened out and Della was accelerating down the mall's outer perimeter service road, slush spraying to either side. Now what? she thought. People must have heard the shots. The lot would be crawling with cops.

But in the meantime—

The lights, bright and blinding, blasted against her mirrors. Della stamped the accelerator to the floor.

This was crazy! This didn't happen to people—not to *real* people. The mall security man's blood in the snow had been real enough.

In the rearview, there was a sudden flash just above the left-side headlight, then another. It was a muzzle-blast, Della realized. They were shooting at her. It was just like on TV. The scalp on the back of her head itched. Would she feel it when the bullet crashed through?

The twins! Kenneth. She wanted to see them all, to be safely with them. Just be anywhere but here!

Della spun the wheel, ignoring the stop sign and realizing that the access road dead-ended. She could go right or left, so went right. She thought it was the direction of home. Not a good choice. The lights were all behind her now; she could see nothing but darkness ahead. Della tried to remember what lay beyond the mall on this side. There were housing developments, both completed and under construction.

There had to be a 7-Eleven, a filling station, *something*. Anything. But there wasn't, and then the pavement ended. At first the road was suddenly rougher, the potholes yawning deeper. Then the slush-marked asphalt stopped. The Subaru bounced across the gravel; within thirty yards, the gravel deteriorated to roughly graded dirt. The dirt surface more properly could be called mud.

A wooden barrier loomed ahead, the reflective stripes and lightly falling snow glittering in the headlights.

It *was* like on TV, Della thought. She gunned the engine and ducked sideways, even with the dash, as the Subaru plowed into the barrier. She heard a sickening *crack* and shattered windshield glass sprayed down around her. Della felt the car veer. She tried to sit upright again, but the auto was spinning too fast.

The Subaru swung a final time and smacked firm against a low grove of young pine. The engine coughed and stalled. Della hit the light switch. She smelled the overwhelming tang of crushed pine needles flooding with the snow through the space where the windshield had been. The engine groaned when she twisted the key, didn't start.

Della risked a quick look around. The Plymouth's lights were visible, but the car was farther back than she had dared hope. The size of the lights wasn't increasing and the beams pointed up at a steep angle. Probably the heavy Plymouth had slid in the slush, gone off the road, was stuck for good.

She tried the key, and again the engine didn't catch. She heard something else—voices getting closer. Della took the key out of the ignition and glanced around the dark passenger compartment. Was there anything she could use? Anything at all? Not in the glovebox. She knew there was nothing there but the owner's manual and a large pack of sugarless spearmint gum.

The voices neared.

Della reached under the dash and tugged the trunk release. Then she rolled down the window and slipped out into the darkness. She wasn't too stunned to forget that the overhead light would go on if she opened the door.

At least one of the boys had a flashlight. The beam flickered and danced along the snow.

Della stumbled to the rear of the Subaru. By feel, she found the toolbox. With her other hand, she sought out the lug wrench. Then she moved away from the car.

She wished she had a gun. She wished she had learned to *use* a gun. That had been something tagged for a vague future when she'd finished her consumer mechanics course and the self defense workshop, and had some time again to take another night course. It wasn't, she had reminded herself, that she was paranoid. Della simply wanted to be better prepared for the exigencies of living in the city. The suburbs weren't *the city* to Kenneth, but if you were a girl from rural Montana, they were.

She hadn't expected *this*.

She hunched down. Her nose told her the shelter she had found was a hefty clump of sagebrush. She was perhaps twenty yards from the Subaru now. The boys were making no attempt at stealth. She heard them talking to each other as the flashlight beam bobbed around her stalled car.

"So, she in there chilled with her brains all over the wheel?" said Tomas, the Hispanic kid.

"You an optimist?" said Chuckie. He laughed, a high-pitched giggle. "No, she ain't here, you dumb shit. This one's a tough lady." Then he said, "Hey, lookie there!"

"What you doin'?" said Huey. "We ain't got time for that."

"Don't be too sure. Maybe we can use this."

What had he found? Della wondered.

"Now we do what?" said Vinh. He had a slight accent.

"This be the West," said Huey. "I guess now we're mountain men, just like in the movies."

"Right," said Chuckie. "Track her. There's mud. There's snow. How far can she get?"

"There's the trail," said Tomas. "Shine the light over there. She must be pretty close."

Della turned. Hugging the toolbox, trying not to let it clink or clatter, she fled into the night.

They cornered her a few minutes later.

Or it could have been an hour. There was no way she could read her watch. All Della knew was that she had run; she had run and she had attempted circling around to where she might have a shot at making it to the distant lights of the shopping mall. Along the way, she'd felt the brush clawing at her denim jeans and the mud and slush attempting to suck down her shoes. She tried to make out shapes in the clouded-over dark, evaluating every murky form as a potential hiding place.

"Hey, baby," said Huey from right in front of her.

Della recoiled, feinted to the side, collided painfully with a wooden fence. The boards gave only slightly. She felt a long splinter drive through the down coat and spear into her shoulder. When Della jerked away, she felt the splinter tear away from its board and then break off.

The flashlight snapped on, the beam at first blinding her, then lowering to focus on her upper body. From their voices, she knew all four were there. Della wanted to free a hand to pull the splinter loose from her shoulder. Instead she continued cradling the blue plastic toolbox.

"Hey," said Chuckie, "what's in that thing? Family treasure, maybe?"

Della remained mute. She'd already gotten into trouble enough, wising off.

"Let's see," said Chuckie. "Show us, Della-honey."

She stared at his invisible face.

Chuckie giggled. "Your driver's license, babe. In your purse. In the car."

Shit, she thought.

"Lousy picture." Chuckie. "I think maybe we're gonna make your face match it." Again, that ghastly laugh. "Meantime, let's see what's in the box, okay?"

"Jewels, you think?" said Vinh.

"Naw, I don't think," said his leader. "But maybe she was

makin' the bank deposit or something." He addressed Della, "You got enough goodies for us, maybe we can be bought off."

No chance, she thought. They want everything. My money, my rings, my watch. She tried to swallow, but her throat was too dry. My life.

"Open the box," said Chuckie, voice mean now.

"Open the box," said Tomas. Huey echoed him. The four started chanting, "Open the box, open the box, open the box."

"All right," she almost screamed. "I'll do it." They stopped their chorus. Someone snickered. Her hands moving slowly, Della's brain raced. Do it, she thought. But be careful. So careful. She let the lug wrench rest across her palm below the toolbox. With her other hand, she unsnapped the catch and slid up the lid toward the four. She didn't think any of them could see in, though the flashlight beam was focused now on the toolbox lid.

Della reached inside, as deliberately as she could, trying to betray nothing of what she hoped to do. It all depended upon what lay on top. Her bare fingertips touched the cold steel of the crescent wrench. Her fingers curled around the handle.

"This is pretty dull," said Tomas. "Let's just rape her."

Now!

She withdrew the wrench, cocked her wrist back and hurled the tool about two feet above the flashlight's glare. Della snapped it just like her daddy had taught her to throw a hardball. She hadn't liked baseball all that much. But now—

The wrench crunched something and Chuckie screamed. The flashlight dropped to the snow.

Snapping shut the toolbox, Della sprinted between Chuckie and the one she guessed was Huey.

The black kid lunged for her and slipped in the muck, toppling face-first into the slush. Della had a peripheral glimpse of Tomas leaping toward her, but his leading foot came down on the back of Huey's head, grinding the boy's face into the mud. Huey's scream bubbled; Tomas cursed and tumbled forward, trying to stop himself with out-thrust arms.

All Della could think as she gained the darkness was, I should have grabbed the light.

She heard the one she thought was Vinh, laughing. "Cripes, guys, neat. Just like Moe and Curley and that other one."

"Shut up," said Chuckie's voice. It sounded pinched and in pain. "Shut the fuck up." The timbre squeaked and broke. "Get up, you dorks. Get the bitch."

Sticks and stones—Della thought. Was she getting hysterical? There was no good reason not to.

As she ran—and stumbled—across the nightscape, Della could feel the long splinter moving with the movement of the muscles in her shoulder. The feeling of it, not just the pain, but the sheer, physical sensation of intrusion, nauseated her.

I've got to stop, she thought. I've got to rest. I've got to think.

Della stumbled down the side of a shallow gulch and found she was splashing across a shallow, frigid stream. Water. It triggered something. Disregarding the cold soaking her flats and numbing her feet, she turned and started upstream, attempting to splash as little as possible. This had worked, she seemed to recall, in *Uncle Tom's Cabin*, as well as a lot of bad prison escape movies.

The boys were hardly experienced mountain men. They weren't Indian trackers. This ought to take care of her trail.

After what she estimated to be at least a hundred yards, when her feet felt like blocks of wood and she felt she was losing her balance, Della clambered out of the stream and struggled up the side of the gulch. She found herself in groves of pine, much like the trees where her Subaru had ended its skid. At least the pungent evergreens supplied some shelter against the prairie wind that had started to rise.

She heard noise from down in the gulch. It was music. It made her think of the twins.

"What the *fuck* are you doing?" Chuckie's voice.

"It's a tribute, man. A gesture." Vinh. "It's his blaster."

Della recognized the tape. Rap music. Run DMC, the Beastie Boys, one of those groups.

"Christ, I didn't mean it." Tomas. "It's her fault."

"Well, he's dead," said Chuckie, "and that's it for him. Now turn that shit off. Somebody might hear."

"Who's going to hear?" said Vinh. "Nobody can hear out here. Just us, and her."

"That's the point. She can."

"So what?" said Tomas. "We got the gun, we got the light. She's got nothin' but that stupid box."

"We *had* Huey," said Chuckie. "Now we don't. Shut off the blaster, dammit."

"Okay." Vinh's voice sounded sullen. There was a loud click and the rap echo died.

Della huddled against the rough bark of a pine trunk, hugging the box and herself. The boy's dead, she thought. So? said her common sense. He would have killed you, maybe raped you, tortured you before pulling the trigger. The rest are going to have to die too.

No.

Yes, said her practical side. You have no choice. They started this.

I put the note under the wiper blade.

Get serious. That was harmless. These three are going to kill you. They will hurt you first, then they'll put the gun inside your mouth and—

Della wanted to cry, to scream. She knew she could not. It was absolutely necessary that she not break now.

Terri, she thought, Tammi. I love you. After a while, she remembered Kenneth. Even you. I love you too. Not much, but some.

"Let's look up above," came the voice from the gully. Chuckie. Della heard the wet scrabbling sounds as the trio scratched and pulled their way up from the stream-bed. As it caught the falling snow, the flashlight looked like the beam from a searchlight at a movie premiere.

Della edged back behind the pine and slowly moved to where the trees were closer together. Boughs laced together, screening her.

"Now what?" said Tomas.

"We split up." Chuckie gestured; the flashlight beam swung wide. "You go through the middle. Vinh and me'll take the sides."

"Then why don't you give me the light?" said Tomas.

"I stole the sucker. It's mine."

"Shit, I could just walk past her."

Chuckie laughed. "Get real, dude. You'll smell her, hear her, somethin'. Trust me."

Tomas said something Della couldn't make out, but the tone was unconvinced.

"Now *do* it," said Chuckie. The light moved off to Della's left. She heard the squelching of wet shoes moving toward her. Evidently Tomas had done some wading in the gully. Either that or the slush was taking its toll.

Tomas couldn't have done better with radar. He came straight for her.

Della guessed the boy was ten feet away from her, five feet, just the other side of the pine. The lug wrench was the spider type, in the shape of a cross. She clutched the black steel of the longest arm and brought her hand back. When she detected movement around the edge of the trunk, she swung with hysterical strength, aiming at his head.

Tomas staggered back. The sharp arm of the lug wrench had caught him under the nose, driving the cartilage back up into his face. About a third of the steel was hidden in flesh. "Unh!" He tried to cry out, but all he could utter was, "Unh, unh!"

"Tomas?" Chuckie was yelling. "What the hell are you doing?"

The flashlight flickered across the grove. Della caught a momentary glimpse of Tomas lurching backward with the lug wrench impaled in his face as though he were wearing some hideous Halloween accessory.

"Unh!" said Tomas once more. He backed into a tree, then slid down the trunk until he was seated in the snow. The flashlight beam jerked across that part of the grove again and Della saw Tomas' eyes stare wide open, dark and blank. Blood was running off the ends of the perpendicular lug wrench arms.

"I see her!" someone yelled. "I think she got Tomas. She's a devil!" Vinh.

"So chill her!"

Della heard branches and brush crashing off to her side. She jerked open the plastic toolbox, but her fingers were frozen and the container crashed to the ground. She tried to catch the contents as they cascaded into the slush and the darkness. Her fingers closed on something, one thing.

The handle felt good. It was the wooden-hafted screwdriver, the sharp one with the slot head. Her auto mechanics teacher had approved. Insulated handle, he'd said. Good forged steel shaft. You could use this hummer to pry a tire off its rim.

She didn't even have time to lift it as Vinh crashed into her. His arms and legs wound around her like eels.

"Got her!" he screamed. "Chuckie, come here and shoot her."

They rolled in the viscid, muddy slush. Della worked an arm free. Her good arm. The one with the screwdriver.

There was no question of asking him nicely to let go, of giving warning, of simply aiming to disable. Her self defense teacher had drilled into all the students the basic dictum of do what you can, do what you have to do. No rules, no apologies.

With all her strength, Della drove the screwdriver up into the base of his skull. She thrust and twisted the tool until she felt her knuckles dig into his stiff hair. Vinh screamed, a high keening wail that cracked and shattered as blood spurted out of his nose and mouth, splattering against Della's neck. The Vietnamese boy's arms and legs tensed and then let go as his body vibrated spastically in some sort of fit.

Della pushed him away from her and staggered to her feet. Her nose was full of the odor she remembered from the twins' diaper pail.

She knew she should retrieve the screwdriver, grasp the handle tightly and twist it loose from Vinh's head. She couldn't. All she could do at this point was simply turn and run. Run again. And hope the survivor of the four boys didn't catch her.

But Chuckie had the light, and Chuckie had the gun. She had a feeling Chuckie was in no mood to give up. Chuckie would find her. He would make her pay for the loss of his friends.

But if she had to pay, Della thought, the price would be dear.

Prices, she soon discovered, were subject to change without warning.

With only one remaining pursuer, Della thought she ought to be able to get away. Maybe not easily, but now there was no crossfire of spying eyes, no ganging-up of assailants. There was just one boy left, even if he *was* a psychopath carrying a loaded pistol.

Della was shaking. It was fatigue, she realized. The endless epinephrine rush of flight and fight. Probably, too, the letdown from just having killed two other human beings. She didn't want to have to think about the momentary sight of blood flowing off the shining ends of the lug wrench, the sensation of how it *felt* when the slot-headed screwdriver drove up into Vinh's brain. But she couldn't order herself to forget these things. It was akin to someone telling her not, under any circumstances, to think about milking a purple cow.

Della tried. No, she thought. Don't think about it at all. She thought about dismembering the purple cow with a chainsaw. Then she heard Chuckie's voice. The boy was still distant, obviously casting around virtually at random in the pine groves. Della stiffened.

"They're cute, Della-honey. I'll give 'em that." He giggled. "Terri and Tammi. God, didn't you and your husband have any more imagination than that?"

No, Della thought. We each had too much imagination. Tammi and Terri were simply the names we finally could agree on. The names of compromise.

"You know something?" Chuckie raised his voice. "Now that I

know where they live, I could drive over there in a while and say howdy. They wouldn't know a thing about what was going on, about what happened to their mom while she was out at the mall."

Oh God! thought Della.

"You want me to pass on any messages?"

"You little bastard!" She cried it out without thinking.

"Touchy, huh?" Chuckie slopped across the wet snow in her direction. "Come on out of the trees, Della-honey."

Della said nothing. She crouched behind a deadfall of brush and dead limbs. She was perfectly still.

Chuckie stood equally still, not more than twenty feet away. He stared directly at her hiding place, as though he could see through the night and brush. "Listen," he said. "This is getting real, you know, *boring.*" He waited. "We could be out here all night, you know? All my buddies are gone now, and it's thanks to you, lady. Who the hell you think you are, Clint Eastwood?"

Della assumed that was a rhetorical question.

Chuckie hawked deep in his throat and spat on the ground. He rubbed the base of his throat gingerly with a free hand. "You hurt me, Della-honey. I think you busted my collarbone." He giggled. "But I don't hold grudges. In fact—" He paused contempla-tively. "Listen now, I've got an idea. You know about droogs? You know, like in that movie?"

Clockwork Orange, she thought. Della didn't respond.

"Ending was stupid, but the start was pretty cool." Chuckie's personality seemed to have mutated into a manic stage. "Well, me droogs is all gone. I need a new gang, and you're real good, Della-honey. I want you should join me."

"Give me a break," said Della in the darkness.

"No, really," Chuckie said. "You're a born killer. I can tell. You and me, we'd be perfect. We'll blow this popsicle stand and have some real fun. Whaddaya say?"

He's serious, she thought. There was a ring of complete hon-esty in his voice. She floundered for some answer. "I've got kids," she said.

"We'll take 'em along," said Chuckie. "I like kids, always took care of my brothers and sisters." He paused. "Listen, I'll bet you're on the outs with your old man."

Della said nothing. It would be like running away to be a pirate. Wouldn't it?

Chuckie hawked and spat again. "Yeah, I figured. When we

pick up your kids, we can waste him. You like that? I can do it, or
you can. Your choice."

You're crazy, she thought. *"I want to,"* she found herself saying aloud.

"So come out and we'll talk about it."

"You'll kill me."

"Hey," he said, "I'll kill you if you *don't* come out. I got the
light and the gun, remember? This way we can learn to trust each
other right from the start. I won't kill you. I won't do nothing.
Just talk."

"Okay." Why not, she thought. Sooner or later, he'll find his
way in here and put the gun in my mouth and—Della stood up.—
but maybe, just maybe—Agony lanced through her knees.

Chuckie cocked his head, staring her way. "Leave the tools."

"I already did. The ones I didn't use."

"Yeah," said Chuckie. "The ones you used, you used real
good." He lowered the beam of the flashlight. "Here you go. I
don't want you stumbling and falling and maybe breaking your
neck."

Della stepped around the deadfall and slowly walked toward
him. His hands were at his sides. She couldn't see if he was
holding the gun. She stopped when she was a few feet away.

"Hell of a night, huh?" said Chuckie. "It'll be really good to go
inside where it's warm and get some coffee." He held the flashlight so that the beam speared into the sky between them.

Della could make out his thin, pain-pinched features. She
imagined he could see hers. "I was only going out to the mall for
a few things," she said.

Chuckie laughed. "Shit happens."

"What now?" Della said.

"Time for the horror show." His teeth showed ferally as his
lips drew back in a smile. "Guess maybe I sort of fibbed." He
brought up his hand, glinting of metal.

"That's what I thought," she said, feeling a cold and distant
sense of loss. "Huey, there, going to help?" She nodded to a
point past his shoulder.

"Huey?" Chuckie looked puzzled just for a second as he
glanced to the side. "Huey's—"

Della leapt with all the spring left in her legs. Her fingers
closed around his wrist and the hand with the gun. "Christ!"
Chuckie screamed, as her shoulder crashed against the spongy
place where his broken collarbone pushed out against the skin.

They tumbled on the December ground, Chuckie underneath,

Della wrapping her legs around him as though pulling a lover tight. She burrowed her chin into the area of his collarbone and he screamed again. Kenneth had always joked about the sharpness of her chin.

The gun went off. The flash was blinding, the report hurt her ears. Wet snow plumped down from the overhanging pine branches, a large chunk plopping into Chuckie's wide-open mouth. He started to choke.

Then the pistol was in Della's hands. She pulled back from him, getting to her feet, back-pedaling furiously to get out of his reach. She stared down at him along the blued-steel barrel. The pirate captain struggled to his knees.

"Back to the original deal," he said. "Okay?"

I wish, she almost said. Della pulled the trigger. Again. And again.

"Where the hell have you been?" said Kenneth as she closed the front door behind her. "You've been gone for close to three hours." He inspected her more closely. "Della, honey, are you all right?"

"Don't call me that," she said. "Please." She had hoped she would look better, more normal. Unruffled. Once Della had pulled the Subaru up to the drive beside the house, she had spent several minutes using spit and Kleenex trying to fix her mascara. Such makeup as she'd had along was in her handbag, and she had no idea where that was. Probably the police had it; three cruisers with lights flashing had passed her, going the other way, as she was driving north of Southeast Plaza.

"Your clothes." Kenneth gestured. He stood where he was.

Della looked down at herself. She'd tried to wash off the mud, using snow and a rag from the trunk. There was blood too, some of it Chuckie's, the rest doubtless from Vinh and Tomas.

"Honey, was there an accident?"

She had looked at the driver's side of the Subaru for a long minute after getting home. At least the car drove; it must just have been flooded before. But the insurance company wouldn't be happy. The entire side would need a new paint job.

"Sort of," she said.

"Are you hurt?"

To top it all off, she had felt the slow stickiness between her legs as she'd come up the walk. Terrific. She could hardly wait for the cramps to intensify.

"Hurt?" She shook her head. No. "How are the twins?"

"Oh, they're in bed. I checked a half hour ago. They're asleep."

"Good." Della heard sirens in the distance, getting louder, nearing the neighborhood. Probably the police had found her driver's license in Chuckie's pocket. She'd forgotten that.

"So," said Kenneth. It was obvious to Della that he didn't know at this point whether to be angry, solicitous or funny. "What'd you bring me from the mall?"

Della's right hand was nestled in her jacket pocket. She felt the solid bulk, the cool grip of the pistol.

Outside, the volume of sirens increased.

She touched the trigger. She withdrew her hand from the pocket and aimed the pistol at Kenneth. He looked back at her strangely.

The sirens went past. Through the window, Della caught a glimpse of a speeding ambulance. The sound Dopplered down to a silence as distant as the dream that flashed through her head.

Della pulled the trigger and the *click* seemed to echo through the entire house.

Shocked, Kenneth stared at the barrel of the gun, then up at her eyes.

It was okay. She'd counted the shots. Just like in the movies.

"I think," Della said to her husband, "that we need to talk."

On the Sidewalk Bleeding

by Evan Hunter

Evan Hunter is one of my favorite writers, and "On the Sidewalk Bleeding" is one of his best short stories. As Ed McBain, of course, Evan Hunter is one of the most influential and best-selling crime writers in the world. And he keeps on getting better; each 87th Precinct novel is richer, deeper, truer than the last. His novel, **He Who Hesitates,** *should be required reading for anybody who ever tries to write fiction.*

First published in 1957

The boy lay bleeding in the rain. He was sixteen years old, and he wore a bright-purple silk jacket, and the lettering across the back of the jacket read *The Royals*. The boy's name was Tony, and the name was delicately scripted in black thread on the front of the jacket, just over his heart.

He had been stabbed ten minutes ago. The knife had entered just below his rib cage and been drawn across his body violently, tearing a wide gap in his flesh. He lay on the sidewalk, with the March rain drilling his jacket and drilling his body and washing away the blood which poured from his open wound. He had known excruciating pain when the knife had torn across his body, and then sudden, comparative relief when the blade was pulled away. He had heard the voice saying, "That's for you, Royal!" and then the sound of footsteps hurrying into the rain, and then he had fallen to the sidewalk, clutching his stomach, trying to stop the flow of blood.

He tried to yell for help, but he had no voice. He did not know why his voice had deserted him, or why the rain had become so suddenly fierce, or why there was an open hole in his body from which his life ran redly, steadily. It was 11:30 P.M., but he did not know the time. There was another thing he did not know.

He did not know that he was dying. He did not know that unless a doctor stopped the flow of blood, he would be dead within a half hour. He lay on the sidewalk bleeding, and he thought only: *That was a fierce rumble. They got me good that time,* but he did not know he was dying. He would have been frightened had he known. But in his ignorance, he lay bleeding. He wished he could yell for help, but there was no voice in his throat. There was only the bubbling of blood from between his lips whenever he opened his mouth to speak. He lay silent in his pain, waiting, waiting for someone to find him.

By midnight, if they did not stop the flow of blood, he would be dead.

He could hear the sound of automobile tires hushed on the muzzle of rain-swept streets, far away at the other end of the long alley. He lay with his face pressed to the sidewalk, and he could see the splash of neon far away at the other end of the alley, tinting the pavement red and green, slickly brilliant in the rain.

He wondered if Laura would be angry.

He had left the jump to get a package of cigarettes. He had told her he would be back in a few minutes, and then he had gone downstairs and found the candy store closed. He knew that Alfredo's on the next block would be open until at least two, and he had started through the alley, and that was when he'd been ambushed. He could hear the faint sound of music now, coming from what seemed a long, long way off, and he wondered if Laura was dancing, wondered if she had missed him yet. Maybe she thought he wasn't coming back. Maybe she thought he'd cut out for good. Maybe she'd leave the jump and go home. He thought of her face, the brown eyes and the jet-black hair, and thinking of her he forgot his pain a little, forgot that blood was rushing from his body. Someday he would marry Laura. Someday he would marry her, and they would have a lot of kids, and then they would get out of the neighborhood. They would move to a clean project in the Bronx, or maybe they would move to Staten Island. When they were married. When they had kids. Someday.

It was 11:35.

He heard footsteps at the other end of the alley, and he lifted his cheek from the sidewalk and looked into the darkness, and tried to yell, but again there was only a soft hissing bubble of blood on his mouth. The man came down the alley. He had not seen Tony yet. He walked, and then stopped to lean against the brick of the building, and then walked again. He saw Tony and came toward him, and he stood over him for a long time, the minutes ticking, ticking, watching him and not speaking.

Then he said, "Whussa matter, buddy-buddy?"

Tony could not speak, and Tony could not move. He lifted his face slightly and looked up at the man, and in the rain-swept alley he smelled the sickening odor of alcohol, and then he realized the man was drunk. He did not feel any particular panic. He did not know he was dying, and so he felt only mild disappointment that the man who had found him was sauced up.

The man was smiling.

"You fall down, buddy-buddy?" he said. You 'sdrunk ezz I am, buddy-buddy? I feel sick. I really feel sick. Don' go 'way. I'll be ri' back."

The man lurched away from Tony. He heard his footsteps, and then the sound of the man colliding with a garbage can, and some mild swearing, and then all was lost in the steady wash of the rain. He waited for the man to come back.

It was 11:39.

When the man returned, he squatted alongside Tony. He studied him with drunken dignity.

"You gonna cash cold here," he said. "Whussa matter? You like layin' in the wet?"

Tony could not answer. The man tried to focus his eyes on Tony's face. The rain spattered around them.

"You like a drink?"

Tony shook his head.

"You had enough, huh?"

Again Tony shook his head.

"I gotta bottle. Here," the man said. He pulled a pint bottle from his inside jacket pocket. He uncorked it and extended it to Tony. Tony tried to move, but pain wrenched him back flat against the sidewalk.

"Take it," the man said. He kept watching Tony. "Take it." When Tony did not move, he said, "Whussa matter? You too good to drink wi' me?" He kept watching him with the flat, blank eyes of a reptile. "Nev' mind," he said at last. "I'll have one m'self." He tilted the bottle to his lips, and then wiped the back of his hand across his mouth. "You too young to be drinkin', anyway. Should be 'shamed of yourself, drunk an' layin' down in a alley, all wet. Shame. Shame on you. I gotta good minda calla cop."

Tony nodded. *Yes, yes,* he tried to say. *Call a cop. Go. Call one.*

"Oh, you don' like that, huh?" the drunk said. "You don' wanna cop to fine you all drunk an' wet in a alley, huh? Okay, buddy-buddy. This time you get off easy. I'm a good Joe, tha's why." He got to his feet. "This time you lucky," he said. He waved broadly at Tony, and then almost lost his footing. "S'long, buddy-buddy," he said.

Wait, Tony thought. *Wait, please, I'm bleeding.*

"S'long," the drunk said again. "I see you aroun'," and then he staggered off up the alley, and Tony watched him go, watched the figure retreat until it passed into the world of red and green neon and automobile tires hushed on the rain-swept muzzle of the street at the end of the long alley far away.

It was 11:41.

He lay and thought, *Laura, Laura. Are you dancing?*

The couple came into the alley at 11:43. They ran into the alley together, running from the rain, the boy holding the girl's elbow, the girl spreading a newspaper over her head to protect her hair. Tony lay crumpled against the pavement, and he watched them run into the alley laughing, and then duck into the doorway not ten feet from him.

"Man, what rain!" the boy said. "You could drown out there."

"I have to get home," the girl said. "It's late, Mario. I have to get home."

"We got time," Mario said. "Your people won't raise a fuss if you're a little late. Not with this kind of weather."

"It's dark," the girl said, and she giggled.

"Yeah," the boy answered, his voice very low.

"Mario . . . ?"

"Um?"

"You're . . . you're standing very close to me."

"Um."

There was a long silence. Then the girl said, "Ohhhhh." Only that single word, and Tony knew she'd been kissed, and he suddenly hungered for Laura's mouth, hungered for it with a fierce, painfully sweet nostalgia. It was then that he wondered if he would ever kiss Laura again. It was then that he wondered if he was dying.

No, he thought, *I can't be dying, not from a little street rumble, not from just getting cut. Guys get cut all the time. All the time in rumbles. I can't be dying. No, that's stupid. That don't make any sense at all.*

"You shouldn't," the girl said.

"Why not?"

"I don't know."

"Do you like it?"

"Yes."

"So?"

"I don't know."

"I love you, Angela," the boy said.

"I love you, too, Mario," the girl said, and Tony listened and thought, *I love you, Laura. Laura, I think maybe I'm dying. Laura, this is stupid but I think maybe I'm dying. Laura, I think I'm dying!*

He tried to speak. He tried to move. He tried to crawl toward that doorway where he could see the two figures in embrace. He tried to make a noise, a sound, and a grunt came from his lips, and then he tried again, and another grunt escaped his body, a low, animal grunt of pain.

"What was that?" the girl said, suddenly alarmed, breaking away from the boy.

"I don't know," he answered.

"Go look, Mario."

"No. Wait."

Tony moved his lips again. Again the sound came from him.

"Mario!"

"What?"

"I'm scared."

"I'll go see," the boy said.

He stepped into the alley. He walked over to where Tony lay on the ground. He stood over him, watching him.

"You all right?" he asked.

"What is it?" Angela said from the doorway.

"Somebody's hurt," Mario said.

"Let's get out of here," Angela said.

"No. Wait a minute." He knelt down beside Tony. "You cut?" he asked.

Tony nodded. The boy kept looking at him. He saw the lettering on his jacket then. *The Royals.* He turned to Angela.

"He's a Royal," he said.

"Let's . . . what . . . what do you want to do, Mario?"

"I don't know. I don't want to get mixed up in this. He's a Royal. We help him, and the Guardians'll be down on our necks. I don't want to get mixed up in this, Angela."

"Is he . . . is he hurt bad?"

"Yeah, it looks that way."

"What shall we do?"

"I don't know."

"We can't leave him here in the rain." Angela hesitated. "Can we?"

"If we get a cop, the Guardians'll find out who," Mario said. "I don't know, Angela. I don't know."

Angela hesitated a long time before answering. Then she said, "I have to get home, Mario. My people will begin to worry."

"Yeah, Mario said. He looked at Tony again. "You all right?" he asked. Tony lifted his face from the sidewalk, and his eyes said, *Please, please help me,* and maybe Mario read what his eyes were saying, and maybe he didn't.

Behind him, Angela said, "Mario, let's get out of here! Please!" There was urgency in her voice, urgency bordering on the edge of panic. Mario stood up. He looked at Tony again, and then mumbled, "I'm sorry," and then he took Angela's arm and together they ran toward the neon splash at the other end of the alley.

They're afraid of the Guardians, Tony thought. *Why should they be? I wasn't afraid of the Guardians. I never turkeyed out of a rumble with the Guardians, I got heart. But I'm bleeding.*

It was 11:49. It was eleven minutes to midnight.

The rain was soothing, somehow. It was a cold rain, but his body was hot all over, and the rain helped to cool him. He had always liked rain. He could remember sitting in Laura's house one time, with the rain running down the windows, and just looking out over the street, watching the people running from the rain. That was when he'd first joined the Royals. He could remember how happy he was the Royals had taken him. The Royals and the Guardians, two of the biggest. He was a Royal. There had been meaning to the title.

Now, in the alley, with the cold rain washing his hot body, he wondered about the meaning. If he died, he was Tony. He was not a Royal. He was simply Tony, and he was dead. And he wondered suddenly if the Guardians who had ambushed him and knifed him had ever once realized he was Tony? Had they known that he was Tony, or had they simply known that he was a Royal wearing a purple silk jacket? Had they stabbed *him,* Tony, or had they only stabbed the jacket and the title, and what good was the title if you were dying?

I'm Tony, he screamed wordlessly. *For Christ's sake, I'm Tony!*

At 11:51, the old lady stopped at the other end of the alley. The garbage cans were stacked there, beating noisily in the rain. The old lady carried an umbrella with broken ribs, carried it with all the dignity of a queen. She stepped into the mouth of the alley, a shopping bag over one arm. She lifted the lids of the garbage cans delicately, and she did not hear Tony grunt because she was a little deaf and because the rain was beating a steady relentless tattoo on the garbage cans. The old lady was a little deaf and a little tired. She had been searching in garbage cans for the better part of the night. She collected her string, and her newspapers, and an old hat with a feather on it from one of the garbage cans, and a broken footstool from another of the cans. And then she delicately replaced the lids, and lifted her umbrella high and walked out of the alley mouth with queenly dignity. She had worked swiftly and soundlessly. When she left the alley, it was only 11:53, only seven minutes from midnight.

The alley looked very long now. He could see people passing at the other end of it, and he wondered who the people were, and he wondered if he would ever get to know them, wondered who it was on the Guardians who had stabbed him, who had plunged the knife into his body."

"That's for you, Royal!" the voice had said, and then the footsteps, his arms being released by the others, the fall to the pavement. "That's for you, Royal!" Even in his pain, even as he collapsed, there had been some sort of pride to knowing he was a Royal. Now there was no pride at all. Now, with the rain beginning to chill him, with the blood pouring steadily between his fingers, he knew only a sort of dizziness, and within the giddy dizziness, he could only think, *I want to be Tony.*

It was not very much to ask of the world. He watched the world passing at the other end of the alley. He lay unnoticed, and the world passed him by. The world didn't know he was Tony. The world didn't know he was alive. He wanted to say, "Hey, I'm alive! Hey, look at me! I'm alive! Don't you know I'm alive? Don't you know I exist?"

He felt very weak and very tired. He felt alone and wet and feverish and chilled, and he knew he was going to die, and the knowledge made him suddenly sad. He was not frightened. For some reason he was not frightened. He was only filled with an overwhelming sadness that his life would be over at sixteen. He felt all at once as if he had never done anything, never seen anything, never been anywhere. There were so many things to do, and he wondered why he'd never thought of them before, wondered why the rumbles and the jumps and the purple jacket had always seemed so important to him before, and now they seemed like such small things in a world he was missing, in a world that was rushing past at the other end of the alley.

I don't want to die, he thought. *I haven't lived yet, so why should I die?*

It seemed very important to him that he take off the purple jacket. He was very close to dying, and when they found him, he did not want them to say, "Oh, it's a Royal." With great effort he rolled over onto his back. He felt the pain tearing at his stomach when he moved, a pain he did not think was possible. But he wanted to take off the jacket. If he never did another thing, he wanted to take off the jacket. The jacket had only one meaning now, and that was a very simple meaning.

If he had not been wearing the jacket, he would not have been stabbed. The knife had not been plunged in hatred of Tony, the knife had hated only the purple jacket. The jacket was a stupid meaningless thing that was robbing him of his life. He wanted the jacket off his back. With an enormous loathing he wanted the jacket off his back.

He lay struggling with the sleek, shiny material. His arms were heavy, and pain ripped fire across his body whenever he moved. But he squirmed and fought and twisted until one arm was free and then the other, and then he rolled away from the jacket and lay quite still, breathing heavily, listening to the sound of his breathing and the sound of the rain and thinking, *Rain is sweet, I'm Tony.*

She arrived with the policeman at 12:05.

She had found him in the alleyway at 12:01, a minute past midnight. She had left the dance to look for him, and when she found him she knelt beside him and said, "Tony, it's me, Laura."

He had not answered her. She had backed away from him, tears springing into her eyes, and then she had run from the alley hysterically, and she had not stopped running until she'd found the cop.

And now, standing with the cop, she looked down at him, and the cop rose and said, "He's dead," and all the crying was out of her now. She stood in the rain and said nothing, looking at the dead boy on the pavement, and looking at the purple jacket that rested a foot away from his body.

The cop picked up the jacket and turned it over in his hands.

"A Royal, huh?" he said.

The rain seemed to beat more steadily now, more fiercely.

She looked at the cop, and very quietly she said, *"His name is Tony."*

The cop slung the jacket over his arm. He took out his black pad, and he flipped it open to a blank page.

"A Royal," he said. Then he began writing.

The Seventh Grave

by Vann Anson Lister

Vann Anson Lister is a name on this story. I know nothing about him other than he lives in the Midwest and is exceedingly polite on the phone. I read this two or three times a year. It never quite leaves me.

First published in 1986

The old-timey wino on the North Avenue Bridge seems to know where he is going. His shoulder bag swings against his baggy corduroys in well-rehearsed rhythm. Beneath the wide-lapel jacket he wears at least six shirts, even though it is not cold.

Looking over the railing at the east end of the bridge, he shakes his head and crosses the street to look over the opposite rail. *Odd,* he thinks. *No trails.*

He eases his frail-looking body around the end of the rail into the thick bushes, and hugging the concrete of the bridge, he pushes his way down the slope to the river.

Since the city of Milwaukee consumes more beer per capita than any city in the U.S., the old wino is very alone. The Milwaukee Road Railway runs along the west bank of the river, so the bridge is high and wide and long, to allow the trains to come and go beneath the bridge, along the river. It is a perfect wino bridge, but this is Beer City, U.S.A., and winos rarely trespass here. Beer drinkers prefer bars or parking lots or alleys or beaches. They never sit under bridges. Bridges are the sole province of the winos of the world.

There is a silent beauty and an art to sitting under bridges that only winos know. The traffic noises and shouting of cabbies and children are muted by the dense foliage and trees along the riverbank. The sounds drift down from another world. Sunlight reflects off the river to dance on the dark belly of the bridge. Between the arched concrete pilings is a bald spot of hard-packed dirt where nothing ever grows, the sun never shines. Here the wino builds a small fire in an ancient circle of stones in the center of the clearing that must surely have been used in bygone days to chart the rising of the moon.

An old coffee can of river water boils gently in the circle of stones. Filleted chunks of catfish churn slowly around in a stew of roots and greens. The fishing line, tied to a crooked limb, still dangles in the water. While the stew cooks, the wino wanders out into the thicket to piss. There are no trails.

Not even adventurous children play here, he realizes. He is thinking he could camp here for weeks, undetected, when he sees a brake-man across the river waving to him, friendly. He watches him walk the train, stooping between boxcars to couple air hoses, climbing steel rungs to release brakes. The brakeman hasn't seen a wino here in Beer City for months. When he clocks out at the yard office he will be inspired to purchase a couple of bottles of wine, for old time's sake.

The wino's name is Sinbad, and he has sailed the seven seas as a merchant seaman. He has a steel plate in his skull where the doctors once peeked into his brain and cut out a black demon that lurked there. He wears a beret to cover the patch of odd-colored skin where no hair will ever grow. The beret is black, to remind him of the demon.

There is a grave where Sinbad is pissing in the bushes. He shakes the last drops away and fumbles with his zipper as he leans through the dense foliage for a closer look. There is a rotting wooden cross with the name Rangoon carved on it, lying fallen on the ground. The grave has been desecrated by some ma-rauding mongrel. The bones of a cat are scattered around a shallow indentation in the soft loam of the forest floor.

Sinbad *reads* the grave. The steel plate in his skull prickles. It is the steel plate, he claims, that gave him this gift; he can know about things just by touching them. He places the scattered bones back in the hole, covers them, and rights the marker, shoving the point deep into the black loam while he *talks* to the ghost of Rangoon, as dappled sunlight plays on the foliage.

Rangoon was a wino; his masters were fond of wine, and often let him drink from their glasses. It is quite appropriate that they buried him here, in wino paradise. They were a young couple, very much in love. They wanted a child, but the girl had problems, ovarian tumors, the doctors said. So Rangoon became a child to them, an only child; a big blue-eyed lynx-point Siamese, terribly intelligent, as near true sentience as only certain Egyptian cats, or a few very old parrots and perhaps porpoises, can be. And terribly pampered . . . until the joyful day the girl announced her proud pregnancy; her impossible, miraculous pregnancy. And Rangoon was no longer pampered. He was all but ignored in the couple's parental bliss. He grew weak and sick and went away and died of loneliness while the couple practiced their Lamaze, Leboyer, and La Leche for natural childbirth. There was no longer room in their lives for a sentient cat. But they wept when a neighbor told them where to find the body, and they carried him in a cardboard box across the North Avenue Bridge from their apartment to bury him on the riverbank. They shared a little bottle of wine under the bridge; a toast to the dead, and to the new life in her belly.

The child was stillborn, and Sinbad finds *that* grave near Rangoon's. Unmarked. The couple had tried to have the child at home, alone, the husband as midwife. They blamed themselves, and their guilt ate them alive.

They had no friends in Milwaukee. The husband's job had brought them here from Houston. They were alone, with no one to share their grief, and they wanted to hide what had happened. It was against the law, after all; they could have been charged with murder for not having an authorized state-licensed doctor present, even though they trained well and studied the books, even though it was not their fault. It was the black demons; tumors.

To hide their shame and guilt they buried the fetus and placenta in a little grave under the bridge, but they hid this grave deeper in the black loam and foliage, and left no marker. They drank a big bottle of wine under the bridge to drown their sorrow.

The husband began drinking heavily, coming home late, missing work. He was a standards analyst, brought in by a local foundry to supervise time studies. He hated it. He wanted to finish and get back home to Texas, but the work dragged on and on.

One night in a drunken rage he struck his lovely wife, too hard, with a half-empty bottle of wine. Sinbad finds *her* grave in the black loam not far from the child. He *reads* it, and knows that she was not sad to die. She could not bear to live with her guilt, and had taunted her husband cruelly, questioning his masculinity in the feeble hope that he would break and lash out at her, end her misery. He did, and only Sinbad knows it was a suicide.

Sinbad has crawled deep into the foliage. His hands and knees are damp and black. Back at his small fire in the circle of stones in the clearing under the bridge there is a dark shadow of a man with a brown paper bag in his hand that can only be a liter of wine. Sinbad's bones, old as the sea, creak like straining mizzen-mast in a high wind as he crawls back toward his fire. The steel plate in his skull stings; tells him the shadowman is not a wayward wino. It is *him.* Sinbad crawls through the dense foliage toward his fate, and cringes suddenly, trembles. He has crawled across another grave. A wino. Stabbed to death when he passed out in a drunken stupor, because he was too near the graves. Stabbed to death by *him:* the shadowman waiting by the fire. Sinbad brushes at the loam and a skull grins up at him through black rotting leaves. *Not just one,* he reads. He glances around through the whispering leaves and sees the skulls of two more winos, drinking black loam wine.

"Howdy," the shadowman says.

"Hello." Sinbad recognizes the brakeman from across the river as he walks toward the fire, brushing black loam from his baggy knees.

"I seen you from across the river, there," the brakeman says, pointing to the tracks across the river. "Don't see many folks over here. I thought you might like to share a jug or two. I sneak down here a lot. It's quiet. Peaceful." He extends the brown-wrapped jug to Sinbad. "Mad Dog? Or Thunderbird?" He pulls another jug, a flat hip flask, from his pocket, offering an alternative.

"Don't talk much, huh? Hungry?" He pulls a can of sardines from his other hip pocket. Sinbad notices the worn black Buck knife sheath on his wide leather belt.

"Well. Just tryin' to be friendly. What was you doin' back in them bushes?"

"Pissing."

"Oh. Nothing personal. Just wondered."

Sinbad accepts the flat bottle of Mogen David 20/20, and sips it carefully. *No. Not poison. That's not his style. The knife on his belt . . . keep an eye on that knife.*

"Gets real lonely down here sometimes," the brakeman says. *I'll bet,* thinks Sinbad. *Terribly lonely.* He drinks long on the Mad Dog, and finally says: "You been a brakeman long?"

"Naw. Couple years. Hey, I'm hungry. Whatcha got boilin'? Can I join you?" The shadowman squats down without invitation on the hard-packed dirt by the fire. "Looks like fish. Smells good." He drinks from the bottle of Thunderbird, swallowing huge gulps like only Texas winos can swallow. Sinbad watches him silently.

"Guess I'll eat these sardines," he says. He pulls the folding Buck Hunter from its black leather pouch, opens it with one hand, and cuts into the lid of the can with the sharp stainless blade, cutting up and down, up and down, expertly. The tin lid crinkles up and away from the sardines.

Sinbad's eyes are riveted on the gleaming blade, up and down, flashing reflections of sunlight from the shimmering river. When he finishes, the man leans forward and places the knife, open, on a rock by the fire, and eats the sardines with his fingers. There is yellow oil on the stainless blade, dripping slowly onto the rock.

"Nice blade," says Sinbad, reaching for it. "Mind if I see?"

The man starts to object, but the knife is already in Sinbad's quick hand. He *reads* it. He *reads* the crushing shame and guilt, and the horrible loneliness of the shadowman. Their eyes meet, and are locked in a fierce embrace. The man sees understanding in Sinbad's eyes.

"You found them, didn't you?"

Sinbad lays the knife back on the rock and sits cross-legged by the warm fire, staring into the shadowman's hollow eyes.

"I'm going to do you a big favor, son."

"Thank you."

Sinbad raises a silver derringer from the baggy folds of his pants and shoots the man in the forehead. The sardine can flies backward to splash into the river, and the man flops sharply back, legs still crossed, to stare unseeing at the reflected sunlight dancing on the dark belly of the bridge. He is smiling.

Sinbad buries him under the bridge near his wife and son, and hops a boxcar headed south. With a bottle of Thunderbird, and a bottle of Mad Dog, he rides the empty car to warmer places, friendlier bridges.

Hot Eyes, Cold Eyes

by Lawrence Block

Lawrence Block is at last finding real and justified fame. He's been a working writer for several decades and has worked in a number of genres with great skill. If you think he's a good novelist, sit down and read a dozen or so of his short stories.

First published in 1978

Some days were easy. She would go to work and return home without once feeling the invasion of men's eyes. She might take her lunch and eat it in the park. She might stop on the way home at the library for a book, at the deli for a barbequed chicken, at the cleaner's, at the drugstore. On those days she could move coolly and crisply through space and time, untouched by the stares of men.

Doubtless they looked at her on those days, as on the more difficult days. She was the sort men looked at, and she had learned that early on—when her legs first began to lengthen and take shape, when her breasts began to bud. Later, as the legs grew longer and the breasts fuller, and as her face lost its youthful plumpness and was sculpted by time into beauty, the stares increased. She was attractive, she was beautiful, she was—curious phrase—easy on the eyes. So men looked at her, and on the easy days she didn't seem to notice, didn't let their rude stares penetrate the invisible shield that guarded her.

But this was not one of those days.

It started in the morning. She was waiting for the bus when she first felt the heat of a man's eyes upon her. At first she willed herself to ignore the feeling, wished the bus would come and whisk her away from it, but the bus did not come and she could not ignore what she felt and, inevitably, she turned from the street to look at the source of the feeling.

There was a man leaning against a red brick building not twenty yards from her. He was perhaps thirty-five, unshaven, and his clothes looked as though he'd slept in them. When she turned to glance at him his lips curled slightly, and his eyes, red-rimmed and glassy, moved first to her face, then drifted insolently the length of her body. She could feel their heat; it leaped from the eyes to her breasts and loins like an electric charge bridging a gap.

He placed his hand deliberately upon his crotch and rubbed himself. His smile widened.

She turned from him, drew a breath, let it out, wished the bus would come. Even now, with her back to him, she could feel the embrace of his eyes. They were like hot hands upon her buttocks and the backs of her thighs.

The bus came, neither early nor late, and she mounted the steps and dropped her fare in the box. The usual driver, a middle-aged fatherly type, gave her his usual smile and wished her the usual good morning. His eyes were an innocent watery blue behind thick-lensed spectacles.

Was it only her imagination that his eyes swept her body all the while? But she could feel them on her breasts, could feel too her own nipples hardening in response to their palpable touch.

She walked the length of the aisle to the first available seat. Male eyes tracked her every step of the way.

The day went on like that. This did not surprise her, although she had hoped it would be otherwise, had prayed during the bus ride that eyes would cease to bother her when she left the bus. She had learned, though, that once a day began in this fashion its pattern was set, unchangeable.

Was it something she did? Did she invite their hungry stares? She certainly didn't do anything with the intention of provoking male lust. Her dress was conservative enough, her makeup subtle and unremarkable. Did she swing her hips when she walked? Did she wet her lips and pout like a sullen sexpot? She was positive she did nothing of the sort, and it often seemed to her that she could cloak herself in a nun's habit and the results would be the same. Men's eyes would lift the black skirts and strip away the veil.

At the office building where she worked, the elevator starter glanced at her legs, then favored her with a knowing, wet-lipped smile. One of the office boys, a rabbity youth with unfortunate skin, stared at her breasts, then flushed scarlet when she caught him at it. Two older men gazed at her from the water cooler. One leaned over to murmur something to the other. They both chuckled and went on looking at her.

She went to her desk and tried to concentrate on her work. It was difficult, because intermittently she felt eyes brushing her body, moving across her like searchlight beams scanning the yard in a prison movie. There were moments when she wanted to scream, moments when she wanted to spin around in her chair and hurl something. But she remained in control of herself and did none of these things. She had survived days of this sort often enough in the past. She would survive this one as well.

The weather was good, but today she spent her lunch hour at her desk rather than risk the park. Several times during the afternoon the sensation of being watched was unbearable and she retreated to the ladies room. She endured the final hours a minute at a time, and finally it was five o'clock and she straightened her desk and left.

The descent on the elevator was unbearable. She bore it. The bus ride home, the walk from the bus stop to her apartment building, were unendurable. She endured them.

In her apartment, with the door locked and bolted, she stripped off her clothes and hurled them into a corner of the room as if they were unclean, as if the day had irrevocably soiled them. She stayed a long while under the shower, washed her hair, blow-dried it, then returned to her bedroom and stood nude before the full-length mirror on the closet door. She studied herself at some length, and intermittently her hands would move to cup a breast or trace the swell of a thigh, not to arouse but to assess, to chart the dimensions of her physical self.

And now? A meal alone? A few hours with a book? A lazy night in front of the television set?

She closed her eyes, and at once she felt other eyes upon her, felt them as she had been feeling them all day. She knew that she was alone, that now no one was watching her, but this knowledge did nothing to dispel the feeling.

She sighed.

She would not, could not, stay home tonight.

When she left the building, stepping out into the cool of dusk, her appearance was very different. Her tawny hair, which she'd worn pinned up earlier, hung free. Her makeup was overdone, with an excess of mascara and a deep blush of rouge in the hollows of her cheeks. During the day she'd worn no scent beyond a touch of Jean Naté applied after her morning shower; now she'd dashed on an abundance of the perfume she wore only on nights like this one, a strident scent redolent of musk. Her dress was close-fitting and revealing, the skirt slit oriental-fashion high on one thigh, the neckline low to display her decolletage. She strode purposefully on her high-heeled shoes, her buttocks swaying as she walked.

She looked sluttish and she knew it, and gloried in the knowledge. She'd checked the mirror carefully before leaving the apartment and she had liked what she saw. Now, walking down the street with her handbag bouncing against her swinging hip, she could feel the heat building up within her flesh. She could also feel the eyes of the men she passed, men who sat on stoops or loitered in doorways, men walking with purpose who stopped for a glance in her direction. But there was a difference. Now she relished those glances. She fed on the heat in those eyes, and the fire within herself burned hotter in response.

A car slowed. The driver leaned across the seat, called to her. She missed the words but felt the touch of his eyes. A pulse throbbed insistently throughout her entire body now. She was frightened—of her own feelings, of the real dangers she faced—but at the same time she was alive, gloriously alive, as she had not been in far too long. Before she had walked through the day. Now the blood was singing in her veins.

She passed several bars before finding the cocktail lounge she wanted. The interior was dimly lit, the floor soft with carpeting. An overactive air conditioner had lowered the temperature to an almost uncomfortable level. She walked bravely into the room. There were several empty tables along the wall but she passed them by, walking her swivel-hipped walk to the bar and taking a stool at the far end.

The cold air was stimulating against her warm skin. The bartender gave her a minute, then ambled over and leaned against the bar in front of her. He looked at once knowing and disinterested, his heavy lids shading his dark brown eyes and giving them a sleepy look.

"Stinger," she said.

While he was building the drink she drew her handbag into her lap and groped within it for her billfold. She found a ten and set it on top of the bar, then fumbled reflexively within her bag for another moment, checking its contents. The bartender placed the drink on the bar in front of her, took her money, returned with her change. She looked at her drink, then at her reflection in the back bar mirror.

Men were watching her.

She could tell, she could always tell. Their gazes fell on her and warmed the skin where they touched her. Odd, she thought, how the same sensation that had been so disturbing and unpleasant all day long was so desirable and exciting now.

She raised her glass, sipped her drink. The combined flavor of cognac and creme de menthe was at once warm and cold upon her lips and tongue. She swallowed, sipped again.

"That a stinger?"

He was at her elbow and she flicked her eyes in his direction while continuing to face forward. A small man, stockily built, balding, tanned, with a dusting of freckles across his high forehead. He wore a navy blue Quiana shirt open at the throat, and his dark chest hair was beginning to go gray.

"Drink up," he suggested. "Let me buy you another."

She turned now, looked levelly at him. He had small eyes. Their whites showed a tracery of blue veins at their outer corners. The irises were a very dark brown, an unreadable color, and the black pupils, hugely dilated in the bar's dim interior, covered most of the irises.

"I haven't seen you here," he said, hoisting himself onto the seat beside her. "I usually drop in around this time, have a couple, see my friends. Not new in the neighborhood, are you?"

Calculating eyes, she thought. Curiously passionless eyes, for all their cool intensity. Worst of all, they were small eyes, almost beady eyes.

"I don't want company," she said.

"Hey, how do you know you don't like me if you don't give me a chance?" He was grinning, but there was no humor in it. "You don't even know my name, lady. How can you despise a total stranger?"

"Please leave me alone."

"What are you, Greta Garbo?" He got up from his stool, took a half step away from her, gave her a glare and a curled lip. "You want to drink alone," he said, "why don't you just buy a bottle ànd take it home with you? You can take it to bed and suck on it, honey."

He had ruined the bar for her. She scooped up her change, left her drink unfinished. Two blocks down and one block over she found a second cocktail lounge virtually indistinguishable from the first one. Perhaps the lighting was a little softer, the background music the slightest bit lower in pitch. Again she passed up the row of tables and seated herself at the bar. Again she ordered a stinger and let it rest on the bar top for a moment before taking the first exquisite sip.

Again she felt male eyes upon her, and again they gave her the same hot-cold sensation as the combination of brandy and creme de menthe.

This time when a man approached her she sensed his presence for a long moment before he spoke. She studied him out of the corner of her eye. He was tall and lean, she noted, and there was a self-contained air about him, a sense of considerable self-assurance. She wanted to turn, to look directly into his eyes, but instead she raised her glass to her lips and waited for him to make a move.

"You're a few minutes late," he said.

She turned, looked at him. There was a weathered, rawboned look to him that matched the western-style clothes he wore—the faded chambray shirt, the skin-tight denim jeans. Without glancing down she knew he'd be wearing boots and that they would be good ones.

"I'm late?"

He nodded. "I've been waiting for you for close to an hour. Of course it wasn't until you walked in that I knew it was you I was waiting for, but one look was all it took. My name's Harley."

She made up a name. He seemed satisfied with it, using it when he asked her if he could buy her a drink.

"I'm not done with this one yet," she said.

"Then why don't you just finish it and come for a walk in the moonlight?"

"Where would we walk?"

"My apartment's just a block and a half from here."

"You don't waste time."

"I told you I waited close to an hour for you. I figure the rest of the evening's too precious to waste."

She had been unwilling to look directly into his eyes but she did so now and she was not disappointed. His eyes were large and well-spaced, blue in color, a light blue of a shade that often struck her as cold and forbidding. But his eyes were anything but cold. On the contrary, they burned with passionate intensity.

She knew, looking into them, that he was a dangerous man. He was strong, he was direct and he was dangerous. She could tell all this in a few seconds, merely by meeting his relentless gaze.

Well, that was fine. Danger, after all, was an inextricable part of it.

She pushed her glass aside, scooped up her change. "I don't really want the rest of this," she said.

"I didn't think you did. I think I know what you really want."

"I think you probably do."

He took her arm, tucked it under his own. They left the lounge, and on the way out she could feel other eyes on her, envious eyes. She drew closer to him and swung her hips so that her buttocks bumped into his lean flank. Her purse slapped against her other hip. Then they were out the door and heading down the street.

She felt excitement mixed with fear, an emotional combination not unlike her stinger. The fear, like the danger, was part of it.

His apartment consisted of two sparsely furnished rooms three flights up from street level. They walked wordlessly to the bedroom and undressed. She laid her clothes across a wooden chair, set her handbag on the floor at the side of the platform bed. She got onto the bed and he joined her and they embraced. He smelled faintly of leather and tobacco and male perspiration, and even with her eyes shut she could see his blue eyes burning in the darkness.

She wasn't surprised when his hands gripped her shoulders and eased her downward on the bed. She had been expecting this and welcomed it. She swung her head, letting her long hair brush across his flat abdomen, and then she moved to accept him. He tangled his fingers in her hair, hurting her in a not unpleasant way. She inhaled his musk as her mouth embraced him, and in her own fashion she matched his strength with strength of her own, teasing, taunting, heightening his passion and then cooling it down just short of culmination. His breathing grew ragged and muscles worked in his legs and abdomen.

At length he let go of her hair. She moved upward on the bed to join him and he rolled her over onto her back and covered her, his mouth seeking hers, his flesh burying itself in her flesh. She locked her thighs around his hips. He pounded at her loins, hammering her, hurting her with the brute force of his masculinity.

How strong he was, and how insistent. Once again she thought what a dangerous man he was, and what a dangerous game she was playing. The thought served only to spur her own passion on, to build her fire higher and hotter.

She felt her body preparing itself for orgasm, felt the urge growing to abandon herself, to lose control utterly. But a portion of herself remained remote, aloof, and she let her arm hang over the side of the bed and reached for her purse, groped within it.

And found the knife.

Now she could relax, now she could give up, now she could surrender to what she felt. She opened her eyes, stared upward. His own eyes were closed as he thrust furiously at her. *Open your eyes,* she urged him silently. *Open them, open them, look at me—*

And it seemed that his eyes did open to meet hers, even as they climaxed together, even as she centered the knife over his back and plunged it unerringly into his heart.

Afterward, in her own apartment, she put his eyes in the box with the others.

Souls Burning

A "Nameless Detective" Story
by *Bill Pronzini*

Bill Pronzini's "Nameless" detective books are among the two or three best private-eye novels being published in America. But hopefully "Nameless" will lead his readers to other aspects of his work as well, which include both some fine westerns and even finer suspense novels, the best of which, Snowbound, *will soon be back in print from Dell.*

First published in 1991

Hotel Majestic, Sixth Street, downtown San Francisco. A hell of an address—a hell of a place for an ex-con not long out of Folsom to set up housekeeping. Sixth Street, south of Market—South of the Slot, it used to be called—is the heart of the city's Skid Road and has been for more than half a century.

Eddie Quinlan. A name and a voice out of the past, neither of which I'd recognized when he called that morning. Close to seven years since I had seen or spoken to him, six years since I'd even thought of him. Eddie Quinlan. Edgewalker, shadow-man with no real substance or purpose, drifting along the narrow catwalk that separates conventional society from the underworld. Information seller, gofer, small-time bagman, doer of any insignificant job, legitimate or otherwise, that would help keep him in food and shelter, liquor and cigarettes. The kind of man you looked at but never really saw: a modern-day Yehudi, the little man who wasn't there. Eddie Quinlan. Nobody, loser—fall guy. Drug bust in the Tenderloin one night six and a half years ago; one dealer setting up another, and Eddie Quinlan, small-time bagman, caught in the middle; hard-assed judge, five years in Folsom, good-bye Eddie Quinlan. And the drug dealers? They walked, of course. Both of them.

And now Eddie was out, had been out for six months. And after six months of freedom, he'd called me. Would I come to his room at the Hotel Majestic tonight around eight? He'd tell me why when he saw me. It was real important—would I come? All right, Eddie. But I couldn't figure it. I had bought information from him in the old days, bits and pieces for five or ten dollars; maybe he had something to sell now. Only I wasn't looking for anything and I hadn't put the word out, so why pick me to call?

If you're smart you don't park your car on the street at night, South of the Slot. I put mine in the Fifth and Mission Garage at 7:45 and walked over to Sixth. It had rained most of the day and the streets were still wet, but now the sky was cold and clear. The kind of night that is as hard as black glass, so that light seems to bounce off the dark instead of shining through it; lights and their colors so bright and sharp reflecting off the night and the wet surfaces that the glare is like splinters against your eyes.

Friday night, and Sixth Street was teeming. Sidewalks jammed —old men, young men, bag ladies, painted ladies, blacks, whites, Asians, addicts, pushers, muttering mental cases, drunks leaning against walls in tight little clusters while they shared paper-bagged bottles of sweet wine and cans of malt liquor; men and women in filthy rags, in smart new outfits topped off with sun-glasses, carrying ghetto blasters and red-and-white canes, some of the canes in the hands of individuals who could see as well as I could, and a hidden array of guns and knives and other lethal instruments. Cheap hotels, greasy spoons, seedy taverns, and liquor stores, complete with barred windows and cynical propri-etors, that stayed open well past midnight. Laughter, shouts, curses, threats; bickering and dickering. The stenches of urine and vomit and unwashed bodies and rotgut liquor, and over those like an umbrella, the subtle effluvium of despair. Predators and prey, half hidden in shadow, half revealed in the bright, sharp dazzle of flourescent lights and bloody neon.

It was a mean street, Sixth, one of the meanest, and I walked it warily. I may be fifty-eight but I'm a big man and I walk hard, too; and I look like what I am. Two winos tried to panhandle me and a fat hooker in an orange wig tried to sell me a piece of her tired body, but no one gave me any trouble.

The Majestic was five stories of old wood and plaster and dirty brick, just off Howard Street. In front of its narrow entrance, a crack dealer and one of his customers were haggling over the price of a baggie of rock cocaine; neither of them paid any atten-tion to me as I moved past them. Drug deals go down in the open here, day and night. It's not that the cops don't care, or that they don't patrol Sixth regularly; it's just that the dealers outnumber them ten to one. On Skid Road any crime less severe than aggravated assault is strictly low priority.

Small, barren lobby: no furniture of any kind. The smell of ammonia hung in the air like swamp gas. Behind the cubbyhole desk was an old man with dead eyes that would never see anything they didn't want to see. I said, "Eddie Quinlan," and he said, "Two-oh-two" without moving his lips. There was an elevator but it had an Out of Order sign on it; dust speckled the sign. I went up the adjacent stairs.

The disinfectant smell permeated the second-floor hallway as well. Room 202 was just off the stairs, fronting on Sixth; one of the metal 2's on the door had lost a screw and was hanging upside down. I used my knuckles just below it. Scraping noise inside, and a voice said, "Yeah?" I identified myself. A lock clicked, a chain rattled, the door wobbled open, and for the first time in nearly seven years I was looking at Eddie Quinlan.

He hadn't changed much. Little guy, about five eight, and past forty now. Thin, nondescript features, pale eyes, hair the color of sand. The hair was thinner and the lines in his face were longer and deeper, almost like incisions where they bracketed his nose. Otherwise he was the same Eddie Quinlan.

"Hey," he said, "thanks for coming. I mean it, thanks."

"Sure, Eddie."

"Come on in."

The room made me think of a box—the inside of a huge rotting packing crate. Four bare walls with the scaly remnants of paper on them like psoriatic skin, bare uncarpeted floor, unshaded bulb hanging from the center of a bare ceiling. The bulb was dark; what light there was came from a low-wattage reading lamp and a wash of red-and-green neon from the hotel's sign that spilled in through a single window. Old iron-framed bed, unpainted nightstand, scarred dresser, straight-backed chair next to the bed and in front of the window, alcove with a sink and toilet and no door, closet that wouldn't be much larger than a coffin.

"Not much, is it," Eddie said.

I didn't say anything.

He shut the hall door, locked it. "Only place to sit is that chair there. Unless you want to sit on the bed? Sheets are clean. I try to keep things clean as I can."

"Chair's fine."

I went across to it; Eddie put himself on the bed. A room with a view, he'd said on the phone. Some view. Sitting here you could look down past Howard and up across Mission—almost two full blocks of the worst street in the city. It was so close you could hear the beat of its pulse, the ugly sounds of its living and its dying.

"So why did you ask me here, Eddie? If it's information for sale, I'm not buying right now."

"No, no, nothing like that. I ain't in the business anymore."

"Is that right?"

"Prison taught me a lesson. I got rehabilitated." There was no sarcasm or irony in the words; he said them matter-of-factly.

"I'm glad to hear it."

"I been a good citizen ever since I got out. No lie. I haven't had a drink, ain't even been in a bar."

"What are you doing for money?"

"I got a job," he said. "Shipping department at a wholesale sporting goods outfit on Brannan. It don't pay much, but it's honest work."

I nodded. "What is it you want, Eddie?"

"Somebody I can talk to, somebody who'll understand—that's all I want. You always treated me decent. Most of 'em, no matter who they were, they treated me like I wasn't even human. Like I was a turd or something."

"Understand what?"

"About what's happening down there."

"Where? Sixth Street?"

"Look at it," he said. He reached over and tapped the window; stared through it. "Look at the people . . . there, you see that guy in the wheelchair and the one pushing him? Across the street there?"

I leaned closer to the glass. The man in the wheelchair wore a military camouflage jacket, had a heavy wool blanket across his lap; the black man manipulating him along the crowded sidewalk was thick-bodied, with a shiny bald head. "I see them."

"White guy's name is Baxter," Eddie said. "Grenade blew up under him in 'Nam and now he's a paraplegic. Lives right here in the Majestic, on this floor down at the end. Deals crack and smack out of his room. Elroy, the black dude, is his bodyguard and roommate. Mean, both of 'em. Couple of months ago, Elroy killed a guy over on Minna that tried to stiff them. Busted his head with a brick. You believe it?"

"I believe it."

"And they ain't the worst on the street. Not the worst."

"I believe that, too."

"Before I went to prison I lived and worked with people like that and I never saw what they were. I mean I just never saw it. Now I do, I see it clear—every day walking back and forth to work, every night from up here. It makes you sick after a while, the things you see when you see 'em clear."

"Why don't you move?"

"Where to? I can't afford no place better than this."

"No better room, maybe, but why not another neighborhood? You don't have to live on Sixth Street."

"Wouldn't be much better, any other neighborhood I could buy into. They're all over the city now, the ones like Baxter and Elroy. Used to be it was just Skid Road and the Tenderloin and the ghettos. Now they're everywhere, more and more every day. You know?"

"I know."

"Why? It don't have to be this way, does it?"

Hard times, bad times: alienation, poverty, corruption, too much government, not enough government, lack of social services, lack of caring, drugs like a cancer destroying society. Simplistic explanations that were no explanations at all and as dehumanizing as the ills they described. I was tired of hearing them and I didn't want to repeat them, to Eddie Quinlan or anybody else. So I said nothing.

He shook his head. "Souls burning everywhere you go," he said, and it was as if the words hurt his mouth coming out.

Souls burning. "You find religion at Folsom, Eddie?"

"Religion? I don't know, maybe a little. Chaplain we had there, I talked to him sometimes. He used to say that about the hard-timers, that their souls were burning and there wasn't nothing he could do to put out the fire. They were doomed, he said, and they'd doom others to burn with 'em."

I had nothing to say to that, either. In the small silence a voice from outside said distinctly, "Dirty bastard, what you doin' with my pipe?" It was cold in there, with the hard bright night pressing against the window. Next to the door was a rusty steam radiator, but it was cold, too; the heat would not be on more than a few hours a day, even in the dead of winter, in the Hotel Majestic.

"That's the way it is in the city," Eddie said. "Souls burning. All day long, all night long, souls on fire."

"Don't let it get to you."

"Don't it get to *you?*"

"Yes. Sometimes."

He bobbed his head up and down. "You want to do something, you know? You want to try to fix it somehow, put out the fires. There has to be a way."

"I can't tell you what it is," I said.

He said, "If we all just did *something.* It ain't too late. You don't think it's too late?"

"No."

"Me neither. There's still hope."

"Hope, faith, blind optimism—sure."

"You got to believe," he said, nodding. "That's all, you just got to believe."

Angry voices rose suddenly from outside; a woman screamed, thin and brittle. Eddie came off the bed, hauled up the window sash. Chill damp air and street noises came pouring in: shouts, cries, horns honking, cars whispering on the wet pavement, a Muni bus clattering along Mission; more shrieks. He leaned out, peering downward.

"Look," he said. "Look."

I stretched forward and looked. On the sidewalk below, a hooker in a leopard-skin coat was running wildly toward Howard; she was the one doing the yelling. Chasing behind her, tight black skirt hiked up over the tops of net stockings and hairy thighs, was a hideously rouged transvestite waving a pocket knife. A group of winos began laughing and chanting "Rape! Rape!" as the hooker and the transvestite ran zigzagging out of sight on Howard.

Eddie pulled his head back in. The flickery neon wash made his face seem surreal, like a hallucinogenic vision. "That's the way it is," he said sadly. "Night after night, day after day."

With the window open, the cold was intense; it penetrated my clothing and crawled on my skin. I'd had enough of it, and of this room and Eddie Quinlan and Sixth Street.

"Eddie, just what is it you want from me?"

"I already told you. Talk to somebody who understands how it is down there."

"Is that the only reason you asked me here?"

"Ain't it enough?"

"For you, maybe." I got to my feet. "I'll be going now."

He didn't argue. "Sure, you go ahead."

"Nothing else you want to say?"

"Nothing else." He walked to the door with me, unlocked it,

and then put out his hand. "Thanks for coming. I appreciate it, I really do."

"Yeah. Good luck, Eddie."

"You, too," he said. "Keep the faith."

I went out into the hall, and the door shut gently and the lock clicked behind me.

Downstairs, out of the Majestic, along the mean street and back to the garage where I'd left my car. And all the way I kept thinking: There's something else, something more he wanted from me . . . and I gave it to him by going there and listening to him. But what? What did he really want?

I found out later that night. It was all over the TV—special bulletins and then the eleven o'clock news.

Twenty minutes after I left him, Eddie Quinlan stood at the window of his room-with-a-view, and in less than a minute, using a high-powered semiautomatic rifle he'd taken from the sporting goods outfit where he worked, he shot down fourteen people on the street below. Nine dead, five wounded, one of the wounded in critical condition and not expected to live. Six of the victims were known drug dealers; all of the others also had arrest records, for crimes ranging from prostitution to burglary. Two of the dead were Baxter, the paraplegic ex-Vietnam vet, and his bodyguard, Elroy.

By the time the cops showed up, Sixth Street was empty except for the dead and the dying. No more targets. And up in his room, Eddie Quinlan had sat on the bed and put the rifle's muzzle in his mouth and used his big toe to pull the trigger.

My first reaction was to blame myself. But how could I have known or even guessed? Eddie Quinlan. Nobody, loser, shadow-man without substance or purpose. How could anyone have figured him for a thing like that?

Somebody I can talk to, somebody who'll understand—that's all I want.

No. What he'd wanted was somebody to help him justify to himself what he was about to do. Somebody to record his verbal suicide note. Somebody he could trust to pass it on afterward, tell it right and true to the world.

You want to do something, you know? You want to try to fix it somehow, put out the fires. There has to be a way.

Nine dead, five wounded, one of the wounded in critical condition and not expected to live. Not that way.

Souls burning. All day long, all night long, souls on fire.

The soul that had burned tonight was Eddie Quinlan's.

A Handgun for Protection

by John Lutz

John Lutz is one of those easygoing writers whose work sort of sneaks up on you. His SWF Seeks Same *was the best urban horror novel of 1991, and his novel* Bonegrinder *remains one of the most unsettling books ever written. He's also author of* Bloodfire, *a piece of virtuoso action writing.*

First published in 1974

I had to have her. Lani Sundale was her name, and for the past three Saturday nights I'd sat at the corner of the bar in the Lost Beach Lounge and listened to her talk to her friends—another girl, a blonde—and a tall, husky guy with graying hair and bushy eyebrows. Once there was an older woman with a lot of jewelry who acted like she was the gray haired guy's wife. They'd sit and drink and gab to each other about nothing in particular, and I'd sit working on my bourbon and water, watching her reflection in the back bar mirror.

It wasn't until the second Saturday night, when she got a telephone call, that I learned her name, but even before that I was—well, let's say committed.

Lani was a dark haired, medium-height, liquid motion girl, shapely and a little heavier than was the style, like a woman should be. But with her face she didn't need her body. She really got to me right off: high cheekbones, upturned nose, and slightly parted, pouty little red lips, as if she'd just been slapped. Then she had those big dark eyes that kind of looked deep into a guy and asked questions. And from time to time she'd look up at me in the mirror and smile like it just might mean something.

The fourth Saturday night she came in alone.

I swiveled on my bar stool with practiced casualness to face her booth. "Where's your friends?"

She shrugged and smiled. "Other things to do." Past her, outside the window, I could see the blank night sky and the huge Pacific rolling darkly on the beach.

"No stars tonight," I said. "You're the shiningest thing around."

"You're trying to tell me it's going to rain," she said, still with the smile. It was a kind of crooked, wicked little smile that looked perfect on her. "I drink whiskey sours."

I ordered her one, myself a bourbon and water, and sat down across from her in the soft vinyl booth. Two guys down the bar looked at me briefly with naked envy.

"Your name's Lani," I told her. She didn't seem surprised that I knew. "I'm Dennis Conners."

The bartender brought our drinks on a tray and Lani raised her glass. "To new acquaintances."

Three drinks later we left together.

It was about four when Lani drove me back to the Lounge parking lot to pick up my car. Hard as it was for me to see much in the dark, I knew we were in an expensive section of coast real estate where a lot of wealthy people had plush beach houses, like the beach house I'd just visited with Lani.

She drove her black convertible fast, not bothering to stop and put up the top against the sparse, cold raindrops that stung our faces. What I liked most about her then was that she didn't bother with the ashamed act, and when we reached the parking lot and the car had stopped, she leaned over and gave me a kiss with that tilted little grin.

"See you again?" she said as I got out of the car.

"We'll most likely run across one another," I said with a smile, slamming the heavy door.

I could hear her laughter over the roar and screech of tires as the big convertible backed and turned onto the empty highway. I walked back to my car slowly.

During the next two weeks we were together at the beach house half a dozen times. The place spelled money, all right. Not real big but definitely plush, stone fireplace, deep carpeting, rough sawn beams, modern kitchen, expensive and comfortable furniture. There was no place the two of us would rather have

been, the way it felt with the heavy drapes drawn and a low fire throwing out its twisted, moving shadows. And the way we could hear that wild ocean curl up moaning on the beach, over and over again. It was a night like that, late, when she started talking about her husband.

"Howard's crippled," she said. "An automobile accident. He'll never get out of his wheelchair." She looked up at me as if she'd just explained something.

"How long ago?" I asked.

"Two years. It was his own fault. Drunk at ninety miles an hour. He can't complain."

"I've been drunk at ninety miles an hour myself."

"Oh, so have I." The shrug and tilted smile. "We all take our chances."

I wondered how much her husband knew about her. How much I knew about her. From time to time I'd marvelled at how skillfully she could cover up the bruises on her face and neck with makeup. She was all that mattered to me now, and it made me ache with a strange compassion for her husband, thinking how it would be watching her from a wheelchair.

"Let's get going," she said, standing and slipping into her suede high heeled shoes. "The fire's getting low."

I yanked her back by the elbow. Then I walked over and put another log on the fire.

Where I lived, at a motel in North Beach, was quite a comedown from the beach house love nest. During the long days of dwindling heat and afternoon showers I'd lie on my bed, sipping bourbon over ice and thinking about Lani and myself. I'm no kind of fool, and I knew what was happening didn't exactly tally. With her money and looks Lani could have had her choice of big husky young ones, her kind. I never kidded myself; I was over thirty-five, blond hair getting a little thin and once-athletic body now sporting a slight drinker's paunch. Not a bad looking guy, but not the pick of the litter. And my not-so-lucrative occupation of water skiing instructor during the vacation season would hardly have attracted Lani. I already owed her over five hundred dollars she never expected to get back.

Maybe any guy in my situation would have wondered how he'd got so lucky. I didn't know or really care. I only knew I had what I wanted most. And even during the day I could close my eyes and lean back in my bed five miles from sea and hear the tortured surf of the rolling night ocean.

"He has more money than he could burn," Lani said to me one night at the beach house.

"Howard?"

She nodded and ran her fingernails through the hair on my chest.

"You're his wife," I told her. "Half of all he owns is yours and vice versa."

"You're something I own that isn't half his, Dennis. We own each other. I feel more married to you than to Howard."

"Divorce him," I said. "You'd get your half."

She pulled her head away from me for a moment and looked incredulous.

"Are you kidding? The court wouldn't look too kindly on a woman leaving a cripple. And Howard's really ruthless. His lawyers might bring out something from my past."

"Or present."

She tried to bite my arm and I pulled her back by the hair. I knew what she'd been talking toward and I didn't care. I didn't care about anything but her. She was twisting her head all around, laughing, as I slapped her and shoved her away. She was still laughing when she said it.

"Dennis, there's only one—"

I interrupted her. "I'll kill him for you," I said.

We were both serious then. She sat up and we stared at each other. The twin reflections of the fire were tiny star-points of red light in her dark eyes. I reached for her.

The beach house was where we discussed the thing in detail, weighing one plan after another. We always met there and nowhere else. I'd conceal my old sedan in the shadows behind a jagged stand of rock and walk down through the grass and cool sand to the door off the wooden sun deck. She'd be waiting for me.

"Listen," she said to me one night when the sea wind was howling in gusts around the sturdy house, "why don't we use this on him?" She opened her purse and drew out a small, snub-nosed .32 caliber revolver.

I took it from her and turned it over in my hand. A compact, ugly weapon with an unusual eight shot cylinder, the purity of its flawless white pearl grips made the rest of it seem all the uglier.

"Whose?" I asked.

Lani closed her purse and tossed it onto the sofa from where she sat on an oversized cushion. "Howard gave it to me just after we were married, for protection."

"Then it can be traced to you."

She shook her head impatiently. "He bought it for me in Europe, when he was on a business trip in a communist block country. Brought it back illegally, really. I looked into this thing, Dennis. I know the police can identify the type and make weapon used from the bullet, only this make gun won't even be known to them. All they'll be able to say for sure is it was a .32 caliber."

I looked at her admiringly and slipped the revolver into my pants pocket. "You do your homework like a good girl. How many people know you own this thing?"

"Quite a few people were there when Howard gave it to me three years ago, but only a few people have seen it since. I doubt if anybody even knows what caliber it is. I know I can pretend I don't."

She was watching me closely as I thoughtfully rubbed the back of my hand across my mouth. "What happens if the police ask you to produce the gun? Nothing to prevent them from matching it with the murder bullet then."

Lani laughed. "In three years I lost it! Let them search for it if they want. It'll be at the bottom of the ocean where you threw it." She was grinning secretively, her dark hair hanging loose over one ear and the makeup under one eye smudged.

"Why not let me in on your entire plan?" I said. "The whole thing would come off better."

"I didn't mean to take over or anything. I just want it to be safe for you, baby, for both of us. So we can enjoy afterward together."

I wondered then if afterward would be like before.

"I know this gun is safe," Lani went on. "No matter where you got another one the police might eventually trace it. But with this one they can't."

"Is it registered or anything?"

"No, Howard just gave it to me."

"But the people who saw him give it to you, couldn't they identify it?"

"Not if they never saw it again." She took a sip of the expensive blended whiskey she was drinking from the bottle and looked up smiling at me with her head tilted back and kind of resting on one shoulder. "I think I've got an idea you'll like," she said. Her lips were parted wide, still glistening wet from the whiskey.

That's how three nights later I found myself dressed only in swimming trunks and deck shoes, seated uncomfortably in the hard, barnacle-clad wooden structure of the underside of the

long pier that jutted out into the sea from Howard Sundale's private beach. To the right, beyond the rise of sand, I could see the lights of his sprawling hacienda style house as I kept shifting my weight and feeling the spray from the surf lick at my ankles. I'd always considered myself small time, maybe, not the toughest but smart, and here I was killing for a woman. There'd been plenty of passed up opportunities to kill for money. I knew it wasn't Lani's money at all; I'd have wanted her rich or poor.

I unconsciously glanced at my wrist for the engraved watch I'd been careful not to wear, and I cursed softly as the white foaming breakers surged out their rolling lives beneath me. It *had* to be ten o'clock!

Lani had guaranteed me that Belson, her husband's chauffeur and handyman, would bring Howard for his nightly stroll out onto the long pier at ten o'clock.

"Belson always wheels him there," she'd said. "It's habit with them. Only this time I'll call Belson back to the house for a moment and he'll leave Howard there alone—for you."

The idea then was simple and effective. I was to climb up from my hiding place, shoot Howard, strip him of ring, watch and wallet, then swim back along the shoreline to near where my car was hidden and drive for North Beach Bridge, where I'd throw the murder gun into deep water.

At first I'd been for just rolling Howard wheelchair and all into the ocean. But Lani had assured me it was better to make it look like murder and robbery for the very expensive ring he was known to wear. Less chance of a mistake that way, she'd argued, than if we tried to get tricky and outwit the police by faking an accident. And Howard's upper body was exceptionally strong. Even without the use of his legs he'd be able to stay afloat and make his way to shore.

So at last we'd agreed on the revolver.

I looked up from my place in the shadows. Something was passing between me and the house lights. Two forms were moving through the night toward the pier: Howard Sundale hunched in his wheelchair, and Belson, a tall, slender man leaning forward, propelling the chair with straight arms and short but smooth steps.

As they drew nearer I saw that the lower part of Howard's body was covered by a blanket, and Belson, an elderly man with unruly curly hair, was wearing a light windbreaker and a servant's look of polite blankness. They turned onto the pier and passed over

me, and I crouched listening to the wheelchair's rubber tires' choppy rhythm over the rough planks.

A minute later I heard Lani's voice, clear, urgent. "Belson! Belson, will you come to the house for a minute? It's important!"

Belson said something to Howard I couldn't understand. Then I heard his hurried, measured footsteps pass over me and away. Then quiet. I drew the revolver from its waterproof plastic bag.

Howard Sundale was sitting motionless, staring seaward, and the sound of the rushing surf was enough to cover my noise as I climbed up onto the pier, checked to make sure Belson was gone, then walked softly in my canvas deck shoes toward the wheelchair.

"Mr. Sundale?"

He was startled as I moved around to stand in front of him. "Who are you?"

Howard Sundale was not what I'd expected. He was a lean faced, broad shouldered, virile looking man in his forties, keen blue eyes beneath wind-ruffled sandy hair. I understood now why Lani hadn't wanted me to risk pushing him into the sea. He appeared momentarily surprised, then wary when I brought the gun around from behind me and aimed it at him. His eyes darted for a moment in the direction of the distant house lights.

"For Lani, I suppose," he said. Fear made his voice too high.

I nodded. "You should try to understand."

He smiled a knowing, hopeless little frightened smile as I aimed for his heart and pulled the trigger twice.

Quickly I slipped off his diamond ring and wristwatch, amazed at the coolness of his still hands. Then I reached around for his wallet, couldn't find it, discovered it was in his side pocket. I put it all in the plastic bag with the revolver, sealed the bag shut, then slipped off the pier into the water. As I lowered myself I found I was laughing at the way Howard was sitting motionless and dead in the moonlight, still looking out to sea as if there was something there that had caught his attention. Then the cold water sobered me.

I followed the case in the papers. Murder and robbery, the police were saying. An expensive wristwatch, his wallet and a diamond ring valued at over five thousand dollars the victim was known always to wear were missing. At first Belson, the elderly chauffeur, was suspected. He claimed, of all things, that he'd been having an affair with his employer's wife and was with her at the time of the shooting. That must have brought a laugh from the law, especially with the way Lani looked and the act she was putting on. Finally the old guy was cleared and released anyway.

The month Lani and I let pass after the funeral was the longest thirty days of my life. On the night we'd agreed to meet, I reached the beach house first, let myself in and waited before the struggling, growing fire that I'd built.

She was fifteen minutes late, smiling when she came in. We kissed and it was good to hold her again. I squeezed the nape of her neck, pulled her head back and kissed her hard.

"Wait . . . Wait!" she gasped. "Let's have a drink first." There was a fleck of blood on her trembling lower lip.

I watched her walk into the kitchen to mix our drinks.

When she returned the smile returned with her. "I told you it would work, Dennis."

"You told me," I said, accepting my drink.

She saw the pearl handled revolver then, where I'd laid it on the coffee table. Quickly she walked to it, picked it up and examined it. There was surprise in her eyes, in the downturned, pouting mouth. "What happened?"

"I forgot to throw it into the sea, took it home with me by mistake and didn't realize it until this afternoon."

She put the gun down. "You're kidding?"

"No, I was mixed up that night. Not thinking straight. Your husband was the first man I ever killed."

She stood for a moment, pondering what I'd said. After a while she took a sip of her drink, put it down and came to me.

"Did the police question you about the gun?" I asked her.

"Uh-hm. I told them it was lost."

"I'll get rid of it tonight on my way home."

"Tomorrow morning," Lani corrected me as her arms snaked around my shoulders. "And we'll meet here again tomorrow night . . . and the night after that and after that . . ."

Despite her words her enthusiasm seemed to be slipping. That didn't matter to me.

Lani was the first one at the beach house the next evening. It was a windy, moon-bright night, only a few dark clouds racing above the yellow dappled sea at right angles to the surf, as she opened the door to my knock and let me in. Her first words were what I expected.

"Did you get rid of the gun?"

"No." I watched her eyes darken and narrow slightly.

"No? . . ."

"I'm keeping it," I said, "for protection."

"What do you mean, Dennis?" The anger crackled in her voice.

I only smiled. "I mean I have the revolver, and I've left a letter to be opened in the event of my death telling a lawyer where it's hidden."

Lani turned, walked from me with her head bowed then wheeled to face me. "Explain it! It doesn't scare me and I know it should."

"It should," I said, crossing the room and seating myself on the sofa with my legs outstretched. "I wiped the gun clean of prints when I brought it here, then lifted it by a pencil in the barrel when I left here after you last night. Your fingerprints are on it now, nice and clear."

She cocked her head at me, gave me a confused, crooked half-smile. "So what—it's my gun. My prints would naturally be on it."

"But yours are the *only* prints on it," I said. "No one could have shot Howard without erasing or overlapping them. Meaning that you had to have handled the weapon *after* the murder—or during. If that gun ever happened to find its way to the police . . ."

Her eyebrows raised.

"I could tell them I found it," she said with a try for spunk, "and then it was stolen from me."

"They wouldn't believe you. And it isn't likely that anyone would take the gun without smudging or overlapping your prints. What the law would do is run a ballistics test on it, determine it was the murder weapon then arrest you. What's your alibi?"

"Belson—"

"You'd be contradicting your own story. And I doubt if Belson would come to your defense now. No one would believe either of you anyway. Then there's that past you mentioned."

I grinned, watching the fallen, trapped expression on her pouting face. A bitter, resigned look widened her dark eyes. When I rose, still grinning, and moved toward her she backed away.

"You're crazy!" Fear broke her voice and she raised her hands palms out before her. "Crazy!"

"It's been said," I told her as calmly as I could.

I made love to her then, while the moon-struck ocean roared its approval.

Afterward she lay beside me, completely meek.

"We were going to be together anyway, darling, always," she

whispered, lightly trailing her long fingernails over me. Her fingernails were lacquered pale pink, and I saw that two of them were broken. "It doesn't matter about the revolver. I don't blame you. Not for anything."

She'd do anything to recover the gun, to recover her freedom.

"I'm glad," I said, holding her tight against me, feeling the blood-rush pounding in her heart.

"It doesn't matter," she repeated softly, "doesn't matter."

That's when I knew the really deadly game was just beginning.

The Crooked Way

by *Loren D. Estleman*

Loren D. Estleman is probably tired of being compared to Raymond Chandler. For one thing, he's tougher than Chandler, with a less forgiving social eye and a much more vivid sense of the real world. He has lately taken to writing historical detective novels, Whiskey River *among them, which is only natural since Loren is also one of our best western novelists and has had plenty of practice using historical incidents as a backdrop.*

First published in 1988

You couldn't miss the Indian if you'd wanted to. He was sitting all alone in a corner booth, which was probably his idea, but he hadn't much choice because there was barely enough room in it for him. He had shoulders going into the next country and a head the size of a basketball, and he was holding a beer mug that looked like a shot glass between his callused palms. As I approached the booth he looked up at me—not very far up—through slits in a face made up of bunched ovals with a nose like the corner of a building. His skin was the color of old brick.

"Mr. Frechette?" I asked.

"Amos Walker?"

I said I was. Coming from him my name sounded like two stones dropping into deep water. He made no move to shake hands, but he inclined his head a fraction of an inch and I borrowed a chair from a nearby table and joined him. He had on a blue shirt buttoned to the neck, and his hair, parted on one side and plastered down, was blue-black without a trace of gray. Nevertheless he was about fifty.

"Charlie Stoat says you track like an Osage," he said. "I hope you're better than that. I couldn't track a train."

"How is Charlie? I haven't seen him since that insurance thing."

"Going under. The construction boom went bust in Houston just when he was expanding his operation."

"What's that do to yours?" He'd told me over the telephone he was in construction.

"Nothing worth mentioning. I've been running on a shoe-string for years. You can't break a poor man."

I signaled the bartender for a beer and he brought one over. It was a workingman's hangout across the street from the Ford plant in Highland Park. The shift wasn't due to change for an hour and we had the place to ourselves. "You said your daughter ran away," I said, when the bartender had left. "What makes you think she's in Detroit?"

He drank off half his beer and belched dramatically. "When does client privilege start?"

"It never stops."

I watched him make up his mind. Indians aren't nearly as hard to read as they appear in books. He picked up a folded newspaper from the seat beside him and spread it out on the table facing me. It was yesterday's *Houston Chronicle*, with a banner:

BOYD MANHUNT MOVES NORTHEAST
Bandit's Van Found Abandoned in Detroit

I had read a related wire story in that morning's *Detroit Free Press.* Following the unassisted shotgun robberies of two savings-and-loan offices near Houston, concerned citizens had reported seeing twenty-two-year-old Virgil Boyd in Mexico and Oklahoma, but his green van with Texas plates had turned up in a city lot five minutes from where we were sitting. As of that morning, Detroit Police Headquarters was paved with Feds and sun-crinkled out-of-state cops chewing toothpicks.

I refolded the paper and gave it back. "Your daughter's taken up with Boyd?"

"They were high school sweethearts," Frechette said. "That was before Texas Federal foreclosed on his family's ranch and his father shot himself. She disappeared from home after the first robbery. I guess that makes her an accomplice to the second."

"Legally speaking," I agreed, "if she's with him and it's her idea. A smart DA would knock it down to harboring if she turned herself in. She'd probably get probation."

"She wouldn't do that. She's got some crazy idea she's in love with Boyd."

"I'm surprised I haven't heard about her."

"No one knows. I didn't report her missing. If I had, the police would have put two and two together and there'd be a warrant out for her as well."

I swallowed some beer. "I don't know what you think I can do that the cops and the FBI can't."

"I know where she is."

I waited. He rotated his mug. "My sister lives in Southgate. We don't speak. She has a white mother, not like me, and she takes after her in looks. She's ashamed of being half Osage. First chance she had, she married a white man and got out of Oklahoma. That was before I left for Texas, where nobody knows about her. Anyway she got a big settlement in her divorce."

"You think Boyd and your daughter will go to her for a getaway stake?"

"They won't get it from me, and he didn't take enough out of Texas Federal to keep a dog alive. Why else would they come here?"

"So if you know where they're headed, what do you need me for?"

"Because I'm being followed and you're not."

The bartender came around to offer Frechette a refill. The big Indian shook his head and he went away.

"Cops?" I said.

"One cop. J. P. Ahearn."

He spaced out the name as if spelling a blasphemy. I said I'd never heard of him.

"He'd be surprised. He's a commander with the Texas State Police, but he thinks he's the last of the Texas Rangers. He wants Boyd bad. The man's a bloodhound. He doesn't know about my sister, but he did his homework and found out about Suzie and that she's gone, not that he could get me to admit she isn't away visiting friends. I didn't see him on the plane from Houston. I spotted him in the airport here when I was getting my luggage."

"Is he alone?"

"He wouldn't share credit with Jesus for saving a sinner." He drained his mug. "When you find Suzie I want you to set up a meeting. Maybe I can talk sense into her."

"How old is she?"

"Nineteen."

"Good luck."

"Tell me about it. My old man fell off a girder in Tulsa when I was sixteen. Then I was fifty. Well, maybe one meeting can't make up for all the years of not talking after my wife died, but I can't let her throw her life away for not trying."

"I can't promise Boyd won't sit in on it."

"I like Virgil. Some of us cheered when he took on those bloodsuckers. He'd have gotten away with a lot more from that second job if he'd shot this stubborn cashier they had, but he didn't. He wouldn't hurt a horse or a man."

"That's not the way the cops are playing it. If I find him and don't report it I'll go down as an accomplice. At the very least I'll lose my license."

"All I ask is that you call me before you call the police." He gave me a high-school graduation picture of a pretty brunette he said was Suzie. She looked more Asian than American Indian. Then he pulled a checkbook out of his hip pocket and made out a check to me for fifteen hundred dollars.

"Too much," I said.

"You haven't met J. P. Ahearn yet. My sister's name is Harriett Lord." He gave me an address on Eureka. "I'm at the Holiday Inn down the street, room 716."

He called for another beer then and I left. Again he didn't offer his hand. I'd driven three blocks from the place when I spotted the tail.

The guy knew what he was doing. In a late-model tan Buick he gave me a full block and didn't try to close up until we hit Woodward, where traffic was heavier. I finally lost him in the grand circle downtown, which confused him just as it does most people from the greater planet Earth. The Indians who settled Detroit were being farsighted when they named it the Crooked Way. From there I took Lafayette to I-75 and headed downriver.

Harriett Lord lived in a tall white frame house with blue shutters and a large lawn fenced by cedars that someone had bullied into cone shape. I parked in the driveway, but before leaving the car I got out the unlicensed Luger I keep in a pocket under the dash and stuck it in my pants, buttoning my coat over it. When you're meeting someone they tell you wouldn't hurt a horse or a man, arm yourself.

The bell was answered by a tall woman around forty, dressed in a khaki shirt and corduroy slacks and sandals. She had high cheekbones and slightly olive coloring that looked more like sun than heritage and her short hair was frosted, further reducing the Indian effect. When she confirmed that she was Harriet Lord I gave her a card and said I was working for her brother.

Her face shut down. "I don't have a brother. I have a half-brother, Howard Frechette. If that's who you're working for, tell him I'm unavailable." She started to close the door.

"It's about your niece Suzie. And Virgil Boyd."

"I thought it would be."

I looked at the door and got out a cigarette and lit it. I was about to knock again when the door opened six inches and she stuck her face through the gap. "You're not with the police?"

"We tolerate each other on the good days, but that's it."

She glanced down. Her blue mascara gave her eyelids a translucent look. Then she opened the door the rest of the way and stepped aside. I entered a living room done all in beige and white and sat in a chair upholstered in eggshell chintz. I was glad I'd had my suit cleaned.

"How'd you know about Suzie and Boyd?" I used a big glass ashtray on the Lucite coffee table.

"They were here last night." I said nothing. She sat on the beige sofa with her knees together. "I recognized him before I did her. I haven't seen her since she was four, but I take a Texas paper and I've seen his picture. They wanted money. I thought at first I was being robbed."

"Did you give it to them?"

"Aid a fugitive? Family responsibility doesn't cover that even if I felt any. I left home because I got sick of hearing about our proud heritage. Howard wore his Indianness like a suit of armor, and all the time he resented me because I could pass for white. He accused me of being ashamed of my ancestry because I didn't wear my hair in braids and hang turquoise all over me."

"He isn't like that now."

"Maybe he's mellowed. Not toward me, though, I bet. Now his daughter comes here asking for money so she and her desperado boyfriend can go on running. I showed them the door."

"I'm surprised Boyd went."

"He tried to get tough, but he's not very big and he wasn't armed. He took a step toward me and I took two steps toward him and he grabbed Suzie and left. Some Jesse James."

"I heard his shotgun was found in the van. I thought he'd have something else."

"If he did, he didn't have it last night. I'd have noticed, just as I notice you have one."

I unbuttoned my coat and resettled the Luger. I was getting a different picture of "Mad Dog" Boyd from the one the press was painting. "The cops would call not reporting an incident like that being an accessory," I said, squashing out my butt.

"Just because I don't want anything to do with Howard doesn't mean I want to see my niece shot up by a SWAT team."

"I don't suppose they said where they were going."

"You're a good supposer."

I got up. "How did Suzie look?"

"Like an Indian."

I thanked her and went out.

I had a customer in my waiting room. A small angular party crowding sixty wearing a tight gray three-button suit, steel-rimmed glasses and a tan snap-brim hat squared over the frames. His crisp gray hair was cut close around large ears that stuck out, and he had a long sharp jaw with a sour mouth slashing straight across. He stood up when I entered. "Walker?" It was one of those bitter pioneer voices.

"Depends on who you are," I said.

"I'm the man who ought to arrest you for obstructing justice."

"I'll guess. J. P. Ahearn."

"*Commander* Ahearn."

"You're about four feet short of what I had pictured."

"You've heard of me." His chest came out a little.

"Who hasn't?" I unlocked the inner office door. He marched in, slung a look around and took possession of the customer's chair. I sat down behind the desk and reached for a cigarette without asking permission. He glared at me through his spectacles.

"What you did downtown today constitutes fleeing and eluding."

"In Texas, maybe. In Michigan there has to be a warrant out first. What you did constitutes harassment in this state."

"I don't have official status here. I can follow anybody for any reason or none at all."

"Is this what you folks call a Mexican standoff?"

"I don't approve of smoking," he snapped.

"Neither do I, but some of it always leaks out of my lungs." I blew at the ceiling and got rid of the match. "Why don't let's stop circling each other and get down to why you're here?"

"I want to know what you and the Indian talked about."

"I'd show you, but we don't need the rain."

He bared a perfect set of dentures, turning his face into a skull. "I ran your plate with the Detroit Police. I have their complete cooperation in this investigation. The Indian hired you to take money to Boyd to get him and his little Osage slut to Canada. You delivered it after you left the bar and lost me. That's aiding and abetting and accessory after the fact of armed robbery. Maybe I can't prove it, but I can make a call and tank you for forty-eight hours on suspicion."

"Eleven."

He covered up his store-boughts. "What?"

"That's eleven times I've been threatened with jail," I said. "Three of those times I wound up there. My license has been swiped at fourteen times, actually taken away once. Bodily harm —you don't count bodily harm. I'm still here, six feet something and one hundred eighty pounds of incorruptible PI with a will of iron and a skull to match. You hard guys come and go like phases of the moon."

"Don't twist my tail, son. I don't always rattle before I bite."

"What's got you so hot on Boyd?"

You could have cut yourself on his jaw. "My daddy helped run Parker and Barrow to ground in '34. *His* daddy fought Geronimo and chased John Wesley Hardin out of Texas. My son's a Dallas city patrolman, and so far I don't have a story to hand him that's a blister on any of those. I'm retiring next year."

"Last I heard Austin was offering twenty thousand for Boyd's arrest and conviction."

"Texas Federal has matched it. Alive *or* dead. Naturally, as a duly sworn officer of the law I can't collect. But you being a private citizen—"

"What's the split?"

"Fifty-fifty."

"No good."

"Do you know what the pension is for a retired state police commander in Texas? A man needs a nest egg."

"I meant it's too generous. You know as well as I do those rewards are never paid. You just didn't know I knew."

He sprang out of his chair. There was no special animosity in his move; that would be the way he always got up.

"Boyd won't get out of this country even if you did give him money," he snapped. "He'll never get past the border guards."

"So go back home."

"Boyd's *mine.*"

The last word ricocheted. I said, "Talk is he felt he had a good reason to stick up those savings-and-loans. The company was responsible for his father's suicide."

"If he's got the brains God gave a mad dog he'll turn himself in to me before he gets shot down in the street or kills someone and winds up getting the needle in Huntsville. And his squaw right along with him." He took a shabby wallet out of his coat and gave me a card. "That's my number at the Houston post. They'll route your call here. If you're so concerned for Boyd you'll tell me where he is before the locals gun him down."

"Better you than some stranger, that it?"

"Just keep on twisting, son. I ain't in the pasture yet."

After he left, making as much noise in his two-inch cowboy heels as a cruiserweight, I called Barry Stackpole at the Detroit *News.*

"Guy I'm after is wanted for Robbery, Armed," I said, once the small talk was put away. "He ditched his gun and then his stake didn't come through and now he'll have to cowboy a job for case dough. Where would he deal a weapon if he didn't know anybody in town?"

"Emma Chaney."

"Ma? I thought she'd be dead by now."

"She can't die. The Detroit cops are third in line behind Interpol and Customs for her scalp and they won't let her until they've had their crack." He sounded pleased, which he probably was. Barry made his living writing about crime, and when it prospered he did, too.

"How can I reach her?"

"Are you suggesting I'd know where she is and not tell the authorities? Got a pencil?"

I tried the number as soon as he was off the line. On the ninth ring, I got someone with a smoker's wheeze. "Uh-huh."

"The name's Walker," I said. "Barry Stackpole gave me this number."

The voice told me not to go away and hung up. Five minutes later the telephone rang.

"Barry says you're okay. What do you want?"

"Just talk. It isn't cheap like they say."

After a moment the voice gave me directions. I hung up not knowing if it was male or female.

I was looking at Suzie. "I'm a private detective hired by your father. He wants to talk to you."

"He's here?" She touched Boyd's arm.

He tensed. "It's a damn cop trick!"

"You're smarter than that," I said. "You had to be, to pull those two jobs and make your way here with every cop between here and Texas looking for you. If I were one, would I be alone?"

"Do your jabbering outside." Ma reversed ends on the shotgun for Boyd to take. He did so and worked the slide.

"Where's the shells?"

"That's your headache. I don't keep ammo in this firetrap."

That was a lie or some of those cartons wouldn't be labeled C-4 EXPLOSIVES. But you don't sell loaded guns to strangers.

Suzie said, "Virgil, you never load them anyway."

"Shut up."

"Your father's on his way," I said. "Ten minutes, that's all he wants."

"Come on." Boyd took her wrist.

"Stay put."

This was a new voice. Everyone looked at Leo, standing in front of the door with his gun still out.

"Leo, *what* in the *hell*—"

"Ma, the Luger."

She shut her mouth and took my gun out of her right coat pocket and put it on the carton with the money. Then she backed away.

"Throw 'er down, Mace." He covered the man in the loft, who froze in the act of raising the rifle. They were like that for a moment.

"Mason," Ma said.

His shoulders slumped. He snapped on the safety and dropped the rifle eight feet to the earthen floor.

"You, too, Mr. Forty Thousand Dollar *Re*ward," Leo said. "Even empty guns give me the jumps."

Boyd cast the shotgun onto the stack of cartons with a violent gesture.

"That's nice. I cut that money in half if I got to put a hole in you."

"That reward talk's just PR," I said. "Even if you get Boyd to the cops they'll probably arrest you, too, for dealing in unlicensed firearms."

"Like hell. I'm through getting bossed around by fat old ladies. Let's go, Mr. *Re*ward."

"No!" screamed Suzie.

An explosion slapped the walls. Leo's brows went up, his jaw dropping to expose the wad of pink gum in his mouth. He looked down at the spreading stain on the bib of his overalls and fell down on top of his gun. He kicked once.

Ma was standing with a hand in her left coat pocket. A finger of smoking metal poked out of a charred hole. "Dadgum it, Leo," she said, "this coat belonged to my Calvin, rest his soul."

I was standing in front of the Log Cabin Inn's deserted office when Frechette swung a rented Ford into the broken paved driveway. He unfolded himself from the seat and loomed over me.

"I don't think anyone followed me," he said. "I took a couple of wrong turns to make sure."

"There won't be any interruptions then. The place has been closed a long time."

I led him to one of the log bungalows in back. Boyd's Plymouth, stolen from the same lot where he'd left the van, was parked alongside it facing out. We knocked before entering.

All of the furniture had been removed except a metal bedstead with sagging springs. The lantern we had borrowed from Ma Chaney hung hissing from one post. Suzie was standing next to it. "Papa." She didn't move. Boyd came out of the bathroom with the shotgun. The Indian took root.

"Man said you had money for us," Boyd said.

"It was the only way I could get him to bring Suzie here," I told Frechette.

"I won't pay to have my daughter killed in a shootout."

"Lying bastard!" Boyd swung the shotgun my way. Frechette backhanded him, knocking him back into the bathroom. I stepped forward and tore the shotgun from Boyd's weakened grip.

"Empty," I said. "But it makes a good club."

Suzie had come forward when Boyd fell. Frechette stopped her with an arm like a railroad gate. "Take Dillinger for a walk while I talk to my daughter," he said to me.

I stuck out a hand, but Boyd slapped it aside and got up. His right eye was swelling shut. He looked at the Indian towering a foot over him, then at Suzie, who said, "It's all right. I'll talk to him."

We went out. A porch ran the length of the bungalow. I leaned the shotgun against the wall and trusted my weight to the railing. "I hear you got a raw deal from Texas Federal."

"My old man did." He stood with his hands rammed deep in his pockets, watching the pair through the window. "He asked for a two-month extension on his mortgage payment, just till he brought in his crop. Everyone gets extensions. Except when Texas Federal wants to sell the ranch to a developer. He met the 'dozers with a shotgun. Then he used it on himself."

"That why you use one?"

"I can't kill a jackrabbit. It used to burn up my old man."

"You'd be out in three years if you turned yourself in."

"To you, right? Let you collect that reward." He was still looking through the window. Inside, father and daughter were gesturing at each other frantically.

"I didn't say to me. You're big enough to walk into a police station by yourself."

"You don't know Texas Federal. They'd hire their own prosecutor, see I got life, make an example. I'll die first."

"Probably, the rate you're going."

He whirled on me. The parked Plymouth caught his eye. "Just who the hell are you? And why'd you—" He jerked his chin toward the car.

I got out J. P. Ahearn's card and gave it to him. His face lost color.

"You work for that headhunter?"

"Not in this life. But in a little while I'm going to call that number from the telephone in that gas station across the road."

He lunged for the door. I was closer and got in his way. "I don't know how you got this far with a head that hot," I said. "For once in your young life listen. You might get to like it."

He listened.

"This is Commander Ahearn! I know you're in there, Boyd. I got a dozen men here and if you don't come out we'll shoot up the place!"

Neither of us had heard them coming, and with the moon behind a cloud the thin, bitter voice might have come from anywhere. This time Boyd won the race to the door. He had the reflexes of a deer.

"Kill the light!" I barked to Frechette. "Ahearn beat me to it. He must have followed you after all."

We were in darkness suddenly. Boyd and Suzie had their arms

around each other. "We're cornered," he said. "Why didn't that old lady have shells for that gun?"

"We just have to move faster, that's all. Keep him talking. Give me a hand with this window." The last was for Frechette, who came over and worked his big fingers under the swollen frame.

"There's a woman in here!" Boyd shouted.

"Come on out and no one gets hurt!" Ahearn sounded wired.

The window gave with a squawking wrench.

"One minute, Boyd. Then we start blasting!"

I hoped it was enough. I slipped out over the sill.

"The car! Get it!"

The Plymouth engine turned over twice in the cold before starting. The car rolled forward and began picking up speed down the incline toward the road. Just then the moon came out, illuminating the man behind the wheel, and the night came apart like mountain ice breaking up, cracking and splitting with the staccato rap of handgun fire and the deeper boom of riot guns. Orange flame scorched the darkness. Slugs whacked the car's sheet metal and shattered the windshield. Then a red glow started to spread inside the vehicle and fists of yellow flame battered out the rest of the windows with a *whump* that shook the ground. The car rolled for a few more yards while the shooters, standing now and visible in the light of the blaze, went on pouring lead into it until it came to a stop against a road sign. The flame towered twenty feet above the crackling wreckage.

I approached Ahearn, standing in the overgrown grass with his shotgun dangling, watching the car burn. He jumped a little when I spoke. His glasses glowed orange.

"He made a dash, just like you wanted."

"If you think I wanted this, you don't know me," he said.

"Save it for the Six O'Clock News."

"What the hell are you doing here, anyway?"

"Friend of the family. Can I take the Frechettes home, or do you want to eat them here?"

He cradled the shotgun. "We'll just go inside together."

We found Suzie sobbing in her father's arms. The Indian glared at Ahearn. "Get the hell out of here."

"He was a desperate man," Ahearn said. "You're lucky the girl's alive."

"I said get out or I'll ram that shotgun down your throat."

He got out. Through the window I watched him rejoin his men. There were five, not a dozen as he'd claimed. Later I learned that three of them were off-duty Detroit cops and he'd hired the other two from a private security firm.

I waited until the fire engines came and Ahearn was busy talking to the firefighters, then went out the window again and crossed to the next bungalow, set farther back where the light of the flames didn't reach. I knocked twice and paused and knocked again. Boyd opened the door a crack.

"I'm taking Suzie and her father back to Frechette's motel for looks. Think you can lie low here until we come back in the morning for the rental car?"

"What if they search the cabins?"

"For what? You're dead. By the time they find out that's Leo in the car, if they ever do, you and Suzie will be in Canada. Customs won't be looking for a dead bandit. Give everyone a year or so to forget what you look like and then you can come back. Not to Texas, though, and not under the name Virgil Boyd."

"Lucky the gas tank blew."

"I've never had enough luck to trust to it. That's why I put a box of C-4 in Leo's lap. Ma figured it was a small enough donation to keep her clear of a charge of felony murder."

"I thought you were some kind of corpse freak." He still had the surprised look. "You could've been killed starting that car. Why'd you do it?"

"The world's not as complicated as it looks," I said. "There's always a good and a bad side. I saw Ahearn's."

"You ever need anything," he said.

"If you do things right I won't be able to find you when I do." I shook his hand and returned to the other bungalow.

A week later, after J. P. Ahearn's narrow, jug-eared features had made the cover of *People,* I received an envelope from Houston containing a bonus check for a thousand dollars signed by Howard Frechette. He'd repaid the thirty-five hundred I'd given Ma before going home. That was the last I heard from any of them. I used the money to settle some old bills and had some work done on my car so I could continue to ply my trade along the Crooked Way.

Exit

by Andrew Vachss

Andrew Vachss is one of the most praised yet controversial writers of our time. In novels such as Blossom *and* Sacrifice, *he offers a view of our society that not everybody wishes to acknowledge.*

First published in 1989

The black Corvette glided into a waiting spot behind the smog-gray windowless building. Gene turned off the ignition. Sat listening to the quiet. He took a rectangular leather case from the compartment behind the seats, climbed out, flicking the door closed behind him. He didn't lock the car.

Gene walked slowly through the rat-maze corridors. The door at the end was unmarked. A heavyset man in an army jacket watched him approach, eyes never leaving Gene's hands.

"I want to see Monroe."

"Sorry, kid. He's backing a game now."

"I'm the one."

The heavyset man's eyes shifted to Gene's face. "He's been waiting over an hour for you."

Gene walked past the guard into a long narrow room. One green felt pool table under a string of hanging lights. Men on benches lining the walls. He could see the sign on the far wall— the large arrow indicating that *EXIT* was just beyond Monroe. They were all there: Irish, nervously stroking balls around the green felt surface, waiting. And Monroe. A grossly corpulent thing, parasite-surrounded. Boneless. Only his eyes betrayed life. They glittered greedily from deep within the fleshy rolls of his face. His eight hundred dollar black suit fluttered against his body like it didn't want to touch his flesh. His thin hair was flat-black, enameled patent-leather plastered onto a low forehead with a veneer of sweat. His large head rested on the puddle of his neck. His hands were mounds of doughy pink flesh at the tips of his short arms. His smile was a scar and the fear-aura coming off him was jailhouse-sharp.

"You were almost too late, kid."

"I'm here now."

"I'll let it go, Gene. You don't get a cut this time." The watchers grinned, taking their cue. "Three large when you win," Monroe said.

They advanced to the low clean table. Gene ran his hand gently over the tightly-woven surface, feeling the calm come into him the way it always did. He opened his leather case, assembled his cue.

Irish won the lag. Gene carefully roughened the tip of his cue, applied the blue chalk. Stepped to the table, holding the white cue ball in his left hand, bouncing it softly, waiting.

"Don't even think about losing." Monroe's voice, strangely thin.

Gene broke perfectly, leaving nothing. Irish walked once around the table, seeing what wasn't there. He played safe. The room was still.

"Seven ball in the corner."

Gene broke with that shot and quickly ran off the remaining balls. He watched Monroe's face gleaming wetly in the dimness as the balls were racked. He slammed the break-ball home, shattering the rack. And he sent the rest of the balls into pockets gaping their eagerness to serve him. The brightly-colored balls were his: he nursed some along the rail, sliced others laser-thin, finessed combinations. Brought them home.

Irish watched for a while. Then he sat down and looked at the floor. Lit a cigarette.

The room darkened. Gene smiled and missed his next shot. Irish sprang to the table. He worked slowly and too carefully for a long time. When he was finished, he was twelve balls ahead with twenty-five to go. But it was Gene's turn.

And Gene smiled again, deep into Monroe's face. Watched the man neatly place a cigarette into the precise center of his mouth, waving away a weasel-in-attendance who leaped to light it for him. And missed again . . . by a wider margin.

Irish blasted the balls off the table, waited impatiently for the rack. He smelled the pressure and didn't want to lose the wave.

Irish broke correctly, ran the remaining balls and finished the game. *EXIT* was glowing in the background. As the last ball went down, he turned:

"You owe me money, Monroe."

His voice trembled. One of Monroe's men put money in his hand. The fat man spoke, soft and cold: "Would you like to play again?"

"No, I won't play again. I must of been crazy. You would of gone through with it. Yes. You fat, dirty, evil sonofabitch . . ."

One of the calmly waiting men hit him sharply under the heart. Others stepped forward to drag him from the room.

"Let him keep the money," Monroe told them.

Gene turned to gaze silently at the fat man. Almost home . . .

"You going to kill me, Monroe?"

"No, Gene. I don't want to kill you."

"Then I'm leaving."

A man grabbed Gene from each side and walked him toward the fat man's chair.

"You won't do anything like that. Ever again."

Monroe ground the hungry tip of his bright-red cigarette deep into the boy's face, directly beneath the eye. Just before he lost consciousness, Gene remembered that Monroe didn't smoke.

He awoke in a grassy plain, face down. He started to rise and the earth stuck to his torn face.

His screams were triumph.

Deathman

by Ed Gorman

First published in 1991

The night before he killed a man, Hawes always followed the same ritual.

He arrived in town late afternoon—in this case, a chill shadowy autumn afternoon—found the best hotel, checked in, took a hot bath in a big metal tub, put on a fresh suit so dark it hinted at the ministerial, buffed his black boots till they shone, and then went down to the lobby in search of the best steak in town.

Because this was a town he'd worked many times before, he knew just which restaurant to choose—a place called Ma's Gaslight Inn. Ma had died last year of a venereal disease (crazed as hell, her friends said, in her last weeks, talking to dead people and drawing crude pictures of her tombstone again and again on the wall next to her death bed.)

Dusk and chill rain sent townspeople scurrying for home, the clatter of wagons joining the clop of horses in retreat from the small, prosperous mountain town.

Hawes strode the boardwalk alone, a short and burly man handsome except for his acne-pitted cheeks. Even in his early forties, his boyhood taint was obvious.

Rain dripped in fat silver beads from the overhangs as he walked down the boardwalk toward the restaurant. He liked to look in the shop windows when they were closed this way, look at the female things—a lace shawl, a music box with a ballerina dancing atop, a ruby necklace so elegant it looked as if it had been plucked from the fat white neck of a duchess only moments ago.

Without quite wanting them to, all these things reminded him of Sara. Three years they'd been married until she'd learned his secret, and then she'd been so repelled she invented a reason to visit her mother back in Ohio, and never again returned. He was sure she had remarried—he'd received divorce papers several years ago—and probably even had children by now. Children— and a house with a creek in back—had been her most devout wish.

He quit looking in the shop windows. He now looked straight ahead. His boot heels were loud against the wet boards. The air smelled cold and clean enough to put life in the lungs of the dead.

The player piano grew louder the closer the restaurant got; and then laughter and the clink of glasses.

Standing there, outside it all, he felt a great loneliness, and now when he thought of Sara he was almost happy. Having even sad memories were better than no memories at all.

He walked quickly to the restaurant door, pushed it open, and went inside.

He needed to be with people tonight.

He was halfway through his steak dinner (fat pats of butter dripping golden down the thick sides of the meat and potatoes sliced and fried in tasty grease) when the tall man in the gray suit came over.

At this time the restaurant was full, low-hanging Rochester lamps casting small pools of light into the ocean of darkness. Tobacco smoke lay a haze over everything, seeming to muffle conversations. An old Negro stood next to the double doors of the kitchen, filling water glasses and handing them to the big-hipped waitresses hurrying in and out the doors. The rest of the house was packed with the sort of people you saw in mining towns—wealthy miners and wealthy men who managed the mines for eastern bosses; and then just hard scrubbed-clean workingmen with their hard scrubbed-clean wives out celebrating a birthday or an anniversary at the place where the rich folks dine.

"Excuse me."

Hawes looked up. "Yes?"

"I was wondering if you remembered me."

Hawes looked him over. "I guess."

"Good. Then you mind if I sit down?"

"You damn right I do. I'm eating."

"But last time you promised that—"

Hawes dismissed the man with a wave of a pudgy hand. "Didn't you hear me? I'm eating. And I don't want to be interrupted."

"Then after you're finished eating—?"

Hawes shrugged. "We'll see. Now get out of here and leave me alone."

The man was very young, little more than a kid, twenty-one, twenty-two at most, and now he seemed to wither under the assault of Hawes's intentional and practiced rudeness.

"I'll make sure you're done eating before I bother you again."

Hawes said nothing. His head was bent to the task of cutting himself another piece of succulent steak.

The tall man went away.

"It's me again. Richard Sloane."

"So I see."

The tall man looked awkward. "You're smoking a cigar."

"So I am."

"So I take it you're finished eating?"

Hawes almost had to laugh, the sonofabitch looked so young and nervous. They weren't making them tough, the way they'd been in the frontier days. "I suppose I am."

"Then may I sit down?"

Hawes pointed a finger at an empty chair. The young man sat down.

"You know what I want?" He took out a pad and pencil the way any good journalist would.

"Same thing you people always want."

"How it feels after you do it."

Hawes smiled. "You mean do I feel guilty? Do I have nightmares?"

The young man looked uncomfortable with Hawes's playful tone. "I guess that's what I mean, yes."

Hawes stared at the young man.

"You ever seen one, son?"

He looked as if he was going to object to "son" but then changed his mind. "Two. One when I was a little boy with my uncle and one last year."

"Did you like it?"

"I hated it. It scared me and the way people acted, it made me sick. They were—celebrating. It was like a party."

"Yes, some of them get that way sometimes."

Hawes had made a study of it all so he considered telling

Sloane here about Tom Galvin, an Irishman of the sixteenth century who had personally hanged more that sixteen hundred men. Galvin believed in giving the crowd a show, especially with men accused of treason. These he not only hanged but often-times dismembered, throwing arms and legs to the crazed on-lookers. Some reports had it that some of the crowds actually ate of the bloodied limbs tossed to them.

"You ever hang two at once?"

"The way they did in Nevada last year?" Hawes smirked and shook his head. "Not me, son. I'm not there to put on a show. I'm there to kill a man." He took a drag on his cigar. "I don't want to give my profession a bad name."

God knew that executioners, as a group, were unreliable. In seventeenth-century England, the executioner himself was put in a jail cell for eight days preceding the hanging—so officials would know he'd show up on time and sober.

"Will you sleep well tonight?" Sloane asked.

"Very well, hopefully."

"You won't think about tomorrow?"

"Not very seriously."

"How the man will look?"

"No."

"Or how the trap will sound when it opens?"

"No."

"Or how his eyes will bulge and his tongue will bloat?"

Hawes shook his head. "I know what you want, son. You want a speech about the terrible burden of being an executioner." He tapped his chest. "But I don't have it in me."

"Then it isn't a burden?"

"No, son, it isn't. It's just what I do. The way some men milk cows and other men fix buggies—I hang people. It's just that simple."

The young man looked disappointed. They always did when Hawes told them this. They wanted melodrama—they wanted regret and remorse and a tortured soul.

Hawes decided to give him the story about the woman. It wasn't the whole story, of course, but the part he always told was just what newspapermen were looking for.

"There was a blonde woman once," Hawes said.

"Blonde?"

"So blonde it almost hurt your eyes to look at her hair in the sunlight. It was spun gold."

"Spun gold; God."

It belonged to Ma Chaney, who greeted me at the door of her house in rural Macomb County wearing a red Japanese kimono with green parrots all over it. The kimono could have covered a Toyota. She was a five-by-five chunk with marcelled orange hair and round black eyes embedded in her face like nail heads in soft wax. A cigarette teetered on her lower lip. I followed her into a parlor full of flowered chairs and sofas and pregnant lamps with fringed shades. A long strip of pimply blond youth in overalls and no shirt took his brogans off the coffee table and stood up when she barked at him. He gaped at me, chewing gum with his mouth open.

"Mr. Walker, Leo," Ma wheezed. "Leo knew my Wilbur in Ypsi. He's like another son to me."

Ma Chaney had one son in the criminal ward at the Forensic Psychiatry Center in Ypsilanti and another on Florida's Death Row. The FBI was looking for the youngest in connection with an armored car robbery in Kansas City. The whole brood had come up from Kentucky when Old Man Chaney got a job on the line at River Rouge and stayed on after he was killed in a propane tank explosion. Now Ma, the daughter of a Hawkins County gunsmith, made her living off the domestic weapons market.

"You said talk ain't cheap," she said, when she was sitting in a big overstuffed rocker. "How cheap ain't it?"

I perched on the edge of a hard upright with doilies on the arms. Leo remained standing, scratching himself. "Depends on whether we talk about Virgil Boyd," I said.

"What if we don't?"

"Then I won't take up any more of your time."

"What if we do?"

"I'll double what he's paying."

She coughed. The cigarette bobbed. "I got a business to run. I go around scratching at *re*wards I won't have no customers."

"Does that mean Boyd's a customer?"

"Now, why'd that Texas boy want to come to Ma? He can deal hisself a shotgun at any K mart."

"He can't show his face in the legal places and being new in town he doesn't know the illegal ones. But he wouldn't have to ask around too much to come up with your name. You're less selective than most."

"You don't have to pussyfoot around old Ma. I don't get a lot of second-timers on account of I talk for money. My boy Earl in Florida needs a new lawyer. But I only talk after, not before. I start setting up customers I won't get no first-timers."

"I'm not even interested in Boyd. It's his girlfriend I want to talk to. Suzie Frechette."

"Don't know her." She rocked back and forth. "What color's your money?"

Before leaving Detroit I'd cashed Howard Frechette's check. I laid fifteen hundred dollars on the coffee table in twenties and fifties. Leo straightened up a little to look at the bills. Ma resumed rocking. "It ain't enough."

"How much is enough?"

"If I was to talk to a fella named Boyd, and if I was to agree to sell him a brand-new Ithaca pump shotgun and a P-38 still in the box, I wouldn't sell them for less than twenny-five hunnert. Double twenny-five hunnert is five thousand."

"Fifteen hundred now. Thirty-five hundred when I see the girl."

"I don't guarantee no girl."

"Boyd then. If he's come this far with her he won't leave her behind."

She went on rocking. "They's a white barn a mile north on this road. If I was to meet a fella named Boyd, there's where I might do it. I might pick eleven o'clock."

"Tonight?"

"I might pick tonight. If it don't rain."

I got up. She stopped rocking.

"Come alone," she said. "Ma won't."

On the way back to town I filled up at a corner station and used the pay telephone to call Howard Frechette's room at the Holiday Inn. When he started asking questions I gave him the number and told him to call back from a booth outside the motel.

"Ahearn's an anachronism," he said ten minutes later. "I doubt he taps phones."

"Maybe not, but motel operators have big ears."

"Did you talk to Suzie?"

"Minor setback," I said. "Your sister gave her and Boyd the boot and no money."

"Tight bitch."

"I know where they'll be tonight, though. There's an old auto court on Van Dyke between 21 and 22 Mile in Macomb County, the Log Cabin Inn. Looks like it sounds." I was staring at it across the road. "Midnight. Better give yourself an hour."

He repeated the information.

"I'm going to have to tap you for thirty-five hundred dollars," I said. "The education cost."

"And it was my duty to hang her."

"Oh, shit."

"The mayor of the town said I'd be hanging a woman, but I never dreamt she'd be so beautiful."

"Did you hang her anyway?"

"I had to, son. It's my job."

"Did she cry?"

"She was strong. She didn't cry and her legs didn't give out when she was climbing the scaffold stairs. You know, I've seen big strapping men just collapse on those stairs and have to be carried all the way up. And some of them foul their pants. I can smell the stench when I'm pulling the white hood over their eyes."

"But she was strong?"

"Very strong. She walked right over to the trapdoor and stood on top of it and folded her hands very primly in front of her. And then she just waited for me to come over there."

"What was she guilty of?"

"She'd taken a lover that spring, and when her husband found out, he tried to kill her. But instead she killed him. The jury convicted her of first-degree murder."

"It doesn't sound like first-degree to me."

"Me either, son. But I'm the hangman; I'm not the judge."

"And so you hanged her?"

"I did."

"Didn't you want to call it off?"

"A part of me did."

"Did she scream when the door dropped away?"

"She didn't say anything."

"And her neck snapped right away?"

"I made sure of that, son. I didn't want her to dangle there and strangle the way they sometimes do. So I cinched the knot extra tight. She crossed over right away. You could hear her neck go."

"This was how many years ago?"

"Ten."

"And obviously you still think about her."

It was clear now the angle the young journalist would be taking. Hangman kills beautiful woman; can't get her out of his mind these long years later. His readers would love it.

"Oh, yes, son, yes, I still think about her."

The excitement was plain on the man's young face. This may just have been the best story he'd ever had.

He flipped the cover of his pad closed. "I really appreciate this."

Hawes nodded.

The young man got up, snatched his derby from the edge of the table, and walked to the rear where the press of people and smoke and clatter was overwhelming.

Hawes took the time for another two drinks and half a Cuban cigar and then went out into the rain.

The house was three blocks away, in the opposite direction of the gallows, for which Hawes was grateful. A superstitious man, he believed that looking at a gallows the night before would bring bad luck. The man would not die clean, the trap would not open, the rope would mysteriously snap—something. And so he didn't glimpse the gallows until the morning of the execution.

Hawes came this way often. This town was in the exact center of the five-hundred-mile radius he traveled as an executioner. So he came to this town three or four times a month, not just when he had somebody to hang here.

And he always came to Maude's.

Maude was the plump giggling madame who ran the town's only whorehouse. She had an agreement with the sheriff that if she kept her house a quarter mile away from town, and if she ran her place clean, meaning no drugs or no black whores or no black customers, then the sheriff would leave her alone, meaning of course he would keep at bay the zealous German Lutherans who made up the town. Maude gave the lawman money but not much, and every once in a while he'd sneak up on the back porch where one of the runaway farm girls she employed would offer the sheriff her wet glistening lips.

He could hear the player piano now, Hawes could, lonely on the rainy prairie night. He wished he hadn't told that pipsqueak journalist about the blonde woman because now Hawes was thinking about her again, and what really happened that morning.

The house was a white two-story job. In front, two horses were tied to a post, and down a ways a buggy dun stood ground-tied.

Hawes went up to the door and knocked.

Maude herself opened it. "Well, for shit's sake, girls, look who's here."

Downstairs there was a parlor, which was where the player piano was, and the girls sat on a couch and you chose them the way you did cattle at a livestock auction.

Hawes always asked for the same one. He looked at the five girls sitting there watching him. They were about what you'd expect for a midwestern prairie whorehouse—young girls quickly losing their bloom. They drank too much and laughed too loud and weren't always good about keeping themselves clean.

That was why he always asked for Lucy.

"She's here, Maude?"

Maude winked at him. "Just taking a bath."

"I see."

"Won't be long." She knew his tastes, knew he didn't want to stay downstairs with the girls and the piano and the two cowboys who were giggling about which girls they'd pick. "You know the end room on the hall?"

"Right."

"Why don't you go up there and wait for her?"

"Good idea."

"You'll find some bourbon in the drawer."

"Appreciate it."

She winked at him again. "Hear you're hanging the Parsons boy in the morning."

"I never know their names."

"Well, take it from me, sweetie, when he used to come here he didn't tip worth a shit. Anything he gets from you, he's got coming." And then she whooped a laugh and slapped him on the back and said, "You just go right up those stairs, sweetie."

He nodded, mumbling a thank-you, and turned away from her before he had to look directly at the small brown stubs of her teeth. The sight and stench of her mouth had always sickened him.

He wondered how many men had lain in this dark room. He wondered how many men had felt this loneliness. He wondered how many men had heard a woman's footsteps coming down the hall, and felt fear and shame.

Lucy opened the door. She was silhouetted in the flickering hall light. "You want me to get a lantern?"

"That's all right."

She laughed. "Never known a man who likes the dark the way you do."

She came in, closed the door behind her. She smelled of soapy bath water and jasmine. She wasn't pretty, but she kept herself clean and he appreciated it.

"Should've just left my clothes off, I guess," she said. "After my bath, I mean."

He could tell she was nervous. The darkness always made her like this.

Wind and rain spattered against the window. The fingers of a dead branch scraped the glass, a curious kind of music.

She came over to the bed and stood above him. She took his hand and pressed it lightly against her sex. She was dry and warm.

"You going to move over?"

He rolled over so there was room for her. He lay on his back and stared at the ceiling.

As usual when they lay there, Lucy smoked a cigarette. She always hand-rolled two or three before coming to see Hawes because many times the night consisted of talk and nothing more.

"You want a drag?" she said.

"No thanks."

"How you doing?"

"All right, I guess."

"Hear you're going to hang a man tomorrow."

"Yes."

Next to him, she shuddered, her whole naked skinny body. "Forgive me for saying so, Hawes, but I just don't know how you can do it."

"You've said that before."

She laughed again. "Yes, I guess I have."

They lay there silent for a time, just the wind and the rain pattering the roof, just the occasional glow of her cigarette as she dragged on it, just his own breathing.

And the darkness; oh, yes, the darkness.

"You ever read anything by Louisa May Alcott?" Lucy asked.

"No."

"I'm reading this book by her now. It's real good, Hawes, you should read it sometime."

"Maybe I will."

That was another thing he liked about Lucy. Where most of the girls were ignorant, Lucy had gone through fourth grade before running away, and had learned to read. Hawes could carry on a good conversation with her and he appreciated that. Of course, she was older, too, twenty-five or so, and that also made a difference.

They fell into silence again.

After a while he rolled over and kissed her.

She said, "Just a minute."

"I can manage it. Is that where they're headed?"

"I hope so. I haven't asked them yet."

I got to my bank just before closing and cleaned out my savings and all but eight dollars in my checking account. I hoped Frechette was good for it. After that I ate dinner in a restaurant and went to see a movie about a one-man army. I wondered if he was available.

The barn was just visible from the road, a moonlit square at the end of a pair of ruts cut through weeds two feet high. It was a chill night in early spring and I had on a light coat and the heater running. I entered a dip that cut off my view of the barn, then bucked up over a ridge and had to stand the Chevy on its nose when the lamps fell on a telephone pole lying across the path. A second later the passenger's door opened and Leo got in.

He had on a mackinaw over his overalls and a plaid cap. His right hand was wrapped around a large-bore revolver and he kept it on me, held tight to his stomach, while he felt under my coat and came up with the Luger. "Drive." He pocketed it.

I swung around the end of the pole and braked in front of the barn, where Ma was standing with a Coleman lantern. She was wearing a man's felt hat and a corduroy coat with sleeves that came down to her fingers. She signaled a cranking motion and I rolled down the window.

"Well, park it around back," she said. "I got to think for you, too?"

I did that and Leo and I walked back. He handed Ma the Luger and she looked at it and put it in her pocket. She raised the lantern then and swung it from side to side twice.

We waited a few minutes, then were joined by six feet and two hundred and fifty pounds of red-bearded young man in faded denim jacket and jeans carrying a rifle with an infrared scope. He had come from the direction of the road.

"Anybody following, Mason?" asked Ma.

He shook his head, and I stared at him in the lantern light. He had small black eyes like Ma's with no shine in them. This would be Mace Chaney, for whom the FBI was combing the western states for the Kansas armored car robbery.

"Go on in and warm yourself," Ma said. "We got some time."

He opened the barn door and went inside. It had just closed when two headlamps appeared down the road. We watched them approach and slow for a turn onto the path. Ma, lighting a cigarette off the lantern, grunted.

"Early. Young folks all got watches and they can't tell time."

Leo trotted out to intercept the car. A door slammed. After a pause the lamps swung around the fallen telephone pole and came up to the barn, washing us all in white. The driver killed the lamps and engine and got out. He was a small man in his early twenties with short brown hair and stubble on his face. His flannel shirt and khaki pants were both in need of cleaning. He had scant eyebrows that were almost invisible in that light, giving him a perennially surprised look. I'd seen that look in Frechette's *Houston Chronicle* and in both Detroit papers.

"Who's he?" He was looking at me.

I had a story for that, but Ma piped up. "You ain't paying to ask no questions. Got the money?"

"Not all of it. A thousand's all Suzie could get from the sharks."

"The deal's two thousand."

"Keep the P-38. The shotgun's all I need."

Ma had told me twenty-five hundred; but I was barely listening to the conversation. Leo had gotten out on the passenger side, pulling with him the girl in the photograph in my pocket. Suzie Frechette had done up her black hair in braids, and she'd lost weight, but her dark eyes and coloring were unmistakable. With that hairstyle and in a man's work shirt and jeans and boots with western heels she looked more like an Indian than she did in her picture.

Leo opened the door and we went inside. The barn hadn't been used for its original purpose for some time, but the smell of moldy hay would remain as long as it stood. It was lit by a bare bulb swinging from a frayed cord and heated by a barrel stove in a corner. Stacks of cardboard cartons reached almost to the rafters, below which Mace Chaney sat with his legs dangling over the edge of the empty loft, the rifle across his knees.

Ma reached into an open carton and lifted out a pump shotgun with the barrel cut back to the slide. Boyd stepped forward to take it. She swung the muzzle on him. "Show me some paper."

He hesitated then drew a thick fold of bills from his shirt pocket and laid it on a stack of cartons. Then she moved to cover me. Boyd watched me add thirty-five hundred to the pile.

"What's *he* buying?"

Ma said, "You."

"Cop!" He lunged for the shotgun. Leo's revolver came out. Mace drew a bead on Boyd from the loft. He relaxed.

Introduction to
The Red Scarf

By Bill Pronzini

Gil Brewer was one of the major voices to evolve from the Gold Medal paperbacks of the fifties. Here, Bill Pronzini, in a piece originally published in Mystery Scene, *charts Brewer's sad life.*

I don't like the *Murder, She Wrote* TV show.

I don't like it because it gives a false and distorted picture of what it's like to be a mystery writer. Dear Jessica effortlessly produces a couple of novels which become instant bestsellers. Critics and readers adore them, every one. Film and play producers flock to her door, offering huge amounts of money. She attends fancy New York parties and everyone knows her name, everyone praises her work. Small towns, ditto. Foreign countries, ditto. Her agent is a prince; so are her U.S. and foreign publishers. She has no career setbacks, no private demons. She writes when she feels like it, which isn't very often, and never has to worry about money. Her life is full of adventure, romance, excitement, joy. It is the kind of life even royalty envies.

Well, bullshit.

You want to know what the life of a working mystery writer is *really* like? Gil Brewer could tell you. He could tell you about the taste of success and fame that never quite becomes a meal; the shattered dreams and lost hopes, the loneliness, the rejections and failures and empty promises, the lies and deceit, the bitterness, the self-doubts, the dry spells and dried-up markets, the

She took him in her arms with surprising tenderness, and held him to her, her soft breasts warm against his chest, and then she said, "Sometimes I think you're my little boy, Hawes. You know that?"

But Hawes wasn't paying attention; he was listening to the chill rain on the dark wind, and the lonely frantic laughter down the hall.

The wind grew louder then, and Lucy fell silent, just holding him tighter; tighter.

"I know."

"It's kind of funny, even."

"It isn't funny to me."

And it hadn't been funny to his wife Sara, either. Once she'd figured out the pattern, she'd left him immediately.

"How'd you figure it out?" he asked.

"I just started keeping track."

"Oh."

"But I won't tell anybody. I mean, if that's what's bothering you."

"I appreciate it. You keeping it to yourself, I mean."

"You can't help the way you are."

"No; no, I guess I can't."

He thought of how angry and disgusted his wife Sara had been when she'd finally figured it, how he was impotent all the time except for the night before a hanging. Only then could he become fully a man.

The snap of the trapdoor; the snap of the neck. And then extinction. Blackness; utter, eternal blackness. And Hawes controlling it all.

In the wind and darkness, she said, "You ever think about how it'll be for you personally?"

"How what'll be?"

"Death."

"Yeah; I guess so."

"You think there're angels?"

"No."

"You think there's a heaven?"

"No."

"You think there's a God?"

"No."

She took a long drag on her cigarette. "Neither do I, Hawes. But I sure wish I did."

From down the hall, Hawes could hear a man laughing, and then a woman joining in. The player piano downstairs was going again.

"Would you just hold me?" Hawes said.

"What?"

"Just hold me in your arms."

"Sure."

"Real tight."

"All right."

She stubbed out her cigarette and then rolled back to him.

She stubbed her cigarette out and then rolled back to him and then they got down to it seriously.

The fear was there as always—could he actually do it and do it right without humiliating himself as usual?—but tonight he had no trouble.

He was good and hard and he got in her with no trouble and she responded as if she really gave a damn about him, and then he came and he collapsed next to her, his breath heaving in the darkness, and him feeling pretty damn good about himself as a man again.

She didn't say anything for a long time there in the wind and rain and darkness, her naked and moist from where his body had been pressing on her, and her smoking a cigarette again, and then she said, "That's why she left you, isn't it?"

"Huh?"

"Your wife. Why she left you."

"I'm not following you." But he was in fact following her and he sensed that she was going to say something he didn't want to hear.

"That time you got drunk up here in the room," she said.

"Yeah? What about it?"

"You told me about your wife leaving you."

"So?"

"But you wouldn't tell my *why* she left you. You just kept saying 'She had a good reason, I guess.' Well, I finally figured out what that reason is."

He was silent for a time again, and so was she.

Obviously she could sense that she'd spooked him and now she was feeling bad about it. "I shouldn't have said anything, Hawes. I'm sorry."

"It's all right."

He was feeling the loneliness again. He wanted to cry, but he wasn't a man given to tears.

"Me and my big fucking mouth," Lucy said, lighting another cigarette.

In the flash of flame, he could see her face. Soft, freckled, eyes the blue of a spring sky.

They lay in silence a long time.

She said, "You mad at me, Hawes?"

"No."

"I'm sorry I said anything."

"I know."

"I mean, it doesn't bother me. The way you are."

constant and painful grubbing for enough money to make ends meet. He could tell you about all of that, and much more. He would, too, if he were still alive. But he isn't.

Gil Brewer drank himself to death on the second day of January, in the Year of Our Lord nineteen hundred and eight-three, at the age of sixty.

. . . Last year [1981] *I nearly croaked; not through drinking, but because I had an infected lung, emphysema, heart failure and pneumonia— all at the same time. It was a rough go at the hospital. Then nearly a year of sobriety and I figured I was ready for work, when things went to pot again. . . . I'm ashamed of all the evil damned things I've done when drinking.* [But] *I'm straight now, and must remain so, because one more drink and Gil Brewer goes down the slot.*

Sure, it's a cliche. Look at all the writers who have destroyed themselves with alcohol. Poe, Stephen Crane, O. Henry, Jack London, Sinclair Lewis, Dorothy Parker. Fitzgerald. Faulkner. O'Hara. And Hammett. And Chandler. And hundreds more. So does it really matter that a minor mystery writer named Gil Brewer also drank himself to death?

Damned right it does.

It matters because he was a gentle, sensitive, vulnerable man who felt too deeply and cared too much.

It matters because he produced some of the most compelling *noir* softcover originals of the 1950s.

It matters because he understood and loved fine writing and hungered to create it himself, to just once write something of depth and beauty and meaning.

It matters because of the writer he might have been with a little luck, encouragement, and the proper guidance, for in him there was a small untapped core of greatness.

It matters because if it doesn't, then nothing does.

. . . For all my seemingly sometimes rattlebrained manner, I am actually deathly sincere and serious about my writing. . . . Am only happy— my only real happiness—at the machine.

Gil Brewer was born in relative poverty in Canandaigua, New York, in November of 1922. He dropped out of school to work, but retained a thirst for knowledge and a love of books; he was an omnivorous reader. At the outbreak of World War II he joined the Army and served in France and Belgium, seeing action and receiving wounds that entitled him to a VA disability pension. After the war, he worked at a variety of jobs—warehouseman, cannery worker, bookseller, gas station attendant—while pursuing a lifelong desire to write fiction.

His early efforts were not crime stories but mainstream and "literary" exercises. He sent some of these to Joseph T. Shaw, the former editor of *Black Mask,* who had become a successful literary agent in the 40s. Shaw liked what he saw and encouraged Brewer to keep writing, though with a more commercial slant to his work.

I began as a "serious" writer, and came close, but married and had to have money so switched to pulp. I was with Joe Shaw at that time. I sold shorts to Detective Tales, *etc. Shaw had my entire career planned. I tried writing a suspense book to see if I could do it, and wrote one single-spaced in five days. Then I wrote* Satin Is a Woman *and Gold Medal bought it and asked for more—Dick Carroll and Bill Lengel—and Joe said to me, "You've already got another one* [finished]. *The five-day book,* So Rich, So Dead. *So GM published that. Then I wrote* 13 French Street *and was off to the races.*

Fawcett was the first and best of the softcover publishers to specialize in original, male-oriented mysteries, Westerns, historicals, and "modern" novels. Their Gold Medal line was in its infancy (the first GM titles appeared in late 1949) when they bought Brewer's first two novels in 1950; but GM's success was already guaranteed. They had assembled, and would continue to assemble, some of the best popular and category writers of the period by paying royalty advances based on the number of copies printed, rather than on the number of copies sold; thus writers received handsome sums up front, up to three and four times as much as hardcover publishers were paying. Into the GM stable came such established names as W. R. Burnett, Cornell Woolrich, Sax Rohmer, MacKinlay Kantor, Wade Miller, and Octavus Roy Cohen; such top pulpeteers as John D. MacDonald, Bruno Fischer, Day Keene, David Goodis, Harry Whittington, Edward S. Aarons, and Dan Cushman; and such talented newcomers as Charles Williams, Richard S. Prather, Stephen Marlowe, and Gil Brewer.

What the Fawcett brain trust and the Fawcett writers succeeded in doing was adapting the tried-and-true pulp fiction formula of the 30s and 40s to post-war American society, with all its changes in lifestyle and morality and its newfound sophistication. Instead of a bulky magazine full of short stories, they provided brand-new, easy-to-read novels in the handy pocket format. Instead of gaudy, juvenile shoot-'em-up cover art, they utilized the "peekaboo sex" approach to catching the reader's eye: women depicted either nude (as seen from the side or rear) or with a great deal of cleavage and/or leg showing, in a variety of provocative poses. Instead of printing a hundred thousand copies of a small number of titles, they printed hundreds of thousands of copies of many titles so as to reach every possible outlet and buyer.

They were selling pulp fiction, yes, but it was a different, up-scale kind of pulp. On the one hand, the novels published by Fawcett—and by the best of their competitors, Dell, Avon, and Popular Library—were short (generally around 50,000 words), rapidly paced, with emphasis on action. On the other hand, they were well-written, well-plotted, peopled by sharply delineated and believable characters, spiced with sex, often imbued with psychological insight, and set in vividly drawn, often exotic locales . . . the stuff of any good commercial novel, then or now. Thanks to writers such as Gil Brewer, the best of the Gold Medal novels are the apotheosis of pulp fiction—rough-hewn, minor works of art, perfectly suited to and representative of their era. What has been labeled as pulp since the early 60s is not the genuine article; it is an offshoot of pulp, or a mutation of pulp, reflective of the "new world" that has been created by the technological and other sweeping changes of the past twenty-five years. The last piece of true-pulp-as-art was published circa 1965.

Readers responded to the Gold Medal formula with enthusiasm and in huge numbers. It was common in GM's first few years for individual titles to sell up to 500,000 copies, and not all that unusual for one to surpass the 1,000,000 mark. Brewer's *13 French Street,* published in 1951, was one of those early million-copy bestsellers, going into eight separate printings and many overprintings.

13 French Street is not his best novel. A deadly-triangle tale of two old friends, one of whom has fallen mysteriously ill, and the sick one's evil wife, it has a thin and rather predictable plot; and too much of the narrative takes place in the house at the title address. Nevertheless, it has all of the qualities that give Brewer's work its individuality and power. The prose is lean, Hemingwayesque (Hemingway's influence is apparent throughout the Brewer canon), and yet rich with raw emotion genuinely portrayed and felt. It makes effective use of one of his obsessive themes, that of a weak, foolish, and/or disillusioned man corrupted and either destroyed or nearly destroyed by a wicked, designing woman. And it has echoes—especially in the use of Saint-Saens' *Danse Macabre* as a leitmotif—of the haunting sur-reality and existentialism that infuses his strongest work.

With the success of *13 French Street,* Brewer was indeed "off to the races." Over the next nine years, Fawcett's editors bought and published a dozen more of his novels, nine under the Gold Medal imprint and three under their Crest imprint generally reserved for hardcover reprints. All but one were contemporary suspense novels; the lone exception is Brewer's only Western novel, *Some Must Die* (1954), an excellent variation on the theme of good people and bad thrown together and entrapped by the elements. (The cover art and blurbs for *Some Must Die* were carefully crafted to give the impression that it was modern-suspense rather than Western-suspense. Brewer's readers weren't fooled, though; *Some Must Die* sold the fewest copies of his early books.)

Despite some lurid titles—*Hell's Our Destination,—And the Girl Screamed, Little Tramp, The Brat, The Vengeful Virgin*—Brewer's 50s GM and Crest novels are neither sleazy nor sensationalized; they are the same sort of realistic crime-adventure stories John D. MacDonald and Charles Williams were producing for GM, and of uniformly above-average quality. Most are set in the cities, small towns, waterways, swamps and backwaters of Florida, Brewer's adopted home. (The exceptions are *Some Must Die* and *77 Rue Paradis* [1954], which has a well-depicted Marseilles setting.) The protagonists are ex-soldiers, ex-cops, drifters, convicts, blue-collar workers, charterboat captains, unorthodox private detectives, even a sculptor. The plots range from searches for stolen gold and sunken treasure to savage indictments of the effects of lust, greed and murder to chilling psychological studies of disturbed personalities.

Probably the best of his Fawcett originals is *A Killer Is Loose* [1954], a truly harrowing portrait of a psychopath that comes close to rivaling the nightmare visions of Jim Thompson. It tells the story of Ralph Angers, a deranged surgeon and Korean War veteran obsessed with building a hospital, and his devastating effect on the lives of several citizens of a small Florida town. One of the citizens is the narrator, Steve Logan, a down-on-his-luck ex-cop whose wife is about to have a baby and who makes the mistake of saving Anger's life, thus becoming his "pal". As Logan says on page one, by way of prologue, "There was nothing simple about Angers, except maybe the Godlike way he had of doing things."

Brewer maintains a pervading sense of terror and an acute level of tension throughout. Although the novel is flawed by a slow beginning and a couple of improbabilities, as well as an ending that is a little too abrupt, its strengths far outnumber its weaknesses. Two aspects in particular stand out: One is the curious and frighteningly symbiotic relationship that develops between Logan and Angers; the other is a five-page scene in which Angers, with Logan looking on helplessly, forces a scared little girl to play the piano for him—a scene Woolrich or Thompson might have written and Hitchcock should have filmed.

A Killer Is Loose—in fact, all of Brewer's early novels—was written at white heat and almost entirely first-draft. This accounts for their strengths, in particular the headlong immediacy of the narratives, and for their various weaknesses. It seemed to be the only way Brewer *could* write: fast, fast, with black coffee and cigarettes and liquor to help him get through the long sleepless periods, and pills to help him come down afterward.

I batted out those Gold Medal books for so very long, never taking more than two weeks on one, and once wrote one in three days—in fact more than one—and often in five or six days—and they all sold. I possibly thought it would continue forever, poor fool that I am, but with never any encouragement toward better stuff, except on one occasion I recall that didn't work.

The 50s was Brewer's decade; satisfied with his work or not, he was a commercial success. In addition to his books for Fawcett, he sold suspense novels to Avon, Ace, Monarch, Bouregy. He continued to write short stories, too, under his own name and such pseudonyms as Eric Fitzgerald and Bailey Morgan, and placed them with most of the digest-sized mystery magazines of the time—*Manhunt, The Saint, Pursuit, Hunted, Accused*—as well as with numerous men's magazines. His new agent (Joe Shaw died in 1952) sold film rights to four of his GM books: *13 French Street, A Killer Is Loose, Hell's Our Destination* (poorly filmed as *Lure Of the Swamps*), and *The Brat*. Almost everything he wrote found a publisher. And almost every one of his novels, if not every one of his short stories, had more than a little merit.

Outstanding among his non-Fawcett books of the 50s, and two of his best overall, are *The Red Scarf* (Mystery House, 1958) and *Nude On Thin Ice* (Avon, 1960). The former title has an interesting history. It was inexplicably rejected by Fawcett and other paperback houses, and eventually sold to the lending-library publisher, Thomas Bouregy, for a meager $300 advance; it was Brewer's second and last book to appear under Bouregy's Mystery House imprint—the first was *The Angry Dream* (1957)—and his second and last U.S. hardcover appearance. After publication of *The Red Scarf*, Fawcett's editors had a sudden change of heart and decided the book was worthwhile after all: they bought reprint rights (presumably for much less money than they would have had to pay Brewer for an original) and republished it as a Crest title in 1959.

The Red Scarf is narrated by motel owner Ray Nichols. Hitchhiking home in northern Florida after a futile trip up north to raise capital for his floundering auto court, Nichols is given a ride by a bickering and drunken couple named Vivian Rise and Noel Teece. An accident, the result of Teece's drinking, leaves Teece bloody and unconscious; Nichols and Vivian are unhurt. At the woman's urging, he leaves the scene with her and the money— and it is only later, back home with his wife, that he discovers Teece is a courier for a gambling syndicate and that the money belongs to them, not to either Teece or Vivian. While he struggles with his conscience, several factions begin vying for the loot, including a Mob enforcer, the police, and Teece. There are some neat plot turns, the various components mesh smoothly, the characterization is flawless, and the prose is Brewer's sharpest and most controlled. Anthony Boucher said in the New York *Times* that the book is the "all-around best Gil Brewer . . . a full-packed story."

Nude On Thin Ice is a much darker and more surreal novel. Set primarily in the Sandia Mountains of New Mexico, it has a deadly-triangle plot reminiscent of *13 French Street*, though much different in execution. The three main characters are drifter Kenneth McCall, the lonely widow of one of his old friends, and a strange and exotic nymphet who enjoys posing naked on ice for men and their cameras. Half a million dollars in cash and an implacable lawyer named Montgomery also figure prominently, as does explosive violence both expected and unexpected. What makes the novel memorable is its brooding narrative, its mounting sense of doom, and an ending that is both chilling and perfectly conceived. The narrator, McCall, is one of Brewer's most striking creations—weak and immoral on the one hand, so sadly tragic on the other that the reader cannot help but empathize with his fate.

At least some of the nightmare, existential quality of *Nude On Thin Ice* can be attributed to Brewer's increasing dependency on alcohol and sleeping pills. By 1960 he was living a private nightmare of his own.

His success had begun to wane. Overexposure, a slowly changing market, the darkening nature of his fiction . . . these and intangibles had led to a steady decline in sales of his Gold Medal and Crest originals after the high-water mark of *13 French Street*, to the point where Fawcett decided to drop him from their list. In his world-by-the-tail decade, he published 23 mostly first-rate novels under his own name, fifteen of those with Fawcett; between 1961 and 1967, he published a total of seven mostly mediocre novels—one last failure with Gold Medal (*The Hungry One,* 1966) and the other six with second-line paperback houses (Monarch, Berkley, Lancer, Banner).

In the late 50s he and his wife, Verlaine, had moved out West. It was not a good move for Brewer. In Florida he had had a coterie of writer friends, among them Harry Whittington, Frank Smith (Jonathan Craig), and Talmage Powell. In Colorado and New Mexico, he missed their counsel and support when he began selling less and drinking more. There was also the fact that he was beginning to be strapped for money; he had lived high off the hog in his salad days, saving and/or investing little. Financial worries combined with the professional frustrations to lead him into protracted binges. More than once he entered a clinic to dry out, only to backslide again after his release. A major crash of some kind was inevitable; it happened in 1964.

. . . *I was drowning in alcohol and drugs, [and then came] the bleary morning I awakened to a tall, cold glass of vodka on the bedside table, left the house for breakfast at a friend's, and was warned loudly by an echoing voice on a corner to "Turn back—go home," which I ignored, only to, an hour later, total a creamy Porsche and pick up 8 broken ribs, 28 fractures, torn lung, etc., in the process. Then the wild, rather ribald, hallucinatory hospitalization . . . peopled with Bozo the Clown, Rhinemaidens, and other happenings that could only be described as otherwordly or science-fictional; a mad doctor, a hospital nightclub, etc.—the beginning of a transfer to hell during which, for a time, at least, I turned out novels and stories, all the while in the very depths of the pit.*

With medical help, he hauled himself out of the pit and he and his wife eventually returned to St. Petersburg, Florida. He was still able to write as well as ever, but his once-flourishing markets, both for novels and short stories, were then dead or dying or had passed him by. He had no marketable skills except those of the professional fictioneer, yet he couldn't sell his own variety of suspense novel and he couldn't afford to take the time necessary to write the serious fiction he yearned to do. He had only one choice, as he saw it: to descend kicking and screaming into hackwork.

He wrote half a dozen sex books under house names for downscale publishers. He wrote stories by the dozens, mostly for the lesser men's magazines, only now and then placing a crime short with *Alfred Hitchcock's Mystery Magazine* and the lower-paying digests. In the late 60s he wrote three novelizations of episodes of the then-popular Robert Wagner TV series, *It Takes a Thief;* published by Ace in 1969 and 1970, these were the last novels to appear under his own name. He wrote four Gothics as by Elaine Evans for Lancer and Popular Library. On an arrangement with Marvin Albert, he wrote two of the Soldato Mafia series published by Lancer under Albert's Al Conroy pseudonym. He ghosted an Ellery Queen paperback mystery, *The Campus Murders* (Lancer, 1969); a Hal Ellson suspense novel, *Blood On the Ivy* (Pyramid, 1971); and five of the novels about the Israeli-Arab war purportedly written by Israeli soldier Harry Arvay. (He had a chance to take over ghosting of the Executioner series as well—what would have been a major source of income—but while his one effort pleased the publisher, it did not please Don Pendelton.)

He hated every minute of this type of work, but he always—or almost always—did the best possible job with the material he had to work with. And at this stage of his fading career, he always—or almost always—delivered as promised and on time.

. . . *I keep hoping for a [subsidiary] sale of some kind; something that might complement the exemplary qualities of my work, ahem. [I'm] up one minute when possibilities of movie rights, or perhaps reprint rights on some lost seed throng my konk, and down the next on Realization Flight 110, knowing that publishers simply are lethargic, fickle, disoriented-and-one-track-oriented. . . . Ah me. (Ah Me's a Chinese philosopher with rancid breath who appears as a ghost at my shoulder—he's from back in 3,000 BC —and forever bids me to go with the tide.) Or maybe better yet, woe is me. At times I do feel exergued. Rats, how I ramble. The notorious Griffin, me, once again, with that dazzling old blue hope, ready to whoop it up at the party, hypostatic, ineffable, even, you might say, but unable to partake of the inducive viands and nectar because of insuforial earth-worms called editors who are, after all, so fucking hidebound, shade-eyed and ponderous it makes me scream—in agony. In agony.*

1976–1977. Even the hackwork was beginning to dry up by this time, the assignments—and the sales—fewer and farther between. He was drinking heavily again—so heavily that he and his wife agreed to separate. They continued to live in the same building, however, in separate apartments. Verlaine also continued to lend moral support, and as much financial support as she was able from a job of her own.

Brewer managed to keep turning out short stories for *Hustler, Chic,* and similar magazines, as well as occasional novel ideas and proposals . . . until the drinking once more slid out of any semblance of control. It not only affected his ability to write, it put him in dangerously poor health. He knew something had to be done, and he did it: he voluntarily joined AA.

The program seemed to work for him, at least for a while. Eventually he was able to return to work on a regular schedule. When his agent wrote to tell him that the Canadian publisher, Harlequin, was looking for mysteries for their new Raven House line, the prospect of once again writing suspense fiction under his own name energized him; he promised to come up with an idea, fifty pages, and an outline. But he soon realized that he was not as attuned to crime fiction as he had once been.

Tried valiantly to read some contemporary suspense stuff, so I'd be up on how character was handled. Tisk. It coddled my fidgeting brain. Awful. Sparse and futile. . . . So many writers are taking old writers' plots these days, like Raymond Chandler's yarns, and rewriting them. I just don't go that way. Perhaps I'm stupid, but it seems a sloppy damned way to make a buck.

And so he couldn't seem to get his head into a book for Harlequin. He had what he felt was a good idea: a novel about the world of bisexuals and homosexuals called *The Skeleton*. The problem lay in putting the right words down on paper.

Suppose you've been wondering why I seem to have been so bloody lax about this Harlequin project. The fact is I had a small relapse—no drinking, or anything like that, just an inability to read one of the [Raven House] books so I could get the formula down pat. Was trying too hard, obviously. Hope you'll excuse any screwy letters dashed off during this hectic interim. Seem to be getting back in place now, for the most part, though my concentration isn't perfect—but believe I'll be at work soon. I have these spells, as you know. . . .

More time passed, and he still couldn't write *The Skeleton* proposal. At length he shelved it in favor of a new novel concept, one that excited him tremendously because it was the sort of serious work he longed to do, and intensely personal and therapeutic as well: an imaginative-autobiographical novel about his alcohol-and-drug-abusing days in the early 60s. The title was to be *Anarcosis*.

It'll be written in sequences of dream-reality, with the dream as reality and the reality as dream . . . It peregrinates all over the U.S. and ends with that bedeviled incarceration in a mental institution back in '64 . . . a big sweep of both subjective and objective shocks, strung with startling characters who, phantom-like, pre-destined and Martian in appeal, connect with me in one way or another—traveling hospitals on the highways of America, a besieged trip to Mexico on sleeping pills and bourbon, various alky wards including the one I call Insanity Ranch in New Mexico, a pack of dogs chasing me at four o'clock in the morning in Albuquerque when I planned to walk to California, and many crazy, firefly incidents that send me screaming through the blinding tunnel of daymare into my own private Gehenna—to survive, or so it seems, anyway. There are dialogues with internationally celebrated dead such as Jack London, Arnold Bennett, Lytton Stratchy, and numerous others, political figures and men and women in the arts; psychic adventures with tortuous conflict, and, at the end, a promise of another book to come called Man on Tape. . . .

He had telephone discussions about the project with his agent, who was impressed enough at its potential to write to the Fine Arts Council of Florida in an (ultimately futile) effort to get Brewer a grant that would ease his financial burden. As excited as Brewer was about the project, however, he had trouble writing it. This led to another, albeit brief and different setback.

. . . *I was on a valium binge. There's been no drinking, but that pill thing was evil—all done for good now. No more of that—ever! No more of anything except life, work, recovery. Recovery from a lifetime of knowing I knew as much as the gods, was, in fact, perhaps, one of them—and all I want to do is write. Write with the knowledge now that I know nothing. Helpless, hopeless exactitudes.*

He managed, finally, to get 35 pages of *Anarcosis* written to his satisfaction and sent them to his agent in February of 1978. The regretful evaluation was that it was "just short of unreadable . . . uncontrolled, hallucinatory dynamism," and it was the agent's suggestion that Brewer rethink it and rewrite it in a more coherent and commercial fashion. The agent also suggested that because of Brewer's financial straits, it would be best if he devoted his immediate energies to short stories for such well-paying markets as *Hustler,* or to the long overdue Harlequin proposal.

At first, Brewer balked at this advice.

. . . *I am going to devote all my energies to* Anarcosis. *I cannot, so help me, face another pulp project—at least, not now. It turns my stomach. It has given me diarrhea; the very thought of it, the attempts to turn a plot again, again, again! I cannot do it.*

It was not long, though, before he relented. He had no choice; as always, he was living hand to mouth—mostly on a VA disability pension and a Social Security disability pension. He forced himself to complete the 50 pages-and-synopsis of *The Skeleton.* Then, encouraged by his agent's favorable response, he wrote a por-tion-and-outline for a second mystery, *Jackdaw.* After that was delivered, he agreed to take on a massive rewrite-and-ghost job —an original manuscript bought by a minor paperback house of which there were two different, unacceptable versions, one of 426 pages and the other of over 1100 pages. He was to rework the mish-mosh pair into an intelligible, publishable book.

The project was a disaster from the beginning. He had long, violent telephonic clashes with the book's editor that eventually, after months of labor and psychic drain, forced him off the job with only nominal payment. As if this bitter pill wasn't enough to swallow, Harlequin rejected *The Skeleton* portion, after holding it for several months, because although they felt it read entertainingly and "would surely make a good mystery novel," the bisexual/homosexual content was deemed unacceptable. *Jackdaw* was not bought either, for more obscure reasons.

These, combined with continuing frustrations with *Anarcosis,* were the final straws.

By mid-1979 Brewer was again drowning in booze. In 1980 one of his writer friends wrote sadly to another, ". . . Gil has drunk the tops off all the vodka bottles and is writing very little, alas." Brewer's redescent into the depths of alcohol and despair continued into 1981, when he nearly died of several different ailments. Then, with Verlaine's help, he managed to lift himself out of the pit for the final time. He rejoined AA; he tried once more to put his life back together.

I no longer drink and attend AA meetings regularly. Last eve a head cheese in the organization suggested I'd be a good speaker. I told him he'd have to wait till I have some front teeth replaced—three have fallen out, God help me [and] I can't afford to go to a dentist.

In late April of 1982 he wrote an abject, rambling, five-page letter to his agent.

I'm hanging by a thread and practically living on noodles and rice with the way things are. The bloody Social Security disability pension and the VA disability pension could give out any time, and I'd be on the streets. I just skin by each month as it is, living like a hermit. Maybe grass, good green grass, I mean, would be a treat. . . .

All I know is, I must write. I love to write. I can sit at the mill again, and I can write the stuff . . . I've got to make money, but in return I'll deliver better goods than ever . . . I have so many terrific books in me! And I no longer drink, nor do I take any drug that would disrupt the scene. I'm sober and ready for work.

But it was too late. Over the previous several years there had been too much conflict, too many failures and missed assignments; and during the dark, alcoholic years of 1979–1981 there had been too many incoherent, angry, pleading letters, too many drunken phone calls. The agent said that his agency and Brewer were "moving in different directions" and wished him well; their thirty-year professional marriage was finished.

In August Brewer wrote Mike Avallone, asking Mike to help him find new representation.

. . . Could you write a brief note to your agent and see if he'd be willing to take me on as a client? I must still have some rep: I've sold over 50 novels . . . about four hundred short stories and novelettes . . . have been published in 26 countries. . . . I have some new, fresh material at hand, and would dearly love an assignment. . . . All I need and want now is an agent, a good one, and a word processor. But at the moment I feel terribly lost and in limbo.

Nothing positive came of this, despite Avallone's efforts. And so, inevitably, Brewer plummeted into the pit for the final time. In December, shortly before Christmas, he placed one last telephone call to his former agent. He was so drunkenly incoherent that the agent had no idea of what he was saying or why he called.

Two weeks later, on the morning of the second day of the new year, Verlaine entered his apartment and found him dead.

That is not quite the end of the Gil Brewer story, however. The gods can be perverse sometimes—damned perverse. This is one bitter instance.

In the years since January 2, 1983, a French film company paid a five-figure advance for film rights to *A Killer Is Loose* and produced it in 1987. Two other early GM novels, *13 French Street* and *The Red Scarf,* were bought for reissue by Zomba Books in England; those two and a number of others were also reissued in France. Black Lizard has expressed interest in reprinting several Brewer titles here. And a number of his short stories were purchased for anthologies edited by the writer of these words. Gil Brewer is dead, but his career, by God, is not; new life has been breathed into it, and it is still on life-support at the time of this writing.

. . . I'm encouraged by how I feel toward really good stuff. It turns me on, as it always has—but I've always denied myself the pleasure of [such] work; forever tied up with one project after the other, facing the stricture of money needed. . . . Everything in my plans hinges on money as a support; I'm tortured out of my skull when the gelt is low. . . .

And the drinking . . . I always imagined it a necessity for my work. I am a terrible fool.

AFTERWORD

The italicized passages in this piece were taken verbatim from letters written in 1977, 1978, and 1982 by Brewer to a number of individuals, primarily his agent and Mike Avallone. None of the letters were addressed to me personally; I had no correspondence with Gil Brewer, did not know him at all.

In retrospect I find this strange, discomfiting, because on numerous occasions from the late 60s to the early 80s I intended to write Brewer a letter; to tell him that I grew up reading his work, admired it, was in fact influenced by it in certain small ways. I *did* write similar letters to such other writers as Evan Hunter, Robert Martin, Jay Flynn, Talmage Powell—but never one to Brewer. In the mid-70s I went so far as to track down his address and type it on an envelope, yet no farther than that. I don't know why.

I wish I *had* written to him, established a correspondence, gotten to know him a little. I might have been able to help him in some small way—bought some of his old stories for anthologies while he was still alive, maybe, or given him an assignment to write an original . . . something. It would have made absolutely no difference in the long run, of course. Just the same, I can't help feeling a bit guilty for my silence.

Maybe I'm a fool, too, in my own way.

Maybe we all are, us real-life working mystery writers. . . .

The Red Scarf

by Gil Brewer

First published in 1958

Chapter 1

About eight-thirty that night, the driver of the big trailer truck let me out in the middle of nowhere. I had stacked in with a load of furniture all the way from Chicago and I should have slept, too. I couldn't even close my eyes. Brother Albert had turned me down on the loan, and all I could think of was Bess holding the fort in St. Pete, and us standing to lose the motel. How could I tell her my own brother backed down on me? The dream. So the driver said if I could make it to Valdosta, then Route 19, the rest down through Florida would be pie. He gave me what was left of the lunch he'd bought in Macon. I stood there under a beardy-looking oak tree and watched him rumble off, backfiring.

It was raining and snowing at the same time; you know, just hard enough to make it real nasty. The road was rutted with slush, and the wind was like cold hands poking through my topcoat. I had to hang onto my hat. I ate the half piece of chocolate cake he'd left, and the bacon and cheese sandwich. I saved the apple.

A couple of cars roared by, fanning the road slop clear up to my knees. I didn't even have a cigarette. I figured this was as broke and low-down as I'd ever be.

My feet were already soaked, so I started walking. I came around a sharp curve in the road and crossed a short wooden bridge. Then I saw the sign.

ALF'S BAR-B-Q
Drinks
Sandwiches

The sign was done in blue lights and it kind of hung like a ghost there in the dripping trees. It swung and you could hear it creak. Just the sign, nothing else.

I kept walking, feeling the change in my pocket, thinking about a cup of hot coffee and some smokes and maybe it would stop raining. Or maybe I could hit somebody for a ride.

Then I saw how I wasn't going to hit anybody for any ride. Not here. Not at Alf's. If a car stopped at this place, they'd either be crazy, or worse off than I was. There was this bent-looking shed with a drunken gas pump standing out front in a mess of mud, and Alf's place itself was a sick wreck of an old one-room house, with the front porch ripped off. You could still see the outline of the porch in the dim light from the fly-freckled bulb hanging over the door. Tin and cardboard signs were plastered all over the front of the place.

I went inside, and it was like being hit across the face with the mixed-up smells of all the food Alf's place had served for the past ten years.

'Ho, ho, ho!' a guy said. He was a big, red-faced drunk, parked on an upturned apple crate beside a small potbellied stove. He looked at me, then at the thin man behind the counter. 'Ho, ho, ho!'

'You best git on along home,' the man behind the counter said to the laughing one. 'Come on, Jo-Jo—you got enough of a one on to hold you the rest of this week and half of next.'

'Ho, ho, ho!' Jo-Jo said.

I brushed some crumbs off one of the wooden stools by the counter and sat down. Alf's place was a compact fermentation of all the bad wayside lunchrooms on the Eastern seaboard. With some additions. He had a coffee urn, a battered juke-box, two stick-looking booths, a chipped marble counter, and a greasy stove. The ceiling was low; the stove was hot.

'What'll it be?' the counterman said. 'I'm Alf. We got some fine barbecue.' His hair was pink and sparse across a freckled skull. He wore a very clean white shirt and freshly ironed white duck trousers.

'Cup of coffee, I guess.'

'No barbecue?'

'Nope.'

Alf shook his head. I turned and glanced at Jo-Jo. He was wearing overalls with shoulder straps. He was a young, rough, country lush. His eyes had that slitted hard-boiled egg look, his mouth broad and loose and his black hair straight and dank, down over his ears. Combed, it would be one of these duck cuts. He was a big guy.

I heard a car draw up outside. Jo-Jo took a fifth of whiskey from his back pocket, uncapped it, drank squinting, and put it away. He stood up, stretched, touching his hands to the ceiling, reeled a little and sat down again. 'Son of a gun,' he said. 'Dirty son of a gun.'

Alf put the thick mug of coffee on the counter. 'Cigarettes?' I said. 'Any kind.'

He flipped me a pack of Camels. I heard a man and woman arguing outside, their voices rising above the sound of a car's engine. A door slammed. The engine gunned, then shut off.

'Damn it!' a man said outside.

The door opened and this girl walked in. She hesitated a moment, watching Jo-Jo, then she grinned and stepped over toward the counter, letting the door slap.

'Ho, ho, *ho!*' Jo-Jo said. Then he whistled. The girl didn't pay any attention. Jo-Jo looked her up and down, grinning loosely, his eyes like rivets. Then the door opened again and a man came in. He stood staring at the girl's back.

'Viv,' he said. 'Please, come on, for cripe's sake.'

She didn't say anything. She was a long-legged one, all right, with lots of shape, wearing a tight blue flannel dress with bunches of white lace at the throat and cuffs. She was something to see. There were sparkles of rain like diamonds on the dress and in her thick dark hair. She half-sat on the stool next to me, and looked at me sideways with one big brown eye.

'You hear me, Viv?' the man said.

'I'm going to eat something, Noel. That's all there is to it. I'm starved.'

'Ho, ho, ho,' Jo-Jo said. I heard him uncap the bottle and drink noisily. He coughed, cleared his throat and said, 'I reckon your woman wants some barbecue, mister.'

The guy breathed heavily, stepped over behind the girl, and just stood there. He was a big-shouldered guy, wearing a double-breasted dark-blue suit, with a zigzag pin stripe. His white shirt was starched. He wore a gray Homburg tilted to the left and slightly down on the forehead.

'Come on, Viv,' he said. He laid one hand on her right arm. 'Please come on, will you?'

'Nuts. I'm hungry, I told you.'

She haunched around on the stool and smiled at Alf. 'I'll try the barbecue. And some coffee.'

'Sure,' Alf said. 'You won't be sorry.'

The guy sighed and sat down on a stool beside her. Alf looked at him, and the guy shook his head.

'You better eat something,' the girl said.

The guy looked at her. She turned front again. I could smell whiskey, but it wasn't from Jo-Jo. They'd both been drinking and driving for quite a while. They had that unstretched, half-eyed look that comes from miles and miles on the highway.

I sat there with my coffee and a cigarette, nursing the coffee, waiting. They were headed in the same direction as I was. I'd heard them come in.

After Alf served her a plate of barbecue, with some bread and coffee, the guy spoke up. He'd been sitting there, fuming. 'You got gas in that pump outside?'

'Sure,' Alf said. 'Absolutely we got gas.'

'How's about filling her up?'

Alf started around the counter, nodding.

'Now, aren't you glad we stopped?' the girl said. 'We won't have to stop later on.'

'Just hurry it up,' the guy said without looking at her. 'Feed your face.'

Alf was at the door. 'You'll have to drive your car over to the pump,' he said.

I looked at him. The guy started toward the door. Jo-Jo was trying to get up off the apple crate. He was grinning like crazy, staring straight at the girl. I looked and she had her skirt up a little over her knees, banging her knees together. You could hear it, like clapping your hands softly.

Neither Alf nor the guy noticed. They went on outside and the door slapped shut. I could feel it; as if everything was getting a little tight. The girl felt it, too, because she paused in her eating and Jo-Jo made it off the apple crate and started across the room.

'Say!' Jo-Jo said. 'You're pretty as a pitcher.'

She took the mouthful of barbecue and began to chew.

Jo-Jo sprawled over against the counter, with his hair hanging down one side of his face, and that bottle sticking out, and he was grinning that way. 'Gee!' Jo-Jo said. 'Cripes in the foothills!'

I got off my stool and walked around to him. 'Come on,' I said. 'Go back and sit down. You're kind of tight.'

He looked at me and gave me a hard shove. I went back across the room and slammed against the wall.

'You?' Jo-Jo said to the girl. He held up two fingers and

wrapped them around each other. He had fingers like midget bananas. 'Me?' he said.

The girl went on eating. She pulled her skirt down over her knees and chewed.

He reached over and took hold of her arm and pulled her half off the stool toward him, like she was a rag doll.

'Girly,' he said. 'I could make your soul sing.'

I nearly burst out laughing. But it wasn't funny. He was all jammed up.

'You wanna drink?' he asked her.

She was struggling. He got up close to her and started trying to paw her. She had a mouthful of barbecue and he started to kiss her and she let him have it, spraying the barbecue all over his face.

He grabbed her off the stool and went to work.

She wasn't doing anything but grunt. He got hold of her skirt and tried to rip it. I was there by then, and I got one hand on his shoulder and turned him and aimed for his chin. It was all in slow motion, and my fist connected. He windmilled back against the counter.

'That dirty ape!' the girl said.

The barbecue was still on his face. When he hit against the counter, the bottle broke. He stood there watching me, with this funny expression on his face and the whiskey running down his leg and puddling on the floor. Then he charged, head down, his hair flopping.

I grabbed his head as he came in, brought it down as I brought my knee up. It made a thick sound. I let him go. He sat down on the floor, came out straight and lay there.

'They grow all kinds, I guess,' the girl said. 'I sure thank you,' she said. 'Thanks a lot.'

'Forget it.'

She kept looking at me. She kind of grinned and lifted one hand and looked at the door. Then she turned and went over to the stool and sat down with her barbecue again.

The door opened, and the guy came in. He saw Jo-Jo. 'What's this?'

'A little trouble,' I told him. 'It's all right now.'

Alf came in and closed the door. He saw Jo-Jo. His face got red. 'What happened?'

I told them. The girl was eating again. Then I noticed she stopped and just sat there, staring at her plate. She turned on the stool and looked at the guy. 'Pay the man,' she said. 'Let's get out of here.'

I looked at her, then at the guy. I had to nick them for a ride. I had to.

'I'm awful sorry, miss,' Alf said. 'He don't really mean no harm. It's just his way.'

Nobody said anything. This guy pulled out his wallet and looked at Alf.

'The gas was six, even,' Alf said. 'The barbecue's a dollar. That's seven. Even.'

The guy counted out a five and two ones. He handed the bills to Alf and Alf took them and stood there with them hanging limply from his hand. Jo-Jo moved and groaned on the floor.

'Come on,' the guy said to the girl.

'Listen,' I said to him. 'How's chances for a lift? I'm going the same way you are. South. There's no—'

'No dice. Come on, Viv.'

I looked at her. She looked at me. 'Oh, let's give him a lift,' she said. 'It's all right, Noel.'

He gave her a real bad look. 'No.'

She bent a little at the waist and brushed at some crumbs. She looked at the guy again. Then she looked at me and winked. 'Come on,' she said to me. 'We'll take you as far as we can.'

'Thanks,' I said. 'I really—'

'You heard me, Viv,' the guy said. 'I told you, no!'

I figured, the hell. If I could get the ride, that's all I cared about. I didn't care about what the guy wanted. Then I saw the way his face was.

'He helped me out,' she said. 'You heard him say what happened, Noel. That dirty ape would have done anything. Suppose this man hadn't been here? What would I have done?'

'Ho, ho, ho,' Jo-Jo said. He was lying flat out on his back, staring at the ceiling.

I looked at the guy and he looked at me.

'All right,' he said. 'Damn it.'

The girl took my arm and we moved toward the door.

It was a Lincoln sedan. The guy, Noel, walked ahead of us, his feet splatting in the mud. He got in under the wheel and slammed his door.

'Don't pay any attention,' the girl said. 'We maybe can't take you far. But it'll help, anyway. In this weather.'

'Anything'll help, believe me.'

She opened the door before I could reach it. She climbed in. I closed the door and opened the rear door.

'Get in front,' the guy said.

She pushed the front door open and I slammed the rear door and got in. She jigged over a little and I slammed the front door and we were off like a bull at a flag.

We struck the highway, slid a little, straightened out. 'Noel,' the girl said. 'Stop the car again.'

I looked at her. She sure was a pip.

'What?'

'I said, "stop the car." So he can take off his hat and coat. He's all wet.'

The car slowed and came to a stop. The windows were closed, heater on, and you could smell the stale cigarette smoke. I remembered my cigarettes back there on the counter at Alf's.

'Throw 'em in back,' she said. 'Okay?'

I opened the door and stepped out into the night and took them off and tossed them in back, beside a couple of suitcases and a brief case on the seat. Then I got in and this time she didn't shove away. In fact, she looked at me and smiled and snuggled down comfortable.

'Is it all right now?' the guy said, real evil.

She didn't say anything.

He popped it to the floor and we roared off.

I sat there without saying anything for about a mile. Just waiting. It wasn't just the cigarette smoke in this car, or the hot air from the heater, either. You could taste the trouble that had been going on between these two.

'I hope you're happy now, Noel.'

'That's enough.'

'Just remember what I said.'

'I told you, Vivian!' He let it come out between his teeth. Not loud; just hard. 'That's enough. You hear?'

She sniffed. 'Just remember.'

He tromped and he tromped. The car bucked and leveled off at eighty-three. We were flying. There wasn't much wind, but you could see that rain and snow whipping up out there.

'Thanks for the lift,' I said. 'It's a rotten night. Not many'd stop in the highway tonight. Any night.'

'One good turn deserves another,' she said, grinning.

You could almost hear him grit his teeth. He was really hanging onto that wheel. I turned and looked at her, putting one arm across the back of the seat. She tipped her head, freeing a good lot of the thick dark hair where my arm squeezed. In the dash lights, there was a sheen on her long slim legs. She looked at me then, with one big brown eye. Then she began watching the road.

You could smell the whiskey in the car. It seemed to have impregnated the upholstery.

'Going far?' the man said.

'Down the coast. St. Pete.'

He breathed heavily, hulked over the steering wheel. I couldn't watch him very well without stretching. He made me nervous.

She laid one hand on my knee. 'Honey. You got a cigarette?'

'There's a carton in the back seat, Vivian. You know that.'

She patted my knee. 'You know? I'm glad you're with us. Least, Noel's not cursing.'

'I'll curse.'

She hitched up and turned and got on her knees on the seat, pawing back there. The dash lights were bright. I looked away.

'On the floor, stupid.'

She came up with the carton and a bottle, turned and sat on my lap, slid off onto the seat and smiled at me again with that one big brown eye. 'Bet you haven't got a cigarette?'

I told her she was right.

She ripped open the carton and handed me a pack. 'Care for a drink?'

'Damn it, Vivian.'

She parked the fifth on my knee. I took it.

'All right,' the guy said. 'All right.'

We drove along for a while, swapping the bottle. I was hitting it hard. She took enough, too. The guy, Noel, was just touching it now and then.

The whiskey got to me good. But I sat there, propped up, smoking cigarettes and letting the night stretch out. Thinking about Bess. She was a good wife, a wonderful girl. And my brother Albert was a twenty-four carat stinker.

Everything was sour inside me. He knew he would have got the money back, if he made the loan. I never welched yet. Knowing Albert, I should never have tried going clear to Chicago to ask him, figuring a personal talk might be better than a long-distance call.

'Roy,' he says. 'You must learn to hoe your own row. I'd gladly help you if I thought it would really be helping you. But you seem to have forgotten that I warned you not to attempt this foolish motel business.'

And Bess down home, maybe even praying. Because if the highway didn't come through by our place, as planned, we were sunk.

And that guy, Potter, at the bank. Hovering behind his desk in a kind of fat gray security. And the way his glasses glinted when he looked at me. 'We're sorry, Mister Nichols, but there's nothing we can do. We've given you one extension, and you're behind again. Another extension would only make matters worse for you in the long run. And as far as another loan of any kind is concerned, you must see the impossibility of that. You've got to make the effort to clear up your debt and meet future payments. The government stands behind you only so far, Nichols. You must do your share.'

'You don't understand, Mister Potter. Everything we own is in that motel!'

'We understand perfectly. We handled your government loan. But remember, when you went into this motel business, we all were assured the new highway would come past your place of business. It seemed a safe risk. Now it's all changed. They've suspended construction, pending the settlement on a new route. And that,' he shook his head, glasses glinting, 'put us all in a bad spot, indeed.'

'But you—'

'We have no choice, Nichols. Place yourself in our position. You're extended far beyond your means now. Either you settle to the date, or we'll be forced to—well, foreclose, to put it plainly. If I were you, I'd make every effort, Mister Nichols—every effort.'

'But the highway may still come through.'

'But when? *When?* And we can't take that risk, don't you see? Suppose you're granted a year's extension? And suppose it *doesn't* come through? What then?' The gentle pause, the clasped hands, the dull gleam of a fat gold ring. 'Surely, you must comprehend. See, here—if we make a loan to you, and you can't pay it—and there's every indication you won't be able to—what then? You'd be worse off than you are now. You'd lose your business, your investment—not only that, you'd have our personal loan to pay. And no way *to* pay. Of course, we could never make that loan. Never. I'm sorry, Mister Nichols. Very sorry, indeed.'

'My name's Vivian. Vivian Rise. This is Noel—'

'Enough, Viv. Snow's letting up. Just rain, now.'

'Teece. That's his last name. Isn't that a sparkler?'

I told her my name. 'Pleased to meet you.'

'We're going South.'

'A good time for it. How far are you going?'

I glanced down and he had his hand gripped on her thigh, giving her a hell of a horse bite. She tried to stand it. But he kept right on till you could see tears in her eyes, and she was panting with the pain. . . .

'Have some more,' he said sarcastically. 'There's another bottle back there.'

'Sure.'

I was floating. I sat there, riding up and down with the bumps, with my eyes half-closed. Trying not to remember Bess, waiting there, running up to me when I got home, her eyes all bright, saying, 'Did you get it? Did you get it?'

I held the bottle up and let it trickle down, warm.

'It's hard drinking it like that. We should have some chasers. Noel, why not stop and get some chasers?'

'Crazy? We've wasted time already.'

Chapter 2

Water splashed and gurgled somewhere. There was an odor of fresh earth and grass and wet leaves.

'Noel?' I heard her say that. Then it was still again. I knew I was on the ground and half of me was in running water. I couldn't move.

'Noel?'

Then a long silence. I went away for a time, then slowly came back again.

'No-o-*eeeel!*'

Somebody was thrashing around. It sounded like a giant with boots on, wading in a crisp brush pile. The rain had stopped. There was a moon now, shedding white on pale trees and hillside as I opened my eyes. I tried to see the road. It was hidden. I didn't dare move. We were in some sort of a gully. I lifted an arm. I turned my head. It hurt.

Something stabbed cruelly into my back. I turned, rolling away from the icy water. I was soaked. I was lying on a car door. There was no sign of the car, the girl, or the man.

Only her voice, some distance away. 'Noel.'

Shivering, I closed my eyes tight, remembering Bess like a kind of sob. Remembering all of it. And then this crazy ride with these two crazy people. Fear washed through me, and I lay there, listening, scared to stand up and look.

Finally I got to my knees. I seemed to be all right. My neck hurt, and my right arm. I glanced at my hand, and saw the blood. I flexed my fingers. They worked.

I moved my shoulders. They hurt, too. When I put weight on my right knee, something stabbed me in the ankle. In the moonlight, I saw the big sliver of glass sticking into my ankle, through the sock. It was like a knife blade, only much broader.

I yanked it out. It hurt and the blood was warm, running into my shoe. I moved my foot and it was all right. It hadn't cut anything that counted. It would have to stop bleeding by itself. My teeth were all there and I could see and hear and move everything.

Except the little finger on my left hand. That was broken and if I touched it, it was bad.

'Mister Nichols?'

I didn't say anything. I got on my knees again, looking around, trying to find the car. Her voice had come from some distance away. Somebody kept thrashing in the brush.

A suitcase and what looked like my topcoat were lying near the door. I looked at the door and it had been torn neatly from the body. Then I saw the other suitcase and I started to get up and saw the brief case.

I kept on looking at that. The clasp was torn open and some kind of wispy scarf was tied to the handle. Only that wasn't what made me look.

It was the neatly bound packets of unmistakable money. I touched them, picked one up and saw the thousand-dollar bill, and put it down.

It was like being hit over the head.

'Mister Nichols?'

I started laughing. Maybe it was the whiskey. I needed money; not a whole lot, compared to this. But plenty for me. And right here was all the money in the world.

'Are you hurt bad?' I asked.

'No. Only my knee. See?'

'Where'd all the blood come from?'

'I don't know. My hand's cut—look at my dress. It's ripped to pieces.' She began to look kind of funny.

'Are you all right?'

'What'll we do?' She started away. I caught her and held her. She fought for a minute, then stopped.

'Now, for gosh sakes. You're all right.'

She turned and ran in the other direction. Her dress sure was a mess. She stumbled in circles all around between the trees. I got it then. She was looking for that brief case. She ran into the open by the stream where I had been. She splashed into the water and out and jumped over the car door.

I went on over there and held her again. 'You're all right. Now, where is he?'

'Down there. Over the edge. He's dead. I saw him. . . . No. Don't go down there.'

She ripped away from me. She had seen the brief case. She went to it, landing on her knees, kind of looking back at me over her shoulder, her hair flopping around.

She shoveled that money back in. The clasp wouldn't work. She got the scarf off the handle and wrapped the scarf around the case and tied it tight.

I went over and dragged her up. She held the brief case, pulling away from me.

'Where is he?'

She pointed in the direction of a bent pine sapling. I turned and walked over there, the blood squashing in my shoe. I came past the pine tree and saw skid marks.

I stopped at the abrupt edge just in time. The car was down there. Not too far, about fifteen feet, lying crumpled on its side, smashed to junk, in a rocky glen with the water splashing and sparkling in the moonlight.

The guy was spread out on the rocks, his feet jammed in the car by the steering wheel. The bright moonlight showed blood all over his face and his suitcoat was gone and his left arm had two elbows. He was more than just dead. He was a mess.

'We'd better get an ambulance.'

She hurried over by me and I got a good look at her face. I never saw anybody so scared in all my life. 'He's dead. What good would an ambulance do? Come on—we've got to get out of here.'

I looked at her and I thought about that money and I knew she was working something; trying to. She turned and walked away from me toward the wooded hill and the road.

A car went by up there and for an instant she was silhouetted against the headlights' glare through the trees. She looked back at me, then slipped and sat down.

I went over to her. She'd lost her shoes and her stockinged feet were muddy. She looked bad. 'Don't you see?' she said. 'We've got to get out of here.'

She tried to get up. I put my hand on top of her head and held her down.

'Whose money?'

'Mine. It's my money.'

'Awful lot of money for one woman to have. 'What about *him?*'

'Never mind about him. It's my money, and we've got to get out of here before they find us.'

'Thought you said that money was yours.'

'It is.'

I held her down with my hand on top of her head. She was so mad, and scared too, you could feel it busting right up out of the top of her skull.

These crazy people. All that money. And Bess and me only needing a little. I wanted to crunch her head like a melon.

I was still bleary from the whiskey and my head was beginning to ache bad. But there was something else in my head besides the ache. I kept trying to ignore it.

'It's taken two and a half years to get that money. We've got to get away from here. Nichols, whatever your name is, you've got to help me.'

'We'll have to get the police.'

She tugged her head away from my hand and stood up. She was still hanging onto that brief case. She grabbed my arm with her other hand. There was a streak of blood down the side of her cheek.

'It's stolen money, isn't it?'

'No. And we can't go to the police.' She began to rock back and forth, trying to rock me with her, trying to make me understand something. Only she didn't want to tell me about it. 'We're up the creek, Nichols.'

I kept trying to figure her. It looked like she was in a real mess.

I tried not to want any part of this. I started away from her. She came after me.

'Please—listen!'

'You're not telling me a damned thing. Look, you two picked me up and fed me whiskey. I shouldn't have taken it. But I got my troubles, too. They're big troubles to me. So now look what's happened. I'm still drunk and I don't even know you. And back there. Your boy friend's dead. How about that? I'm getting out of here.'

'Don't you see? If you hadn't seen the money—then you'd have helped me.'

'We'd go to the police. Like anybody else. You got to report an accident like this. There's a dead man down there. Don't you realize that?'

'He doesn't matter.'

'Somebody was following you, weren't they? We saw somebody in Valdosta and you'd just turned off the main southern route, too. Only you turned back, and we were followed. That's why this happened.'

She looked as if she might cry. Well, why didn't I call the police then? Why didn't I do what I should have done?'

'They'll be back.'

'You stole that money.'

'You're wrong, Nichols. You've got to believe me.' She stood perfectly still and got her voice very calm and steady. 'It won't hurt you to help me. If you knew who Noel was, you'd understand that it doesn't matter about him being dead.'

There was one thing: Her fear was real.

'We'll take the suitcases and get out of here. Down the road somewhere. Change clothes. His clothes'll fit you.'

'Oh, no.'

'But you can't go any place the way you are. Look at you. Mud —blood. Neither can I. We'll clean up and get dressed. Then we'll find the nearest town and you can help me get a hotel room.'

'Lady, you're nuts.'

She dropped the brief case then, and faced me. She put both hands on my arms and looked me in the eye. Straight.

'Nichols,' she said, 'there's absolutely no other way. He's dead down there and I'm all alone. I'll bet you can use some money. I've got plenty and I'll pay you well. If you don't help me, they'll find me.'

'Let them. This is too much for me.'

And I wanted it to be too much. But the sight of that money was like catching cold and knowing it would turn into pneumonia. If only that guy had lived, then I'd have an excuse.

We stood there and the moonlight was bright on her face. Her dress was all torn, her hair mussed up, and there was this streak of blood on her cheek. There was something about it. It got me a little. She looked so damned alone and afraid, her eyes big and pleading. And there she stood, hanging onto that brief case, like that.

Chapter 3

Well, near the edge of the town, there was this big billboard beside the concrete. It was at the bottom of a shallow slope, across a small creek. We were walking tenderly, me with the blood drying in my sock. And Vivian in her stocking feet, on tiptoe. A car passed us, but by that time we were behind the billboard out of sight.

She took off her dress. 'Turn your back, Nichols,' she said, 'and get some clothes out of his suitcase. We've got to get away from here. Hurry!'

I was afraid if I sat down I'd never get up. I staggered around, having trouble with the one sock. Finally when I yanked at it, it peeled like adhesive, but was stiff as cardboard. There was quite a hole where the glass had stuck in, and it was bleeding again. The hell with it. Only that was the whiskey still talking.

After she got through, I scrubbed off the blood and mud. My ankle kept bleeding. I fumbled in the suitcase and found a handkerchief and tied it around my ankle.

I kept glancing over there at that brief case. 'I'll help you find a room. That much.'

Still trying to convince myself. I got dressed in his clothes, transferred my wallet and stuff and put my coat and hat on again.

She bundled the old clothes together and walked away into the trees. When she came back, she didn't have them. Her movements were still jerky. You could tell by the way she moved and looked that she was living in a pool of fright.

'No kidding, where'd you get that money?'

'It's mine.'

We closed the suitcases.

She picked up the brief case and started out around the billboard. Then she glanced back. The moonlight was on her—fur jacket, long black hair, high heels and scared.

'All right,' I grabbed the two suitcases, forgetting about my pinky. It hurt like hell. I went on after her, dressed in a dead man's clothes.

I kept trying hard not to think of what Bess would think of this business. It wasn't much good. Then I looked at that brief case in Vivian's hand again. 'You'll have to take one of these suitcases.'

'Why?'

'Because my finger's busted, that's why. I can't handle the both of them.'

She took hers and went on. I didn't want all that money. Just a part of it. Her heels rapped real loud on the asphalt. She had a long stride and she walked with her chin up.

On the road we kind of half-ran, half-walked. She kept looking behind us, and trying to see ahead. She had me as nervous as herself.

She was taking some kind of big chance.

So was I. But she knew what it was, what the odds were. I was playing it blind.

There was more to the town than I'd figured, but it still wasn't much. All the houses were asleep and her heels made terrific echoes in the still cold.

A car came down the main drag and she gave me a shove into a store front. I listened to her breathe, with her face pressed right up to mine. It was kids in the car, with the radio blaring.

'Off the main street, Nichols.'

We turned away from the car tracks. There was a hotel down there with a rusty-looking marquee and white bulbs saying: *Hotel Ambassador.* Three bulbs in the 'D' were smashed. She stopped under the marquee and faced me. 'You can't just leave me.'

'Why can't I?'

'You've come this far. It's not going to hurt you.'

I looked at her, saying nothing.

'Is it, Nichols? How could it?'

The wind blew down the street, dusting along the curb, blowing newspapers and small trash past the hotel.

'Look, Nichols. You can't imagine the jam I'm in.'

'That's any reason why I should be in it with you?'

'I'm not asking that.'

I looked down at the brief case, then remembered what she'd said about paying me. 'I was just on my way home,' I said.

'I know that. St. Pete, wasn't it? Well, you can't start home now, anyway, Nichols. You're tired. I'm not asking a whole lot. I can't do it myself. You'll have to help me. I've got to get out of the country.'

'Honest to God, you sound crazy.'

'That's the way it is. I'll pay for it. I'm not asking you to do it for nothing.'

'I've already—'

'That's what I mean. Listen, I'm so scared that it's all I can do to walk. If I told you, you'd understand.'

'I don't want to know.'

'But I've got to tell you.'

We stood there, and the accident and the dead guy sat there in the back of my mind. I'd already come this far, and it was a long way.

Her knuckles were white, she was holding the brief case that tight. The wind started to blow in her hair. She set her suitcase down and lifted her hand and brushed some hair off her cheek. She was an absolute knockout.

'Well?'

Chapter 4

It had to be one room. When I said something about getting separate rooms, you could see the fear bubbling up inside her like acid. She wouldn't leave me for a second.

I felt pretty bad. I needed a drink and I was sick. Only there wasn't any chance of getting a drink, and I kept thinking more and more all of a sudden, about that dead guy back there in the gully, bloody and broken.

'I'll pay you well, Nichols.'

'Get off it, will you?'

So we were Mr. and Mrs. Ed Latimer on the register. I couldn't see as it mattered much. The clerk yawned and blinked and tossed me the keys and said, 'Two-oh-two.'

But when we went up the stairs, I glanced back and he was watching her legs from under his hand.

It sure was a dingy place.

She sat on the bed and said, 'Cripes!'

I didn't say anything. There was the bed, a straight-backed chair, a paint-peeling, battle-scarred bureau with an empty water pitcher and a pencil on the bare top. There were brown curtains on the window, and the walls were painted blue. There was one lamp by the bed with a frothy pink shade, and the bathroom looked older than the hotel.

She sat there on the bed and I stood by the closed door and it was cold. Finally she got up and went over and peeked out the window, around the shade, and turned with her hands clasped together like she was praying.

'They won't find me here. Not only one night.' She looked at me, then she took off her fur jacket and hung it in the closet. She opened her suitcase and said, 'Here.' She had a bottle. 'It didn't break,' she said. 'Noel always had a lot of bottles.'

'Get off him.'

'He might even have another in his bag, there.'

Something came up in me. It was like fighting, and you get in a good punch. This punch was aimed at that something inside me. I hadn't been able to level off. But now I had a flash of that old white logic.

I turned and went over to the door and opened it. 'The hell with this. I'm taking off.'

I walked out and closed the door and started down the hall. The door opened and her heels rattled down the hall after me. 'Nichols!'

'No.'

She grabbed my arm. I dragged her a couple of steps and stopped.

'It's my money. I'm afraid.'

'You're lying like hell. You expect me to believe something like that?'

'Make it business, then—let's say I hired you.'

'Let go.'

We were standing next to a door. The door opened and a guy stuck his head out and stared at us. 'Will you two please shut up?'

We went back into the room and I stood by the door, holding it open, and looked at that brief case leaning against the night table. She had the bottle. The scarf she'd tied around the brief case was red, bright red.

She began to look as if she'd fall to pieces. It was all jammed up inside her and she didn't know what to do. Then she set the bottle on the bureau. There was a woolen blanket folded at the foot of the bed. She took it out and spread it and opened the bed.

'I'm freezing, Nichols.'

I went and sat in the chair and looked at the bottle. Then I took it and opened it and had a long drink.

I looked at her and she was standing there in the middle of the room, staring at the wall. She had her hands together like that. She kept staring, lost.

The color of the dress she'd put on was taffy. Some sort of soft material. It stuck to her. She had a lot of chin, too, and a broad soft mouth and these great big frightened eyes.

'You're going to tell me, lady. Who was it following us? What's it all about?'

'I'd better have some of that, Nichols.'

She took a sip out of the bottle, and I went over and closed the door and took off my coat and hat. She sat down on the edge of the bed and stared at the floor. I could see her getting ready to lie again. Then she crossed her legs and leaned back on her elbows. She cleared her throat, and I looked at that brief case again.

'So Noel was my boy friend. You can call it that. I've known him for three years. He took money down this way every two months.'
'Why?'
'The people—the people he worked for.'
'Yeah. But who?'
'Well.' She folded her fingers together and bent her hands back and swallowed. I took a drink, watching her. As she watched me, her eyes kind of hazed over with thinking, Can I get away with a lie? And then her eyes cleared, and she wasn't going to lie. You could see that little bit of relief in her, too. And I couldn't get that money out of my mind. She cleared her throat again. 'Well,' she said, 'Noel, he worked for the syndicate. He was a courier.' She paused. 'My God,' she said, 'the things that can happen!'
'Go on.'
'I don't care. Anyway, they had him making runs through the South. The syndicate runs gambling places in the South, see? It's a very carefully controlled business. For instance, there's a place in Baltimore, and Atlanta, too. Well, every two months it was Noel's job to make the run with working capital. He carried cancelled checks, papers, notifications of change, stuff like that. Sometimes he'd pick up a part of the take, sometimes not. He never really knew what would happen till he reached each place.'
I watched her, listening, and not liking it.
She said, 'So I thought of how Noel and I could get this money. He would carry quite a pile on these trips, only they always watched him, tailed him. He never knew where, either. Listen, I was never mixed up in it. I just wanted to get him clear of them.'
'Sure.'
'It's nobody's money that'll do any hurt. I mean, it's not stealing. Not like—' She stopped.
I took another drink. She was tight. I don't mean drunk, I mean scared, all tied up inside; frozen. You could feel it and she kept swallowing as she talked. The whiskey was reaching me, though.
I kept feeling lower all the time. I kept remembering Bess, and her wondering where I was. This was five days now. Tomorrow would be six. Damn that Albert!
She began to tremble. 'Noel said he'd maybe try it. All right. So when they got so they trusted him, then we'd take the money and leave the country together. So every trip, he'd watch how they kept track of him. And we wanted a trip where he skipped the

Baltimore and Atlanta places, see? One straight through. And this was it, this one. Only they must have caught on—there in Valdosta. We were going to New Orleans, along the coast and Noel made the wrong turn and one of them was waiting for that. Noel turned back, all right, but it was too late and he knew it. You couldn't explain it, see? And with you in the car, too? And then, he made the run, and that was the worst, when Noel panicked. So that's who was following us.

'Listen, they won't stop at anything now. You can't just give them back the money. It's too late for that. It's too late for the stop at Tampa. That's where he was supposed to go, and me with him. I wasn't supposed to be with him. It's too late for anything, but getting away.' She paused, looking at me, bent over a little, her eyes wide and bright. 'I've got to get away.' She shook her head. 'You can't possibly understand. But right this minute, they're hunting. It's a lot of money. It was always in cash, see? It had to be that way for them, and Noel was a trusted courier. God, maybe they've missed the car, the wreck. So that'll slow them down. But they're hunting. And they know how to hunt. They'll kill me.'

Maybe some of it was lies. But basically it was the truth, because you could see it all through her.

'Noel wanted to back out, but I kept at him. It's my fault. We'd been arguing in the car when we stopped at that place. That's half why he let you come along, I think, to—to shut me up. We were going right on to New Orleans.'

She didn't say anything for a time. I took another long one from the bottle and glanced at the brief case.

'A lot of money?'

'A terrible lot. But they've got crazy ethics. A thing like this is unpardonable. It's like any business—except you know what they do to somebody who crosses them? You know what they do to a woman who crosses them?' She looked away, her face pale and expressionless. Then she looked at me again. 'But I've got that money and I'm keeping it. It took two and a half years to get this far.'

'Not very damned far, huh?'

She put both hands against her face and turned around.

I looked at her back and I knew just why I was sticking here. It was the money, all the way. I'd seen it, and I couldn't get it out of my head. Bess and I needed money so damned bad, and there it was right by my foot, leaning against the night table.

It was crazy, maybe. She was crazy to think she could get away with it. And telling me all this, but she had nobody to turn to. In the back of my mind I began to know I was going to help her. It didn't really matter where she got that money.

I got up and went into the bathroom and found a glass. I washed the glass and filled it with water and came back and sat down in the chair again. I was drunk. I drank some of the water. It tasted like dust.

'If you're lying—I'll quit on you.'

She just looked at me.

'I been a bum. Before I met Bess. She's my wife.'

She didn't move. She was thinking.

'That's right. I was in the Merchant Marine, and the war. I been around enough to know. You think I don't read you?'

'You can get a car in the morning. I'll give you the money, so you can buy a car.'

'I met Bess in New Mexico, where her folks lived. A little town. We had that thing and we got married without a cent. I worked in a gas station and we bought a trailer, and I got hold of some dough and we bought a house. We sold the trailer. Then I couldn't make it again, so we sold the house and bought a car and came to Florida. I worked the shrimpers. We saved a lot. Then I heard of this thing.'

I was drunk and running off at the mouth. I couldn't stop. I felt sad. I was trying to convince myself out loud that this was the thing to do. It was crazy, all right. But it was happening.

'So finally I got a line on this place, a motel. Somebody'd built it in the wrong place and went broke. Then news got around they were going to put a new highway through. It's coming right through in front of the motel. Twenty apartments. Bedroom, living room, kitchen and bath. Real nice.

'So I'd never used my G.I. loan, see? So it was tough, but I got that and right along in there Bess's old man died. He left her quite a bit. We used it all. I went into hock all around. We managed to get this place. We met the down payment. It's nice. We're happy. No money, but happy. Then payments begin to come due.'

'Mmmm.'

'We just manage, sweating out the highway. They began work, see? Then we don't manage and I had to start stalling. I got an extension from the bank, all right. But then that time went. I tried to get a job. I couldn't find one that would pay enough.' I took a long drink. 'So they suspended work on the highway.' I told her about the bank refusing a personal loan; how it was.

'Why are you telling me all this?'

'Just want you to know.'

'You don't know what trouble is, Nichols. . . . Well, go ahead. Finish.'

'Well,' I said, 'this highway will sure be something, if it does come through. We're right on it. We'll get the business. From the North, straight through to Miami. They started work, sure. Only the 'dozers sit out there and the tar vats, and nobody's working. Nothing happens, because that damned commissioner wants a different route. Meantime, if I don't have the money, we lose the place. We lose the place—I'm done.'

She leaned over and pushed her plump lips to my ear and said, 'Nichols.'

'So I went up to Chicago.' I told her about Albert.

'Tomorrow I'll give you enough for the car. We'll drive on down. Then you can see about plane tickets. Or a boat, or something so I can get out. I'll pay you well, Nichols.'

The bottle was empty. I dropped it on the floor.

She reached over and put her palm against my face and turned my head. We looked at each other.

I slumped back in the chair and watched her.

She took her suitcase and went into the bathroom and when she came out I was still sitting there. She set her suitcase down and opened the other one. She was wearing a red polka-dot negligee. She found the bottle she'd mentioned and set it on the night stand and turned the light off. Then she moved by me to the window and raised the shade and opened the window. A cold wind yawned into the room. She went back and got into the bed. The sign from the hotel outside lit up the room.

I got up and took the bottle and returned to the chair. I opened it and had a drink. Then I got the glass of water and drank some and set it on the bureau. I sat in the chair with the bottle and watched her.

'You'll freeze.'

'You wouldn't understand.'

'The bed's warm.'

I took a drink and set the bottle on the bureau and fell off the chair. I got up on the chair again and watched her.

'Nichols?'

'What?'

'You can't sit there all night!'

'Shut up.'

Then she was standing by me, pulling at my arm. I stood up

and fell flat on my face. The floor was grimy and there was no rug. . . .

In the morning I was hung over bad, and plenty sick. She gave me the money and I went out and found a car. I wasn't thinking yet. I couldn't think.

It was a good car. It was a Ford sedan and it hadn't taken more than a half-hour to get the papers changed. The used-car dealer took them to the courthouse himself, while I waited on the lot.

He came back, smiling through the flaps of his jacket collar, turned up against the cold. He was a tall guy with bloodshot eyes and he was happy over the sale.

'You've got a good car,' he said. 'A good car.'

'Thanks.'

'Boy!' he said. 'Everybody's running out to the other end of town this morning. Big wreck out there. Police are going out there now, I reckon. Maybe I'll run out there. Somebody spotted a smashed-up Lincoln out there. Sailed right over the damned pine trees.'

'Oh. Anybody—? They find anybody?'

'I don't know. I'm going to run out there.'

So I looked at him, and it was like something clicked inside my head. Maybe it was just the cold morning. But I suddenly didn't want any part of this. It scared the hell out of me, just standing there. I'd gone too far, and I wanted to get home to Bess. Money or no money.

I took the papers he'd given me and put them in the glove compartment of the car. Then I turned to him again.

'Look,' I said. 'Do me a favor?'

'Sure.'

'You got an envelope?'

He went into the little office and came out with an envelope, frowning. I turned away and took what money there was left and put it in there and sealed it and handed it to him.

'Do me a favor,' I said. 'Take this, and the car. Drive the car over to the Ambassador Hotel, all right? Leave the envelope at the desk for Mrs. Ed Latimer. Got that?'

'Yes. Sure, but—'

'Better yet. Take it up to room two-oh-two, see? The envelope, of course, with the car keys and papers. She'll tip you. Tell her you brought the car over. All right?'

'But, I don't understand.'

'You don't have to. All right?' I repeated the names. 'Take your time. There's no hurry. Wait an hour or so.'

We looked at each other. I turned away and started walking fast down through town toward the main southern route.

I wasn't on the corner under the stop light more than three minutes, when this convertible came along with an old guy and his wife. They were headed for Key West. Sure, they'd be glad to take me to St. Pete. I got in and sat quiet.

It wasn't till we were way down in Florida that I remembered I'd bought that Ford in my name. So the rest of the way, I sat there sweating with that, trying not to think about it. Then trying to think what to do about it. Nothing.

It wasn't much good, I'll tell you. The old guy and his wife knew I was sick. Getting to St. Pete didn't help, either.

Chapter 5

They let me out on Lakeview. They were headed for the Sunshine Skyway bridge, and if it hadn't been for Bess, I'd have stayed with them. 'We'd be glad to take you wherever you live,' the woman said.

'Thanks. It's all right.'

The old guy wanted to move on. His wife wanted to talk. I grinned at them and started across the street. They started off toward their happy, unworried vacation.

I crossed to the sidewalk and began walking down Lakeview. It was off schedule for the bus, so I'd probably have to walk all the way home. It was afternoon. The sun slanted across a stately row of royal palms along the street and the air was warm. Two girls in shorts went riding by on bicycles, jabbering at each other. Cars hissed past on the asphalt. Over there between patches of green jungle, beyond cool-looking homes, you could see Lake Maggiore, pale blue and shadowed in the sun.

I moved along, trying not to think. I'd have to face Bess with this, and with the rest of it in the back of my mind. Vivian and that damned money. I'd been that close to a solution, and then turned away from it. Maybe it was wrong. I felt bad and I wanted to feel good. I'd done the right thing, it had to be. But did it matter? *What was I going to tell her?*

How do you tell them you've failed them at the last ditch? especially when they depend on you; when they're sure of the way you do things—banking on you, like they do.

I remembered that guy, Teece, lying twisted in the wreck, and I began to feel better. I needed something to fasten my mind to. I was well clear from them both and that had to be right.

Crossing another block, it was plenty warm. I paused under a young banyan and started peeling my coat. I turned and glanced back there along Lakeview to see if a bus might be along.

A Ford sedan slid into the curb, tires scraping, steam frothing white and hot from under the fenders and hood. Vivian looked at me, pale-faced, and beeped the horn.

I looked away, shrugged back into my coat, and started walking. It wouldn't do any good. There was no place to run, and anyway, you don't run. There were about fifteen more hot blocks to my place. I heard the cars peel by through the shadows and the sunlight.

'Nichols—'

The car door slammed and I heard her running lightly across the grass and down the sidewalk after me, her heels snicking. A young guy and his girl came strolling out of a nearby house. They stopped, whispering, watching. The guy grinned behind his shoulder.

She caught up with me, grabbed my arm.

'Go away, will you?'

'You ran out on me before. You can't run out on me now.'

I kept staring down the street. In the back of my mind, I knew nothing was going to work. She'd found me, just like that—and it was only natural she would come on down here. I looked at her and she was plenty worried. Worse than before, even.

She began to laugh. It was a kind of strained, muted, hysterical laughter. 'Nichols. Come back to the car!'

'What d'you want with me?'

'You know what I want.'

I figured I should have had sense enough not to try and get away from this one.

'Come on,' she said. 'Will you?' She stood there watching me with her eyes all shot full of worry and waiting. 'The minute that man from the car lot drove up to the hotel, I knew,' she said. 'I knew even before that. I got one of those feelings.'

We went back to the car and she climbed under the wheel and sat there. You could hear the steam hissing, and the engine creaked a lot.

'I'm going to stay right at your place, Nichols.'

I turned and looked at her. She didn't bother looking at me. 'Like hell,' I told her.

'It's got to be that way. I've got to be able to get to you.' Then she turned to me and her voice had that dead seriousness she was able to get. 'How could you run out on me like that? After all I've told you?' She turned away and hid her head down against the steering wheel. She was going through plenty. Vivian kept her head pressed against the wheel.

'You can't stay at my place,' I heard myself say. 'What about my wife?'

'God, I thought I'd lost you. I got to thinking, suppose he lied to me. Suppose he doesn't live down here at all. There was no way of telling. Nichols, I'm about dead from driving. I didn't know what I was going to do. I had to find you.'

'What about my wife?'

'She doesn't have to know.'

'Your damn right. She isn't going to know. Hear?'

'Don't worry. I'm going to pay you. That's all you want—money.'

I'd made up my mind, now. 'That's for sure.' Well, all right. I'd let her stay at the motel. She'd be a customer. Somehow. A guest. Some guest. Then I told her about how they'd spotted the wreck.

She came around in the seat like a shot. 'Why didn't you tell me?'

I didn't say anything. She started the car. It took some starting, it was that hot. Finally she got her going and you could feel the fear in her and the dead tiredness.

'Where's your place, Nichols?'

She was sitting up on the edge of the seat, staring at the windshield as if she were hypnotized. It was hard to figure her as a woman who would play it this tight. She was nice looking; more than that.

She sure had fouled me up.

I had her park the car on a side street, three blocks from the motel. The car was still steaming. I told her to get some water and she didn't say a word. I got out and leaned in the window and looked at her.

'You wait a while, then just drive up front. Give me enough time. It's the Southern Comfort Motel.'

'All right. Some name, Nichols.'

We watched each other. She had her hands clenched tight on the wheel.

I turned and took off my hat and coat and started down the block toward home. It hadn't turned out the way I'd wanted. You

get caught in something like this and you get in deeper and
deeper, and you begin to accept it.

Traffic had been rerouted off the main street past our place.
The bricks were torn up and there was a tractor sitting silent
across the way.

I walked along, alone and beat and kind of lost. Everything was
cockeyed, but there was that money. I kept thinking about that. It
had to work, now.

My head ached and I needed a shave and I was in a dead man's
clothes. It's real great, the things that happen to you. You don't
even have to look for it hard.

Southern Comfort
Motel
Vacancy

I could see it down there.

'Vacancy.' That was a hot one. We'd never once used the *'No
Vacancy'* sign. But it did look good down there. The lawn would
have to be mowed. I'd have to get at it right away. And some
fronds on two of the plumosas needed trimming.

Walking along, I began to feel a little better. Sanctuary down
there. And it was Bess who made it that way, made me feel good.

It took up a whole block. Boy! Nichols, the land baron.

Why didn't they put that highway through? I wasn't the only
one, there were other motel owners going through the same
thing. But most of them had been in business for quite a while.
They had a nest egg.

You *could* limp along the way the road was before. But with it
shut off and the detour, you had nothing.

The hedges needed trimming, too. I hadn't noticed that before
I left. Then I saw the hedge that ran along the side nearest me
had been trimmed about halfway.

Bess again. I'd told her never to do that. I started walking
faster, unconsciously.

It was good to be home.

So then it all rushed back into my mind, maybe worse than
before, like it does sometimes. Her, in the Ford, waiting back
there. The wreck. The brief case with all that money. And Teece
—Noel Teece, lying there dead with his two elbows on one arm.

Bess was sitting on the steps by the office. She had on a slipover and a pair of red shorts, just sitting there holding a broom, staring at nothing. I whistled at her.

She looked up and saw me and flung the broom and came running.

Then, watching her, I knew I'd done the right thing, after all. It had worked out right. I wasn't coming home empty-handed and I knew now I never wanted that to happen. Now she'd have what she deserved, or as near to it as I could deliver. It had been in my mind all along, I guess. If I'd come home the way I'd started, without Vivian—it wouldn't have been good.

'Roy!'

It seemed odd and sort of wonderful, hearing her call me that —after all that 'Nichols' business.

How Bess could run! She wasn't too tall, just right, and built just right, too. With light blond hair that the sun was dancing in, and bright blue eyes, her slim legs churning. And those red shorts. She came running across the lawn past the sign, and down the sidewalk.

She hit me hard, the way she always did, jumping into my arms. 'Roy—you're back!'

I kissed her and held her and we started walking across the lawn toward the office. We had the apartment behind the office.

Like I say, the sun was in her hair and it was in her eyes, too. She had on a white terry-cloth slip-over, and walking across the lawn she kept swatting me with her hip.

'Did you get it, Roy?'

'Sure.'

She stopped again and jumped up and hung on my neck, kissing me. Bess was the way I wanted it and I never wanted it any other way. Just Bess.

I dropped my hat and she let go. 'You mean, Albert gave you the money?'

I nodded.

She picked up my hat and looked at me and there was a flash of suspicion, only she chased it away. 'That's a different suit, Roy. Where'd you get the suit?'

'It's—'

'Doesn't fit you quite right.'

She reached out and flicked the jacket open and grabbed the waist of the pants and yanked. She was that way; quick as anything and I stood there, looking down at the gap. He'd been a lot bigger around the middle than I was.

'Al gave it to me.'

'Oh?'

'Like it?'

'Where's your other suit?'

'I gave it the old heave-ho.'

'But, Roy! That was your best suit.' She began to look at me that way again.

'My only. And three years old. It fell apart.'

'Oh, Roy!'

I grabbed her again and kissed her and we went on over to the office and on inside. I had a desk in here, and a couple chairs. It was a small front room.

Bess looked at me kind of funny, and took my coat. She flipped the coat on a chair and plopped the hat on it, and looked at me again.

'It's good to be home.'

'You know it.'

I took her in my arms as she walked up to me. She pressed against me, and when she kissed me, she really let me know. I got my hand snarled up in her hair and yanked her head back, looking down into her eyes.

'Gee, Roy!'

'Yeah.'

'He came through!'

'That's right. He's going to send the money down. Don't know what got into him.'

'You were right, then—in going up there. Instead of writing or just phoning, like I said at first.'

I kissed her again, kissing her lips, her chin, with my hand snarled in that golden hair.

'Roy, you better stop.'

I was trying to hold the rest of the bad stuff away from my mind. It was rough, because I hated lying to Bess. I remembered Vivian, and kissed her again and said, 'You son-of-a-gun!' Then I let go of her and turned around, looking at the office, rubbing my hands together. 'Boy, it's sure good to be back! Any customers?'

'A couple. Listen, you're not getting away that easy. How come you're late? I figured the day before yesterday. Where've you been?'

'Got a ride down. It saved some money. Folks coming south to Tampa, and I bummed over from Tampa.' I cleared my throat. 'For free. I drove them down, see?'

She kept looking at me. 'What did your brother say?'

I shrugged. 'Well, I laid the cards on the table. I told him what kind of a fix we were in. He saw it, all right.' I laughed. 'Wouldn't trust me with the money, bringing it down myself. Thinks I'm still wild, or something. Said he'd send it.'

She came over and put her arms around me again. 'You're sure he will, Roy?'

I nodded. 'Anything new about the road?'

She shook her head, laying her cheek against my chest. 'I missed you, Roy. And you look sick. You need a shave and you're pale. Is something the matter?'

'I'm fine. No sunshine up there. Freezing. Snowing in Georgia, even.'

I kept trying to look out the window. I knew damned well that Ford would be along any minute. She was plenty anxious. Then I got to thinking, 'What if she doesn't come? What then?' It hit me just exactly how much I was depending on that money. It was like caving in—I had to have it.

'You went and started trimming the hedge. I told you not to do that.'

'It's just started growing again. I had to do something.'

'Yeah, I guess.' I caught myself pacing.

'Roy, you sure you feel all right?'

I turned and looked at her. 'Just happy, getting home and all.'

She started to come over to me and I heard the car drive up out in the street. Bess looked at me. I didn't look out the window, I didn't dare.

'Somebody's stopped out front,' Bess said. 'Maybe business is picking up.' She yanked her sweater down and headed for the door. 'I'll go see, Roy.'

'No. You take it easy. I'll check this one.'

We stood there, looking at each other, by the door.

'You listen to me,' she said. 'One look at you, and you'd scare anyone clear down to Key West. You look like you've been shot out of a cannon. So I'll see who it is. You sit right here and relax.'

The screen door slammed. I watched her cross the lawn, her legs scissoring, the red shorts in and out of shadow.

Sweat popped out all over me. I stood watching them through the window. Vivian got out of the car and stood there, looking at the motel. When she saw Bess coming across the lawn, she kind of shrunk back against the car, then straightened and reached for her purse on the seat. She turned as Bess stepped up.

They were talking, and I sweated and sweated, sitting at the desk, my head propped on my fist, watching Bess and Vivian. Vivian was nodding about something. Her hair was real black. Bess was shorter than Vivian, standing there with her hands on her hips.

They both started up toward the office.

It was all wrong. I got up and walked out of the office, into our living room. I couldn't stay there, so I came back. They were talking out on the front lawn. It was enough to drive you nuts.

I had to have a cigarette. I found a pack in the desk drawer and lit up and stood there sweating and fuming. I went out into the kitchen and got a drink of water.

I didn't want to see the two of them together. Not now, I couldn't face that. Bess was too wise.

I heard the front screen door slam. I walked as slow as I could back to the office. Bess was beside the desk, counting some money.

'Two weeks!' She turned and waved the bills and smiled. 'Just like that. Isn't it swell? I gave her number six. A woman, all alone. She's a real looker, too. You stay away from her door, Roy. Hear?'

I looked at her, but she had her eyes on the money. She took it over and put it in the cigar box in the desk drawer. I felt real bad about this. Now it was beginning.

'She's coming over to register.'

The blood began to pound behind my ears. 'Did you tell her where to park the car?'

'No. You can show her later.'

'I think I'll take a shower, Bess.'

'Right. I'll take care of her. I'll fix a good dinner.' Then she left the desk and came over by me. 'It's swell about Albert. Maybe we can make it now.'

'Sure, we'll make it.' I kissed her and gave her a good smack with both hands and went back into the apartment and closed the door. In the bathroom I started to take that suit off; I'd never put it on again.

I was taking off my shoes, when I remembered the broken finger and the ankle. Bess hadn't said a word about that finger. It looked like a miniature baseball bat and it was as black as midnight. She couldn't have missed seeing it.

The ankle was a mess. I took the sock off, then untied the handkerchief. When I yanked the handkerchief, it started bleed-

ing again. I got a Band-Aid and fixed it up with some iodine and
then remembered the shower.

I'd fouled things up just dandy.

'You can show her the garage, Roy.'

'All right. Did she register?'

'You bet.'

'You didn't say anything about my finger.'

'Uh-uh. I saw it, though. Did Albert bite it?'

'It's busted. Caught it in the car door, coming down. Not my
fault, either. This old biddy slammed the door on it.'

She looked at it. 'You'll have to see a doctor.'

Then she looked up and smiled at me. 'You look lots better,
shaved and in your own clothes. They fit, at least.'

I had on sneakers, a pair of gray slacks and a T-shirt. 'Fix some
dinner, huh?'

'She's out by her car. Go show her the garage.'

I went on out there, walking across the lawn like it was a big
basket of eggs. The sun was way down now, right smack in your
eyes from across the street in the park, glinting between the
branches of the oak trees—long slices of fiery orange peel.

'Hello, there.'

I nodded at her.

'Wonder if you could show me where to park the car?'

'I'll drive it around. Get in.'

She slid under the wheel and over to the other side of the seat
and I climbed in after her. I slammed the door, not looking at
her, started the engine and took it down around the block and in
the drive behind the apartments.

'Nice wife you have, Nichols.'

I showed her the garage for number six. I drove the car inside
and got out and stood there in the semi-dark. She got out on her
side and came around and stood in the doorway, looking at me.
She wasn't self-conscious.

'You've got a swell place. You're very lucky.'

'Thanks. And listen: Be careful around my wife.'

'Relax, Nichols. I'm a woman, too.'

She was telling me! 'You go that way, I'm going around the
other way.'

'But, Nichols—!'

'You heard me.'

'You've got to stay by me. Suppose somebody—?'

I left her standing there and cut around the other side of the garage. She worried me plenty. I heard her walking the other way on the gravel. It wasn't good having her here. I had to keep elbowing out of my mind who she really was, the things she'd been mixed up in, the people she knew. But that money kept chewing away at me.

I headed for the back door. Bess was waiting, holding the door for me. 'I've got my eye on you, Roy.'

I knew she was kidding. Bess was real smart, but she was usually trusting. I wondered just how far that could go. It made me sweat, the way she was standing there and the way she said that.

Chapter 6

With Vivian in number six, my nervous system started to kick up. I couldn't stay still. Thing was, I didn't know what she might do. She was scared and wound up tight and anxious to get on the move. There was always the chance she might crack and come running over to our place, yelling, 'Nichols—Nichols!'

That would be all I'd need.

I couldn't see any way to get to her tonight. If I took a chance and went over there, Bess might wise up. She was watching me like a cat, anyway. I figured she was thinking about what I'd done up in Chicago. She probably thought I'd got drunk.

'Last day I was up there, I stayed in a cheap hotel. Waiting for these folks to get ready for the trip down. I bought a bottle, Bess. I shouldn't have, but I felt like celebrating.'

She seemed to take it all right. Celebrating! That was a hot one, all right.

'It was bad stuff. I got sick.'

'You looked pretty bad when you came home. Lots better now, though.'

'When I saw you, I felt better right away.'

'Now, Roy, you know what whiskey does to you. You shouldn't take the chance in a strange town. You don't have any sense when you're drunk. Somebody tell you, "Let's rob a bank," you'd be all for it. Whoopee!' She shook her head, standing there by the oven in the kitchen with the roast going. 'No sense at all, Roy.'

'Let's not talk about it. All right?'

We looked at each other. Then she started smiling and she laughed and it was all right. For a minute there, she had me worried. The way she looked at me.

It was a good dinner. Roast beef, mashed potatoes, fresh peas in a cream sauce, apple pie and coffee.

'Wonder what she's doing down here?'

'Who?'

'That woman I put in number six. One that came in before dinner.'

'Oh. Why?'

'All alone, like that. You don't see them like her alone. Miss Jane Latimer, from Yonkers, New York.'

'That's her name?'

'Didn't you introduce yourself?'

I shook my head.

Bess drank some coffee. 'She didn't go out for dinner. She hasn't left the place.'

'It's early yet. Who else we got aboard?'

'There's an old guy in number fifteen. He's a shuffleboard bug. I think you ought to clean off the courts. He'd play all by himself. His wife's going to join him in a month or so. They're looking for a house down here. So we've got him for a month. Mr. Hughes, he is. . . . Say—maybe I should introduce him to Miss Latimer?'

I began to wish she'd lay off.

'Then there's a couple—middle-aged. The Donnes. She drinks an awful lot, always got one in her hand. I don't blame her, though. The way her husband sits and broods. They came down from New York, so he could get some rest. They never do anything, just sit. Every day a taxi comes up with a load of papers for him. He's an editor. Some New York publishing house. Got great big circles under his eyes. He walks up and down, talking to himself. She told me she's scared he's going to crack up.'

'Anybody else?'

'Honeymooners in eleven, only here for a couple of days. Real cute. And a woman whose husband just died, in nineteen. That's all.'

'I think that's damned good, the way things been.'

After supper I got out on the lawn and monkeyed with the sprinkler system, trying to work myself over by number six, so I could see what was going on. It was real quiet over there, but she had a light burning.

I turned the sprinklers on. I knew if I was going to speak with her, it would have to be fast, while Bess was doing the dishes.

We had the floodlights cut off to save juice, what with the electric bill we had. They turn them off on us, and it'd really be rough, but I had the lights turned on the lawn at the two corners of the block. And the sign was a big one.

What I did was turn all the sprinklers off, then start turning them on, one at a time, by hand. I followed around, working toward number six. The sprinklers ticked and swished. They looked real good. If only there was lots of traffic, and I could have put the floodlights on. It looked good from the road, but the road was like a mortuary.

'*Psst!* Nichols!'

I almost went right out of my skin. She was standing there behind one of the double hibiscus bushes at the corner of number seven.

'Get back.'

'I've got to see you.'

I just walked straight off across the lawn. I leaned against the royal palm by the sign. I heard her go back toward number six. So then I went over to the sprinklers again. I got the one by seven going, then moved on down beside six. It was in shadow.

It wasn't good to whisper and sneak. But it wasn't good to play it straight, either. Let Bess catch me running over here every chance, she'd put the clamps on—trusting or not.

I heard Vivian breathing through the screen windows from inside number six. She had the lights shut off except for one burning in the kitchen.

'You've got to get a move on,' she said. 'I mean it. I can't stay here forever.'

'I'm not doing nothing till tomorrow. That's the way it is.'

I could still hear her breathing; kind of rough, like she was breathing across a washboard. 'I haven't anything to eat.'

'Well, go out and buy yourself something. You got enough money.'

'I can't go out, Nichols. You'll have to get me some groceries. Something. Buy me a hamburg.'

'Get it yourself.'

Her voice crackled, high and shrill, whispering through the window. 'I can't go out, damn you! They'll be watching! My God, they'll—!'

'They won't be in St. Pete.'

'But I can't take that chance!'

'All right. I'll be in front of our place. You come on over there —by the office, and ask me real loud. Hear? And bring some money. And no hundred-dollar bills.'

She started to say something, but I was already walking away toward the office.

Well, I waited and nothing happened. She didn't come and she didn't come.

'Roy?'

The front screen door slammed. It was Bess, coming around front where I stood. Now, *she* would come. That's the way it always goes.

'Roy, that Latimer girl asked if you wouldn't go someplace and buy her some groceries.'

'What?' It was a good thing she didn't get a close look at my face.

'She came to the back door. Not feeling well, but she's hungry. Tired from the trip down. She made a list, here. And here's some money.

'The corner store's still open. I told her you'd be glad to do it.'

So I got the Chevie out of the garage and bought her groceries and came back. She and Bess were talking out in front of the office, on the lawn. I wanted to talk with Vivian.

I came across the lawn. 'Here you go.'

'Oh, fine. Thanks so much.' She was wearing white slacks and a black cardigan sweater.

'Well, don't stand there,' Bess said. 'Take them inside for her.'

I went on across and into number six. There were the two suitcases, sitting in the middle of the floor, one of them open. I didn't see anything of the brief case. I left the groceries on the table in the kitchen, with the change, and started out.

She came in the front door. She didn't say anything. She just stood there, wringing her hands. 'I feel trapped.'

'Tomorrow. I'll do something tomorrow.'

'You've got to get me out of here fast.'

'Leave, then.'

'I can't just leave. Nichols, I've got to get a plane, or a boat, or something. And I can't do it myself. They'll have every place covered!'

'You're nuts. They can't do that. You think they got the U.S. Army?'

'It's worse than that.' She stood there, not looking at me. 'I wish you were staying with me tonight. I'm scared, Nichols.'

'Where's the money?'

'Under the seat of that chair.'

I could see the tip of the brief case and some of the red scarf.

'Why don't you fix the clasp on that brief case? Give you something to do.'

'Better the way it is. I've had that scarf for years. It's a kind of talisman.'

'What in hell's a talisman?'

'Good luck charm, like.'

Bess was coming back from the curb, brushing off her hands. She was looking toward number six, squinting a little.

'We'll work something out tomorrow.'

She turned and kind of leaped at me, both hands out. I got over by the door. 'Nichols. I'm scared.'

I watched her for a second, then went on outside. That Vivian, scared of her own shadow! How could they cover all the airports? They didn't even know she was down here. Maybe they didn't even know she existed. It was Teece they would be wondering about. And they wouldn't wonder about him for long. They would wonder about the money.

But who were 'they?' she was really frightened, there was no getting around that.

Well, I'd have to get her out of here. And I was going to hit her hard for doing this. It was costing me a few years.

I went on out and put the Chevie in the garage.

'I phoned the doctor.'

'What?'

'About your finger. You've got an appointment for tomorrow afternoon. Two o'clock. I tried to get it earlier, but he was filled up.'

Bess closed the Venetian blinds on the bedroom windows.

The next morning I couldn't get near number six no matter how hard I tried. She came out and walked around and you could see the nerves. She had on the white slacks and the black sweater.

The best we could do was wave at each other. There was so much to do, I didn't really accomplish anything, what with the worrying.

The front of number twenty was beginning to peel. I mixed some paint, trying to get the same pastel shade of blue it was in the first place. When it began to dry, it was a lot darker. It looked bad.

'You'll have to paint them all, Roy. They need it anyway.'

And all the time Vivian was back there in number six, going crazy. Every time I walked past on the lawn, she'd come out on the little porch, kind of frantic, making eyes. I didn't even dare look at her much.

Roy this; Roy that. The grass needed cutting. The garage roof leaked in two places. The hedges needed trimming and the fronds were withered and brown on all the palms. The lights had gone bad in ten. The sink was plugged up in number five. Mister Hughes said his toilet wouldn't flush.

I ran around the place, getting nowhere, and then it was one-thirty.

'How'd you do this to your finger, Mister Nichols?'

'Well, Doc, you see, I caught it in a car door.'

He looked at me, blinking his eyes behind enormous black-framed glasses. He was a young guy, heavy-set, with shoulders like a fullback, with those eyes that say you're lying no matter what you say. He kept looking at the finger and shaking his head.

'Have to set it. Have to get the swelling down first.'

'Anything. Listen, just set it.'

'With the swelling, the pain would be bad.'

'Go ahead—go on.'

Well, he liked to kill me. So there I was, finally, with it in a neat little cast. My finger sticking out so it would be in the way of everything.

'Bill me, Doc.'

'Well, all right, Mister Nichols. And, say—be careful of car doors after this.'

His grin was real sly. . . .

His office was alongside the Chamber of Commerce building. I went on out to the car, figuring I'd have to see Vivian if I was ever going to get my hands on any of that money. I climbed into the car and started her up.

The sun was bright and hot.

I looked back to check traffic and happened to glance over toward the front door of the Chamber of Commerce building.

It was like being shot in the face. But it was no mistake. I would never forget that face.

Noel Teece was limping across the sidewalk.

Chapter 7

I sat there, staring, with my foot jammed against the gas pedal, my hand just resting on the gearshift. The engine roared and roared without moving.

Teece was limping badly, dressed in a white Palm Beach suit. His left arm was in a big cast and sling. One side of his face was bandaged, so he only could use one eye.

I didn't know what to do. All the things Vivian was afraid of were beginning to come true.

He walked right by the front of the car, starting across the street. Then he looked directly at the windshield, and you could see him frown with the way the engine was tearing it up. I let go on the gas. He turned away. The sun was on the windshield, so he hadn't seen me. Then he went on across the street, limping, moving in a slow slouch.

He was real beat up and in pain. You could tell.

I watched him go on across the street and stand on the corner. He stood there arranging the sling, kind of staring at his arm as if it was something foreign. Then he patted the bandages by his left eye. He was wearing a Panama hat and it rode on top of the bandages on his head. He kept trying to pull the brim down.

I had to tell Vivian. When I did, there was no telling what she'd do. I sure didn't like seeing Noel Teece—alive.

Because I knew why he was in this town.

'You get your finger fixed?'

'Yeah.'

I had tried bringing the car around to the garage, figuring I'd be able to sneak over to number six. Bess must have seen me coming, or else she was just waiting back there. Anyway, she watched me park the car in the garage.

'That's good.'

'The doc set it. It sure hurt.'

'Tough,' Bess said.

I looked at her. She had on a two-piece white swim suit. She'd been working in the back lawn while I was gone, and she was wet from the sprinklers. Only there was something else in her eyes. She had some mud on one hand, and she wiped her face and some of the mud smeared off.

We stood there watching each other. Finally I started for the house. Somehow I had to get to Vivian, because Noel Teece knew my name. I remembered telling him in the Lincoln. All he had to do was check a little, and he'd be along.

'Where you going?'

'Inside. This damn finger. You wouldn't think a little finger could hurt so much.'

She came along behind me, her feet swishing on the grass. 'Roy?'

I stood there holding the screen door open, half inside the kitchen. You could tell it from the tone of her voice. She had something on her mind. 'A letter came for you.'

'Oh?'

'It's in on the desk.'

'Well, fine.'

She just stood there. She didn't say anything.

I went on into the kitchen and let the screen door slam. It was like everything had gone out of the place, all life. There just wasn't any sound at all.

I kept thinking of Vivian. I went in and the letter was on the desk. There wasn't another thing on the desk. Just that letter. Now, I knew Bess was pulling something.

It was from Albert, and it was open.

I started reading and I heard her coming. It was short and sweet, just like that creep. Explaining everything, just fine.

'Why did you lie, Roy?'

'What in hell else could I do?'

'You could have told me he wouldn't give you the money. I didn't mean to open it. I thought it was all right. I thought it was the check.'

Albert had said how sorry he was about not giving me the money. The same old line all over again. Hoe your own row. Maybe some time ten years from now. . . .

'Roy?'

'Huh?'

'You didn't answer me. Why'd you tell me he was sending the money?'

I stood there with my mouth open. Vivian was walking across the front yard. She went over by a palm tree and stood there. I could see her gnawing her lip.

'You want a telescope, Roy?'

'Cut it out!'

'Answer me, then.'

I had to get Vivian back into the apartment. My God, what if Teece came along now? She didn't even know. All day long she'd been waiting for me to do something and I hadn't even been able to talk with her.

I turned to Bess. 'I had to lie to you. How could I tell you the way he acted? It was lousy—crumby. You never saw anything like it. My own brother!'

'You don't have to talk like that, Roy.'

'Well, damn it, it's true. I didn't know what to do.'

'So you let me get my hopes up. And the suit, Roy. Did he give you the suit of clothes, too?'

'Sure, he did. Certainly. My gosh, Bess!'

'Don't blame me. I don't know what to believe any more.'

She came over and perched herself on the corner of the desk. Her hair was all messed up and there was that mud on her face. 'Take it easy, Bess.'

'I'm taking it easy. I'm just so damned mad I could choke you.'

Vivian was staring over here at the office. Then she started back across the lawn toward number six. She paused and glanced toward the office again.

'You notice? She cut off her slacks and made a pair of shorts. She's got nice legs. Hasn't she?'

'Bess, for gosh sakes!'

She came off the desk and started toward the kitchen, and whirled and stood there. 'You saw him four days ago. Where were you all that time, Roy?'

'I told you—waiting for a ride down here. Listen, I didn't have much money, you know that. The hotel bill took everything. I had just enough for that damned bottle. So I bought it. Not enough dough to get home, even. I didn't even eat, Bess. Last night was the first meal in two days.'

'All right,' she said. 'I'm sorry.' She walked up to me and put her arms around me. She was soaking wet, but I held her tight and kissed her.

'Forgive me, Roy?'

'Sure. What's there to forgive?'

'I shouldn't be that way. Only you were gone so long, up there in Chicago. And I know Chicago, remember? I thought all sorts of things. Then to find this out—that you didn't get the money.'

I kissed her again.

'What are we going to do, Roy?'

'I'm figuring something. But I can't tell you now. Something'll work out.'

'All right. I'll lay off. I'm going to take a shower. I'm sorry what I said about her, too. But she's been walking around in those home-built shorts of hers. She cut them so close up it's a wonder they don't gag her.'

'Go take your shower.'

The minute I heard the water running behind the closed door, I started over toward number six.

Hughes was a fine-looking old gent. He stopped me right outside the office. I tried to let him know I was in a hurry, but he wasn't having any nonsense.

'Mister Nichols?'

I nodded and tried to brush by.

'Wait. I want a word with you.'

'What is it?'

He was tall and thin and stooped a little; the scholarly stoop. He had on a gray business suit and a red bow tie and his eyes were like a busy chipmunk's. 'It come to me that you should do something about that shuffleboard court of yours, there. Now, if you like, I could get to work and clean it up just fine. We could—'

'All right, you just go right ahead and do that.' I could still hear the shower going, but it wouldn't be for long.

'Now, there's one thing—'

'I'm sorry. I've got to run.'

'Well, it's just—'

I whacked him a light one on the shoulder. He darned near collapsed, but I was already cutting across the front of the apartments.

'Teece is alive.'

She was sitting there in a chair, with a newspaper in her hand. It was shaking like crazy.

'I knew it,' she said. 'I knew it.'

'I saw him. Downtown.'

'Oh, God—Noel.'

'You'd better stay inside and not go out.'

She dropped the paper on the floor and Bess had sure been right about those shorts. Then she grabbed the newspaper up and shook it at me.

'It's in the paper about the wreck. They found the Lincoln, Nichols. Only they didn't find anybody in it. . . . Nichols! What in God's name am I going to do?'

She stood up and threw the paper down. I picked it up and she pointed to the little news item.

According to the report, there'd been blood all over everything. The pine trees were sprinkled with it. They'd found a smashed whiskey bottle, and that was supposed to account for the wreck. There had been no sign of any of the car's occupants. They located a trail of blood leading up along the bank of the stream to the road and down the road, only it stopped. They had no idea what happened, but decided the person or persons involved had picked up a ride on the highway.

Vivian was breathing down my neck, trying to read it again over my shoulder, trying to thoroughly digest the bad news. Then she stepped away, flopping that thick black hair around. 'You've got to get me out of here, Nichols.'

'Relax a minute, will you? Let me think.'

'There isn't time to think. Noel's after that money, now. He's out to find me. He'll be here. You *know* he'll be here!'

'Quiet.' I remembered Bess. I had to get out of the apartment. 'We can't talk here. You just stay inside. There's nothing to worry about. If he comes, I'll talk with him. He may not even come.'

'Stop it!' she said. 'Will you please stop it!'

'Well, we can't talk now. If my wife spots us together and thinks anything at all, she'll have me boot you out of here—and quick.'

She had her hands folded the way she did, praying again.

'If I didn't move you out, she'd call the cops.'

She shook her head. 'Oh, no, Nichols. I'd tell her you slept with me night before last. In that hotel. How would she like that?'

'You think she'd believe you?'

'Nichols, we've got to hide the money. At least you can do that much?'

She had me going. It was like my mind had shut down like a door. What she'd said about telling Bess had jarred me. Because Bess would believe it, the way things had been going. I tried to calm down inside, so I could think straight. I couldn't do it. I was all tied up and everything was going wrong.

She'd never let me try to ditch her and back out on this now. And Teece was alive and he knew me.

I had to take the chance of Bess finding me here, so I told Vivian I'd help her hide the money. I didn't know what good it would do. But if Teece did raise any hell, at least he wouldn't get that money.

'You know,' she said. 'It's not just that brief case any more, Nichols. It's me, now. And it's you. Noel's not dumb. He's probably worked it out, what's happened.'

We hid the money in the bureau. I took the top drawers out and wedged it in against the back of the bureau. The drawers wouldn't close all the way, so I took some of her clothes and dribbled them over the drawer. It looked like the drawer was jammed with black lace.

'Now, I've got to scram.'

'Nichols, Nichols.' She got her arms around my neck and slung herself against me. 'I'm scared.'

I pulled her off and checked the back way from the kitchen door. No sign of Bess. I went on outside and started toward our place. Bess stepped onto our back porch from the kitchen, and looked at me. She had on a bright-colored skirt and a peasant blouse. Her hair was brushed to a soft gold.

'Where've you been, Roy?'

'Just checking the paint on the rest of the place. Sure needs a paint job.'

'Wait, I think I heard a car stop out front.'

It felt as if the porch steps began to rock and heave.

"Roy, you're pale as a ghost. What's the matter?'

'Nothing, honey. Nothing at all.'

I pushed past her on the porch. She followed me through the house and I was sweating all over. Sure enough a car had stopped out front. It was a big black baby, a Cadillac, and the sun shot off it like a mirror. It was huge.

I stared till my eyes watered. Then a man got out and stood there a minute, staring at the motel sign. It wasn't Teece.

'Look at that car. It's like a hearse.'

I didn't answer. My heart gradually began to slow down and we stood there together, watching him.

'Think he's coming here?'

He was. He threw a cigar away, turned and started up across the grass. He was a big guy, wearing a single-breasted powder-blue suit and a light gray felt hat. I didn't like it, the way he came at the office. His head kept going back and forth, his gaze checking.

'Could it be somebody from the bank?'

'I don't know.'

'Well, go out and meet him, Roy. He probably wants an apartment.'

'His kind don't stay at motels.'

I went on outside and waited. He saw me and his face didn't change expression. Then he grinned and paused by the porch steps. I came down a step.

'Roy Nichols?'

'That's right.'

'My name's Radan; Mister Nichols. I've just come over here from Tampa. That mean anything to you?'

'No. Why?'

He pursed his lips and lifted one foot to the first step of the porch. Then he took off his hat and held it in both hands on his knee and watched me. His hair was immaculate. It was black hair and it was perfectly combed. His eyes were level and steady. There were tiny nips at the corners of his mouth and, standing there, he gave an impression of great leisure.

I heard Bess moving around inside. 'Looking for a place to stay?'

He shook his head gently. 'Nothing like that. Not yet, anyhow.'

'Well, what is it?'

'That's not the question, Mister Nichols.'

'Maybe we'd better talk inside?'

'That's up to you. I believe perhaps it might be best that we talk alone, privately. At least, for now.'

'Oh?'

He took his foot down and lightly banged his hat against his leg. He seemed to be waiting for something.

I stepped down beside him. He edged a little toward the front lawn, looking at me with his head a shade to one side. Then we both walked out on the lawn.

'Is that your wife inside, Mister Nichols?'

'Yes.'

'I didn't want to embarrass you.'

I didn't say anything.

'I understand how these things are, Mister Nichols. Now, where is Vivian?'

'Vivian?'

'Yes. Vivian Rise. You know what I mean, Mister Nichols.' He cleared his throat carefully. Unless you *would* rather go back inside and discuss it with your wife.'

'I don't get you.'

'I'm sorry about this,' he said. He kept his voice low and his manner was apologetic. 'But I can't do anything about it. You see, I've been sent over here to clear this up. You recall Noel Teece, don't you, Mister Nichols?'

The screen door slammed and I heard Bess coming toward us. 'Roy? Could I be of any help?'

The guy turned and jerked his head in a neat little bow. 'We'll see, Mrs. Nichols. We'll see.'

Bess smiled at this Radan. She had slash pockets in her skirt. She jammed her hands into the pockets and stood there, smiling and rocking back and forth on her heels.

Vivian might not know who Radan was. More than likely she'd never heard of him. So all she had to do was wander out here now, in those shorts of hers and make things just right. I got a tight feeling at the base of my skull, as if somebody'd put a clamp on there and was screwing it tighter and tighter.

Radan cleared his throat. 'You have a very nice place here.'

'Thank you. We love it, don't we, Roy?'

'Oh, yes.'

Radan looked at me and smiled pleasantly. He banged his hat against his leg. He looked at his fingernails. He banged his hat against his leg. He looked at his fingernails, and then at the apartments. He checked the roofs, glancing at Bess from the corner of his eye.

'Thinking of staying in St. Pete?' Bess said.

He frowned at her.

I glanced over at number six. There was no sign of life. But I knew she was there, behind the Venetian blinds, watching, waiting.

'Let's see around back,' Radan said. 'I'd like to have a look at your garage, Mister Nichols.'

I started to say something and changed it fast. I didn't want him to see the Ford with Georgia plates. If he got a look at that, there was no telling. I didn't know exactly who he was, but I had a good enough idea. I wished to God I was out of this. But there was no way out right now.

'All right.'

'Sure,' Bess said. 'We'll show you.'

'Well—Mrs. Nichols.'

'Bess, you know—' She stared at me.

I tried to give her the eye, making it look as if this guy was nuts. As if I didn't know anything about what he wanted, one way or the other. I winked at her.

'Guess I'll see about dinner, Roy.'

Radan nodded and Bess went back inside.

We walked on across the grass toward the far side of the block, over to the edge of the apartments. 'I'm afraid you're in over

your head, Mister Nichols. I don't think you have any idea what
you're really mixed up with. Or have you?'

I didn't say anything.

'You understand?'

'I don't believe so.'

He paused and got in front of me and lightly tapped the brim
of his hat against my chest. Then he pursed his lips and turned
and walked toward the corner of the apartments. The shuffleboard courts were just beyond, under some pines.

'Come along, Mister Nichols.'

We went on past there. I had this one court. Hughes was on his
hands and knees on a pad, scrubbing the cement with a G.I.
brush. He was working with a pail of soapy water, wearing khaki
shorts. He kept coughing as he worked. There was soap and
water all over everything. He was really scrubbing.

'Now, Mister Nichols,' Radan said. 'You've got to understand
that we want to know where this girl is.'

Hughes saw me. He got up, straightening like a rusty hinge,
and came toward us, stooping. He waved the brush and a string
of soap and water dribbled wildly. 'Mister Nichols?'

'We'd better go the other way.'

Hughes reached us. Radan sighed.

'How you like that, Mister Nichols? Getting her really cleaned
up around here.' Hughes' eyes sparkled. He waved the brush and
a long stream of soapy water sprinkled on Radan's suit. Radan
kept on smiling, brushing at it with his hat.

'I'm sorry,' Hughes said. 'Excited, I guess. You can't blame me,
getting the courts all fixed up and all.'

Hughes moved in closer and stood there, holding the brush so
it dribbled gobs of soap on Radan's shiny right shoe.

'I'll have her cleaned up in a jiffy. Then I can play. We'll get up
a game, right, Mister Nichols? You and your wife can come out
and we'll have a fine time. I think the Donnes are becoming
interested in the sport.' Then Hughes nudged my arm, looking at
Radan. 'Is this somebody new—going to stay here, Mister Nichols?'

I shook my head.

'I'm afraid not, sir,' Radan said. He walked toward the rear of
the apartments, past some benches I'd put beside the shuffleboard court.

'Mister Nichols?' Hughes called.

We kept going. At the corner of the apartments, Radan paused.
He got out a handkerchief and bent down, rubbing at the soap

and water on his shoe. It took all the shine off. 'I don't exactly go for this,' he said.

'Sorry.'

He straightened. 'You smash your finger in the wreck, Mister Nichols?'

'What wreck?'

'That won't do any good. There's no use pretending. We know all about it. Either you take action, or we take action. That's the way it is.' He was still very apologetic.

'You haven't made yourself clear.'

'Whether you like it or not, you're mixed up in it now, Mister Nichols. I don't believe you realize that.'

'I still don't understand.'

'Yes. You do. Don't be foolish. We don't like to get rough. It's silly, this day and age. You should understand that.'

'Are you threatening me about something?'

'Mister Nichols, for Lord's sake! Now, look—you certainly wouldn't want to see your place burned down, would you? Your motel, I mean? Now, would you?'

He talked very pleasantly. He was almost pleading, and very matter-of-fact about everything. Looking at him, talking with him, you would think he was some kind of a businessman. He was obviously prosperous. But there was something about him.

'We just can't let it go on, Mister Nichols.'

I could hear Hughes working on the cement with the scrub brush, and his dry, papery cough.

'All right,' Radan said. 'I take it that I have your answer. Right?'

I still said nothing.

'All right,' he said. 'You've had your chance. I was told to give you ten minutes, and I have. You've used them up, playing this all wrong. Now, where's Vivian Rise?'

'Never heard of her.' He was beginning to make me mad, now. Damned if I'd tell him anything.

'Have you seen Noel Teece, Mister Nichols?'

I didn't say anything.

Radan put his hat on. He watched me levelly. 'You've had it, Nichols.'

He turned and walked rapidly away. I started after him. He walked on past Hughes, then paused and stepped over beside the court. Hughes was on his knees, scrubbing the cement.

Hughes looked up and saw Radan and smiled and bobbed his head. Radan looked at him for a long moment, then he lifted his foot, placed it against the old man's head and shoved. Hughes slipped down onto the soapy cement.

'Listen here!' I said, going after him. Radan paused and looked back at me, turned sharply and cut across the lawn. He reached his car. I stood in the middle of the lawn by the sign and watched him get in the car.

Radan took a last look at the motel, started the engine and made a fast rocking U-turn on the broken road. He vanished around the corner, the engine hissing.

I went over to Hughes. 'I'm sorry about that.'

'It's all right, Mister Nichols. I could tell he was a sorehead when I spilled that soap on him. He didn't hurt me. There's all kinds in this world. Now, listen—I think the court should be renumbered. Have you any white paint? I'm really good at lettering.'

'You'll find some in the garage for number one.'

He nodded happily and I started back toward the office. I had to see Vivian again, but I didn't know how I was going to get to her.

This Radan was a beaut.

'Roy?'

'Yes?'

'What did he want?'

'Oh, that guy? Kind of a funny character. Says he, well—wanted to build a motel. Comes from over in Tampa. He's been riding around looking at motels. He likes this one. Asked me a few questions, that's all.'

'Sure peculiar.'

'I know it. Hard to figure. Wants to build a motel. He sympathized with us, being stuck the way we are, with the road not through yet. He mentioned taxes.'

'Please. Don't even speak of them. What'll we do, Roy? What are we going to do about money?'

'I'll think of something.'

We were in the office and she was standing in the doorway leading to our living room. She turned and went back into the kitchen.

I wished I could think of something to send Bess out for, so I could go talk with Vivian. But there wasn't a thing I could do. And there she was in the doorway again. When Bess looked at me, it was in that funny way that I didn't like.

'Roy, you look sick. Honestly, I never saw you look so bad. Try not to worry about things. Everything'll be all right. You wait and see. Hasn't everything always worked out all right?'

'Sure.'

'Or is it just that you had a hot time up there in Chicago?'

'Nothing like it. I just got drunk, that's all. But it was bad stuff. Maybe I can't take it any more.' I had to get away from her and think. Try to.

'You don't suppose that man had anything to do with the bank?'

'No.' She was so worried, and there was nothing I could do to straighten her out about things. Not now. I wanted to and I couldn't.

'Maybe they've put the place up for sale, or something. Without telling us about it.'

'Stop it, Bess!' My voice was hoarse. 'They can't do a thing like that. You know that.'

'What's the *matter* with you, Roy?'

I went outside and stood on the porch and looked down across the lawn. There was no sign of Vivian. I knew that was no way to act if I wanted to keep Bess quiet. I went back inside. She was standing by the kitchen table with both hands flat on top. She didn't look up as I came in.

'I'm sorry about that.'

'It's all right.'

'Everything's got me down. Trying to figure a way out of this mess.'

'I know.'

Oh God, I thought, if she only did know. . . .

A few minutes later she was in by the desk; checking the bills. 'Roy—that man just drove past again.'

I went over by the desk. 'What?'

She turned and looked at me, frowning. 'The man in the hearse, Roy. I've seen him go by the place twice now.'

I stared out the window. It was quiet on the street, but I knew she had seen him. And I began to know she would keep on seeing him.

Chapter 9

'Mrs. Nichols. I've got to see your husband.'

'Oh, hello, Miss Latimer.'

'Is Mister Nichols around?'

'Yes. He's in the other room. What is it?'

'Well—I think he'd better have a look at my stove. There's something wrong with the stove.'

'What seems to be the matter?'

I went on out there. She was on the back porch, talking with Bess. She was still wearing the shorts and she looked wild. Her hair was like she'd been combing it with her fingers. She had on lots of lipstick, but the rest of her face was the color of flour.

She saw me over Bess's shoulder and her eyes got kind of crazy. Bess heard me and turned, holding the door open.

'Miss Latimer's having trouble with her stove.' She gave me the eye.

'Well, all right. You want me to have a look?'

'Would you?' Vivian said. 'I hate terribly bothering you like this.'

'Sure.' I brushed past Bess. Vivian went off the porch onto the grass and Bess stepped after me. I didn't dare say anything. If Bess came along, there was nothing you could do.

'Think I'll see how Hughes is making out with the shuffleboard courts,' Bess said.

'Every time I light the gas, it pops,' Vivian said.

'Air in the line.'

Bess went off along the rear of the apartment.

'God. Nichols!'

'Wait'll we get over there.'

As soon as we were in her kitchen, she whirled, and it was like somebody was running a knife in and out of her. 'I saw him, Radan! That's Wirt *Radan!* I know about him. I know why he's here. You don't even have to tell me. He's famous, Nichols— famous! I met him once in New York. He moves around the country. You know what he is?' She was breathing quickly, her eyes very bright, and she had her fists bunched tight against her thighs. 'He's a killer.'

'Cut it out. . . .'

'Sure. You wouldn't believe that. I knew you wouldn't, you're such a damned square. But it's true. That's his job. He's one of them that works to a contract. You think they don't do that any more? Do you? You're crazy, if you think that!'

'Take it easy.'

'Noel told me about him just a few days ago.' She paused and turned and held her back to me that way, and her shoulders began to shake. She whirled on me again and I thought for a second she was going to yell. She didn't. She just kept talking, with her voice held down in her throat, and she was really scared now. 'Noel said Wirt Radan was getting so tough the men are afraid to work with him, even.'

'And you told me you weren't mixed up in any of this.'

'I'm not. I was Noel's girl. That's all.'

'Only that wasn't enough.'

'Nichols! You've got to get me out of here!'

I wanted that as much as she did. Only, how? 'Did you ever stop to think of the mess you've got me in?' I said. 'Did you?'

'I'm paying you. Remember?'

'Vivian, all you think about is that money. Money can't take care of everything.'

'You're thinking about it, too! Plenty. True, Nichols?'

'All right. How do you want to work it?'

'I want plane tickets to South America—Chile, probably. You'll have to get me to the airport, see me on the plane. Somehow. Then you'll get yours.'

'Why not just get the tickets? Can't you get them yourself, for that matter? You can drive to the airport yourself. It's not far.'

'Can we still get them now? You think it's open, downtown? The ticket office?'

'I guess so.'

'Then let's get going. I can't go alone. I know they'll be at the airport.'

I just stood there. She turned and rushed out of the room and I heard her in the bedroom, yanking the bureau drawers. I went in there.

She had the brief case. She got her suitcase off a chair, snapped it shut without putting anything extra back inside, and looked at me. 'Let's go, Nichols.'

She was off her rocker. She wasn't thinking; traveling in some kind of a vacuum, she was like a hound dog on the scent, flying like the crow.

But I thought about that money, and not only that—if I could get her out of here now, I could tell Bess I'd taken her downtown. Tell her anything. Because she'd be gone and there wouldn't be any chance for argument.

She glanced down at her shorts, turned abruptly, dropped the brief case and opened the suitcase and whipped out a blue skirt. Her anxiety was almost comical, except you knew how real it was.

I heard Bess call to me from outside.

'No,' Vivian said. 'Please—don't go.' She grabbed me. 'Tell her something—anything. You know I've got to leave here now.'

I shoved her and she went windmilling across the bedroom and landed against the wall. I beat it out into the kitchen and Bess was just coming up on the porch. I opened the door. Bess tried to look past me. I let her look.

'Did you fix her stove all right?' There was a slight touch of sarcasm in her voice. But as she looked at me, she began to smile.

I grinned at her. 'You go fix dinner. I'll be along.'

She turned and went back toward our place. Vivian came out of the bedroom wearing the blue skirt. That wild look was still in her eyes. There was something about the way she held her mouth, too; a tenseness that told you a little about what went on inside her. Just a young kid, really—only not a kid—and her life all twisted out of shape. And she was trying to save her life in the only way she knew. Watching her, I felt a sense of hopelessness.

'All right. Let's get going.'

She picked up the brief case and the suitcase and I saw the filmy red scarf fall softly, lazily, from the brief case to the floor. She jammed the case under her arm and we went out into the kitchen.

'Wait'll I check.' I looked outside. Nobody. 'All right. You get in your car. I'll be along in a minute, so it won't look so bad. Make it fast, now, to the garage.'

'Yes.' She gave me a quick harried look, turned and went outside. I watched her cross the grass swiftly and slip between the garages toward the drive, her shoulders held rigid, as if she were trying to hide behind them. Twinkletoes.

I waited another moment. I knew it was better this way. She'd be gone, and the worry would be gone with her. She'd carry that part wherever she went, but it would be off my back. Somehow, I knew it was going to work out all right.

I stood there, trying to get my breath evened out, and then I went on outside and closed the door and started across the grass. She came running at me.

She tripped, stumbling, and the suitcase fell out of her hand. She made a wild grab for it, missed, and came on, her mouth open and her eyes stricken and sick.

'Get back!' She kept running. 'He's out there. Radan just drove through the alley!' She came past me and rushed inside.

I went on out and got the suitcase and made it back to the porch. I entered the kitchen and looked at her. 'Did he see you?'

'No. No, he didn't see me.' She kind of turned and bent over like an old woman, and let her head hang, and went into the living room, moaning to herself. She still had the brief case plugged under her arm.

'Did he stop?'

'No. I saw him coming. I was right out in the drive, there. He'd just turned in off the street with that big black car. I could see his face—looking. Not at me, though. Oh, *damn it!*'

'That's bad.'

'I'll never be able to get out of here now. He'll watch, and he'll watch.' She flopped down into a chair, hugging the brief case and she began to cry. It was wild, angry, hurt crying.

'The money. We'd better hide the money again,' I said. 'But not in the bureau. I got a better place. Come on.'

She just sat there. I went over and grabbed her arm, pulled her up, and she leaned against me, shuddering. She was an awful sight and I felt sorry for her.

'The apartment next door's empty. That'll be a better place—just in case. We'll have to run for it again. The front way this time. So come on.'

We went outside, and there was no sign of Radan. The sun was beginning to dip. Another day gone, and things just that much worse.

We went in next door. It was hot and stuffy. It hadn't been aired in weeks, and our footsteps were loud on the floors. 'Suppose somebody moves in here?'

'They won't. I'll see to that. Listen, I'm going to drain the tank behind the toilet, shut it off, and we'll put the brief case in there.'

She was lost again, praying. I got the brief case and there was an immediate thrill, knowing what was inside it. It was heavy and full and it made you want to run some place, hanging onto it. I took it into the bathroom, turned the water off, flushed the john, and put the money in the tank.

'What are you doing over here, Miss Latimer?'

'I—we—he's checking the stove for something.'

I came out of the bathroom, dodged into the kitchen and stood there sweating. Bess was talking in the living room now, about it being so hot. I went out the back door and let it slam real hard. I went over to number six, and stood there fiddling with the stove, turning it on and off, hating every minute of this and wishing I didn't have to treat Bess like a stranger. I could hardly see the stove.

Pretty soon they came along. Bess entered the kitchen first and I didn't look at her. I got out a match and lit the stove, and the gas caught just fine.

'Hi. She's okay now.'

'That's fine,' Bess said.

'Thanks so much, Mister Nichols. Honestly, I hate all this trouble I'm causing.'

I looked at Bess. Boy, was she sparking! Vivian moved past us, on into the living room and stood by the front window.

'You just call me if there's any more trouble.'

Bess and I went outside.

'You're sweating, Roy.'

'Roy. She's got a man's suitcase in there.'

'What?'

'Miss Latimer. She's got a man's suitcase, and it's full of a man's clothing.'

'What've you been doing in her apartment?'

'I just looked in, that's all, while you were next door. I saw it. What would she be doing with another suitcase, like that?'

'Darned if I know. Maybe it's her husband's. Maybe she's married, just doesn't want to say anything. Some women are like that.'

'She acts pretty queer, if you ask me. Has she said anything to you about being married?'

'No.'

I had to shut her up, or get away from her. I couldn't take it, because I knew now that I was in on everything with Vivian, and I was scared. Just plain scared. I didn't know what to do. With Radan skulking around like that. Only you couldn't call the cops. Not on a thing like this, not even if you did want to back out of the bad part.

Besides, that money. It was there, and I *had* to have some of it. Somehow. It was the only way I could see—even if it was a wrong way. When the taxes for this property came due, we'd really be in the soup. I didn't want to lose this motel. I wasn't going to lose it. I couldn't let Bess take it on the chin any more. She'd never had any peace, never—all our married life, it had been like this. From one thing to another, never any peace, and by God, she was going to have peace and some of the things she wanted.

One way or another.

Even if I had to get hold of the brief case myself, and run. . . .

God, I was in a sweet mess and I knew it. But something had to be done.

'Roy,' Bess said, 'I hate to keep at you like this. But I know darned well something's the matter with that woman. You must have seen that. She's afraid of something. We've got enough around here without somebody tossing their troubles in our laps.'

'How do you mean?'

'I don't know. I can't figure her out, but I do know something's wrong. You think I should ask her?' I knew Bess had been doing a lot of thinking. There was no way of her catching onto the truth, but I didn't like her this way. It was my problem, not hers. She said, 'I'll bet she's in some kind of trouble, Roy.'

'Well, maybe so. But let's not stick our noses in, huh?'

'Yes. I know you're right.'

I went into the bedroom and lay down. I finally dozed a little. Once I heard Bess come in, very softly, and stand there looking at me. I didn't open my eyes. She went away.

I woke up and it was dark. I could hear Bess breathing quietly. I rolled off the bed carefully, so as not to disturb her and stood there in the dark. It was after midnight by the clock ticking away on the dresser. I had conked off for sure. I hadn't even eaten and Bess had let me sleep. The poor kid was plenty worried about everything.

I started to undress, then looked at her again. She was really knocking it, breathing deep and heavy.

I left the room. In the office, I looked out through the window. The sign was still lit up and I sat down at the desk for a while, trying to think of something. I got nowhere.

It was real quiet, inside and outside. And it got real lonely.

I finally got up and went and looked into the bedroom again. She was sleeping quietly. There was a dim shaft of light down across her face, from where one of the slats in the Venetian blinds was tilted open. She looked worried, even in sleep. I knew she was catching on to things, to something anyway, and it troubled her plenty, even if she didn't know what it was. She knew me too well, and she trusted in me too much, and God, I loved her and I wanted her to be happy.

I left the room and slipped out of the back door and around between the apartments. It was quiet over at number six, but there was a light inside. I went up onto the porch and kept checking out there on the lawn. I opened the door and stepped inside, and closed the door.

'Yeah,' Noel Teece said. *'Yeah.* Here he is now.'

They were sitting there. She was on a chair, with her hands clenched in her lap, holding her thumbs, staring up at me, round-eyed and hopeless-looking.

Teece was humped on the studio couch. He was all bandaged up, the way I'd seen him. His hat was on, jutting above the bandages on his face.

Chapter 10

Teece had an evil-looking eye.

That eye watched me, blinking under the hat brim, and you kind of wished you could see the other eye, too. But the bandage covered that. The eye that watched me was bloodshot and tired, yet kind of frantic and steady, even behind the blinking. His cheek was mottled and his lips were pale and thin and he needed a shave. He just sat there, blinking that damned eye at me.

'Noel just came in. He sneaked in the back way,' Vivian said. 'Noel, honey—we thought you were dead. You know we thought that.'

He kind of laughed. It sounded a little like he was crying inside.

'You two been happy?'

Neither of us said anything. I didn't like the looks of him at all. Like I say, there was something frantic about the way he looked. As if he was out of hand and knew it and didn't care. He was breathing pretty fast.

'All afternoon I've been trying to get in here, you two. Now, I'm here.'

His eye was watering. Vivian just sat there, holding onto her thumbs.

'Thought I was dead, did you? Well, I'm not dead.'

Still we didn't speak.

'You know why I'm here?'

Vivian began nodding slowly.

Teece stood up. Now I could see what it was. The man was scared. He was so scared he didn't know what to do next. It was knocking the hell out of him, the way he was.

'I talked with them on the phone,' he told us. 'I can't go see them. They'll kill me. Oh, yes. But if I get that money back to them, maybe I can swing it. Maybe they'll understand.'

He said it like that, but you could tell he didn't really believe himself. He knew they wouldn't understand. That's what you could read in the half of his face that showed, and in the way he began prowling up and down the room.

'All right. Where's the money, Viv?'

She looked across at me.

'We haven't got it,' I told him. I heard myself say it and went along with it. 'They beat you here, Teece. You worked too slow.'

He was like an animal. His mouth came open and the way I'd said that had hurt him. He stood there, blinking, with the light gleaming in that bloodshot eye.

'We gave the money to some guy called Radan.'

'Wirt Radan?' He turned on her and she bobbed her head fast.

'That's right, Noel. He came and we gave the money to him. We had to.'

'But, he's—'

'Radan said they were going to get you, Teece.'

'You lie! Both of you lie! You and Viv, you think I can't see through this? You're planning it together. But you're not getting away with this. Now, where's that money?' He reached into his coat and came up with a gun. It wasn't very large, but it wouldn't have to be. Only he wasn't sure of himself. He wasn't certain that we were lying.

'That's not going to do a damned bit of good. I told you, this fellow Radan came here today. This afternoon. He drives a big black Caddy. He knew all about everything—you, the accident, the works. We gave him the money, and that's it.'

He moved his head slightly from side to side.

'It's the truth, Noel.' She came up out of the chair, with an imploring look on her face. It was a real art, the way she did it. 'It's true, Noel.' She stood there, looking straight into his eye. 'He told us what they were going to do. There wasn't any other way. *You know Radan.* Sure, I was going to try and get away with the money. Wouldn't you have done the same thing? What else was there to do?'

He kept on moving his head from side to side.

'Noel, honey. We thought you were dead. I did the only thing I could do. I've been trying to get Nichols to help me, see? So I was going to pay him to help me get out of the country. He needs the money for his motel, here. Can't you understand that?'

The gun began to droop a little and the head-shaking slowed down almost to a stop.

'So, then Radan came here this afternoon. He burst right in here, Noel. He saw the brief case we had the money in—remember? I gave it to him. There was nothing else to do.'

A crafty look came into the eye. 'Radan just took the money? Didn't he do anything else?'

I said, 'He threatened a lot of things. Maybe it's all still up in the air. He hasn't been back. That's why I came over here now, to ask her what we should do.'

He wheeled on me with the gun, and it scared me. I made a pass at the gun with one hand. It connected. The gun clattered on the floor.

'Don't!'

He came at me with that one arm, his head back, cursing. It was comical. Him with his arm in a sling and his head all bandaged up and that scared look in his one bloodshot eye. But he swung, just the same.

I tried to hold him off. Then I took a poke at him, shying away from his face. I hit him in the chest. He staggered back toward the door and the door opened and Bess stood there, blinking sleepily and hitching at her housecoat over her pajamas.

'I heard a noise,' she said.

He fell against her. She shoved him off and looked at us. He turned and saw her and his face reddened.

'What's going on?'

'It's nothing, Bess. It's all a mistake.'

Teece eyed me and swallowed and looked at Bess.

There was the gun on the floor, but Bess hadn't seen it. Vivian saw the gun and she stepped over and stood just beyond it, so Bess wouldn't be able to see it even if she looked down there.

'But, Roy—' Bess said.

'Yes,' Vivian said. 'Sure. Look, this man—' she motioned toward Teece—'is a friend of mine. Mister Nichols must have heard something and made a mistake.'

'That's right, Bess. I couldn't sleep after I woke up. I went out to get some air and I saw this guy snooping. I thought he was a prowler. Actually, I guess all he was doing was looking for Miss Latimer's apartment. I'm sorry I was so bull-headed.'

Teece's eyebrow shot up.

'He'd planned on coming down,' Vivian said. 'He was supposed to meet me here. He met with an accident on the way. Maybe you've noticed how worried I've been? Well, this is why. Mister Nichols thought he was doing the right thing. He came to help me.'

Bess stood there and took it all in. Then she turned and stepped out onto the porch. 'I'm sorry,' she said through the screen door. 'You coming, Roy?'

'Sure. Just a minute.'

She went away and we looked at each other.

'The money,' Teece said.

'We told you. Radan's got it.'

Teece went over and picked up the gun and looked at it. He put it away.

'Radan, huh?' he said, and there was this funny new look in that eye of his. He stared at Vivian for a second and she looked right back at him, nodding slightly. Then he turned away and went outside. He disappeared along the side of the apartment, back toward the garages. I started for the door.

'Don't leave me alone!'

'I've got to get out of here.'

I opened the door and stepped out on the porch. She came up to the door and stood there, scratching her fingernails on the screen.

'Don't you see?' she said. 'I can't leave now. I can't leave!'

I went down off the porch and around toward the garage. I heard a car start up out in the alley. It drove away fast, showering gravel. I listened to it until I couldn't hear it any more, then I went back to our place. . . .

'Roy, I'd like you to ask Miss Latimer to leave. I'd appreciate it if you'd go over there now and ask her to pack her things.'

'Bess, don't be silly. I know how it looked. It bothered me, too. But everything's all right now.'

'I'm sorry. But I'm asking you to do this for me. I don't like it, the way things are over there. Are you going to do it for me?'

'Look. Let her stay till morning.' I reached out and drew her close, and kissed her, but she was kind of cold about it.

'Morning?'

'All right. In the morning, you go over there the first thing, Roy.'

Chapter 11

In the morning I figured she forgot about what she'd said. Either that, or maybe thought better of it. I didn't get much sleep. I lay there thinking it through, but trying to stay away from the real part—how it was working out. I kept trying to figure how I could have got my hands on some of that money, or all of it, without this mess. There was no use telling myself I didn't want that money. There were too many reasons why I needed it.

The big thing I kept figuring was that it was crooked money to begin with. Somehow that made me feel better. I kept coming back to that, trying to figure some way. And then I remembered that was how Vivian had talked in the hotel room. It wasn't money that really belonged to anybody, she'd said. Or to that effect. And she was right.

But, there was no way. Not unless I went over there and took it and got out of here. I thought about that. How I could grab the money and run. Then I could mail Bess enough to pay off the motel, and . . . only it wasn't any good. It didn't have that part I wanted—the peace of mind part.

Because without the peace, you had nothing. And you couldn't buy that, either.

Anyway, all I wanted out of this world was Bess and the motel. The motel. That was a laugh, and I lay there with Bess asleep beside me, thinking of her, and how I could make some decent kind of life for us together. . . .

I figured I'd done enough to belong to a part of that brief case, anyway. Not a big part. Just enough to take care of immediacies. Where did that come from?

And then I saw that Radan's face, like it was hanging up there on the ceiling of my mind. And I knew what kind of a guy he was. I didn't want to mix with him.

It was all real crazy. Albert, and the Lincoln and Vivian and Noel Teece, and now Radan, like a parade through the bloody twilight. And the brief case with that red scarf tied around it. Only she'd dropped the scarf. Talisman.

'Go to sleep, Roy.'

'Yeah.'

What in hell was I going to do? The emptiness got filled with a kind of frantic rushing and my heart got to going it, lying there. I wanted to yell and crack my knuckles, or sock somebody.

Because it was all closing in. I could tell.

You recognize the landmarks, because you've seen them before, if you've been around enough. You go along trying to hold it all gutted up and hard and ignoring it all, then one fine day it busts wide open. And there you are. You got to do something, and there's nothing to do. You can't think even.

Southern Comfort Motel—crawling with fright.

That Vivian was a dilly, sure enough. Getting herself messed up like she had. Shooting the works to Teece, and so scared now with what she'd done, she could hardly stand up.

It was like I didn't quite know them and I didn't want to. Just that brief case. A piece of that. . . .

So I finished breakfast and she didn't say a word about anything. My second coffee, I said, 'Maybe mow the lawn today.'

She clinked the plates and coffee cups to the sink. She ran the water. She shut it off. She had on a kind of blue-flowered house-coat and she looked nice, only worried.

'Roy?'

'Yeah?' Here it was.

'Have you forgotten what I said last night?'

I kind of ran my hand across my face, trying to remember what she meant, letting her think that was it.

'You know what I mean. About Miss Latimer. I want you to go over there and ask her to leave.'

'I figured that was just a pipe dream.'

'It's no dream. You want me to do it? If you won't, I will.'

She sure had me there. Now what was I going to do? Tell Vivian that, and she'd freeze over there in number six, and you couldn't get her out with a derrick.

'Well?'

'You'd have to give her back her rent money.'

'A pleasure.'

She left the kitchen. 'We can't have people like her running around, Roy. She'll hurt the name of the place. Imagine, that wreck of a man coming in the middle of the night. Maybe she picked him up off the street, how do you know?'

I tagged along and she went into the office, to the desk, and counted the money out of the cigar box and looked over at me.

'I'd appreciate it if you'd do it, Roy.'

I took the money. 'Can't we give her a little more time?'

'You want her staying here? That it? With her nice tight shorts and everything?'

I looked at her.

'I'm sorry I said that, Roy. Honest. I didn't mean it.' She stared down at the desk, then up at me again. 'It's just she worries me, being here. She isn't right, and you know it.'

'Okay.'

I left the office and let the screen door slam.

I came along by number six and looked it over. It was quiet. What was I going to do? I had to tell her what Bess said, but there was no saying how she'd take it. I knew how she'd take it. It had to be Bess's way.

Well, she sure had that red scarf tied around her neck.

Vivian was right there on the floor in the doorway between the living room and the bedroom hall. She was all crumpled up in a twisted knot, the blue skirt up to her belly, and her face was a hell of a color. Her eyes bugged and her mouth was open, her tongue all swelled up like a fat pork chop.

I turned around, wanting to run, then stopped. The scarf was tied around her neck so tight the flesh bulged around it. I got over there, still holding her refund money in my hand, and I touched her.

She was cold.

Chapter 12

Well, Vivian was gone, all right. Only it wasn't exactly the way Bess had wanted her to go.

I knelt there for a long time, dizzy and half sick. Her shirt was torn at one shoulder and there were bruises on her arms. She was crumpled on the floor like paper gets crumpled.

That red scarf. Vivian's good luck. Her talisman.

Then I remembered the brief case. I got out of there, still carrying the rent refund wadded in my hand. I shoved it into my pocket and cut over next door. I kept thinking. What now—What now—? I went next door, let myself in and headed for the bathroom.

I got the lid off the tank and there was the brief case. All I could think was, maybe she told whoever did this where the money was. I got it out of there, and the money was inside. I put the lid back on the tank, turned the water on and headed for the rear of the apartment.

I had to hide it again. But where?

I got out in the garage and stood there, wondering what to do with the brief case. So finally I climbed up on the hood of the Chevy and grabbed a beam and snaked myself up there where I had some lumber piled. I crawled back into the corner under the eave and shoved the brief case under some of the boards. You wouldn't find it unless you knew it was there. They'd tear the whole motel apart first.

They? They—who? And it kept hitting me that the law would be in on this now. There wasn't anything I could do about that. I climbed down onto the car again, and hit the dirt. There was no sign of anybody. I made a run for it, down between the garages and to the back door of number six. It was open. I walked through the kitchen, and she was still lying there on the floor.

'Roy?'

It was Bess. She called again from out front. I stepped past the body and walked through the living room fast, and out the door. I stood on the porch.

Bess came across the lawn. She'd been talking with Mrs. Donne who was settled in her beach chair, a half-filled drink in her hand.

'Well, did you tell her?'

I didn't say anything.

'All right. *I'll* tell her!' She tried to push past me. I got hold of her and held her still. She had on a white dress and she looked fresh and lovely, but I couldn't remember ever seeing her look so worried. Her eyes had that kind of not-quite-looking-at-you way they get.

'Don't go in there, Bess. Bess—' I couldn't bring myself to say it.

'I certainly *am* going in there! I'm going to tell her. Didn't you say anything to her at all? What'd you do, just stand there?' She pulled away from me and started for the door of number six. I turned and went after her. 'Is *he* still inside?'

'No.'

'Then, what—?' She knocked lightly on the door, brushing some hair away from her forehead.

'Nobody's going to answer,' I said softly.

Bess opened the door and went on inside. I followed her, thinking, What am I going to do? Bess just stood there, staring and I could see her start to yell. If she yelled, that was her business. She didn't. She cut it off and turned and looked at me and blinked. 'She's dead.'

'Yes.'

Well, she just stood there, staring. She didn't cry or scream or carry on at all, like a woman might. And I was proud of her—that she was my Bess. Then she looked at me again and swallowed.

'Well,' I said. 'That's the way I found her.'

She shook her head and went over and slumped into a chair. I got over there and pulled her up and held her. She was trembling a little. I held her tight.

'What d'you suppose happened, Roy?'

'That's better.'

I wondered for a moment if she'd thought I'd done this. Sometimes they can cook up some weird things in their heads.

She looked over there again and whipped her head away. 'It's awful!'

She didn't even begin to know how awful. It was just hitting her, what had really happened. You could see it come across her face. A shadow of fear, and something like hate.

'Mrs. Nichols?'

I whirled and it was the young girl who was on her honeymoon, in number eleven. We hadn't seen anything of them, but now here she was. Her yellow dress was one of these fluffy things, and she had brown hair and brown eyes and she smiled and said, 'Mrs. Nichols.'

'No,' I said. 'Wait.'

But she was already coming through the door. Bess started toward her with one hand out.

The girl said, 'I was just looking for you. I saw you come in here, so I—' and she stopped. She saw that over there on the floor and she screamed.

She put both hands against her face and filled her lungs and let it rip. It rocked the house. She really had lungs. Her face got red and she kept on screaming. She turned and ran smack into the screen door, and got it open and went outside, screaming and running for number eleven.

I looked out the window. Mrs. Donne was standing out there by the beach chair. She held the glass in her hand, but it had all spilled down her front. She watched the girl run across the lawn, trying to brush the spilled drink off her dress. Then she looked over here at number six.

'We've got to phone the police.'

'Wait.'

'What d'you mean, wait, Roy? We can't wait.'

'Wait, anyway.' I went and sat in the chair and held my head. I felt blocked. I knew there was something I could do. There had to be—

'We've got to phone the police right now. Is there any reason why we shouldn't?'

'Wait.' I didn't want her to call the cops. I couldn't help it, I just didn't want it, and there was nothing I could do about it.

'Roy, let's get out of here. I don't want to stay in this place.'

'Yeah.'

She came over and grabbed my arm. I stood up and we walked over to the door. 'What's the matter with you, Roy?'

'All right.'

The girl from number eleven was standing down there by her porch. She was talking with her husband through the window, waving her arms around. I quit looking at her, but I could hear her damned piping voice talking and talking.

We got over to the office and Bess sat down at the desk. 'What'll I say?'

I stood there watching her.

'Roy!'

'Just go ahead. Call them.'

So she did. . . .

'How long d'you think it'll take them to get here, Roy?'

I sat there on the couch, staring at the floor. I could see Bess' feet going back and forth on the rug, back and forth. She walked up and down.

'Roy. You just sit there.'

I stared.

'Did—did you touch her?'

'Yeah. She's cold.'

'What could have happened? It must have been that man, the one with his arm in the sling. This is awful, Roy! It can ruin business here, too.'

Business. Business.

'Here come the honeymooners.'

I looked up and they came along and knocked on the office door. Bess went over and started to open the door, then decided against it.

'We're leaving,' the guy said. He was a tall, thin guy, dressed in a gray suit. He had red hair and freckles, and the girl stuck close to him. 'We were going to stay another week, but now we want this week's rent back. We've decided to move along. That's how—'

'All right,' Bess said. There was a kind of a sting to the way she said it. 'Come on in.'

'No,' the girl said.

They stood there, shuffling on the doorstep. Bess looked at them for a moment, then went and counted some money out of the cigar box and looked at me and went over and opened the door. She handed the guy the money.

They turned quickly and walked away without a word. The girl was talking like crazy the minute they were on the front lawn. I sure didn't envy him his married life with that one. A few more years and she'd really be a dilly.

'I wish they'd come.'

'They will, don't worry.'

'Roy. Who d'you think she was? Murdered—murdered right here in our place. I didn't hear a thing. Did you hear anything after we came back from over there?'

'Nope.'

I got up and went out into the kitchen and washed my hands in the sink. I dried them on the dish towel. Then I took a glass down from the cupboard and filled it with water and stood there drinking. You could taste the chlorine, and the water wasn't very cold.

'What are you going to tell them, Roy?'

'What *can* I tell them?'

She was in the doorway. She came over and stood by the kitchen table. I didn't want to look at her. At the same time, I wanted to tell Bess everything I knew, all I'd been through with Vivian.

'You're spilling water all over the floor, Roy.'

Well, I took that damned glass and I let her go. It whizzed across the room and smashed against the cupboards and busted, and water and glass showered.

She didn't move. Just stood there, watching me.

'Honey,' she said, 'what's the matter?'

'It's all right,' I said. 'It's nothing. I'm sorry I did that. It's just things, that's all. *Just things!*'

Chapter 13

We stood there for a time without saying anything. It began to scare me a little, understanding how easy it is to start a canyon of doubt between two people. We'd been as close as any two people can get in every way, and now I could sense the separation because of doubt, and because I couldn't, or wouldn't tell her about things. I couldn't. And then I knew I wouldn't ever let it be like that.

'It's nothing, Bess. I'm just wrought up, I guess. Not getting the money from Albert, and then I went and lied to you about it all, and he writes. All the money we owe, and I can't see my way clear.'

I went over to her and put my arms around her. She was kind of stiff, then she let loose and laid her head on my chest and it was like old times.

'And now this,' I said. 'Can you understand how I feel?'

'It scares me, Roy.'

'It's damned well enough to scare anybody.'

'I mean the way she looked. She was beautiful, Roy.'

'I guess maybe she was.'

'How could anybody *do* a thing like that? And us finding her. Why? Why?'

I patted her head and squeezed my hand on her arm. I wanted it to be right with us. But how could it ever be right from now on in?

So finally I let her go, and went in and flopped down on the bed. And I kept seeing that face, red and black. With the tongue.

Well, you either win—or you lose.

'Roy, that man in the car like a hearse drove by again.'

'Oh? Yeah? Him?'

'He just keeps driving by. It's the third time I've seen him today, Roy. Maybe he's gone past other times. Just driving by, like he's going around and around the block. I wonder what he's up to?'

'I don't know.'

'Well, he's sure up to something.'

'Maybe.'

'Please don't act that way, Roy!'

I lay face down on the bed, with my head buried in the pillow.

'I wish the police would come. Why don't they hurry up?'

They came quick enough for me. They came to the office and Bess went out there. I stuck with the bed. She told them about number six and they went over there. You could hear them, like elephants.

You could hear them talking.

There's something about the voice of the law. It's a jumble of solemn and righteous sound. It reached me all the way in the bedroom and I lay there, listening, wondering what I was going to do. What would I tell them? My mind was all cluttered up with that brief case, and how it had been for the past few days. I kept being with Noel Teece and Vivian in the Lincoln, off and on, cracking up on the Georgia road. And then the hotel room, and the brief case again, around and around.

'Roy?'

I didn't move. She came into the bedroom and over to the bed. After a little while, she sat on the bed and put her hand on my shoulder. What did she figure was the matter with me? I'd make a fine crook, all right—running off and trying to hide my head like an ostrich.

'They're still over there,' she said. 'One of them says he wants to talk with you. He said he'd be over here.'

'Okay.'

'They're going to take the body away. They've been over there an awful long time.' She paused, then said, 'I think you'd better come into the office—kind of show yourself. That one, he said—'

'I heard you.'

'Don't snap so.' Her hand rubbed on my shoulder, the fingers squeezing. I rolled over and looked at her and she grinned at me. So I grinned at her, and it was like she'd come back to me, after she'd been away a long time. And then I knew she wasn't really back at all. Because she still didn't know. But she was with me. That much of it paid for a lot.

I sat on the edge of the bed. 'Okay, honey,' I said. 'Thanks.'

We watched each other, and she put her hand on mine and I took her hand and squeezed it and it was almost as if she knew everything and was with me. So I knew everything was all right, even if she didn't know.

'What are you going to tell them?'

I kept looking at her, kind of drinking her in. Then I grunted and got up and went into the bathroom. When I came back, she was still sitting there on the bed.

'They took the body away. I told them we found it together.'

'But, Bess—we didn't.'

'I told them that, though.'

'Well, all right.'

'I haven't seen him drive by any more, Roy—not since the police have been here.'

I looked at her and she looked at me, then down at the floor, then up at me again. I grinned at her and turned and went into the office and sat down at the desk. I felt plenty shaky inside. Maybe she really thought I did it. She was acting funny. Acting good, but—would they think that?

I heard her come through the hall. She leaned against the jamb in the doorway, with her hands together just the same way Vivian used to do. 'Here he comes, Roy.'

'Okay. Everything's going to be all right, now.'

'*Shhh!* Here he comes!'

I stared at her. Her eyebrows were all hiked up and my God, I didn't know what to do. Really, I hadn't done anything, and yet she suddenly had me feeling so guilty and I was rotten with it. And then I knew it wasn't her fault. She was trying to do right by me, and I was kicking her for it. . . .

Knock—knock. . . .

Bess went across the room, stumbling once on the rug, and opened the door. 'Yes, Officer?'

'Mrs. Nichols, hate to bother you again. Is your husband awake yet?'

So, I'd been asleep. Great.

'Yes, Officer.' She held the door open, stepping out of the way, and he came into the office and took his hat off. He stood in the doorway, so she couldn't close the door. He looked over at me. 'Mister Nichols?'

'Yes?'

He stepped into the room and she closed the door and leaned back against it. I could hear old Hughes talking from outside.

The plain-clothes cop was a little guy, not big at all. His voice was very soft, kind of like purring. He wore dark-brown pants and a light sand-colored jacket, white shirt, and a clean maroon tie. The tie was clipped halfway down with a silver sword and his coat was open so you could just see the hump and the edge of the butt of his holstered revolver. On the left side, for a cross draw.

'Could we talk for a little?'

'Sure thing.'

He had a moon face and it was buttered like a bun with sweat. There were little pouches under his eyebrows, and his eyes looked at you through slits in the pouches. Brown, bright eyes. This was the man whom I'd deal with.

I couldn't help staring at him. I'd been waiting to meet him for a long time. Almost ever since that Lincoln picked me up on the Georgia road. . . . His hat was brown, like a chocolate drop.

'I'm Ernest Gant.'

I got up and went around the desk and stuck out my hand. He transferred his hat and we shook once and dropped clean. He had a waistline shake, palm down.

'Well, I guess I'll be in the kitchen,' Bess said.

'That's all right, Mrs. Nichols. You needn't leave.'

'I just thought—'

He smiled at her, then looked at me. 'I wonder if you'd just step over to the other apartment with me a moment, Mister Nichols?'

'Sure thing.'

He grabbed the door and held it open and grinned at Bess again. The grin went away and we were outside and the door was closed.

'What do you think?' I asked him.

He didn't say anything. We walked across the grass. A uni-formed cop hurried across the lawn toward an official car parked by the curb. The Southern Comfort Motel had become a busy place.

Gant was nearly as tall as I was, after all—it was just that he seemed smaller, somehow. He wasn't, though. Not really.

We went inside number six. There was nobody there. The body was gone.

'Your wife tells me you found the body together?'

I started to go along with that. Then there was something in the tone of his voice, in the way he looked at me. It gave me a queer feeling and a certain respect for him, too. 'I want to clear that up. She said that, but it wasn't quite that way. I came in first.'

'I understand.'

He went over and stood by a chair. Then he sat down. His actions seemed to be thought out beforehand. He put his hat over his knee and patted his pockets. He came up with a crumpled package of cigarettes.

'Smoke, Mister Nichols?'

'No, thanks.'

'Sure?'

'Well, all right—I guess I could.' I took one and fumbled for a match. By the time I found one, he had a Zippo going under my nose. It was nice and steady with a big flame. He went over and sat down again.

'Why don't you sit down?'

I got over on the couch. I kept looking toward the hall door-way, the area drew my gaze. They had cleared the body away and there wasn't a trace.

Somebody came clomping heavily through from the back way. I looked up and it was another harness cop. He walked into the room, his leather creaking, and stepped around the place on the floor where the body had been.

'You want anybody posted outside, Lieutenant?'

'You stick around, all right?'

'Burke's with me.'

'Tell him to stick around, too. I'll let you know. They're finished with the floor?'

'I guess so.'

The cop looked at me. He was a man of perhaps thirty-five and there was nothing at all in his look, the way they look at you. He had very pale blue eyes, and his cap was on very straight. 'We'll be out in the car, then.'

Gant nodded and went on smoking. He had very dark hair,

parted neatly on one side and brushed straight back. 'You came in first?'

'That's right.'

'When was that? What time, about?'

'This morning.'

'This is this morning. Could you narrow it down some?'

'Well.' I didn't have any idea about time. Time was suddenly all run together like syrup. 'Maybe nine?'

He smoked. He would come back to the time later, after I'd thought about it a while. He really had me thinking about time now. When *had* I come in here?

'And your wife? When did she come in?'

'A little after I came in.'

'Oh. I see. Let me get this straight. I thought you both came over here together, and you came in first. But she—?'

'No. That's not right. I came over alone.'

He nodded. 'That's straight enough. Then your wife came along. That it?'

'Well, she—yes. That's right.'

'You just kind of—well, waited around until she decided to come and find the body, too—huh?'

I looked at him.

He held his hand up. He grinned. The grin went away and he began to smoke again, really working on the cigarette. He would take a drag and inhale, and hold it and then let it out, and stare at the cigarette, and do it all over again. The cigarette was finished, with that treatment. He held the lungful of smoke and ground the cigarette out in a standing ash tray. Then he let the smoke out in a long sigh, down into his shirt.

I was getting mixed up, and it made me mad.

'What did you do when you found the body of this woman—girl—in here?'

I started to blurt something, then paused, and that was all he needed. I could see it in his eyes, no real expression, just a shadow. I wanted to cover it, he was thinking. You couldn't cover it. You make your slip just once and it stands there, laughing, sneering at you for the rest of your life.

'Did you touch it?'

'No. Of—yes. Yes, I did.'

'Why?'

'I don't know why, I just touched it, that's all. Wouldn't you touch it?'

'*I* would. But then, that's my job. It doesn't matter, Mister

Nichols. Don't misunderstand, please. I've got to get everything as straight as I can. You see, your wife was rather, well—nervous? She tried not to be, but she was. A normal reaction.'

I nodded.

His voice was soft, like velvet. Honest, it purred like a little well-oiled motor. There was nothing sleepy about his eyes. He just seemed to be holding cards, that's all. He hadn't said anything to make me know that for sure, but I couldn't help believing it. I was guilty of a lot of stuff that had to do with this crime, and it was stuff I didn't want known. I had to catch hold of myself, and keep the grip.

There was something about Gant . . . I didn't like him. So what could I do about that?

'Was the body cold?'

'Yes.'

'Then what?'

'How do you mean?'

'What did you do then?'

I started to say something and he leaned back in the chair and held up his hand and cleared his throat. 'Wait. I mean, let's get back a little bit. Why did you come over here?'

'Didn't my wife tell you anything about—?'

'Just answer the question.'

'I don't have to answer anything.'

He sighed and stared down into his lap. He lifted his hat and rapped it on his knee and looked out the window. Then he tipped his head a little to one side and said, 'Would you really mind answering a few questions, Mister Nichols? You'll have to sooner or later. Why not now?'

'I didn't say I wouldn't. I just—'

'Fine! That's the way to talk.'

I could feel the shaking start in my stomach and spread. 'No reason in the world why I wouldn't answer some questions.'

'Look,' he said. 'I have to go about this in my own way. This is a serious thing.'

'I know it.'

'This woman was murdered. Somebody choked her to death with a silk scarf. She took quite a beating, too.'

'I know.'

'Oh. You know.'

'I saw the bruises.'

'Mister Nichols, don't you think you'd better put that cigarette out? It's going to burn your fingers. It makes me nervous.'

Chapter 14

'Let's relax. All right?'

I jammed the cigarette into the dirt around the cactus plant on the table by the couch. I wanted to relax. I had to get hold of myself, but it wasn't working right. Like if I tried to lean one way, I'd really be leaning in the opposite direction. I looked at my hands and they seemed steady, yet I could feel them tremble. The shaking was all through me. I couldn't control it.

If I refused to answer his questions, it would only make things worse.

'You have a nice place here.'

'Thanks.'

'Been here long?'

'Oh, not too long.'

'Must be expensive, the upkeep.' He shook his head. 'Especially now. Must be a headache, with the highway all torn up. Hasn't that done something to your business?'

'It's knocked it off a little.'

He wasn't looking at me. Then he did. 'Mrs. Nichols said something about a man's suitcase being in here.'

I didn't say anything.

'Did you see it?'

'I didn't really notice.'

'Did Miss Latimer mention anything about a man?'

'No.'

'Nothing like her being married, anything like that?'

'I didn't talk with her much.'

It troubled me that he thought her name was Latimer. I didn't know why. Then I began to realize just how snarled up things were. With me smack in the middle. And I was already off on the wrong track with Gant. There was nothing to do about that, either.

'What about this man who was here last night?' He had left it open. I didn't know what to say. 'You met him, didn't you?'

'Yeah—I met him.'

'How did you happen to meet him?'

I told him how I'd thought he was a prowler and had gone to see if Miss Latimer was all right. Telling it to him that way, it came out easy. Then after it was out I sat there and felt the sweat. Every word I said, it got deeper. Why couldn't I just tell him? Tell him everything?

I knew why, and it was hell. That money hidden in the garage. There was no reason why the law should ever find it, because they knew nothing about it. It didn't concern them. The only thing they were after was the killer of Vivian. I couldn't tell them that, either. Sooner or later they'd find out. And I hadn't killed her, so I was all right.

'Were they arguing, Mister Nichols?'

'Who?'

'This man and Miss Latimer. Did you notice whether or not they got along—seemed to?'

'Oh, sure. There might have been some argument.'

'Your wife said something about it. When she came in she said you—'

'Oh, that. Well, the guy sort of resented my bursting in like that. You understand.'

'I see.'

All I had to do was keep that brief case hidden the way it was and everything would be all right. Even if Gant was a snoop, and I was pretty sure he was. Then I remembered something.

I looked at him and it came to me and I almost fell off the couch. I had never had any thought hit me this hard.

'What's the matter, Mister Nichols?'

'Nothing. Pain in my stomach.'

'Oh?'

'Cramp, like.'

I put my hand on my stomach and made a face. 'Listen, would you excuse me a minute?'

He looked at me and frowned slightly.

All I could think was, The car. The Ford. With Georgia plates taken out in my name. It was beautiful.

'I won't be long. Just wait right here, Lieutenant. I get these pains every once in a while. There's some stuff over at the house.'

'All right.'

We got up and stood there.

'I'm not through talking with you, though,' he said. 'I'll be out front in the car.'

'Fine.'

I went on out quick and cut toward our place. He walked across the grass to the police car at the curb. When his back was turned, I started down between the apartments, toward the garage. I ran.

Sure as the devil, they'd trace those plates. If they found them in my name, how could I explain that? If I could just hang on long enough, I felt sure something would turn up. They'd find

Teece; they'd find who she was and they'd get him for it. If I could just hang on and keep them off my neck, so I wouldn't have to spill about that money.

They'd never say anything about that money to the law. They wouldn't dare, not a one of them.

I reached the garage for number six. Her car was there, all right, with the door closed and nobody'd been around yet. Her car hadn't been mentioned. Maybe they thought she'd come down by train, or plane. Maybe they wouldn't ever ask about her car.

Don't be a complete idiot, I told myself. You know better than that. But they might play it out that way. Worse things have happened than the cops slipping up.

I worked as fast as I could. I was so excited I really did begin to get cramps.

I went along the front of the garages to our garage and got back in there by my work bench. Under the bench I knew I had a last-year New York plate. Some folks had left it here. There was week before the time expired in Florida, so it would still be okay down here.

I couldn't find the plate. I got down under the bench and rummaged around in the junk box. It wasn't there. Then I got up and saw it sitting on a side beam, like a decoration. I grabbed it and headed for number six garage.

I had to come back for a pair of pliers and a screw driver. I was kind of sobbing to myself by then, soaked with sweat, running against time. He'd begin wondering where I was and I didn't want him to wonder.

The Georgia plate came off easy. They had it snapped on with a kind of coil spring deal, so I didn't need the screw driver and pliers, after all. I flung them across the alley into a field beside a house. I got the plates changed and stood there with the Georgia plate.

I started back for number six and Bess came around the corner of the garage, emptying the garbage. She had the little tin bucket from the house and she was just taking the lid off the big garbage can by the garage, when she heard me.

'Roy.'

I had the plate jammed into my belt, in back, up under my shirt.

'You through talking with the detective?'

'No.'

'What are you doing back here?'

'I was just—oh, hell—I had a cramp.'

'What?'

'Stomach-ache. I don't know.'

I started past her.

'You want me to fix you something?'

'I was just coming over to the house. I'll have to get back there. I told him I'd be right back.'

She looked back down the line of garages, then at me. She didn't say anything. I kind of grinned at her and patted her shoulder. I left her standing there and went for the house. As soon as I was around the corner of the garage. I ran again.

In the house, I had that damned plate. I didn't know what to do with it. I had to hide it. There didn't seem to be any place and Bess would be back in a minute. I heard her coming across the yard, then, the handle on the kitchen garbage bucket squeaking and her feet hushing on the grass.

I went into the office, still with that plate cutting into my back. I looked outside. He was leaning against the car, talking with them, watching the office.

The kitchen door opened.

I went over to the studio couch, lifted a cushion and jammed the plate down in back. I pushed it as far as it'd go and something ripped. I jammed it down in there and put the cushion back and sat on the couch to see if it was all right. It was, and I was plenty tired all at once.

'Your stomach any better, Roy?'

'It'll be all right. I was just going.'

'Be glad to fix you something. Bicarb, maybe?'

'No. Never mind.'

She stood there watching me and I could see she wanted to help, only I couldn't let her do anything. I didn't half know what I was doing. I got up and went out and across to number six. Gant saw me and started back over the lawn, walking with a kind of head-down shuffle, holding his hat.

I waited for him, trying to ease my breathing.

'Feel better, Mister Nichols?'

'Lots better. Thanks.'

Then I saw the front of my T-shirt, and my hands. There was dust on my shirt and my hands were black with dirt and grease. He hadn't noticed yet, but he would.

'Wait a second. I'm going to turn on the sprinklers.'

He looked at me and frowned with that nice way he had. I paid no attention, went down by the main faucet and turned the sprinklers on. Then I turned on the spare faucet that I used for the hose, and washed my hands the best I could and splashed some up on my shirt. I saw old Hughes walking around the corner of the apartments, toward the shuffleboard court.

'Can you talk now?' Gant said.

'Sure. Fire away.'

'Let's start from where we were.'

'Shall we go back inside?'

'Let's just stand out here.'

I didn't like the tone of his voice now. It had changed; there was something new in it. It was no longer so soft. 'This man who was in the apartment with Miss Latimer. You didn't happen to hear his name?'

'Not that I know of.' It came out like that and I wished I hadn't lied about that. But I couldn't correct myself, not without making it worse, so I'd have to let it ride.

'What did he do? I mean, when you came in. Did he want to fight you?'

I laughed. 'He couldn't fight so well. He had one arm in a sling. His face was all bandaged up.'

It made me feel good to tell the truth for a change.

Gant went over and leaned against the wrought iron railing on the small porch of number six. He looked like a man who had maybe worked hard at his studies, always treating everything very seriously, and now he was exactly where he wanted to be. He seemed certain of where he was going now, and what he was going to do. He was a thinker, keeping everything peacefully and quite seriously to himself.

'Did he want to fight?' Gant said.

'Well, yeah. I guess he did. I took a little jab at him, just to warn him.'

'Your wife said you almost warned him right through the door.'

'Well, it might have been harder than a jab. I mean, he was off balance.'

'Mister Nichols.' He looked at me and took his hat off again, then put it on again, fooling with the crown until he was satisfied. 'This is no way to go about things. Honest.' He shook his head. 'I know you don't feel well, but you've got to get your thinking arranged better than this. You keep making me think things.'

I didn't say anything.

'The way you act, anybody would think you killed that Latimer girl.'

'I didn't.'

'All right, then. Why don't you make an attempt to help me? This is my job, and I like it. But you're making things tough for me.'

'I'm just answering your questions.'

'No. You're not. You're thinking just as fast as you can, and you're saying the first thing that comes into your head. Are you trying to cover up something? Because, if you are, it won't do any good. We *always* find out, Mister Nichols. It'll just save lots of time if you'll play it straight with us.'

'I'm not covering up anything. What right have you to say that?'

'There you go again.' He sighed and stared down at his shoes. 'We deal with things like this all the time. I'm with Homicide, and sometimes we have to talk and talk. But I can't recall ever having talked with a guy just like you, Mister Nichols. You say one thing and you must know your wife has told me different. Why do you do that?'

'Well, I don't know. I didn't realize it.'

'Are you trying to shield your wife from something?'

'No. Listen, I've got a motel to run. There's a million things—'

He held up his hand and stepped closer. 'I don't want to have to run you down to headquarters, Mister Nichols. But if this keeps up, we'll have to. We question a little bit different down there. And you wouldn't be able to take care of the motel by remote control.' He looked around. 'Anyway, there's not really much to take care of. Your wife says business isn't good at all. I don't see many people around.'

He began to scare me now.

'Now, try not to get excited,' he said. 'I never saw anybody get so excited and pretend they aren't.'

I didn't dare say anything. I wanted to either poke him or walk away. I didn't do either, because I was beginning to see how I looked to him. From his side, I'd either done this thing, or I'd done nothing. I was just a motel owner, a guy who was a near-witness to a murder, and he was trying to learn what he could from me. But with the amount of lying stuff I had inside me, it was difficult to act right. I *was* trying to think every minute—I *was* saying the first thing that popped into my head. And now I knew it couldn't be any other way.

'Your wife says Miss Latimer drove down here in what looked like a Ford sedan. That right?'

I nodded, and the world seemed to tilt a little. 'That's better. What say we have a look at the car?'

I motioned with my hand and we started walking toward the garage. Boy, it was that close. If only I wouldn't make any slips now. He wasn't fooling me now. He scared me some, but I was still ahead of him. And I had to keep it that way. That brief case was Bess's and mine, from now on straight down the line. It had to be.

Now, just take it easy . . . easy is the way.

Because the thought I kept on hanging to was that *I hadn't done anything*. Not anything real bad. Of course not. . . .

'You're sure lucky, Mister Nichols. Having a place like this. I'd give my eyeteeth for something like this.'

'Thought you liked your job.'

'Well, sometimes it catches up with me.' He didn't look at me when he said that. We came around by the garages and walked up to number six.

'You always leave the garage doors open?'

'I guess she must have left it open. I didn't check.'

He nodded and we stood there and looked at the Ford. The New York plate on the back bumper would knock your eye right out, it was that bright. He looked at that and went up and flicked it with his fingers. It clanged. Then he stretched his neck to look into the back seat through the rear window.

'Don't touch the car. We'll have to dust it for prints. No use messing it up any more than it probably is.'

'Oh.'

'Probably won't find anything. Hardly ever do. We'll have to check it, though, just the same.'

'I understand.' Sure, with my prints all over it. 'I drove it around here and parked it in the garage for her.'

'Oh, well, that won't matter. Person would have to be in the car for a time, to really lay any prints worth while. Anyway . . .'

He didn't finish that.

He looked the car over, looking in every window, hanging his head in the open windows. He kept looking at me, now and then. I just stood there and waited, thinking about things.

His attitude was lousy. He had no right acting the way he did, saying those things he'd said. He was getting me on the defensive and keeping me there. He didn't have anything on me. There was something speculative in the way he'd look at me, kind of like he was trying me out on things.

I turned away and walked along the garages. He could come

and get me when he wanted me. The hell with him, and the hell with everybody.

'Nichols?'

He called from back there. I waited for him and he came up.

'Didn't you hear a thing last night?'

'No.'

'Well, this is a hell of a one, all right. It must have been that guy who was here last night. But why?'

'She said she'd been waiting for him to show up. She didn't say he was her husband, anything like that. Just waiting.'

'And your wife claims she saw a man's suitcase in the apartment before he came?'

I waited while he thought that over. He shoved his hat back and scratched his head, looking at me through those slits of eyes.

'Look,' he said. 'There's something I've got to check on. Then I'll want to see you again. So don't go away.'

'What did he want?'

'Just questions, honey. He thinks he's a hot-shot.'

'I didn't get that impression.'

I went into the bedroom and sat down on the bed. Then I flopped back and lay there looking up at the ceiling. She came in and sat down on the bed. I wished she would go away. Then I cursed myself for even thinking such a thing.

'Roy,' she said. 'You got to tell me if there's something troubling you.'

I didn't say anything. I reached out and patted her arm and let it go at that.

Gant had left things hanging, because he was planning something. I knew damned well that's what it was. There'd been a crafty look in his eye and he'd practically run back out to the curb to get in the car. What could it be? I had to stay a jump ahead of them.

'If there's anything you think you should tell this man, Gant, Roy—I wish you would.'

I cocked my head up and looked at her. She had on her red shorts now, and a yellow blouse. She looked real good and she was smiling at me. Her eyes were very bright.

'What d'you mean?'

'Nothing. Just that you should try to help all you can.'

'What do you mean?'

She shrugged. I sat up and grabbed her arm. 'You mean something. You're trying to say something.'

'No, I'm not, honey. You're reading something into what I say.'

We watched each other. She kept on smiling and I began to feel better. I'd thought for a minute there—but I'd been wrong.

'Roy?'

'Yeah?'

'Why do you think somebody killed her?'

'I don't know.'

'You don't even like to talk about it. Do you?'

I didn't say anything.

'Roy, I hear somebody.'

She started up. I heard somebody step on the office porch and then the rattle of knuckles against the door.

'You answer it, Roy. It's probably Gant again.'

Somehow I didn't want to answer that door. I did, though. It was Wirt Radan.

Chapter 15

Radan stood there in the doorway and looked at me. He didn't smile; he didn't do anything. His face was without expression and he was wearing a gray suit and a blue hat, this time. He had switched colors, but he looked as natty as ever—and the threat in him was as quiet and contained as before.

'Hello, Mister Nichols.'

I waited.

'Would you mind opening the door?'

I opened the door and went on inside. I heard Bess come into the office and glanced back.

'Hello, there, Mrs. Nichols,' Radan said. He touched one finger to his hatbrim and the corners of his mouth pinched up a little.

'Oh,' Bess said. 'It's you.' She smiled at him. 'Won't you come in?'

'He wants to see something outside,' I said. We went out onto the lawn. Bess stood by the screen door, then I heard her walking toward the rear of the apartment.

'Well, well,' Radan said. 'Here we are again.'

'What is it this time?'

'It's like this,' he said. 'I saw them take her out. Feet first. She was here and Teece was here. What do you figure you'll do about this?'

'Take who out?'

'Let's get away from here,' he said. 'Come on.' He started down toward the rear of the apartments. 'Come along, Mister Nichols.'

I followed him and he had that same jaunty walk as before. His shoulders leaned forward just a shade with each step, and he didn't look around to see if I was coming.

He paused by some bushes. 'Where's the money?' he said.

'You killed her, didn't you?'

'Be careful how you talk to me, Nichols,' he said, and something peculiar came into his eyes. It was only there for an instant, then it was gone. Something had come over his face, as if the skin had shrunk in that brief moment. Then it relaxed. But I'd seen all I needed to see. I knew that if you touched him, he'd be like a piece of steel ready to spring. There was that warning emanating from him, from the way he looked at you and the way he stood. It hadn't shown so much before, but now it did show. Just enough to let you know. He didn't seem to have any satisfaction about it, either. It was, as was everything else about him, quite matter-of-fact, edgily contained.

'You're learning,' he said. 'Aren't you?'

I wanted to get away from him. I'd read about them, the way he was, but I'd never really met up with one. He was a killer, and in no joking sense. It was written in every line of the man. He was woodenly conscienceless.

'Where's the money?' he said.

I still didn't say anything, but I moved slightly away to not say it.

'We can save time, Mister Nichols—and energy. Your energy, if you'll just tell me quickly.' He sighed and shoved his hands into the pockets of his jacket and stood there looking at me with his shoulders hunched. 'You know,' he said. 'I've never met a guy just like you.' He shook his head. 'You know who I am, and why I'm here—yet you act this way. It's a dumb way to act. I wish you wouldn't do it.'

I grinned at him. He didn't move.

'Was she here when I was here last time?'

'Did it ever occur to you I won't be pushed?' I said.

'No.'

I didn't say anything.

He took a single step, bringing him up close to me. His eyes were very clear, the whites as clear and innocent looking as a baby's. 'Mister Nichols,' he said. 'You know the kind of a man I am, and you know the job I'm on. I'm paid very well for this job, believe me.'

'So?'

'I'm going to kill you right here in your own yard, if you don't tell me what I want to know.'

He waited. That's all there was to it. You knew absolutely that he would do exactly as he said. It would be, to him, like turning around and walking away. A single movement.

'We gave the money to Teece. You're too late.'

'You're not lying?'

'It's the truth. I swear it. We gave it to this Teece. All right, yes —she had it. I didn't. I didn't have anything to do with this. She told me about it—wanted me to do some damned thing for her. She gave it to Noel Teece. It was in a brief case.'

He kept standing there like that, watching me. I saw the skin on his face shrink up again and stay that way, and his color under the tan was pale. There were tiny pinpoints of perspiration on his nostrils. Otherwise, he didn't change at all. He didn't move.

'What did she tell you about it, Mister Nichols?'

'Nothing. She just wanted me to help her.'

He thought about that for a time, watching me steadily.

'This is something that has to be cleaned up right away,' he said. 'You can believe that, can't you? And it's not getting cleaned up—not at all. It's getting gummier all the time.'

'The hell with you, Radan.'

'You can say that, yes.'

I turned and walked away from him.

'All right,' he said, from back there. 'I'm going to move in.'

'What?'

'I want her apartment. Number six.'

I paused, then went back to where he was standing. 'The hell you say!'

'I'll take the one next door, for now. As soon as the law's through, then I'm moving into her apartment. You can understand what that means, of course?'

'You can't do that!'

He laughed quietly, reached out and tapped me on the arm. 'Come on,' he said. 'Will you show me the apartment? Or shall I take care of that myself?'

I just had to stand here and take this, along with all the rest. And it was getting to be too much. Wouldn't the law know him? Apparently not. He wouldn't be here if they did, and he was damned certain I wasn't going to say anything. He had me over a barrel.

'Let's do it right,' he said. 'Like any decent landlord, Mister Nichols.'

He started walking out toward the front of the motel. Then he turned. 'You going to change your story, Nichols?'

'She gave Teece the money. Honest to God she did. He did something, threatened her—listen, she wanted me to help her get out of the country. That's how I got mixed up in this. It's all over now. It's done, can't you see? Teece is probably in South America, by this time. Can't you go away and leave us alone?'

'Nobody got that money, Nichols. You're lying.'

'I'm telling you—'

'All right. I'm moving in. We'll see. I'll have to work it out.'

Well, he moved into number seven. And the first thing he did, with me right there, was walk into the bathroom and lift the lid off the toilet tank and take a look. He clanked it back on and didn't say a word.

'I have some things out in the car,' he said. 'Come on, help me carry it in.'

'You can go to hell.'

'All right.' He shrugged and went out, whistling. He got into the car and started it and drove off. My cripes, was he leaving? I rushed out there and watched him drive along and turn the corner. I waited. He turned into the alley and I heard the plump tires of his Caddy on the gravel back there and I heard him stop at the garage for number seven. The door squeaked as he slid it open. He drove inside.

Pretty soon he came along, carrying two great big suitcases, so he'd figured on something like this. He walked past me without looking at me and went on into number seven.

I went after him. I stood in the doorway. He had taken the suitcases into the bedroom, and he came back into the living room and glanced at me, then went over and opened the blinds.

'You can't stay here,' I said.

'Why don't you prevent me?'

'I told you all I know.'

He began to whistle. It was shrill and harsh on the ears, tuneless. Just ceaseless, endless, hard. He walked around and put all the blinds open, took off his hat and set it on an end table, with care. Then he took his jacket off and went into the bedroom. When he returned, he wasn't wearing the gun, either. It had been a big gun.

'I like these assignments, Nichols. Everybody knows what's going on, and only one is lying or not lying, and eventually you find out.'

He wasn't sure about believing me. I could tell the way he looked at me. His instinct told him I was lying, and his instinct was right. Only he had to believe me.

'Too bad I can't have a dame around here,' he said. 'But I'm traveling under orders, like I said. Too bad. It'll be lonely—unless something happens. And it probably will.'

We stood there and watched each other. He reached up and loosened his tie, stretching his jaw, his eyes never leaving mine. Where his shoulder harness for the gun had been, his shirt was wrinkled. It was no light harness, either; it was thick-strapped and Radan was a tried gunman. You knew it, you didn't have to be told. And there didn't seem to be any fear in the man, and he wasn't ignorant.

'There a phone in the office, Nichols?'

'No.'

He shoved by me and went on outside. I had thought about shoulder pads in his suit jacket. It wasn't so. Radan's shoulders were broad, pushing at the seams of his shirt. He was loaded with energy, and very fit, and I felt that in his own secret way, he was very proud of this. So far, I hadn't seen him smoke. I wondered if he drank.

He started across the lawn toward the office. I went after him and caught up with him.

'Listen: Be careful what you say over the phone. My wife's around.'

He didn't bother answering. He stepped jauntily up on the porch and opened the door and called, 'Mrs. Nichols—I'd like to use your phone. Will it be all right?'

Bess came into the office. 'Why, hello, there.'

'I've moved into your motel, Mrs. Nichols.'

She looked at me and I nodded. 'Number seven.'

She swallowed and said, 'You've probably heard what happened here this morning.'

'Wipe it straight off your mind. The phone?'

She pointed to the desk and he went over and picked it up and dialed once and asked the long-distance operator for a Tampa number. Then, waiting, he looked first at me, then at Bess.

Bess tugged at my arm. We were bothering him, and after all, when a person's phoning, you should have the common decency not to listen in. 'Hello,' he said into the phone. He waited as somebody spoke on the other end. 'Yes,' he said. 'All present and accounted for. I moved in. Yes.' He hung up, turned and grinned at Bess.

'Thanks,' he said. He stood there by the desk and said, 'How much for a week? I figure a week should take care of it.' He looked at me when he said that.

She told him and he paid her, and he went outside, whistling. 'He's rather nice, in a funny way, isn't he?' Bess said.

'Yeah, sure.'

'What did he say when you told him about what happened?'

'Nothing, Bess. It didn't seem to trouble him.'

'You think they've caught the man, yet?'

'How's about fixing something to eat?'

She hesitated, watching me. Her eyes were soft and blue. I looked at her and there was this expression of patience on her face, in her eyes, and she smiled at me. Then she came up to me and put her arms around me. I held her tight, wanting to crush her, loving her maybe more than I ever thought I could love her. I was lost and all these things were crowding me. I didn't know what to do now. And she didn't know what it was all about and I couldn't tell her. That's what hurt most, I guess. I wanted to tell her—but I never could. She believed in me and trusted me, and I'd slipped up.

Only the money was out there, and it was our money. I wasn't going to lose that now.

Her lips were warm and I kissed her temples, feeling the soft golden hair against my lips, and her forehead and her chin. I pulled her tight against me.

'I love you, Roy.'

We stood there like that.

And him over there in number seven, with his gun and his suitcases, waiting for God knew what. And Gant. And Noel Teece.

Remembering Teece brightly was like a kind of added pain.

Maybe if I could talk Bess into taking a vacation. Just close the place down, kick them all out, and go away. Let it all blow over. We could take what money we had and just leave that brief case. When we came back, Lieutenant Gant would have the murder solved, and we could . . .

After we ate, I went around trying to catch up with things. Trying to keep my mind off what was happening—what could happen. It didn't work. I'd be in the yard and find myself sneaking around the apartments to have a look at the outside of the garage. Six or seven times I went into the garage, for nothing. Just to find myself standing there by the Chevy, staring up there at the beams where that brief case was. Or I'd look over at number seven, and sometimes he'd be standing on the porch with a tall glass in his hands. He'd look across at me and I'd turn away.

Once he waved and called, 'Hot, isn't it?'

I began to quit trying to duck everything, and face it up instead. I'd have to, sooner or later. And maybe right then, for the first time, I really began to understand what I was up against. I'd thought I had before. Now it all came up into me like a big choke. These people who had sent Radan over here weren't fooling, and I'd been kidding with it. And Radan had said he had a plan.

What kind of a plan? I didn't want to think about that. I began to get scared, more than ever before in my life, and I knew I had good reason. Bess was in there and what was she thinking? And Gant, what was he going to do—would he be back today? I went back inside our place and just sat. Bess would come and look at me, then go away. I didn't care what she thought. It didn't matter.

I felt empty inside, as though there wasn't anything left—no place to go. Yet, I had to hang on. If I weakened now, then it was all shot and we wouldn't have anything. It was the chance I had to take. All down through the years there'd never been anything but fight, fight, fight—for nothing. Whenever we got anything, we'd lose it.

Now, just this once . . . !

I'd sit there and Bess would come in and look at me. Sitting on the couch in the office, waiting. I didn't know what for. For the guy over there in number seven to do whatever it was he was going to do—or for Gant to come back and shackle me and I'd still fight, and if I fought, I'd have to lie. And that would put me in deeper and deeper, only I couldn't stop.

It happens that way sometimes. If you ever have it that way, then you'll know what I mean.

And there was a deep concern in Bess's eyes; something I couldn't quite read. It bothered me, but what was I going to do?

'Come and eat, Roy. Supper's ready.'

'All right.'

I went into the kitchen and sat down and stared at my plate. I didn't want to eat. There was this rotten black feeling all through me and I couldn't shake it.

'Eat something, Roy. What's the matter?'

'Nothing. I just don't feel so hot.'

I wanted to go over and take this guy Radan and knock the hell out of him. Only I knew I wouldn't. You know when it's not ready; you know when something's going to happen.

Something had to happen. It was like before a big storm, with the black clouds out there on the horizon. Everything goes calm and dead, and then . . .

It happened about four o'clock in the morning. It was still dark when somebody began pounding on the office door.

I got up and wandered around, kind of hazy, there in the bedroom. They pounded on the door. I didn't want to go out there. Finally I put on a robe and went.

I opened the door and a cop stood there, his face shining in the darkness. I saw a car out by the curb, with the headlights gleaming cold and brilliant on the road.

'Get some clothes on, Mister Nichols,' he said. 'Lieutenant Gant wants you to come along with me.'

Chapter 16

We went out to the car. There was nobody inside. The motor was quietly idling and the door on the driver's side was open. He sure didn't give a hang about the city paying for his gas. I went around and climbed in and he got in and we slammed our doors at the same time.

He started up and we went down the street and took the turn at the corner and headed toward Tampa Bay. He drove along through the quiet Southside residential section, his face turned rigidly front.

'Well,' I said. 'What's up?'

He didn't answer.

It makes you feel like hell when they act that way. They get that superior air and I suppose they teach them that. Only I was a taxpayer, at least on the books, and I paid his salary.

'Lieutenant Gant, eh?'

'Look, Mister Nichols. It won't do you any good to keep asking. I'm not going to tell you anything. Those are my orders, and I reckon I'll keep them.'

We turned left on the street along the park by the bay and he stepped it up a bit. You could see the reddish halo of light across the bay, over Tampa. Like a hooded, glass-enclosed Martian city, maybe—or just a pale hell on the not-too-distant horizon.

The park looked shadowed and quiet.

Then it changed.

There were some cars parked along the curb up there. Men were grouped in three or four places and they wore dull uniforms upon which sparks of light winked. Two spotlights were shining a silvery wash down there in the park, focused on the ground just beyond a tremendous live oak. The light was somehow off-white, bringing that odd cast of known green but seen gray to the brain and eye. The two cars were parked down there in the park on the grass.

We rolled along and he put on the brakes. He scraped the curb with the tires and we stopped.

'Get out, Nichols.'

I got out and waited, looking across the park where the spotlights were. A man detached himself from a group down there and the group dispersed. The man came along with a kind of head-down shuffle.

He came along and flipped his hand at me. 'Something I want you to see, Nichols.'

It was ominous and I didn't like it. This Gant was too somber. He motioned to the cop and the cop went around and got behind the wheel of the car and drove off. For a moment Gant and I stood there. The palms along the road sent crazy shadows leaping from the streetlights. 'Come on,' Gant said.

I started along with him, down through the park. There was nobody down there where the spotlights from the police cars shone. I couldn't see where we were going, because there was a huge bush in the way.

We came into the beams of the spots. We rounded the bush and Gant looked at me, waiting.

Well, it was Noel Teece.

He had been what you might say torn limb from limb. A long streamer of bandage from the cast on his left arm lay tugging and fluttering in the wind, up along the grass. The cast on his arm had been smashed. His eyes were half-open. The bandage had been torn off his face and it was all scabs. He was lying flat on his back, looking up into the dark sky.

Then I saw how he'd been slit up the middle with a knife, or maybe an axe. I turned and walked behind the bush and was sick.

When I came back, Gant hadn't moved. He was standing there, looking at Teece.

'Like a fish,' he said. 'Just like a fish.'

'What'd you bring me down here for?'

'Don't you know?'

I couldn't look at him again.

'Go ahead,' Gant said, 'Look at him. That's Noel Teece, Nichols. He's the man who was down to your place, visiting that Latimer dame. Recognize him?'

I still couldn't say anything.

'He's a little hard to recognize, I admit,' he went on. 'But that's him, all right.' He turned and looked at me and frowned. 'Do you say it's him, Nichols?'

'I don't know.'

'Well, make up your mind. We brought you down here just to make sure. Not like there's two of them running around, dressed the same—and with a broken arm and a patched-up head. What do you say?'

'It might be.'

' *"It might be!"* You—' He paused and rubbed his hand across his face. 'All right. We'll bring your wife down here. She saw him, remember?'

'I guess it's him, all right.' I still didn't look down there again. 'I'm sorry. I don't know why I said that.'

'Thanks. For nothing.' He turned and started away, then whirled and came up to me again. 'Why do you do this? Why do you act this way? Isn't it enough—?' He shook his head, breathing hard, real mad.

I felt like hell. I wanted to help him. But if I helped him, I'd be helping myself right out of that money.

Then I thought of Radan and it was as if the back of my neck turned to wood. He'd done this, as sure as hell—Radan. So why hadn't he come to me? If he did do this, he sure would head for me right after, because by now he'd know Teece didn't have the money. And that was all Radan wanted.

I could hardly move, the way I felt.

'What's the matter, Nichols? What's cooking in that peaceful little mind of yours?'

'If you know who this guy was, why'd you bring me down here? What's the point of that?'

'Nichols, I wish to God you weren't what they call a citizen! I'd run you in and I'd work you over.'

'Why don't you? I'd like to know what you're getting at. You act like I've done something.'

He went absolutely still. His mouth hung open and his eyes got wide and he shoved his hat back on his head. Then his eyes went normal again. 'Done something,' he said. 'You're lying, Nichols. You know something. You're scared. There's something inside you that's eating at your guts till you can hardly stand it. It's going to bust out, too. Wait and see.'

'You think I did this to that guy?'

'I don't know.' He turned and walked away again. I went up by him and he turned and stopped me with his hand out. 'Why don't you come clean, Nichols? This is getting you no place. *What is it you're trying to hide?*'

'You've got it wrong. A woman was murdered at my motel. Now you think I'm mixed up in it.'

'We're running lab tests, Nichols. What are you going to do then? Because I know we're going to find something. All right, suppose this one killed the Latimer girl. Then who killed him? And why? Why at your place? Why do you act so scared? Why do you lie about things that don't matter, that couldn't matter to you? I'll tell you—it's because they somehow *do matter.* Do you know who that dead man is? Noel Teece. Do you know who *he* was? We know, Nichols. We know all about him, and why he was going to end up this way, for sure. You think it's going to take long to find out all the rest of it?'

'Who was he?'

He just made another face and I was plenty sick about the whole thing. 'You're damned good at this,' I said. 'You've got it all straight in your mind, haven't you? You've got the guilt all leveled at me. You can do that fine. What do you do about protecting the public from things like this?'

He cursed in a soft whisper, watching me. 'Yes,' he said. 'You'd say something like that, too. But I'll tell you—even you, and you know what I'd like nothing better than to do to you, Nichols— even you . . . I have two men stationed by your place all night —just waiting. Know what they're there for? For your health, Nichols—so you won't get hurt, because we might be wrong, and you might be right, and that's the job the way I see it. I have to do that. And it was done because you were a suspect in the killing of that girl, too.'

Now I saw why Radan hadn't been around. Radan would be half nuts with wanting to get at me. I hadn't seen any guards by the house, but Radan would know. It explained a lot of things. And now what was going to happen when I got home?

Radan wouldn't move too quickly; haste could mean a big bill of waste in this instance. He had orders to get the money. He knew I wasn't going any place with the law barking down my collar. So he would wait until everything was clear. Then he would move in on me, because he knew now that I'd lied to him abut the brief case.

'Nichols?' Gant said. 'You aren't listening.'

'What?'

'I said, "What happened to your finger?" '

'It's broken.'

'That's damned enlightening, I mean, how broken?'

'I caught it in a car door.'

'When?'

'What's that to you?'

'See, Nichols? See what I mean?'

We stared at each other.

'Nichols, there's hardly a thing I can ask you about that you don't get scared and want to run. *What is it!* God, I'll bet you can't bring yourself to tell me about that finger, even. Not the truth. You can't force yourself to tell me how it got caught in what door, or when, or where? Right?'

I didn't say anything. He had me really going. I wanted to pile into him, and I couldn't. And that was bad, because I knew I was the one who was wrong.

He was doing his job. He had every right to be this way, and I could see that much of it clear now. And I was withholding the very grains of knowledge he had to have.

'Nichols, all I have to do is ask your wife.'

My neck got hot. If he asked her, she'd tell him about my going to Chicago. I felt trapped.

'Well?' he said. 'Where *did* you bust your finger?'

There was a kind of gleeful tone to his voice, as though he was really enjoying this, or maybe a little crazy or something. And I knew he wasn't enjoying it.

'A car door.'

' "A car door." '

He turned sharply and started up toward the road, muttering to himself. I watched him go with this tight new feeling of being trapped inside me. If he went to Bess, what then? I hadn't done anything! I wanted to yell it at him. If he really had anything on me, he'd have to run me in fast. I knew that. So I was all right. I was still ahead of them—'way ahead.

Only how long would they keep it up?

All I had to do was tell them. Only I couldn't tell them a thing, and they didn't know that. And by keeping my mouth shut and lying, it looked as if I was really mixed up in this. Maybe even committed murder.

I started on up across the park toward Gant.

So Vivian was dead. and now Teece, too. And it struck me what Radan might be doing, and I was damned well scared. I wanted to get home. . . .

'I'm going to haunt you, Nichols.'

'Listen, if I could help you, I would. There's nothing I can do to help you. You think I know a lot of things that I don't. You're reading a lot into this that isn't there. I mean it. Why should I want to stand in your way?'

He turned to a cop standing about ten feet off on the curb. 'Pete, will you run Mister Nichols home?'

'Listen,' I said, rapping his arm. 'You didn't answer me.'

He looked at me and grinned. 'I'm going to haunt you,' he said. Then he turned and walked off across the park toward where the spotlights were focused.

'Coming, Mister Nichols?' the cop said.

'Yeah.'

Way off there toward the Gulf, you could see the pale, gray-pink line of dawn, blurring the horizon.

I headed for our place in a hurry. I hoped that Gant still had his guards posted. But it could be that Radan would wait to make certain about everything.

Bess lay there in bed with her eyes closed. But she was awake. Already the gray morning was probing through the Venetian blinds. Still fuzzy with sleep, she sat there on the bed, staring at me, her pale golden hair mussed, and looking as warm and cozy as crackers.

'Wh-what did Gant want in the middle of the night?'

While I undressed, I told her about Teece, and she put her hand up to her mouth, her eyes round. 'Roy,' she said, and her voice broke a little, 'I've had all this on my mind and I can't stand it. . . .'

I could feel the sudden tensing behind my solar plexus.

'Will you tell me? Will you?'

'What, Bess?'

'You're mixed up in something, I know you are. How long do you think I can go along with you like this? You knew that girl, Roy—I know you did.'

'I don't get you at all.'

'Listen, Roy. I've been playing dumb, for your sake. But it can't

go on. I live with you. I love you. I can't help feeling things—
knowing something's wrong. All I know is this—you're in trouble
and you won't tell me what kind of trouble.'

'Listen, Bess,' I said finally, 'if there was anything I had to tell
you, I would. I didn't know that girl, and I'm not mixed up in
anything. Now, just relax, and let's try to get a little sleep before
we have to get up. Huh?'

She turned over and didn't answer. I could tell she was mad,
and she knew darned well she was right about a lot of things and
all of it was eating at her. Just like things were troubling me. . . .

Well, just for now, to hell with them. I was real beat, and I had
to get some rest in, because God knew what was coming up in a
few hours. Before anything else, I had to check the garage. Just
an hour or two of sleep. . . .

Chapter 17

Maybe when you get in more real trouble than you can handle
and get dead beat-out the law of subconscious gravity or something slides the whole load off somewhere. Anyhow, I didn't
know a thing until dark, and Bess brought me some stuff in on a
tray, like I was an invalid. It made me feel worse than ever, and
now all the things were catching up with me, and I got dressed,
and carried the tray out to the kitchen. But I couldn't eat. I had
some black coffee and all the worries were crowding me again.

I was telling Bess that she should have gotten me up, when
someone knocked on the office door up front. I went over and
swung it open.

Gant stood there. He nodded at Bess, who had come up behind me. He gnawed his lower lip and thrust his hands into his
pockets. 'Mind if I step inside your place for a few words? The
two of you together?' He looked carefully at me when he said
that.

'Sure.' I stepped aside and he came in.

'Shall I go make some fresh coffee?'

We both looked at Bess and Gant smiled pleasantly. He took
his hat off. 'That would be nice. But would you mind waiting a
moment?'

She nodded and her gaze sought mine.

There was something in the air that I didn't like. Something
smug about Gant and the way he spoke. He walked across the
room and stood by the studio couch.

'Sit down,' he said. 'There are a couple of things I'd like to clear up.'

'But,' Bess said. 'I don't understand. About what?'

He smiled. 'Please, sit down and take it easy.' And he sat down on the couch and there was this *clang!*

He stood up immediately. The *clang* had come from behind the couch. I knew what it was right off; that Georgia license plate, and my world quietly exploded.

'What could that have been?' Bess said. She went over by the couch. It had been much too loud to be ignored.

Gant frowned and stepped away from the couch.

'Let it go,' I told Bess. 'Probably just a spring busted.'

'No; it wasn't that. Here, help me move the couch.'

Gant frowned and frowned.

I went over there like a sleepwalker and helped her move the couch. She skinned behind there, up against the wall, and bent over and came up with the plate. 'Why, it's a license plate. It slipped through the back, where the lining's torn.'

Gant was already halfway over the back of the couch. He snatched it from her and looked at it and started nodding his head. I went across the room and sat down. Bess put one hand against her face and stared at me. She came out from behind the couch and shoved it back with her knee, as easy as anything, and stood there.

Gant looked at me and sighed. 'This shouldn't take long to check, should it, Nichols?'

I sat there and stared at him. I felt this grin form on my face and I couldn't erase it. He tapped the plate against his other hand and stepped over to the telephone.

He called police headquarters and asked them to run an immediate check on that plate and he read the numbers.

'How ever did that get there, Roy?'

I didn't bother answering that. Gant hung up and moved to the couch again and sat down. He laid the license plate across his knees. 'Bright and new, too. Hardly used at all. Odd.' He patted his pockets and came up with a package of cigarettes. He didn't offer me one. He took one and lit up.

Bess watched me closely and I hated seeing the look in her eyes. She didn't know what was up, but she knew that whatever it was, it was no good.

'Mrs. Nichols, why don't you go make that coffee you mentioned? I reckon I could go for some. I reckon we all could.'

'Sure thing.'

'We may have a little wait, here.' He paused and glanced my way, not quite meeting my eyes. 'All of us.'

She left the room, her heels smacking the floor.

'Well, Nichols. You want to say anything?' He had lowered his voice and I liked him for that.

'No.'

'All right. We'll just wait. You see, Nichols, it's a funny thing. License plates was exactly what I came to see you about. We checked that New York plate through.' He shook his head and smiled to himself. 'Thought we had it all in a hat. Boy, how wrong can you get? Where'd you think it would get you? Never mind, you'd lie like hell, anyway—we'll find out.' He shook his head again. 'That New York plate was owned by people living right here in town, Nichols. They were staying here at your motel a while back and they bought their Florida plate and exchanged them in your garage. Maybe you even helped them, hey?'

'No.'

'Boy, you've got a real stubborn streak, haven't you?' He stood up. 'Second thought, I'm afraid I'll have to take you downtown. Might have a long wait and I don't think this is the best place.'

He waited. I stood up. 'Whatever you say, Lieutenant. You're the boss.'

'How right,' he said. Then he turned and called to Bess. She came into the hallway. She was very pale.

'Your husband and I are going to run downtown for a while. I'm sorry about the coffee. All right?'

'But—Roy?'

'It's all right. I'll be back.'

'Sure,' Gant said. 'Sure.' He looked at me.

'Roy.'

I didn't look at her. I moved across the office and out the door and he came with me. Bess ran over to the door and called my name again.

'It's all right, honey. I'll be right back.'

'Good-night, Mrs. Nichols.'

We walked out across the lawn. He kept banging that license plate against his leg. We climbed into the car and he started the engine and drove off.

'You want to hold this, Nichols?' He handed me that Georgia plate. 'You're not going to try anything, are you, Nichols? You're not *that* crazy, I hope.'

I just sat there, trying to think.

'Gee. It's sure something, isn't it, Nichols?'

It was a small room, not much larger than a good-sized closet.
There were no windows and only one doorway, with no door. At
one end of this room, there was a platform perhaps ten inches
high. On the platform was a straight-backed chair, nailed to the
floor.

I was on the chair.

Over my head, swinging about a hand's breadth, was a 150-
watt bulb, with a green tin shade. Nobody had touched the bulb,
hanging from the high ceiling by a black length of wire, but it
never stopped swinging and their shadows leaned and length-
ened and shortened against the wall, breaking up against the
ceiling. And my shadow was on the floor. It was crazy, any way
you looked at it.

Gant had brought me in here, and for quite a while I sat alone,
brooding. Then one by one they came and looked at me. They
would stand in the door, with their uniforms all creased and their
harness creaking, and just look at me.

They talked in the other room. Now and again one of them
who had looked in once before, would come and stick his head in
and then step away again.

Gant finally came into the little room and stood against the far
wall, watching me. It was a little hard to see him, because of the
light. The light was hot, too. Then another man in plain clothes
joined him. This was a big one, smoking a stub of cigar and he
looked like the nasty kind. He was in his shirt sleeves.

'This is Armbruster,' Gant said. 'Armbruster, meet Nichols.'

'Hello, Nichols.'

I nodded.

Armbruster smoked his cigar, standing there. He had a red
face, round and beefy, and when he breathed it made quite a
noise. He had a barrel chest and it was like he had a pain in his
stomach. He would kind of groan a little to himself every now
and then.

'You want to say anything, Nichols?'

'What in hell is there to say?'

'Still chipper,' Armbruster commented.

'Oh, he's chipper.'

They stood there. Armbruster smoked and Gant just leaned
against the wall, looking at me. It's pretty bad when people just
stand and stare at you, like that. It begins to annoy you. You itch.

You try to look away. You can't do anything. You begin to sink into the chair. You sweat. You think of a million things to do, all of them wrong.

'They've traced the plate,' Gant said.

'Oh?'

'Yes. It didn't take long, did it? The Ford car was in your name. Roy Nichols.'

'Isn't that something?' Armbruster said.

I swallowed. I wanted a drink of water, but I knew better than to ask for one.

'That's all there is to it. Just that quick. We made it with two phone calls. Now, what do you say, Nichols?'

'Hell, man,' Armbruster said. 'Don't be a damned fool. Tell us about it.'

A uniformed cop pushed past Armbruster and looked at me. 'Why'd you do it, Nichols?' he said. 'Why'd you kill Vivian Rise?'

He went away. I stared at the space where he had been. They knew her name.

'Yes,' Gant said. 'Vivian Rise. Did you know a girl by that name, Nichols? Or did you just know her as Jane Latimer? Or are you really Ed Latimer? Or what?'

'Or what?' Armbruster said.

'Come on, Nichols,' the cop said, sticking his head in the doorway. 'Why did you do it?' He looked at me for a minute, his face without expression. Then he stepped inside the room. He took a package of cigarettes out of his pocket. 'Have a smoke, Nichols?'

'Thanks.'

'That's all right.' He lighted my cigarette, put the lighter away, stood there a moment, then left.

'Well, Nichols?' Armbruster said. 'Are you Ed Latimer, late of the Ambassador Hotel?'

Gant looked down at the floor. 'Come on. Let's not be here all night long.'

Armbruster looked at Gant. They both left me sitting there.

The cop came in, the one who had given me the cigarette. He stood in the doorway, smoking and looking at me. 'We know you didn't kill her,' he said. 'But how about the other one? Did he make you mad? That it? Was he going to tell your wife about her? That it?'

I looked at him and opened my mouth. He turned quickly away and I heard him walk across the room.

They began talking out there. I couldn't make out what they

were saying. I dropped the cigarette and stepped on it and sat there, staring at my hands. What to do?

That money. I had to keep it. Somehow.

It beat like a very small drum in the back of my head. A small and very distant drum. . . .

Chapter 18

Armbruster came and stood in the doorway.

'Tell Lieutenant Gant I want to see him.'

'Sure thing, Nichols.'

He went away. A telephone rang. I could hear them talking out there. I was in a terrible sweat and I was going to tell it—my way. I had to tell something, and it would look all right. Anyway you looked at it, that money was still up there in the garage.

Gant came into the room and stood there.

'All right,' I said. 'Here's the story.' I told it to him straight. All of it. Only I left out the money and I left out Radan. 'I don't know why she wanted me to help her. She wouldn't say. She just said she'd pay me. That's all. I need money. I need it bad. So I told her all right, it was a go.'

'You thought this Teece was dead?'

'Yes.'

'Did you check to make sure?'

'He looked dead. I thought he was dead, that's God's truth, Lieutenant. But he wasn't, that's all.'

'It could happen. Then why in hell did you keep on lying after she was dead?'

'I don't know. I was scared.'

'Oh, hell, Nichols. You don't scare that easy. I can tell.'

'It's the truth. I was scared for Bess—my wife.'

'And how about when you saw Teece dead?'

'I didn't know what to do. I figured you thought I'd killed him.'

'Hey, Ernie!' one of them called.

Gant left the room. Pretty soon he came back. He looked at me for a long time. 'You telling me the truth, Nichols?'

I could sense something. It smelled good. But I had to doubt it.

'Yes. It's the truth.'

'Get out of the chair and come on.'

I stood up. My back was stiff. I followed him through the other room, past Armbruster and three cops who were standing there.

They didn't look at us. I followed Gant and he led me out and into a hall. We walked down the hall, our heels echoing on the marble floors.

We reached the front doors and the street was out there, with cars going up and down. A girl and a guy walked along the street out there, holding hands. He kissed her on the cheek and she laughed and they walked along out of sight. A truck went by, backfiring.

'All right,' Gant said. 'Go on home, Nichols.'

I looked at him. 'But, what in hell?'

He turned and walked back down the hall. And I smelled a rat. A great big dead rat. But I went on through the doors, and onto the street. It was like just waking up in the morning.

Down the street I hailed a cab and went home. During the ride, I sat there and I was numb. I couldn't figure it. And I knew I had to do something.

It was crowding me hard. I knew it wasn't over.

Not yet . . .

'You're back, Roy!'

'Yeah. I'm back.'

Bess had been sitting on the studio couch, waiting. When I opened the door and saw her, she looked up, scared to death, with worry all over her face. Then she ran across the room and jumped into my arms, like the old days.

'What did they want you for, Roy?' Her voice was tight.

I held her away, looking into her eyes. 'About those two murders. They thought I was implicated.'

'But you weren't—*you weren't!*'

'No. Listen, Bess—I've got something to tell you. Something I should have told you long ago.'

'Yes?' She was smiling. I grabbed her and held her as close as I could. Then I thrust her away again and led her over to the couch. We sat down.

'I'm not asking you to forgive me,' I told her. 'But I've been lying to you, Bess. Up and down and crosswise. I'm in a terrible jam. But I want you to know the truth. All of it. The police already know.'

'You've told them?'

'Yes. Only not all of it. Not the part I'm going to tell you.'

And I told her. I gave it to her straight and hard, without any holding back. The whole business, from the very beginning on the Georgia road when the truck driver let me off, to the barbecue joint and the Lincoln. The hotel room. Vivian and me, in that room, and the money. I told her everything and she sat there, listening, with no change in expression and her eyes got wet just as I finished. 'So, I'm not asking you to forgive, unless you can. If you can't, I understand. I had to tell you. I just found out I had to tell you, coming home tonight from the police station. I was sitting in the cab and I knew you had to know. That's why I've been like I've been. I couldn't stand it. That girl—it was only the one night, I want you to understand that.'

'You were drunk, weren't you?'

'It makes no different. I'm not making excuses.' I wasn't. She had it in her lap now. All of it. 'That guy Radan, he's right next door.'

The only thing I didn't tell her was where the money was.

'All right, Roy.'

She got up and turned her back to me and I saw her shoulders stiffen a little. She walked over to the hallway, turned and looked at me. She wasn't saying anything. Her eyes were a little cold now. I couldn't blame her. It was bad, but she had it straight, anyway.

'I've known something was wrong for a long time,' she said. 'I just didn't know what. You told the police about the money?'

'No.'

'But Roy—!'

'It's our money, Bess. You're not going to tell them, either. I've been through too much for that money. It's got to be somebody's money, and it's ours.'

'No, Roy.'

'I mean it.'

'Where is it?'

'I'm not saying. If you tell the cops, Bess, I'll say it's all the bunk. I'll lie up and down, all over again. They'll *never prove different*. I mean it, honest to God, I do.'

'Yes. You and that girl. Yes.'

I watched her put her hands to her face. But she didn't cry. She brought her hands back down and came over to the couch and stood there in front of me.

'You've got to tell the police, Roy. You've got to!'

I shook my head. 'I'm sorry, Bess. I can't do it. I've had that out with myself. It means too much for us, and they don't know anything about that.'

She turned around and stood with her back to me. I looked at her hair, falling thickly to her shoulders, and the line of her back and her legs and her feet. I saw her hands along her sides, the fists half-clenched and she was perfectly still. I wasn't sure how she was taking it, or what she was thinking.

'All this time—' she said.

'That's right. I've lied, and I've lied.'

'When that girl was here, Roy. Did you go over to number six and be with her? Did you?' She turned and looked at me, then. 'Because, if you did—if you—'

'No.'

'I believe you. God only knows why.'

I couldn't look at her face. I didn't feel any better, having told her. I felt worse, because it was hurting her. I didn't want that. Yet, she had to know.

'Roy,' she said. She came to the couch and sat down and looked at me. Her voice was pitched low. 'You've got to tell them. We don't want that money. It'll stand in the way of everything for the rest of our lives. We'd never be happy with it.'

'We'll never be happy without it. We've been without it all along, and it's not going to be that way any more.'

'Roy, I'm telling you—you've got to listen.'

'I'm not listening.' I stood up.

'For me, Roy.'

'Not for you—not for anybody. The money's ours. It stays that way.' I leaned over and looked her in the eye. 'I went through a lot to keep it. And now we've got it.'

'Not "we", Roy. You. You've got it.'

I turned and walked out of the office, and down the porch steps. On the grass, I half expected her to come after me. She didn't. I looked back in the screen door and she was sitting there on the studio couch, staring vacantly at the wall. I walked away from there.

I heard the hiss of feet on the grass and somebody grabbed my arm, whirling me around. 'Nichols.'

It was Radan.

I was mad and I went straight into him. He stepped back and I saw the gun.

'Take it easy, will you?' he said softly.

I stopped, watching him.

'Come on, now,' he said. He stepped up to me and rammed the gun into my back. 'Move. Over to number seven.'

In the apartment, he closed the door and looked at me. He needed a shave, and he looked harried and I realized he'd been drinking a lot more than he should. But that gun was very steady, and so were his eyes.

'What do you want?'

'You know what, Nichols. You're going to tell me where that brief case is. You're the one who hid it, and we know that. You're going to tell me—all alone—just me.'

'That's what you think.'

'So. At last you admit it.'

We watched each other. He stepped in toward me and brought the gun down. It raked across my face. I grabbed his wrist and he grunted a little and his other fish flashed around and I saw the brass knucks.

I went down and sat against the wall. My face was ripped open and bleeding from the knucks.

'All right, Nichols. Tell me.'

Chapter 19

He stood up there looking down at me with the gun in one hand and the brass knuckles in the other. I was seeing Wirt Radan for the first time. I brought my hands down, braced against the wall and pushed. He wouldn't use the gun, I was sure.

I hit him hard in the legs. He didn't fall, but his fist did. The gun bounced off my skull and the pain flashed through me. I raked at him with my arms and got a leg and pulled. He fell on top of me.

I felt the quick impact of the knucks against my head. *Once— twice—three* times and I got groggy and lay back on the floor, staring up at him. He brought his foot back and let me have it hard in the head. My teeth jarred and I bit my tongue. I tried to catch his foot, but it was like working in slow motion. My head was one great big knot of pain and the pain shot down in my chest.

Then it was quiet and I gradually began to hear him breathing. I looked up and he was over there, sitting on the edge of the couch, resting, holding the gun, and the knucks glistened in the dim light from the lamp on the end table. He still wore his suit jacket and his tie wasn't even out of place. His breathing began to slow down.

'Where is it, Nichols? You may as well tell me. I think you understand that by now?'

I didn't say anything. I just lay there, looking up at him, trying to get my breath and let the pain chip away. The pain came into my head in great sheeting waves, and my eyeballs hurt. Finally I began to get up. He rose quickly and stepped over and lashed out with the gun barrel, hitting and raking, back and forth. He did it mechanically, without emotion—as you might swing a hammer at a nail. I tried to catch his wrist.

I caught it and the knucks landed again. I was on the floor, flat out again. He was killing me. He was quick and I knew he wanted that money, and if he got it he would kill me, and that would be that.

It was quiet. I heard water dripping in the kitchen sink and the sound of our breathing whispered harshly in the room. There was no other sound. It was as if everything was dead and gone and there was only this pain, throbbing inside me.

'You'd better tell me,' he said. 'You're going to, you know.' He cleared his throat gently. 'Honestly, you really are, Nichols. Can you believe that?'

I watched him. 'I gave it to Teece.'

'No, you didn't. I killed Teece, Nichols. Just as I'm going to do to you. He told the truth, I know that. He was crying and pleading like a small child. He said he didn't have the money. Those were his last words, Nichols.'

'He lied.'

'We know he didn't. I've been sent on this job, and I'm going to finish it. I always do. It's my turn for the brief case now.'

'The double cross from you?'

'Only halfway. They aren't sure how much is in that brief case.'

I came up off the floor and at him fast. I got him. I sank one into his gut and chopped with my other fist and he started to go down. I saw it in his face, the hanging on. Those damned knucks flashed again.

I lay there. He leaned down and smashed at me with the gun. Then he stood up and cleared his throat. Then he waited.

'All right. I wasn't going this far, Nichols. But now I am. I'm going to tie you up and I'm getting your wife over here. Then you're going to watch something. And you'll talk Nichols. They always do. It's the last thing we try. We don't have any other way. But it's a good way. It produces.'

I looked at him and I knew he meant it. There was nothing to do.

'O.K., Nichols? You know I would?'

'Yes. All right. I'll show you.'

'One wrong move. That will be all.'

'It's all right. I've got the money.'

'Get up.'

'I can't, yet.'

He waited. After a time the pain began to drift away and I got to my knees. Finally I got up on my feet. The blood was in my eyes and I rubbed my hands across my face, knowing it was all done.

I'd let myself down. And Bess, too. I should have got Radan before, on my own. It had been the only way, and I'd missed it.

'Coming, Nichols?'

We went on out the door. I staggered off the porch and nearly fell. He stood back. He watched while I hung onto the porch railing, trying to see right. I couldn't see right.

'Around back, Radan.'

We started down between the apartments. It was a cool night and the wind washed against my face. Everything was a big blank, and I had drawn it There was no use.

We came around behind the apartments. I still couldn't walk right. Something inside my skull kept crackling, and my teeth hurt bad. I knew I was spitting blood and I didn't give a damn, not any more.

We came by the garage and I reached up and grabbed the door and flung it open. 'You climb on the hood of the car. Then pull yourself up by a beam and the brief case is up there under the far eave, under some loose boards.'

'Stand right there, Nichols. Remember, I've got a gun. I can see you against the light. Don't go away.'

I didn't say anything. I stood there waiting. I knew I was waiting for a slug. It was almost as if I didn't care about that, either. He would kill me as sure as the night was dark. Then I thought, Maybe he won't.

He was up on the hood of the car. 'Stay right there,' he said. 'I can see you.'

I watched him pull himself up. Now was my chance to run. I didn't. I waited. I heard him up there, prowling around in the darkness. He was on the boards, over against the eave.

'God!' he said. 'I've got it.'

He came down fast, in a single leap from the beams to the car's hood to the ground. I turned and started walking toward the house.

'Nichols!'

'The hell with it.'

I started up along the side of our apartment, heading toward the office door. I heard him coming fast on the grass.

'Nichols!'

Somebody else said, 'Hold it right there, Radan!'

I whirled and saw him lift his gun and fire at the dark. He fired twice and I flattened myself against the side of the house and he came by me, running like hell.

He took a shot at me as he passed. It *thocked* onto the wooden side of the house. A car moved along out in front by the curb and a spotlight blinked on, coming slowly bright and it picked him up.

I ran out after him. I saw him stand there on the front lawn all alone, with that brief case swinging and he fired at the spotlight and missed.

'Stop—*Radan!*' I recognized Gant's voice.

Radan didn't stop. Somebody fired rapidly twice from down by the corner and Radan turned and knelt down and fired. Somebody fired from the car out there in the street. Radan stood and whirled on the car and his gun clicked empty.

The front sign went on, bright and glowing. Then the floodlights came on and it was like daylight out there on the grass and he stood there holding his empty gun. He drew his arm back and flung the gun sailing at the car. He turned and started across the lawn, running toward the far corner and I saw the brief case come open. That broken clasp. Money streamed and tumbled out as he ran.

They shouted for him to stop. They gave him every chance.

But he didn't stop. They cut him down. He skidded into a pile right by one of the floodlights, landing on his face.

Then everything became still. It had been sudden. Now it was over. I walked out across the lawn.

'You all right, Nichols?'

'Sure.'

It was Lieutenant Gant. He came across the lawn in a steady shuffle, putting his gun away. I walked over to Radan, lying on the ground. There was nothing left inside me.

We stood there and looked at him. About six slugs had nailed him. He was crumpled over on his face, with his grip still tight on the handle of the brief case, only most of the money had spilled out. He'd left a scattered green trail of it all the way across the lawn.

A cop started toward us, picking up the packets of money, softly whistling through his teeth.

'Well?' I said.

Gant looked at me. He shrugged. 'It was your wife. She knew about that money, Nichols. She saw you put it in the garage. She checked and found the money, only she didn't tell us until just now, when she phoned. We'd freed you, thinking maybe you'd lead us somewhere. She wanted you to find it in yourself, to straighten it out without any help. That's why she never said anything to you about the money. I don't know. The hell with it. You know how women are. You should know how your wife is.'

'Yeah. I know.'

'She's over there. I'm not sure whether she wants to see you, though. Can't say as I blame her.'

Bess was standing there by the royal palm at the near corner of the sign. She was watching me. I lifted one hand toward her and let it drop. She didn't move.

Three officers came across the lawn.

The one who'd been picking up the money went over by the dead man and got the brief case loose from his fingers. He began packing the money inside the case, still whistling through his teeth.

'I'm afraid you'll have to come along with us,' Gant said. 'We know Teece killed the girl and Radan killed Teece, all that. We couldn't move in any quicker because we didn't really have anything on Radan, see? We've wanted him for a long while, Nichols. As I say, you'll have to come along, too. There'll be some sort of a trial. Maybe you'll get a suspended sentence. Maybe not.'

I turned and walked over by Bess. There was just nothing left inside me, but her. And she didn't want any part of me.

We looked at each other.

'Lieutenant Gant says the highway's coming through,' she said. 'He told me that tonight, when we were talking about you. Why you did all this.'

'I'm sorry, Bess.'

She looked up at me. We stood there that way for a second or two. Then I saw Gant coming toward us.

'It's all right, Roy.'

I didn't know what to say. It was all over.

'It's all right. I'll be here, Roy.'

Gant touched my arm. 'Coming, Nichols?'

We started off across the lawn toward the curb. 'There are a few things you'll have to clear up,' Gant said. 'I don't exactly get it all yet.'

'Me either, Lieutenant.'

As we got into the car, I looked over across toward the sign. Bess was still standing there. She waved her hand.

Gant slammed the car door. His voice reached me through a haze. 'You care for a cigarette, Nichols?'

But You'll Never Follow Me

by Karl Edward Wagner

Karl Edward Wagner's fiction is almost always informed by a soft, quiet sorrow. Even in his action novels involving Kane, there's a melancholy and a darkness you don't soon forget. He's a better writer than even his fans understand, and he's never been better than in this story.

First published in 1990

I t wasn't the smell of death that he hated so much. He'd grown used to that in Nam. It was the smell of dying that tore at him. Slow dying.

He remembered his best buddy stuck to the paddy mud, legless and eviscerated, too deep in shock to cry out, just gulping air like a beached fish, eyes round with wonder and staring into his. Marsden had closed those eyes with his right hand and with his left he put a .45 slug through his friend's skull.

After that, he'd made a promise to himself never to kill again, but that was as true a promise as he'd ever made to anyone, and never-intended lies rotted together with the never-realized truths of his best intentions.

Marsden found a moment's solitude in the slow-moving elevator as it slid upward to the fourth floor. He cracked a zippered gash into his bulky canvas flight bag, large enough to reach the pint bottle of vodka on top. He gulped down a mouthful, replaced the stopper, and then replaced the flask, tugged down the zipper—all in the space of four floors. Speed was only a matter of practice. He exhaled a breath of vodka as the elevator door opened.

Perhaps the middle-aged couple who waited there noticed his breath as he shouldered past them with his bag, but Marsden doubted it. The air of Brookcrest Health Care Center was already choked with the stench of bath salts and old lady's perfume, with antiseptics and detergents and bouquets of dying flowers; and underlying it all was the veiled sweetness of urine, feces, and vomit, physically retained in bedpans and diapers.

Marsden belched. A nurse in the fourth floor lounge scowled at him, but a blue-haired lady in a jerry cart smiled and waved and called after him: "Billy boy! Billy Billy boy!" Michael Marsden shut his eyes and turned into the hallway that led to his parents' rooms. Somewhere along the hall a woman's voice begged in feeble monotone: "O Lord, help me. O Lord, help me. O Lord, help me." Marsden walked on down the hall.

He was a middle-aged man with a heavyset frame that carried well a spreading beer gut. He had mild brown eyes, a lined and long-jawed face, and there were streaks of gray in his short beard and in his limp brown hair where it straggled from beneath the Giants baseball cap. His denim jacket and jeans were about as worn as his scuffed cowboy boots.

"You'd look a lot nicer if you'd shave that beard and get a haircut," Momma liked to nag him. "And you ought to dress more neatly. You're a good-looking boy, Michael."

She still kept the photo of him in his uniform, smiling bravely, fresh out of boot camp, on her shelf at the nursing home. Marsden guessed that that was the way Momma preferred to hold him in memory—such of her memory as Alzheimer's disease had left her.

Not that there was much worth remembering him for since then. Certainly the rest of his family wouldn't quarrel with that judgment.

"You should have gone back to grad school once you got back," his sister in Columbus had advised him with twenty-twenty and twenty-year hindsight. "What have you done with your life instead? When was the last time you held on to a job for more than a year?"

At least she hadn't added: Or held on to a wife? Marsden had sipped his Coke and vodka and meekly accepted the scolding. They were seated in the kitchen of their parents' too-big house in Cincinnati, trying not to disturb Papa as he dozed in his wheelchair in the family room.

"It's bad enough that Brett and I keep having to drive down here every weekend to try to straighten things out here," Nancy had reminded him. "And then Jack's had to come down from Detroit several times since Momma went to Brookcrest, and Jonathan flew here from Los Angeles and stayed two whole weeks after Papa's first stroke. And all of us have jobs and families to keep up with. Where were you during all this time?"

"Trying to hold a job in Jersey," Marsden explained, thinking of the last Christmas he'd come home for. He'd been nursing a six-pack and the late night movie when Momma drifted into the family room and angrily ordered him to get back to mowing the lawn. It was the first time he'd seen Momma naked in his life, and the image of that shrunken, sagging body would not leave him.

"I'm just saying that you should be doing more, Michael," Nancy continued.

"I was here when you needed me," Marsden protested. "I was here to take Momma to the nursing home."

"Yes, but that was after the rest of us did all the work—finding a good home, signing all the papers, convincing Papa that this was the best thing to do, making all the other arrangements."

"Still, I was here at the end. I did what I had to do," Marsden said, thinking that this had been the story of his life ever since the draft notice had come. Never a choice.

They hadn't wanted to upset Momma, so no one had told her about the nursing home. Secretly they'd packed her things and loaded them into the trunk of Papa's Cadillac the night before. "Just tell Momma that she's going for another checkup at the hospital," they'd told him to say, and then they had to get home to their jobs and families. But despite her advanced Alzheimer's, Momma's memory was clear when it came to remembering doctors' appointments, and she protested suspiciously the next morning when he and Papa bundled her into the car. Momma had looked back over her shoulder at him as they wheeled her down the hall, and her eyes were shadowed with the hurt of betrayal. "You're going to leave me here, aren't you?" she said dully.

The memory of that look crowded memories of Nam from his nightmares.

After that, Marsden had avoided going home. He did visit Momma briefly when Papa had his first stroke, but she hadn't recognized him.

Papa had survived his first stroke, and several months later had surprised them all again and survived his second stroke. But that had been almost a year ago from the night Marsden and his sister had sat talking in the kitchen while Papa dozed in his wheelchair. That first stroke had left him weak on one side; the second had taken away part of his mind. The family had tried to maintain him at home with live-in nursing care, but Papa's health slowly deteriorated, physically and mentally.

It was time to call for Michael.

And Michael came.

"Besides," Nancy reassured him, "Papa only wants to be near Momma. He still insists on trying to get over to visit her every day. You can imagine what a strain that's been on everyone here."

"I can guess," said Michael, pouring more vodka into his glass.

"Where are we going, son?" Papa had asked the next morning, as Marsden lifted him into the Cadillac. Papa's vision was almost gone now, and his voice was hard to understand.

"I'm taking you to be with Momma for a while," Marsden told him. "You want that, don't you?"

Papa's dim eyes stared widely at the house as they backed down the driveway. He turned to face Michael. "But when are you bringing Momma and me back home again, son?"

Never, as it turned out. Marsden paused outside his mother's room, wincing at the memory. Over the past year their various health problems had continued their slow and inexorable progress toward oblivion. Meanwhile health care bills had mushroomed—eroding insurance coverage, the last of their pensions, and a lifetime's careful savings. It was time to put the old family home on the market, to make some disposal of a lifetime's possessions. It had to be done.

Papa called for Michael.

"Don't let them do this to us, son." The family held power of attorney now. "Momma and I want to go home."

So Michael came home.

The white-haired lady bent double over her walker as she inched along the hallway wasn't watching him. Marsden took a long swig of vodka and replaced the pint bottle. Momma didn't like to see him drink.

She was sitting up in her jerry cart, staring at the television, when Marsden stepped inside her room and closed the door. They'd removed her dinner tray but hadn't cleaned up, and bits of food littered the front of her dressing gown. She looked up, and her sunken eyes showed recognition.

"Why, it's Michael! She held out her food-smeared arms to him. "My baby!"

Marsden accepted her slobbery hug. "I've come for you, Momma," he whispered as Momma began to cry.

She covered her face with her hands and continued weeping as Marsden stepped behind her and opened the flight bag. The silencer was already fitted to the Hi-Standard .22, and Marsden quickly pumped three hollow-points through the back of his mother's head. It was over in seconds. Little noise, and surely no pain. No more pain.

Marsden left his mother slumped over in her jerry cart, picked up his canvas bag, and closed the door. Then he walked on down the hall to his father's room.

He went inside. Papa must have been getting up and falling again, because he was tied to his wheelchair by a bath towel about his waist. "Who's that?" he mumbled, turning his eyes toward Marsden.

"It's Michael, Papa. I'm here to take you home."

Papa lost sphincter control as Marsden untied the knotted towel. He was trying to say something—it sounded like "Bless you, son"—then Marsden lovingly shot him three times through the back of his skull. Papa would have fallen out of the wheelchair, but Marsden caught him. He left him sitting upright with the Monday night football game just getting underway on the tube.

Marsden finished the vodka, then removed the silencer from the pistol and replaced the clip. Shoving the Hi-Standard into his belt, he checked over the flight bag and left it with Papa.

He heard the first screams as the elevator door slowly closed. Someone must have finally gone to clean Momma's dinner off her.

A uniformed security guard—Marsden hadn't known that Brookcrest employed such—was trying to lock the lobby doors. A staff member was shouting into the reception desk phone.

"Hold it, please! Nobody's to leave!" The guard actually had a revolver.

Marsden shot him through the left eye and stepped over him and through the glass doors. Marsden regretted this, because he hated to kill needlessly.

Unfortunately, the first police car was slithering into the parking lot as Marsden left the nursing home. Marsden continued to walk away, even when the car's spotlight pinned him against the blacktop.

"You there! Freeze!"

They must have already been called to the home, Marsden thought. Time was short. Without breaking stride, he drew his .22 and shot out the spotlight.

There were still the parking lot lights. Gunfire flashed from behind both front doors of the police car, and Marsden sensed the impact of buckshot and 9mm slugs. He was leaping for the cover of a parked car, and two more police cars were hurtling into the parking lot, when the twenty pounds of C4 he'd left with Papa went off.

The blast lifted Marsden off his feet and fragged him with shards of glass and shattered bricks. Brookcrest Health Care Center burst open like the birth of a volcano.

Two police cars were overturned, the other on fire. The nursing home was collapsing into flaming rubble. No human screams could be heard through the thunder of disintegrating brick and steel.

Marsden rolled to his feet, brushing away fragments of debris. He retrieved his pistol, but there was no need for it just now. His clothes were in a bad state but they could be changed. There was no blood, just as he had known there would not be.

They couldn't kill him in Nam, that day in the paddy when he learned what he was and why he was. They couldn't kill him now.

Was it any easier when they were your own loved ones? Yes, perhaps it was.

Michael Marsden melted away into the darkness that had long ago claimed him.

The Tunnel of Love

by Robert Bloch

Robert Bloch tells me that this was literally a "lost" story for years. He forgot all about writing it. Then it turned up and he put it into one of his anthologies and it found a whole new audience. Here's my favorite kind of Bloch story, ironic, sad, and dark in the way of the paperback fifties.

First published in 1948

The entrance to the tunnel had been painted to resemble a woman's mouth, with Cupid's-bow lips bordering it in vivid red. Marco stared into the yawning darkness beyond. A woman's mouth—how often had he dreamed of it, this past winter?

Now he stood before the entrance, stood before the mouth, waiting to be engulfed.

Marco was all alone in the amusement park; none of the other concessionares had come to inspect their property and put it in working order for the new season. He was all alone, standing before the mouth; the scarlet mouth that beckoned him to come, be swallowed, be devoured.

It would be so easy to run away, clear out and never come back. Maybe when the summer season opened he could sell the concession. He'd tried all winter long, but there'd been no takers, even at a ridiculously low price. Yes, he could sell out and go away, far away. Away from the tunnel, away from the red mouth with its black throat gaping for some human morsels.

But that was nonsense, dream-stuff, nightmare. The Tunnel of Love was a good stand, a money-maker. A four-months' take was enough to support him for an entire year. And he needed the money, needed it more than ever since he'd married Dolores.

Perhaps he shouldn't have married her, in view of his troubles, but in a way that's just why he had to marry her. He wanted something to cling to, something to shut out the fears that came to him at night. She loved him, and she would never suspect; there was no need for her to suspect if he kept his own head. Everything was going to be all right once the season started. Now all he needed to do was check up on his equipment.

The ticket booth was in good shape; he'd opened it and found no damage through leaking or frost. A good coat of paint would help, and he'd put a new stool inside for Dolores. She'd sell the tickets next season and cut down on his overhead. All he need bother about would be running the boats through; shoving them off and docking them for the benefit of the giggling couples who eagerly tasted the delights of the Tunnel of Love.

Marco had checked the six gondolas stored in the shed behind the boards fronting his concession. All were sound. The treadmill motor was oiled and ready. The water intake and outlet were unrusted. He had dragged one of the flat-bottomed gondolas out and it lay ready for launching once he flooded the channel and started the treadmill operation.

Now he hesitated before the tunnel entrance. This was it. He had to make up his mind, once and for all. Would he . . .

Turning his back deliberately on the jaws of the monster (he had to stop thinking like that, he *had* to!) Marco stepped over and opened the water. It ran down into the channel, a thin brown trickle, a muddy jet, a gushing frothy stream. The tunnel swallowed it. Now the treadmill was obscured; the water rushed into the tunnel full force. It rose as it flowed until the normal depth of three feet was attained. Marco watched it pour into the mouth. The mouth was thirsty. Thirsty for water, thirsty for . . .

Marco closed his eyes. If only he could get rid of that crazy notion about mouths! Funny thing, the exit of the tunnel didn't bother him at all. The exit was just as big, just as black. The water would rush through the entrance, complete the circuit of the tunnel, and emerge on the other side from the exit. It would sweep over the dry treadmill, clean out the dirt and the debris, the accumulation of past months. It would sweep it out clean, bring everything from the tunnel, it was coming now, yes, he could hear it now; he wanted to run, he couldn't look!

But Marco had to look. He had to know. He had to find out what floated on that bubbling, gurgling stream; had to see what bobbed and twisted in the torrent that emerged from the tunnel exit.

The water trickled, eddied, churned, swept out in a raging and majestic tide. Marco knelt in the gutter and stared down at the flow. It would be a hemorrhage, it would be blood, he knew that; but how could it be? Marco stared and saw that it wasn't blood. Nothing emerged from the tunnel but dirty water—dirty water carrying caravels of leaves, a fleet of twigs, a flotilla of old gum-wrappers and cigarette butts. The surface of the water was rain-bow-veined with oil and grease. It eddied and mingled once again with the steady flow from the faucets leading back into the tunnel. The level rose to the markings on the side of the treadle-pit.

So the tunnel was empty. Marco sighed gratefully. It had all been a nightmare; his fear were groundless. Now all he needed to do was launch the single gondola and go through the tunnel for an inspection of the lights on his exhibits.

Yes, all he had to do was sail into the waiting mouth, the hungry mouth, the grinning jaws of death—

Marco shrugged, shook his head. No use stalling, he had to go through with it. He'd turn the lights on; he could use the hand-switches en route to stop the treadle if needs be. Then he could inspect the cut-off and see if everything was barricaded off. There was nothing to worry about, but he had to be quite *sure*.

He slid the heavy gondola off its truck and into the channel. Holding it with a boat-hook, he stooped again and switched on the motor. It chugged. The treadle groaned under the water, and he knew it was moving. The deep, flat-bottomed gondola rested on the moving treadle-struts. Marco let the boat-hook fall and stepped into the forward seat of the boat. It began to move forward, move towards the red lips, the black mouth. The entrance of the tunnel loomed.

Marco leaped from the boat with a spastic, convulsive tremor agitating his limbs. Frantically, he switched off the motor and halted the gondola at the lip of the tunnel. He stood there, all panting and perspiration, for a long moment.

Thank God, he'd thought of it in time! He'd almost gone into the tunnel without remembering to turn on the lights. That he could never do, he knew; the lights were necessary. How could he have forgotten? *Why* had he forgotten? Did the tunnel want him to forget? Did it want him to go into the blackness all alone, so that it could . . .

Marco shook his head. Such thoughts were childish. Quite deliberately, he walked into the ticket booth and plugged in the cord controlling the tunnel light circuit. He started the treadle going and jumped into the moving boat, barking his left shin. He was still rubbing the sore spot as the boat glided into darkness.

Quite suddenly Marco was in the tunnel, and he wasn't afraid any more. There was nothing to be afraid of, nothing at all. The boat bumped along slowly, the water gurgled, the treadle groaned. Little blue lights cast a friendly glow at intervals of forty feet—little blue lights behind the glass walls of the small papier-mâché exhibit booths set in the tunnel sides. Here was Romeo and Juliet, here was Antony and Cleopatra, here was Napoleon and Josephine, here was the cutout . . .

Marco stopped the boat—halted the treadle, rather, by reaching out and pulling the handswitch set near the water's edge in the left wall of the tunnel.

Here was the cutout . . .

Formerly the tunnel had contained an extra loop; a hundred and twenty feet more of winding channel through which boats had doubled back on an auxilliary treadle. Since November this channel had been cut out, boarded up, sealed up tightly and cemented at the cracks by Marco's frantic fingers. He had worked until after midnight to do the job, but it was well done. Marco stared at the wall. It had held. Nothing leaked into the cutout, nothing leaked out of it. The air of the tunnel was fetid, but that was merely a natural musty odor soon to be dispelled—just as Marco's fears were dispelled now by the sight of the smooth walled surface.

There was nothing to worry about, nothing at all. Marco started the treadle. The boat swept on. Now he could lean back in his double seat and actually enjoy the ride. The Tunnel of Love would operate again. The bobby-soxers and the college kids, the sailors and the hicks would have their romance, their smooching, their dimes'-worth of darkness. Yes, Marco would sell darkness for a dime. He lived on darkness. He and Dolores would be together; just like Romeo and Juliet, Antony and Cleopatra, Marco and—but *that* was over.

Marco was actually grinning when the boat glided out into the light of day again.

Dolores saw the grin and thought it was meant for her. She waved from the side of the channel.

"Hello, darling!"

Marco gaped at the tall blonde in the flowered print dress. She waved at him, and as the boat drew up opposite the disembarking point she stooped, stopped the motor, and held out her arms to the man in the gondola. His grin disappeared as he rose.

"What are you doing here?"

"Just thought I'd surprise you. I guessed where you'd be going." Her arms pressed his back.

"Oh." He kissed her without giving or receiving any sensation.

"You aren't mad, are you, darling? After all, I'm your wife— and I'm going to be working here with you, aren't I? I mean, I'd like to see this old tunnel you've been so mysterious about."

Lord, she was a stupid female! Maybe that's why he loved her; because she was stupid, and uncalculating, and loyal. Because she wasn't dark and intense and knowing and hysterical like . . .

"What on earth were you doing?" she asked.

The question threw him off balance. "Why, just going through the tunnel."

"All alone?" Dolores giggled. "What's the sense of taking a boat ride through the Tunnel of Love by yourself? Couldn't you find some girl to keep you company?"

If you only knew, thought Marco, but he didn't say it. He didn't care. "Just inspecting the place," he said. "Seems to be in good shape. Shall we go now?"

"Go?" Dolores pouted. "I want to see, too."

"There's nothing to see."

"Come on, darling—take me thought the tunnel, just once. After all, I won't be getting a chance after the season opens."

"But . . ."

She teased his hair with her fingers. "Look, I drove all the way down here just to see. What're you acting so mysterious about? You hiding a body in the tunnel, or something?"

Good Lord, not that, Marco thought. He couldn't allow her to become suspicious.

Not Dolores, of all people.

"You really want to go through?" he murmured. He knew she did, and he knew he had to take her, now. He had to show her that there was nothing to be afraid of, there was nothing in the tunnel at all.

And why couldn't he do just that? There *was* nothing to fear, nothing at all. So—"Come along," said Marco.

He helped her into the boat, holding the gondola steady in the swirling water as he started the treadle. Then he jumped into the seat beside her and cast off. The boat bumped against the sides of the channel and swayed as he sat down. She gasped.

"Be careful or we'll tip!" she squealed.

"Not a chance. This outfit's safe. Besides the water's only three feet deep at most. You can't get hurt here."

Oh, can't you? Marco wiped his forehead and grimaced as the gondola edged toward the gulping black hole of the Tunnel of Love. He buried his face against her cheek and closed his eyes against the engulfing darkness.

"Gee, honey, isn't it romantic?" Dolores whispered. "I bet you used to envy the fellows who took their girls through here, didn't you? Or did you get girls and go through yourself?"

Marco wished she'd shut up. This kind of talk he didn't like to hear.

"Did you ever take that girl you used to have in the ticket booth in here with you?" Dolores teased. "What was her name—Belle?"

"No," said Marco.

"What did you say happened to her at the end of the season, darling?"

"She ran out on me." Marco kept his head down, his eyes closed. They were in the tunnel now and he could smell the mustiness of it. It smelled like old perfume—stale, cheap perfume. He knew that smell. He pressed his face against Dolores's cheek. She wore scent, but the other smell still came through.

"I never liked her," Dolores was saying. "What kind of a girl was she, Marco? I mean, did you ever . . ."

"No—no!"

"Well, don't snap at me like that! I've never seen you act like this before, Marco."

"Marco." The name echoed through the tunnel. It bounced off the ceiling, off the walls, off the cutout. It echoed and reechoed, and then it was taken up from far away in a different voice; a softer voice, gurgling through water. *Marco, Marco, Marco,* over and over again until he couldn't stand it.

"Shut up!" yelled Marco.

"Why . . ."

"Not you, Dolores. Her."

"Her? Are you nuts or something? There's nobody but the two of us here in the dark, and . . ."

In the dark? How could that be? The lights were on, he'd left them on. What was she talking about?

Marco opened his eyes. They *were* in the dark. The lights were out. Perhaps a fuse had blown. Perhaps a short circuit.

There was no time to think of possibilities. All Marco knew was the certainty; they were gliding down the dark throat of the tunnel in the dark, nearing the center, nearing the cutout. And the echo, the damned drowned echo, whispered, *"Marco."*

He had to shut it out, he had to talk over it, talk against it. And all at once he was talking, fast and shrill.

"She did it, Dolores, I know she did it. Belle. She's here now, in the tunnel. All winter long I felt her, saw her, heard her in my dreams. Calling to me. Calling to me to come back. She said I'd never be rid of her, you'd never have me, nobody and nothing could take me away from her. And I was a fool—I came back, I let you come with me. Now we're here and she's here. Can't you feel it?"

"Darling." She clung to him in the dark. "You're not well, are you? Because there's nobody here. You understand that, don't you? Belle ran away, remember, you told me yourself. She's not here."

"Oh yes she is!" Marco panted. "She's here, she's been here all along, ever since last season. She died in this tunnel."

Dolores wasn't clinging to him any more. She drew away. The boat rocked and bumped the channel sides. He couldn't see anything in the perfumed blackness, and he had to get her arms around him again. So he talked faster.

"She died here. The night we took a ride together after I closed the concession. The night I told her I was going to marry you, that it was all over between her and me. She jumped out of the boat and tried to take me with her. I guess I fought her.

"Belle was hysterical, you must understand that. She kept saying it over and over again, that I couldn't leave her, that she'd never give me up, never. I tried to pull her back into the boat and she choked me and then she—drowned."

"You killed her!"

"I didn't. It was an accident, suicide, really. I didn't mean to hold her so tight but she was fighting me—it was just suicide. I knew it looked like murder, I knew what would happen if anyone found out. So I buried her, walled her up behind the cutout. And now she's coming back, she won't let me go, what shall I do, Dolores, what can I do?"

"You . . ."

Dolores screamed.

Marco tried to put his arms around her. She moved away, shrieking. The echo shattered the darkness. He lunged at her. The boat rocked and tipped. There was a splash.

"Come back, you fool!" Marco stood up, groping in darkness. Somewhere Dolores was wailing and gurgling. The gondola was empty now. The blackness was spinning round and round, sucking Marco down into it. He felt a bump, knew the boat had stopped. He jumped out into the water. The treadles were slippery with slime. Cold waves lapped about his waist. He tried to find Dolores in the darkness, in the water. No wailing now, no gurgles.

"Dolores!"

No answer. No sound at all. The bumping and the lapping ceased.

"Dolores!"

She hadn't run away. There was nowhere to run to, and he would have heard the splashing. Then she was . . .

His hands found flesh. Wet flesh, floating flesh. She had fallen against the side of the boat, bumped her head. But only a few seconds had passed. Nobody drowns in a few seconds. She had passed out, poor kid.

He dragged her into the boat. Now it moved away, moved through the darkness as he propped her on the seat beside him and put his arm around the clammy, soggy wetness of her dress. Her head lolled on his shoulder as he chafed her wrists.

"There, now. It's all right. Don't you see, darling, it's all right now? I'm not afraid any more. Belle isn't here. There's nothing to worry about. Everything will be all right."

The more he said it, the more he knew it was true. What had he done, frightening the girl half to death? Marco cursed the slowness of the treadles as the boat bumped its way out of the tunnel. The mechanism wasn't working properly. But there was no time to bother about that. He had to bring Dolores around.

He kissed her hair. He kissed her ear. She was still cold. "Come on, honey," he whispered. "Brace up. This is the Tunnel of Love, remember?"

The boat bumped out into the daylight. Marco stared ahead. They were safe now. Safe from the tunnel, safe from Belle. He and Dolores . . .

Dolores.

Marco peered at the prow of the bumping gondola as it creaked over the treadles. He peered at the obstruction floating in its path; floating face upward in the water as if tied to the boat with a red string running from its gashed forehead.

Dolores!

She had fallen in the water when she jumped out of the gondola, fallen and struck her head the way Belle had struck her head. It was Dolores's body that bumped against the front of the boat and retarded its progress. She was dead.

But if that was Dolores out there in the water, then what . . .

Marco turned his head, ever so slowly. For the first time he glanced down at the seat beside him, at what lay cradled in his arms.

For the first time Marco saw what he had been kissing . . .

. . . the boat glided back into the Tunnel of Love.

Tony

by William Relling

William Relling is currently a screenwriter in Hollywood where he continues to write quite good horror stories that seem, slowly, to be edging more toward the crime category. He has his own style and it is nowhere more evident than in his fine horror novels.

First published in 1990

They found what was left of the night nurse, the pretty one named Theresa, stuffed in a linen closet near the tub room on the second floor. She wasn't very pretty when they found her. One of the housekeepers opened the door and saw her first, and she screamed and screamed. They let her go home early for the day.

Judy, the head nurse on the day shift, called the police. A couple of orderlies took Theresa's body down to the hospital morgue on a stretcher, covered with a white sheet that they brought with them. They couldn't use any of the ones from the closet where they found Theresa. They were all red and sticky.

The orderlies didn't take her body away until after the first policemen came, the ones who wore uniforms. The policemen who came later wore suits and ties. One of them had a camera, and another had something that looked kind of like a fishing tackle box. He took out some kind of powder and they brushed it around the closet. He was looking for fingerprints, just like they do on television.

Another one was with Dr. Woodburn when he came to do his rounds. The policeman went into the conference room with Dr. Woodburn after the doctor had stopped off at the nurses' station and got all of his patients' charts. I didn't find out that the man with Dr. Woodburn was a policeman until later.

Dr. Woodburn called me into conference after he had talked to Lila. I sat down in my same seat as always. Dr. Woodburn sat in his seat at the other end of the table. The policeman was sitting next to him. I pulled an ashtray over next to me and lit a cigarette.

"Are you feeling all right today, John?" asked Dr. Woodburn. He had my chart open in front of him.

"Not so bad now," I said.

He paged through my chart. Then he looked at me, and he made a noise like he was clearing his throat. "John," Dr. Woodburn said, "this man is a police detective. A homicide detective. I think it will be all right if he asks you some questions."

I sort of smiled, then nodded to them.

"My name is Sergeant Stephens," said the policeman.

"How do you do," I said.

"I'm fine," he answered. He had a funny look on his face, like he wasn't sure what to say to me.

"You don't have to be afraid to talk to me, Sergeant," I said. "I know where I am and why I'm here. And I don't rant or rave or hit myself or make trouble. And I know why *you're* here, too."

He looked at Dr. Woodburn.

"He didn't tell me anything," I went on. "We *all* know. And I'm not stupid. I'm just crazy."

Sgt. Stephens got that funny look again.

"Mr. Garbo knows what he's saying, Sergeant," Dr. Woodburn said softly.

The policeman took a deep breath. "Okay, Mr. Garbo," he said to me. "You know about Nurse Caputo?"

I nodded.

"Did you know her personally?" he asked.

"Sure," I answered. "She'd been here for almost a year."

Sgt. Stephens looked surprised. "You've been here that long?"

I laughed. "Of course not," I said. "At least not this time. But I've been here before. They *do* allow us to talk to the nurses, Sergeant. Even at night."

"John," Dr. Woodburn warned me.

"Sorry," I said. I turned back to Sgt. Stephens. "Yes. I knew Theresa."

"Did you know her very well?"

I shrugged. "As well as any of the rest of the staff, I suppose.

She was a pleasant enough person. Not really any different from anybody else."

"Did you like her?"

"We weren't friends, Sergeant, if that's what you mean. I'm a patient. She's a nurse. She had her job . . ." I smiled again. "And I have mine."

He was writing in a brown notebook that he'd pulled from one of the pockets in his suit coat. "Is there anything else you can tell me about last night?" he asked.

"Like what?"

"Like did you see anything or did you hear anything—"

"You mean 'out of the ordinary'?" I cut in. I was smiling again. "You know, Sergeant," I said, "this is really a lot more like television than I thought it would be."

"Did you see anything, Mr. Garbo?" he asked.

I crushed my cigarette in the ashtray.

"Answer him please, John," said Dr. Woodburn.

"All right," I said, giving in. I was angry with them. "There was nothing unusual about last night. Lila had a fit because she was out-voted and didn't get to watch *Happy Days.* And my brother Rod and his wife came to see me, but they left about eight-thirty. I went to my room and read until about eleven o'clock, and then I feel asleep. I woke up when I heard Mrs. Thompson screaming, which was about six this morning. They made us all stay in our rooms, and we didn't get breakfast until after eight. My cereal was soggy." I pointed at his notebook. "Be sure you get that down, Sergeant," I said. "I want to register a complaint."

He frowned at me and closed the notebook. "Thank you, Mr. Garbo," he said. He wasn't happy.

"That's all, John," Dr. Woodburn said, dismissing me.

"Wait a minute," I said. " 'That's all'? You're not going to talk to me, Doctor . . . ?"

"Not today."

"Now just hold on . . ."

I paused. They were looking at me sternly. They wanted me to leave.

I looked down at the ashtray. "I know who killed Theresa," I said.

"I didn't hear you, John," said Dr. Woodburn.

"I said I know who killed Theresa, dammit!" I slammed a fist on the table. They both jumped.

The policeman looked from Dr. Woodburn to me, then back to

Dr. Woodburn again. I thought for a minute that he looked scared.

I shook my head. "I'm sorry . . ."

"It's all right, John," said Dr. Woodburn.

"Do you?" Sgt. Stephens asked me. "Do you know who killed Miss Caputo?"

I lit another cigarette. Neither of them saw my hand shaking. I made it stop before they could see it.

"Yes, Sergeant," I said calmly. "I know."

"Who?" he asked. He was leaning way forward over the table.

I looked to Dr. Woodburn. "Do you know something, John?" he asked me.

The policeman was staring hard at me. He began to push himself up out of his chair, but Dr. Woodburn put a hand on his arm to stop him. He shook it off and stood up.

"Mr. Garbo," the policeman said in a voice that was *very* official, "you didn't see Miss Caputo's body, did you? But you knew her. Do you want to know how she looked when we found her?"

Dr. Woodburn said, "Hold on, Sergeant—"

The policeman snapped at him: "No, Doctor! If *he* knows something then *I* want to know!"

Sgt. Stephens turned to me again. "An animal killed her, Mr. Garbo," he said. "She was ripped to pieces."

I was still calm. "An animal?" I said.

"That's right. Now, I don't know anything more about you than what your doctor told me before you came in—"

"Paranoid schizophrenia," I said helpfully.

His eyes flashed angrily. "I don't care about that!" he shouted. "But I don't think that you're too crazy to understand that everybody here is in danger until we catch Theresa Caputo's killers!"

"Touche, Sergeant," I said.

He demanded: "If you know something about this maniac—"

Dr. Woodburn grabbed the policeman by the arm. "That's enough, Sergeant," he said harshly. "This is a psychiatric unit and John is a patient. He's not a criminal. I'd appreciate it if you would keep that in mind."

The policeman fell back into his chair. "I apologize, Mr. Garbo," he said.

Dr. Woodburn looked down the table at me. "Do you know something, John?" he asked quietly.

I was looking down at the ashtray again. "I know," I said.

Dr. Woodburn said, "I can't hear you when you mumble."

"I *said* 'I know'."

The policeman leaned forward "You know who killed her?"
I nodded. "Yes, I know. He told me."
"Who told you?"
"Tony."
"Tony who?"
It surprised me that he was so stupid. "Tony, Tony," I said.
"How many Tonys are there here?"
The policeman turned to Dr. Woodburn and questioned the
doctor with his eyes. Dr. Woodburn shrugged. "I don't have any
patients named Tony in the unit," he said.
"A woman's name, maybe?"
"Perhaps," said Dr. Woodburn. He got up out of his chair. "It
may be another patient, belonging to another doctor. I can check
the register at the nurses' station."
On his way out of the conference room Dr. Woodburn paused
when he reached my chair. "Help him, John," he whispered.
"Tell him what you know." Dr. Woodburn walked out of the
room and closed the door behind him.
I was turned around in my chair, looking at the door.
"Tony who?" the policeman said to my back.
I spun around.
He was glaring at me. "Tony who?" he repeated.
I shook my head. "You know, Sergeant," I said, "you're not as
smart as I first thought you were."
He came out of his chair. "Listen to me," he spat angrily. "If
you're just screwing around with me . . . I don't give a damn if
you're supposed to be sick or not—but you know something *and
you're gonna tell me!*"
He was shaking a finger at me and his eyes were popping. I
thought that his face would explode.
"I told you already," I said. "Tony."
His face was bright red with rage. "Tony *who!?!*"
I gave him as hard a look as I could manage. "You're *so* stupid," I said.
That's when he slapped me.
Like last night, in the middle of the night, when Theresa
slapped me. When all I wanted to do was touch her, and she
slapped me and called me an animal.
So Tony killed her. Like an animal.
The conference room was soundproofed, but that didn't mat-
ter. Tony never gave Sgt. Stephens a chance to scream.
Dr. Woodburn was the first one in there. The other policemen
were still on the unit, and the doctor called them in right away.

Sgt. Stephens lay on the table. His head hung over the edge, right at the point where his throat had been chewed open, after he had been strangled. His throat was gaping, and the air from his windpipe made the blood bubble over his suit. His eyes were open.

Then they saw me.

I was sitting in Dr. Woodburn's chair. I smiled at them.

They were staring at my face.

I wiped my mouth with the back of my hand then looked down at it. My hand was bloody. I smiled again.

I told them. It was an animal, just like Sgt. Stephens said. It was Tony.

Like in Tony the Tiger. You know: *Grrrrrrrreeeeeaat!*

Then I growled.

By the Hair of the Head

by Joe R. Lansdale

Joe R. Lansdale is the Mark Twain of the suspense field—dark as he gets, there's always laughter in the grief; and violent as he gets, there's always dignity, and even redemption, in the finale. There's nobody else like him. He's going to be big-big, and soon.

First published in 1983

The lighthouse was grey and brutally weathered, kissed each morning by a cold, salt spray. Perched there among the rocks and sand, it seemed a last, weak sentinel against an encroaching sea; a relentless, pounding surf that had slowly swallowed up the shoreline and deposited it in the all-consuming belly of the ocean.

Once the lighthouse had been bright-colored, candy-striped like a barber's pole, with a high beacon light and a horn that honked out to the ships on the sea. No more. The lighthouse director, the last of a long line of sea watchers, had cashed in the job ten years back when the need died, but the lighthouse was now his and he lived there alone, bunked down nightly to the tune of the wind and the raging sea.

Below he had renovated the bottom of the tower and built rooms, and one of these he had locked away from all persons, from all eyes but his own.

I came there fresh from college to write my novel, dreams of being the new Norman Mailer dancing in my head. I rented in with him, as he needed a boarder to help him pay for the place, for he no longer worked and his pension was as meager as stale bread.

High up in the top was where we lived, a bamboo partition drawn between our cots each night, giving us some semblance of privacy, and dark curtains were pulled round the thick, foggy windows that traveled the tower completely around.

By day the curtains were drawn and the partition was pulled and I sat at my typewriter, and he, Howard Machen, sat with his book and his pipe, swelled the room full of grey smoke the thickness of his beard. Sometimes he rose and went below, but he was always quiet and never disturbed my work.

It was a pleasant life. Agreeable to both of us. Mornings we had coffee outside on the little railed walkway and had a word or two as well, then I went to my work and he to his book, and at dinner we had food and talk and brandies; sometimes one, sometimes two, depending on mood and the content of our chatter.

We sometimes spoke of the lighthouse and he told me of the old days, of how he had shone that light out many times on the sea. Out like a great, bright fishing line to snag the ships and guide them in; let them follow the light in the manner that Theseus followed Ariadne's thread.

"Was fine," he'd say. "That pretty old light flashing out there. Best job I had in all my born days. Just couldn't leave her when she shut down, so I bought her."

"It is beautiful up here, but lonely at times."

"I have my company."

I took that as a compliment, and we tossed off another brandy. Any idea of my writing later I cast aside. I had done four good pages and was content to spit the rest of the day away in talk and dreams.

"You say this was your best job," I said as a way of conversation. "What did you do before this?"

He lifted his head and looked at me over the briar and its smoke. His eyes squinted against the tinge of the tobacco. "A good many things. I was born in Wales. Moved to Ireland with my family, was brought up there, and went to work there. Learned the carpentry trade from my father. Later I was a tailor. I've also been a mason—note the rooms I built below with my own two hands—and I've been a boat builder and a ventriloquist in a magician's show."

"A ventriloquist?"

"Correct," he said, and his voice danced around me and seemed not to come from where he sat.

"Hey, that's good."

"Not so good really. I was never good, just sort of fell into it. I'm worse now. No practice, but I've no urge to take it up again."

"I've an interest in such things."

"Have you now?"

"Yes."

"Ever tried a bit of voice throwing?"

"No. But it interests me. The magic stuff interests me more. You said you worked in a magician's show?"

"That I did. I was the lead-up act."

"Learn any of the magic tricks, being an insider and all?"

"That I did, but that's not something I'm interested in," he said flatly.

"Was the magician you worked for good?"

"Damn good, m'boy. But his wife was better."

"His wife?"

"Marilyn was her name. A beautiful woman." He winked at me. "Claimed to be a witch."

"You don't say?"

"I do, I do. Said her father was a witch and she learned it and inherited it from him."

"Her father?"

"That's right. Not just women can be witches. Men too."

We poured ourselves another and exchanged sloppy grins, hooked elbows, and tossed it down.

"And another to meet the first," the old man said and poured. Then: "Here's to company." We tossed it off.

"She taught me the ventriloquism, you know," the old man said, relighting his pipe.

"Marilyn?"

"Right, Marilyn."

"She seems to have been a rather all-round lady."

"She was at that. And pretty as an Irish morning."

"I thought witches were all old crones, or young crones. Hook noses, warts . . ."

"Not Marilyn. She was a fine-looking woman. Fine bones, agate eyes that clouded in mystery, and hair the color of a fresh-robbed hive."

Odd she didn't do the magic herself. I mean, if she was the better magician, why was her husband the star attraction?"

"Oh, but she did do magic. Or rather she helped McDonald to

look better than he was, and he was some good. But Marilyn was better.

"Those days were different, m'boy. Women weren't the ones to take the initiative, least not openly. Kept to themselves. Was a sad thing. Back then it wasn't thought fittin' for a woman to be about such business. Wasn't ladylike. Oh, she could get sawed in half, or disappear in a wooden crate, priss and look pretty, but take the lead? Not on your life!"

I fumbled myself another brandy. "A pretty witch, huh?"

"Ummmm."

"Had the old pointed hat and broom passed down, so to speak?" My voice was becoming slightly slurred.

"It's not a laughin' matter, m'boy." Machen clenched the pipe in his teeth.

"I've touched a nerve, have I not? I apologize. Too much sauce."

Machen smiled. "Not at all. It's a silly thing, you're right. To hell with it."

"No, no, I'm the one who spoiled the fun. You were telling me she claimed to be the descendant of a long line of witches."

Machen smiled. It did not remind me of other smiles he had worn. This one seemed to come from a borrowed collection.

"Just some silly tattle is all. Don't really know much about it, just worked for her, m'boy." That was the end of that. Standing, he knocked out his pipe on the concrete floor and went to his cot.

For a moment I sat there, the last breath of Machen's pipe still in the air, the brandy still warm in my throat and stomach. I looked at the windows that surrounded the lighthouse, and everywhere I looked was my own ghostly reflection. It was like looking out through the compound eyes of an insect, seeing a multiple image.

I turned out the lights, pulled the curtains and drew the partition between our beds, wrapped myself in my blanket, and soon washed up on the distant shore of a recurring dream. A dream not quite in grasp, but heard like the far, fuzzy cry of a gull out from land.

It had been with me almost since moving into the tower. Sounds, voices . . .

A clunking noise like peg legs on stone. . . .

. . . a voice, fading in, fading out . . . Machen's voice, the words not quite clear, but soft and coaxing . . . then solid and firm: "Then be a beast. Have your own way. Look away from me with your mother's eyes."

". . . your fault," came a child's voice, followed by other words that were chopped out by the howl of the sea wind, the roar of the waves.

". . . getting too loud. He'll hear . . ." came Machen's voice.

"Don't care . . . I . . . ," lost voices now.

I tried to stir, but then the tube of sleep, nourished by the brandy, came unclogged, and I descended down into richer blackness.

Was a bright morning full of sun, and no fog for a change. Cool clear out there on the landing, and the sea even seemed to roll in soft and bounce against the rocks and lighthouse like puffy cotton balls blown on the wind.

I was out there with my morning coffee, holding the cup in one hand and grasping the railing with the other. It was a narrow area but safe enough, provided you didn't lean too far out or run along the walk when it was slick with rain. Machen told me of a man who had done just that and found himself plummeting over to be shattered like a dropped melon on the rocks below.

Machen came out with a cup of coffee in one hand, his unlit pipe in the other. He looked haggard this morning, as if a bit of old age had crept upon him in the night, fastened a straw to his face, and sucked out part of his substance.

"Morning," I said.

"Morning." He emptied his cup in one long draft. He balanced the cup on the metal railing and began to pack his pipe.

"Sleep bad?" I asked.

He looked at me, then at his pipe, finished his packing, and put the pouch away in his coat pocket. He took a long match from the same pocket, gave it fire with his thumbnail, lit the pipe. He puffed quite awhile before he answered me. "Not too well. Not too well."

"We drank too much."

"We did at that."

I sipped my coffee and looked at the sky, watched a snowy gull dive down and peck at the foam, rise up with a wriggling fish in its beak. It climbed high in the sky, became a speck of froth on crystal blue.

"I had funny dreams," I said. "I think I've had them all along, since I came here. But last night they were stronger than ever."

"Oh?"

"Thought I heard your voice speaking to someone. Thought I

heard steps on the stairs, or more like the plunking of peg legs, like those old sea captains have."

"You don't say?"

"And another voice, a child's."

"That right? Well . . . maybe you did hear me speakin'. I wasn't entirely straight with you last night. I do have quite an interest in the voice throwing, and I practice it from time to time on my dummy. Last night must have been louder than usual, being drunk and all."

"Dummy?"

"My old dummy from the act. Keep it in the room below."

"Could I see it?"

He grimaced. "Maybe another time. It's kind of a private thing with me. Only bring her out when we're alone."

"Her?"

"Right. Name's Caroline, a right smart-looking girl dummy, rosy cheeked with blonde pigtails."

"Well, maybe someday I can look at her."

"Maybe someday." He stood up, popped the contents of the pipe out over the railing, and started inside. Then he turned: "I talk too much. Pay no mind to an old, crazy man."

Then he was gone, and I was there with a hot cup of coffee, a bright, warm day, and an odd, unexplained chill at the base of my bones.

Two days later we got on witches again, and I guess it was my fault. We hit the brandy hard that night. I had sold a short story for a goodly sum—my largest check to date—and we were celebrating and talking and saying how my fame would be as high as the stars. We got pretty sicky there, and to hear Machen tell it, and to hear me agree—no matter he hadn't read the story—I was another Hemingway, Wolfe, and Fitzgerald all balled into one.

"If Marilyn were here," I said thoughtlessly, drunk, "why we could get her to consult her crystal and tell us my literary future."

"Why that's nonsense, she used no crystal."

"No crystal, broom, or pointed hat? No eerie evil deeds for her? A white magician no doubt?"

"Magic is magic, m'boy. And even good intentions can backfire."

"Whatever happened to her, Marilyn I mean?"

"Dead."

"Old age?"

"Died young and beautiful, m'boy. Grief killed her."

"I see," I said, as you'll do to show attentiveness.

Suddenly, it was as if the memories were a balloon overloaded with air, about to burst if pressure were not taken off. So, he let loose the pressure and began to talk.

"She took her a lover, Marilyn did. Taught him many a thing, about love, magic, what have you. Lost her husband on account of it, the magician, I mean. Lost respect for herself in time.

"You see, there was this little girl she had, by her lover. A fine-looking sprite, lived until she was three. Had no proper father. He had taken to the sea and had never much entertained the idea of marryin' Marilyn. Keep them stringing was his motto then, damn his eyes. So he left them to fend for themselves.

"What happened to the child?"

"She died. Some childhood disease."

"That's sad, I said, "a little girl gone and having only sipped at life."

"Gone? Oh no. There's the soul, you know."

I wasn't much of a believer in the soul and I said so.

"Oh, but there is a soul. The body perishes but the soul lives on."

"I've seen no evidence of it."

"But I have," Machen said solemnly. "Marilyn was determined that the girl would live on, if not in her own form, then in another."

"Hogwash!"

Machen looked at me sternly. "Maybe. You see, there is a part of witchcraft that deals with the soul, a part that believes the soul can be trapped and held, kept from escaping this earth and into the beyond. That's why a lot of natives are superstitious about having their picture taken. They believe once their image is captured, through magic, their soul can be contained.

"Voodoo works much the same. It's nothing but another form of witchcraft. Practitioners of that art believe their souls can be held to this earth by means of someone collecting nail parin's or hair from them while they're still alive.

"That's what Marilyn had in mind. When she saw the girl was fadin', she snipped one of the girl's long pigtails and kept it to herself. Cast spells on it while the child lay dyin', and again after life had left the child."

"The soul was supposed to be contained within the hair?"

"That's right. It can be restored, in a sense, to some other object through the hair. It's like those voodoo dolls. A bit of hair or nail parin' is collected from the person you want to control, or if not control, maintain the presence of their soul, and it's sewn into those dolls. That way, when the pins are stuck into the doll, the living suffer, and when they die their soul is trapped in the doll for all eternity, or rather as long as the doll with its hair or nail parin's exists."

"So she preserved the hair so she could make a doll and have the little girl live on, in a sense?"

"Something like that."

"Sounds crazy."

"I suppose."

"And what of the little girl's father?"

"Ah, that sonofabitch! He came home to find the little girl dead and buried and the mother mad. But there was that little gold lock of hair, and knowing Marilyn, he figured her intentions."

"Machen," I said slowly. "It was you, was it not? You were the father?"

"I was."

"I'm sorry."

"Don't be. We were both foolish. I was the more foolish. She left her husband for me and I cast her aside. Ignored my own child. I was the fool, a great fool."

"Do you really believe in that stuff about the soul? About the hair and what Marilyn was doing?"

"Better I didn't. A soul once lost from the body would best prefer to be departed I think . . . but love is sometimes a brutal thing."

We just sat there after that. We drank more. Machen smoked his pipe, and about an hour later we went to bed.

There were sounds again, gnawing at the edge of my sleep. The sounds that had always been there, but now, since we had talked of Marilyn, I was less able to drift off into blissful slumber. I kept thinking of those crazy things Machen had said. I remembered, too, those voices I had heard, and the fact that Machen was a ventriloquist, and perhaps, not altogether stable.

But those sounds.

I sat up and opened my eyes. They were coming from below. Voices. Machen's first. ". . . not be the death of you, girl, not at all . . . my only reminder of Marilyn . . ."

And then to my horror. "Let me be, Papa. Let it end." The last had been a little girl's voice, but the words had been bitter and wise beyond the youngness of tone.

I stepped out of bed and into my trousers, crept to the curtain, and looked on Machen's side.

Nothing, just a lonely cot. I wasn't dreaming. I had heard him all right, and the other voice . . . it had to be that Machen, grieved over what he had done in the past, over Marilyn's death, had taken to speaking to himself in the little girl's voice. All that stuff Marilyn had told him about the soul, it had gotten to him, cracked his stability.

I climbed down the cold metal stairs, listening. Below I heard the old, weathered door that led outside slam. Heard the thud of boots going down the outside steps.

I went back up, went to the windows, and pulling back the curtains section by section, finally saw the old man. He was carrying something wrapped in a black cloth and he had a shovel in his hand. I watched as, out there by the shore, he dug a shallow grave and placed the cloth-wrapped object within, placed a rock over it, and left it to the night and the incoming tide.

I pretended to be asleep when he returned, and later, when I felt certain he was well visited by Morpheus, I went downstairs and retrieved the shovel from the tool room. I went out to where I had seen him dig and went to work, first turning over the large stone and shoveling down into the pebbly dirt. Due to the freshness of the hole, it was easy digging.

I found the cloth and what was inside. It made me flinch at first, it looked so real. I thought it was a little rosy-cheeked girl buried alive, for it looked alive . . . but it was a dummy. A ventriloquist dummy. It had aged badly, as if water had gotten to it. In some ways it looked as if it were rotting from the inside out. My finger went easily and deeply into the wood of one of the legs.

Out of some odd curiosity, I reached up and pushed back the wooden eyelids. There were no wooden painted eyes, just darkness, empty sockets that uncomfortably reminded me of looking down into the black hollows of a human skull. And the hair. On one side of the head was a yellow pigtail, but where the other should have been was a bare spot, as if the hair had been ripped away from the wooden skull.

With a trembling hand I closed the lids down over those empty eyes, put the dirt back in place, the rock, and returned to bed. But I did not sleep well. I dreamed of a grown man talking to a wooden doll and using another voice to answer back, pretending that the doll lived and loved him too.

But the water had gotten to it, and the sight of those rotting legs had snapped him back to reality, dashed his insane hopes of containing a soul by magic, shocked him brutally from foolish dreams. Dead is dead.

The next day, Machen was silent and had little to say. I suspected the events of last night weighed on his mind. Our conversation must have returned to him this morning in sober memory, and he, somewhat embarrassed, was reluctant to recall it. He kept to himself down below in the locked room, and I busied myself with my work.

It was night when he came up, and there was a smug look about him, as if he had accomplished some great deed. We spoke a bit, but not of witches, of past times and the sea. Then he pulled back the curtains and looked at the moon rise above the water like a cold fish eye.

"Machen," I said, "maybe I shouldn't say anything, but if you should ever have something bothering you. If you should ever want to talk about it . . . Well, feel free to come to me."

He smiled at me. "Thank you. But any problem that might have been bothering me is . . . shall we say, all sewn up."

We said little more and soon went to bed.

I slept sounder that night, but again I was roused from my dreams by voices. Machen's voice again, and then the poor man speaking in that little child's voice.

"It's a fine home for you," Machen said in his own voice.

"I want no home," came the little girl's voice. "I want to be free."

"You want to stay with me, with the living. You're just not thinking. There's only darkness beyond the veil."

The voices were very clear and loud. I sat up in bed and strained my ears.

"It's where I belong," the little girl's voice again, but it spoke not in a little girl manner. There was only the tone.

"Things have been bad lately," Machen said. "And you're not yourself."

Laughter, horrible little girl laughter.

"I haven't been myself for years."

"Now Catherine . . . play your piano. You used to play it so well. Why, you haven't touched it in years."

"Play. Play. With these!"

"You're too loud."

"I don't care. Let him hear, let him . . ."

A door closed sharply and the sound died off to a mumble, a

word caught here and there was scattered and confused by the throb of the sea.

Next morning Machen had nothing for me, not even a smile from his borrowed collection. Nothing but coldness, his back, and a frown.

I saw little of him after coffee, and once, from below—for he stayed down there the whole day through—I thought I heard him cry in a loud voice, "Have it your way then," and then there was the sound of a slamming door and some other sort of commotion below.

After a while I looked out at the land and the sea, and down there, striding back and forth, hands behind his back, went Machen, like some great confused penguin contemplating the far shore.

I like to think there was something more than curiosity in what I did next. Like to think I was looking for the source of my friend's agony; looking for some way to help him find peace.

I went downstairs and pulled at the door he kept locked, hoping that, in his anguish, he had forgotten to lock it back. He had not forgotten.

I pressed my ear against the door and listened. Was that crying I heard?

No. I was being susceptible, caught up in Machen's fantasy. It was merely the wind whipping about the tower.

I went back upstairs, had coffee, and wrote not a line.

So day fell into night, and I could not sleep but finally got the strange business out of my mind by reading a novel. A rollicking good sea story of daring men and bloody battles, great ships clashing in a merciless sea.

And then, from his side of the curtain, I heard Machen creak off his cot and take to the stairs. One flight below was the door that led to the railing round about the tower, and I heard that open and close.

I rose, folded a small piece of paper into my book for a marker, and pulled back one of the window curtains. I walked around pulling curtains and looking until I could see him below.

He stood with his hands behind his back, looking out at the sea like a stern father keeping an eye on his children. Then, calmly, he mounted the railing and leaped out into the air.

I ran. Not that it mattered, but I ran, out to the railing . . .

and looked down. His body looked like a rag doll splayed on the rocks.

There was no question in my mind that he was dead, but slowly I wound my way down the steps . . . and was distracted by the room. The door stood wide open.

I don't know what compelled me to look in, but I was drawn to it. It was a small room with a desk and a lot of shelves filled with books, mostly occult and black magic. There were carpentry tools on the wall, and all manner of needles and devices that might be used by a tailor. The air was filled with an odd odor I could not place, and on Machen's desk, something that was definitely not tobacco smoldered away.

There was another room beyond the one in which I stood. The door to it was cracked open. I pushed it back and stepped inside. It was a little child's room filled thick with toys and such: jack-in-the-boxes, dolls, kid books, and a toy piano. All were covered in dust.

On the bed lay a teddy bear. It was ripped open and the stuffing was pulled out. There was one long strand of hair hanging out of that gutted belly, just one, as if it were the last morsel of a greater whole. It was the color of honey from a fresh-robbed hive. I knew what the smell in the ashtray was now.

I took the hair and put a match to it, just in case.

Red Light

A Ms. Tree Short Story
by Max Allan Collins

Max Allan Collins' Stolen Away *is one of this year's major crime novels, and one almost guaranteed to bring him the wide public he's long deserved. Collins works in a variety of forms, including short stories, of which he's quickly becoming a master. This is one of the few "Ms. Tree" tales written in prose. Artist Terry Beatty and Collins do "Ms. Tree" in graphic-novel form for DC Comics.*

First published in 1984

I was stopped at a light, on my way home from working late at the office, when the guy climbed in on the rider's side and pointed his gun at me.

It wasn't much of a gun, but then he wasn't much of a guy: He was chocolate-black and had Michael Jackson's curls and approximate weight and a similar plastic beauty. Only I didn't figure him for a rock star, or a Jehovah's Witness, either.

"You oughta keep your doors locked, babe," he said, flashing his caps. It was a dazzling smile, I had to give him that much; but it was a nervous smile. And there was blood spattered on his blue satin shirt and skinny white leather tie; also on one satin sleeve there was a tear, or rather a slash, just below the bicep, and a circle of red dampness grew around it. His white leather pants were spotless, however.

"Cut yourself shaving?" I asked.

His smile faded and only the nervousness remained. "You're a pretty cool customer, babe, that much I got to hand you."

"The meter's running," I said. "Where to?"

He was looking back over his shoulder. "Take a left when the light changes, then cut through the alley and double back to Wells."

Red turned to green, and I did what he said.

He smiled smugly as he continued looking back over his shoulder. "Think we lost 'em. Just keep driving. You know where the Skyview Hotel is?"

"Out by the airport?"

"You got it.

"That where we're going?"

"That's where we're goin', babe."

I got on the expressway; it was well after rush hour—lights blinked nervously in the night, though not as nervously as my passenger with the gun. For a skinny little man who obviously fancied himself cool, my main man here was a beat away from coming apart at the seams.

"How long have you been a pimp?" I asked him.

He shot me a narrow-eyed look that was at once angry and frightened. "Just drive, bitch," he said.

"Hey, and here I thought I was your 'babe.' "

He studied me; the gun in his hand—a nickel-plated .32 with a pearl-handle—studied me, too. "Ain't I seen you someplace before?"

"That's a pretty smooth line," I said, smiling over at him. "Is that how you reel in the little girls from Michigan when you pick 'em up at the bus station?"

"Shut-up," he said. There was almost a pout in his voice. He was beginning to think he'd climbed in the wrong car.

He was right.

"Anybody following us?" I asked.

He was looking behind him again. "Not that I can see. But step on it. Just don't attract any sirens."

I shrugged. "I go sixty-five along here all the time. Never been picked up yet."

"Do it, then!" He almost spit the words.

"Nice teeth you got there. How much they cost you?"

He put the gun in my neck. Leaned into me. He smelled good. "You're a nice-looking piece of work, but you got a smart-ass mouth. And I don't like that in my ladies."

"No offense. I'm just . . . nervous. It's not every day a guy jumps in my car and holds a gun on me."

"You ain't nervous enough, far as I'm concerned."

"We all show our nervousness in different ways, to different degrees. With me, it comes out in wisecracks. Now, you, you don't seem nervous at all."

That was a lie, of course, but it was also sort of a compliment. It isn't true that you can't bullshit a bullshitter, you know.

"But I wouldn't blame you if you *were* nervous," I said. "A situation like this, who wouldn't be?"

He let air out. Pulled the gun away from my neck. Slid back over by his window.

"Well, I'm not," he said, wincing as he flexed the bleeding arm. "Nervous."

"It's five minutes to the airport. Care if I smoke?"

"Light up. Die of cancer. See if I give a shit."

I punched in the lighter; a few seconds later it popped out of the dash. I pulled it out and pressed it to the hand holding the gun. Skin sizzled, he screamed, shot himself in the leg, and I slammed on the brakes.

The windshield didn't shatter, when his head slammed into it, but it made a lovely lace-like effect, as if the most artistic spider in the world had had a hand in it. And here my passenger had managed it all with a simple nod of the head.

I ended up my sliding skid along the roadside. Other cars glided by in the cool night, not noticing us, or not caring, as I hopped out and went around on the driver's side and pulled him out onto the shoulder. There was blood in his pretty curls, but he wasn't dead. I had my gloves on, so picking up the little gun he'd dropped in my car was no problem. I gave him a nudge or two with my foot and he rolled down the embankment into the ditch. Then I went back to the car, got my own gun out of my purse and went down to see how my main man was doing.

He was on his back, just beginning to rouse. He pushed up on one elbow, touched his bloody head, looked up groggily.

"Who . . . who the fuck are you, anyway?" he managed.

I removed the clip from his automatic; emptied the bullets in one cupped hand, tossed them into the night. Put the clip back, tossed it in his lap. Then I bent over and, holding my gun on him, edged a money clip from out of his tight white pants. I peeled off a hundred, tossed the clip back at him.

"That's for my windshield," I said. "And my name's Michael Tree."

"Oh, shit. . . ."

"You might've seen my picture in the paper. Every now and then I kill somebody I don't like."

"I didn't do anything to you . . ."

"Not enough to kill you over." I turned away. "I'll see you around."

From behind me his voice was a razor cutting the night.

"You're one cold bitch, ain't you?"

I didn't turn when I spoke. "That coming from a pimp I take as high praise indeed."

I started up the embankment.

A red Cadillac came careening up, and three women jumped out, almost simultaneously: a redhead, a blonde, a brunette. All of them had spandex pants on and various skimpy, spanglely tops. All of them wore expressions so intensely angry the make-up on their pretty faces was cracking.

The redhead had a knife in her hand and the blade was bloody.

"We saw him get in your car waving his gun," she said breathlessly. "Figured he made you drive him."

"You figured right," I said.

The brunette said, "We thought we lost you, but then we figured he might head back to the Skyview so we got on the expressway and . . ."

The redhead cut in, nodded toward my car. "What happened?"

"That's my line," I said.

"He killed Candy," the blonde said. She was maybe twenty and had a face harder than the gun in my hand.

"He said she was holding out on him," the brunette said, her mouth a thin red line, her eyes full of water, "and he shot her!"

The redhead said, "And I took this out of my bag and cut him! Then he ran . . ."

"Can't blame him," I said.

"Where is he?" the redhead with the knife demanded.

I pointed down the embankment. "Down there. Waiting for you."

And I drove off and left them to it.

Taking the Night Train

by Thomas F. Monteleone

Thomas Monteleone is writer, raconteur, editor, and (lately) publisher. But mostly, he's a writer. He's got this tight, paranoid city voice that makes him a direct descendant of Cornwell Woolrich. I think he's got a major crime novel in him and I hope he soon makes the shift over from horror. In the meantime, he's writing literally dozens of tales as dazzling as this one.

First published in 1981

It was after 3:00 A.M. when Ralphie Loggins scuttled down the stairs, into the cold sterility of his special world.

Holding the railing carefully so that he would not slip, as the November night wind chased him, he entered the Times Square subway station. Ralphie always had to be watchful on steps because the elevated heel on his left shoe was constantly trying to trip him up. He fished a token from the pocket of his Navy pea jacket and dropped it into the turnstile, passing through and easing his way down the last set of stairs to the platform.

Ralphie walked with his special clump-click-slide to a supporting girder by the tracks and waited for the Broadway–Seventh Avenue local, noticing that he was not alone on the platform. There were few travelers on the subways in the middle of such winter nights, and he could feel the fear and paranoia hanging thickly in the air. Turning his head slowly to the left, Ralphie saw a short, gray man at the far end of the station. He wore a tattered, thin corduroy jacket insulated with crumpled sheets of the *Daily News.*

To Ralphie's right, he heard footsteps approaching.

Just as he turned to look, he felt something sharp threatening to penetrate his coat and ultimately his kidneys. At the limits of his peripheral vision he was aware of someone tall and dark-skinned looming over him, the stranger's breath heavy and warm on his neck.

"Okay, suckah!" came a harsh whisper, the words stinging Ralphie's ear. "You move and you *dead!* Dig?"

Ralphie nodded, relaxing inwardly since he knew what would come next. When he did not move, the man pressed his knife blade a little more firmly into the fabric of the coat, held it there.

"Now, real easy like . . . get out your bread, and give it up. . . ."

Ralphie slipped his left hand into his back pocket, pulling out his wallet, and passed it back over his shoulder to the mugger. It was snatched away and rifled cleanly and quickly. The tip of the blade retreated, as did the tall, dark presence of the thief. His footsteps described his flight from the station, and Ralphie was alone again. He looked to the end of the platform where the gray old man still stood in a senile, shivering daze.

A growing sense of loss and anger swelled in Ralphie. He felt violated, defiled, *hurt* in some deeply psychic manner. The mugger had reinforced his views of life in the city and all the dead hours within it. A silence pervaded the station, punctuated by a special kind of sadness and futility. Stifling his anger and his pain, Ralphie smiled ironically—it was most fitting that he be robbed in the subway, he thought.

Time seemed to lose its way beneath the streets of Manhattan, flowing at a rate completely its own, and it seemed to Ralphie that there might be a reason for it. He felt that there was some-thing essentially *wrong* about the subways. As though man had somehow violated the earth by cutting these filthy pathways through her, and that the earth had reacted violently to it. Ralphie believed this, because there was a feeling of evil, of fear, and of something lurking beneath the depths of the city that *everyone* felt in the subways. Ralphie knew that others had sensed it, felt it, as they descended into the cold, tomblike stations.

His thoughts were shattered by the approaching roar of the train. A gust of warmer air was pushed into the station as the local surged out of the tunnel, jerked to a halt, opened its doors. The old man shuffled into a distant car; Ralphie entered the one closest to him. As he sat on the smooth plastic seat, the doors sighed shut, and the train rattled off into the darkness, under the belly of the beast, the city. The only other passenger in Ralphie's car, an old woman in a ragged coat, a pair of stuffed shopping bags by her high-topped shoes, looked at him with yellow eyes. Her face was a roadmap of wrinkles, her lips so chapped and cracked they looked orange and festering.

Ralphie kept watching the old woman, wondering the usual thoughts about members of her legion. Where did she live? What did she carry in those mysterious bags? Where did she come from? Why was she out riding the night trains? The rocking motion of the cars was semi-hypnotic, soothing, and Ralphie felt himself unwinding from the tension of the robbery. He allowed himself to smile, knowing that the mugger had gotten nothing of value—his left pants pocket still held his money clip and bills, whereas the wallet had contained only some pictures, business cards, and his library card. He had not been counting the local's stops, but he had been riding the train for so many years that he had an instinctive feeling for when his station would be coming up. It was not until the train reached Christopher Street–Sheridan Square that Ralphie began staring through the dirty glass into the hurtling darkness. Houston Street would be next.

Then it happened.

The lights in the car flickered and the motion of the car slowed. The old shopping-bag lady seemed to be as still as a statue, and even the sound of the wheels clattering on the tracks seemed softer, *slower*. The warm air in the car became thicker, heavier, and Ralphie felt it was becoming difficult to breathe. He stood up, and it felt as if he were underwater, as though something were restraining him. Something was *wrong*. The train seemed to be slowing down, and he looked out the windows, past the reflection of the interior lights, to see something for the briefest of moments—a platform, a station with no sign, no passengers, only a single overhead bulb illuminating the cold beige tiles of its walls.

For a second, Ralphie imagined the train was trying to stop at the strange station, or that something was trying to stop the train. There was a confluence of forces at work, and time itself had seemed to slow, and stretch, while the train struggled past the place. Then it was gone, replaced by the darkness, and the train was gathering speed, regaining its place in the time flow.

The air thinned out, the old lady moved her head, gripped her bags more tightly, and Ralphie could move without interference.

The train was loud and full of energy once again. Ralphie felt a shudder pass through him. It was as though something back there had been reaching out, grasping for the train, and just barely failing. The image persisted and he could not stop thinking about it. He knew that the image of the stark, pale platform and the single naked bulb would prey upon him like a bad dream. He knew he had passed a place that no one ever saw, that no one even knew existed; yet he had *seen* it, felt its power. . . .

The local lurched to a halt, its doors slamming open. Ralphie looked up and saw the Houston Street sign embedded in the wall tiles. Jumping from the car, he hobbled across the deserted platform, wedged through the turnstile, and pulled himself up the steps. The cold darkness of the street embraced him as he reached the sidewalk, and he pulled his collar tightly about his neck. The street was littered with the remnants of people's lives as he threaded his way past the overturned trash cans, discarded toys, heaps of eviction furniture, stripped cars, and empty wine bottles. This was the shabby reality of his neighborhood, the empty shell that surrounded his life. He walked to the next corner, turned left, and came to a cellarway beneath a shoe repair shop. Hobbling down the steps, he took out his key and unlocked the door to his one-room apartment. He flipped on the light switch and a single lamp illuminated the gray, tired room. Ralphie hated the place, but knew that he would never escape its prison-cell confines. Throwing his coat over a straight-backed chair, he walked to a small sink and medicine chest, which had been wedged into the corner of the room. His hands were trembling as he washed warm water over them, chasing the stinging cold from his bones. In the spotted mirror he saw an old face, etched with the lines of defeat and loneliness. Only thirty-one and looking ten years older, his sandy hair was getting gray on the edges, his blue eyes doing the same. He tried to smile ironically, but could not manage it. There was little joy left in him, and he knew it would be better to simply crawl beneath his quilt on the mildewed couch and sleep.

That night he dreamed of subway trains.

It was late in the afternoon before he awakened, feeling oddly unrefreshed. He could not forget the baleful image of the empty station, and he decided that he would have to investigate the place. When he took a train up to midtown, he asked the trainman about it. The IRT employee said he had never heard of that particular platform, but that there were countless places like that beneath the city: maintenance bays, abandoned stations, old tunnels that had been sealed off. Somebody must have left a light on, that's why Ralphie had seen it at all. The trainman seemed unimpressed, but Ralphie had not told him how he had felt something reaching out from that place, trying to take hold of the train. . . .

After having coffee in a small shop off Fifty-second Street, Ralphie walked the streets aimlessly. He knew that he should go to the public library and get a new card, but he felt too restless today. His mind was too agitated to read, even though it was one of his only pleasures. When he had been a child, living with his uncle, the old man had taught him the wonders of books, and Ralphie had educated himself in his uncle's library. When the old man died without a will or an heir, Ralphie was turned out on the street, a victim of New York State Probate Court at the age of seventeen, with nothing. A string of odd jobs leading nowhere, combined with his crippled leg, had beaten him down until he didn't seem to care anymore. He identified with the desperation of characters from Dostoevski and Gogol, the self-inflicted terror and pain of characters from Hawthorne and Poe. The world had been different when those writers had lived, he often thought, and people knew how to *feel,* and think, and *care.* In the city, Ralphie wondered if people even cared about themselves anymore.

Evening crept into the streets, and Ralphie worked his way toward Times Square, watching the faces of those he passed on the crowded sidewalks. Some said that it was an unwritten law that you did not look at anyone you passed in the city, but Ralphie knew that was untrue. *Everyone* looked at everyone else. Only they did it furtively, secretly, stealing glances at one another like thieves. They walked behind masks of indifference, like Gogol's "dead souls," playing the parts assigned them in the mindless dollhouse of the city. It was like a disease, thought Ralphie, which had infected us all.

Down Broadway, he turned left at Forty-second Street, already ablaze with the flashing lights and colors of the theaters and porn shops. The crowds of tourists and theatergoers mingled with the panhandlers, the hustlers, and the legions of blacks and Puerto Ricans carrying suitcase-sized radios at full volume. Dealers hung in doorways or strutted and leered at passersby. The sidewalks were speckled with trash and dark wet patches that could be any number of things. In the middle of the block, Ralphie entered the glass, satin-lined doors of the Honey Pot, to be swallowed up in the sweaty darkness and loud music of the bar. The lyrics of a song pounded at him, and he listened to the words without wanting to:

> *I want to grab your thighs . . .*
> *I want to hear your sighs . . .*
> *M-m-m-make luuuuuv to you! . . .*

Ralphie shook his head sadly to himself, took off his coat, and walked past the bar, which was already half-filled with patrons. Behind the bar was a light-studded runway, backed by a floor-to-ceiling mirror, where the girls could watch themselves while they danced. Brandy was strutting back and forth across the runway, wearing only a pair of spike heels and a silver-sequined G-string. She was short and lithe, with stringy dark hair, boyish hips, and pendulous, stretch-marked breasts that seemed absurdly large for her small frame. She half walked, half pranced to the beat of the music, causing her breasts to bounce and loll in what to Ralphie was a most unerotic manner. Once in a while she would smile at the patrons, or lick her lips and pout, but it was an empty, hollow gesture. Ralphie had seen all the girls pretending to like the customers and he hated the whole game, hated that they were trapped in it, as was he. Empty exchanges, devalued emotions, flensed of meaning and feeling.

When he reached the end of the bar, his boss, Mr. Maurice, spotted him. "Hey, Ralphie boy! You're early tonight. . . ."

"Hello, Mr. Maurice. You want me to start anyway?"

Maurice, a broad-shouldered, overweight, and balding man, smiled and shook his head. "Naw, there ain't nothin' out there yet. Go on in the back and get a coffee. I'll call ya when I need ya."

He dismissed Ralphie with a turn of the head, resuming his conversation with one of the new dancers, who was sitting on a barstool by her boss, clothed only in a bra and panties.

"Okay," said Ralphie, walking into the darkness beyond the bar, and through a door to the girls' "dressing" rooms, to a small alcove where a coffee maker and Styrofoam cups could be found. As he poured the black liquid into his cup, someone entered behind him. Turning, he saw it was Brandy, completely nude, going to the dressing room.

"Hi, Brandy. . . . How are you?"

The girl looked at him and smiled, but said nothing, then disappeared behind the door. She treated him as all the girls did

—like a mascot or a pet dog. Funny, he thought, but he had never grown accustomed to the way people treated him. Just because he was a short, dough-faced cripple didn't mean that he had less of a need for warmth and a little caring. . . . Ralphie shook his head slowly, embarrassed that he could indulge so easily in self-pity. He walked from the back room to one of the vacant tables farthest away from the bar, sat down, and sipped his coffee. A half hour passed under the haze of cigarette smoke and the sheets of loud music as Ralphie ignored the laughter and the whistles from the bar patrons. His thoughts kept returning to the Broadway local, and that abandoned station—there was something about the place that would not leave him. It was as though there were something down there, waiting. Waiting for him, perhaps. . . . He knew it was a crazy thought, but it felt so strong in him that he could not get rid of the idea. He had *felt* something, damn it, and he had to know what it had been.

Maurice appeared by his shoulder, slapping him in mock friendliness. "S'after eight . . . ya better get out there and bring in some rubes, huh? Whaddaya say, Ralphie boy?" Another slap on the arm.

"Yeah, okay, Mr. Maurice." He stood up from the table and pulled on his coat, wrapped his scarf about his neck. Ralphie hated his job, but it was by far the best-paying gig he'd ever had. If he didn't need the money so badly, he would have quit long ago.

Walking past the bar, he saw that Chrissie was dancing now. She had long legs which seemed too thin when she wore a dress, but looked all right when she was nude. Her face was long and thin, making her eyes look large and forlorn. She was not what you would call pretty, but she had, as Maurice phrased it, "a big rack," and that was what the guys liked.

He pushed through the glass doors and felt the wind sting his face, the brilliance of the lights cut his eyes. Even in the cold November night, there were thousands of people, mostly men, out looking for warmth—or whatever could be passed off as the same. Ralphie held open the door to the Honey Pot and began his spiel, the words so automatic that he never thought of them anymore: "All right, fellas! No cover, no minimum! Take a peek inside! We got the best show in town! Young girls for *you!* All nude, and that means *na*ked!"

He would pause for a moment, and then repeat his message to the ever-changing surge of topcoated bodies. Sometimes he would stare into the men's faces, especially the ones who listened to his patter, the ones who slipped through the open door with heads bowed as if entering a church. He always saw the same things in their eyes. Our eyes betray us always, he thought, and he saw in their expressions a searching for something, for something lost and becoming unrecognizable. He also saw sadness. Sadness and shame.

On and on, he repeated his litany of the flesh, until the night had whipped past him and the traffic thinned out, the pedestrians disappearing. Maurice came up behind him and tapped his shoulder. "Okay, Ralphie. Nice job, let's pack it in, baby."

He entered the bar, walked past the hunched row of men. They were the hangers-on, the ones who closed the bars, the loneliest of the lonely. This last crowd watched Jessie work through her final number, wearing only a pair of gold-glitter platform heels as she swished her hips and played with her blond pubic hair. She had an attractive face, but it was flawed by her empty-eyed stare, her artlessly constructed smile.

Ralphie sat at the back table after getting a cup of coffee from the back room. As he used its heat to warm his hands before sipping it, more thoughts of the Broadway local ripped through his mind, and he feared that he was becoming obsessed with it. There were whispers and giggles behind him as the girls were emerging from the dressing room, putting on their coats, and preparing to leave. They filed past him, ignoring him as they always did, but this night the gesture seemed to eat at him more than usual. He knew that he should have become accustomed to the treatment, but he never did. The strange thing about it was that for the first time he felt himself disliking them, almost hating them for their lack of compassion, of simple, honest feeling. And that scared him.

Finishing his coffee, he left the bar, not saying good night to anyone, and no one seeming to notice his departure. Out in the Broadway night, fleets of cabs battled for one last fare, and the fringe people of the dark hours huddled in doorways and on street corners. Ralphie descended into the Times Square station, dropped a token through the stile, and held the railing as he went down to the platform. He was thinking that he should quit the Honey Pot, knowing that he had hung on there so long only because it was easier than looking for something better, or even taking courses during the day so that he could be qualified for something with more of a future. But that would mean getting out and interacting with the people of the day, and that might mean more pain and indignation. At least the people of the night considered him almost invisible, and did not actively hurt him. But they *did* hurt him, he thought, only to a lesser degree. To everyone, Ralphie was a loser, a hunched-up, bummy-looking clubfoot. He was one of the semi-human things that inhabited the shadowy parts of all cities, one who did not think or feel, but only slinked and scrabbled and hustled for an empty existence.

He would show them someday how wrong they were, he thought.

A rattling roar filled the station as the local rumbled to a stop. The train was a sooty, speckled nightmare covered with spray-paint graffiti—an old, dying beast. Its doors opened and Ralphie stepped inside, moving to a hideously colored turquoise seat. The air in the car was heavy with the smell of cheap wine and vomit, but the only other passenger, a dozing, fur-coated pimp in a droopy-brimmed hat, did not seem to notice. Ralphie took a seat near the doors and stared at his reflection in the smeared glass window across the aisle.

Penn Station. Twenty-eighth Street. Twenty-third. The night train hurtled down the tunnel, and Ralphie felt his pulse quickening. Would it happen again? Would he see that station with no name? The questions dominated his thoughts. Eighteenth Street. Then Fourteenth. Sheridan Square was next, and the train seemed to be going slower already. He hoped that it was not just his imagination.

When the train stopped at the Square, several passengers boarded. Two were teenaged girls wearing almost identical suede jackets with fur collars and Calvin Klein jeans with butterflies embroidered down the legs. Rich girls out slumming, thought Ralphie, as one of them looked into his eyes and smiled. He felt something stir in his heart, and smiled back at the pretty young girl.

"You're kind of cute," said the girl. "Come here often?"

Ralphie couldn't believe what she said. He could only stare for a moment. "What?" he asked dumbly.

The girl giggled and nudged her friend, who looked at Ralphie, then whispered loudly to the first girl, "Hey, watch it, you're getting Quasimodo excited!"

They both laughed, and Ralphie looked away, feeling something shatter inside, breaking and turning to dust. The train was moving again, and he wanted to ask them why they had acted that way, but his thoughts were racing ahead as he sensed the train approaching that secret place once again. There was something new smoldering in his heart; it was a new feeling, still unrecognized. He looked past the reflections in the glass into the rumbling darkness, and suddenly it was happening again.

He felt a *slowness* come over him, and he looked to the other passengers, the pimp and the two girls. Why didn't *they* feel it too!? He could feel the train itself struggling to get past that place, that station with no name. Watching and waiting, Ralphie sensed something tugging at the fibers of time itself. There came a flicker of light beyond the car and, for an instant, an illuminated rectangle. The image burned into his mind: the single bulb, the cold yellow tiles, the empty platform.

And then it was gone.

The train seemed to be regaining its speed, the sound of the girls giggling and the wheels clacking. How could they not have *seen* it? *Felt* it? He stood up, grabbing the center pole as his vision fogged for a moment, and he fought the sensation that he was going to black out. He swayed drunkenly, fighting it, still looking out the windows. Then the train was jerking to a halt, its doors opening at Houston Street.

Forcing his legs to move, Ralphie limped from the car and stood on the concrete platform, rubbing his forehead. The vertigo had passed and the cooler air of the station seemed to help. The doors whooshed shut, and the local clattered from the station, leaving him alone, staring down the black shaft from which he had just come. It was so close, he thought. It could not be far from where he now stood. . . .

There would be no trains for fifteen minutes. He had the time. He was alone in the station, and no one saw him ease off the platform and slip down to the tracks. The electrified rail was across the roadbed and he could easily avoid it, but ahead of him the black tunnel hung open like a mouth waiting to devour him. Driven by the need to find the abandoned station, he walked forward into the darkness, trying not to think of what it would be like if a train rushed him ahead of schedule.

The tracks curved to the left and soon the lights from the Houston Street station were completely obscured and Ralphie was moving in total darkness. There was not even the dim eye of a signal semaphore to give him direction, and he felt his stomach tightening as he moved clumsily, keeping his left hand in touch with the cold, slightly moist, slightly slimy wall of the tunnel. He lost all sense of time, becoming engrossed with the darkness, the uneven roadbed, and the dead touch of the wall. He felt more terribly alone than he had in his entire life, and he knew in his gut that he was walking to a place where no man had ever walked before.

Something was taking shape ahead of him, rimmed by faint light: he saw that it was the outline of a support girder along the wall. Another came into view, and then another. With each step the light grew stronger, and he could see the shine of the rails ahead of him. The wall curved to the left again, and he was upon the place: a rectangle of light suspended in the darkness. It looked unreal, like a stage devoid of props and actors.

He pressed forward and pulled himself up over the edge of the platform, instantly aware of a *coldness* about the place which transcended temperature. It was a chilling sense of timelessness that touched his mind rather than his flesh. Looking about, Ralphie saw that the platform was not deep, nor were there any exit stairs. Only a seamless wall of cold tiles trailing off into the shadows beyond the perimeters of light from the solitary bulb.

He knew that it was into the shadows he must walk, and as he did so, he became more acutely aware of the silence of the place. The mechanical clop of his elevated heel seemed so loud, so obscenely loud. He should have felt fear in this place, but it was replaced by a stronger emotion, a *need* to know this place for whatever it was. Then there was something touching his face. Out of the shadows it languished and played about his cheek like fog. It became a cold, heavy mist that swirled and churned with a glowing energy of its own, and it became brighter the deeper he probed it. He could sense a barrier ahead of him, but not anything that would stop him, but rather a portal through which he must pass.

He stepped forward . . .

. . . to find himself standing upon a narrow, rocky ledge, which wound across the sheer face of a great cavern. Above him, like the vault of a cathedral, the ceiling arched, defined by the phosphorescent glow of mineral veins. To his right a sheer cliff dropped off into utter darkness; to his left was a perfectly vertical wall. Ralphie followed the narrow winding path, each step bringing him closer to an eerie sound. At first it was like a gently rising wind, whispering, then murmuring, finally screaming through the cavern. An uncontrollable, eternal wailing.

Ralphie recognized the sound—it was the sound of utter loneliness. It was a sound made by something totally alien, and simultaneously all too human. It was a sound that, until now, he had heard only in the depths of his own mind. Such a primal, basic sound. . . . He became entranced by it, moving closer to its source, until he saw the thing.

The ledge had widened ahead of him, becoming a ridge that sloped gently upward to another sheer cliff face. Affixed to the face of the cliff, upon a jagged outcropping of rock, by great shining chains was the thing. Even from a distance it looked monstrously huge. Its arms and legs gave it a vaguely human form, but its true shape was amorphous, indistinct. There was a shimmering, almost slimy aspect to its body as it writhed and strained against the chains that bound it to the rock.

Moving closer, Ralphie now saw a bird thing perched upon a piece of the jagged rock, balancing and swaying, and batting the air with its leathery wings. It was skeletal, reptilian, its head hideously out of proportion to its thin body. All curved beak and yellow, moon-pool eyes.

The creature paid no attention to Ralphie's approach, continuing with its task in dead earnest—savagely tearing out the chained one's entrails. With each rooting thrust of the bird's beak, Ralphie heard the wailing fill the chamber louder than the last. One foul creature feeding upon the other. Ralphie watched the nightmare for a moment and knew it for what it was.

The thing on the rock must have perceived Ralphie's recognition, for it turned away from the cause of its agony long enough to look down at Ralphie with fierce white eyes. It regarded him with a coldness, a calmness, which seemed to say: *So you have come at last.* . . .

Ralphie looked into its eyes, human and yet inhuman, seeing the eons of suffering, millennia of pain and loneliness. And deep within the eyes he could also see the disillusionment, the brooding coals of hate and retribution waiting to be unleashed.

There was a sensation of betrayal which radiated from those monstrous eyes, and Ralphie could feel a bond with the tortured figure on the rock. Watching it, Ralphie saw it change. Less amorphous now, a head and face appeared vaguely. The emotions in its eyes seemed to alter.

When the bird swung its beak savagely into the thing's middle once again, it flinched, but there was no sound of pain this time, no agony in its eyes, which remained fixed upon Ralphie, as though speaking to him.

Set me free, said its eyes. *And I shall right the wrongs.*

Ralphie understood, nodding, almost smiling. Slowly he approached the bird on its perch, seeing that it was almost equal in size to him and could tear him to ribbons with razorlike talons. A man would normally fear this thing from the myth time, but Ralphie was beyond fear now. He had peered into the eyes of the thing on the rock, sharing the greatest pain, the hate, and the betrayal. Ralphie could feel these things pulsing out of the creature, especially the hate, which had been bubbling like lava for untold ages. It raged to be free upon the world that had twisted its gift, forgotten its sacrifice. It reached out and touched Ralphie, suffusing him with strength, and he stepped closer to the bird, his left foot sliding upon the cavern floor.

Hearing the sound, the bird paused, turning its skullish head, cocking it to the side, to regard the odd little creature that stood below it. As it watched, Ralphie bent to pick up a fist-sized rock. In one motion he stood and hurled it at its head, striking one of its great yellow eyes, puncturing it like the delicate yolk of an egg. The bird screamed as its empty socket oozed, then launched itself upward with a furious beating of its thick wings. It shrieked as it hovered for a moment above Ralphie, then it rose up into the darkness, leaving only the echo of its wings smacking the dead air.

Once again, Ralphie looked up to the figure on the rock, transfixed by its ravaged entrails and the stains on the stone below, where the excess of its torture had dripped for millennia. Stepping forward, he touched one of the chains; it was hot to his touch. There was a large pin holding the chain to a hasp cut into the rock, and Ralphie pulled upon it. He could hear a chinking sound as the chain fell free, and the great thing with the eyes that spoke to him surged against the remaining bonds. Its wailing had ceased, replaced by a gathering vortex of excitement and power. The sensation grew like an approaching storm, filling the cavern with a terrible static charge.

Ralphie reached up and loosed another pin; the chain fell away from the harnessed body as it moved against the last two restraints. It gave out a great cry—a cry born of eons of humiliation and defeat, but now almost free. The cavern walls shook from the power of the cry and the remaining chains exploded in a shower of metallic fragments. Ralphie backed away, for the first time awed by the power he had unleashed, seeing that its face had changed into something dark and nameless. For an instant, the thing's eyes touched him, and he felt immediately cold. Then there was an eruption of light and a clap of thunder. Ralphie fell backward as the great thing leaped from its prison rock, past him, and toward the exit from the depths.

Darkness and cold settled over Ralphie as he lay in the emptiness of the cavern. He knew where the thing would be going, and he knew what terrible lessons it would wreak upon the world, what payments would be exacted upon the dead souls. All the centuries of twisted vision would soon be put aright. His thoughts were coming slower and his limbs were becoming numb as he surrendered to the chilling darkness. He knew that he was going to fall asleep, despite the rumblings in the earth, despite the choirlike screams that were rising up from the city.

And when he awoke, he was not surprised to find himself upon a rock, bound by great chains of silver light, spread-eagled and suspended above the cavern floor. The air was filled with the smells of death and burning, of unrelenting pain, but he did not mind.

Out of the darkness, up from Gehenna, there came a deliberate flapping. It was the sound of wings, beating against the darkness, closer, and closer, until Ralphie could see the skull-like face, the beak, and the one good eye.

Stoner

by William F. Nolan

William F. Nolan has been writing since the fifties and getting better as he goes. He's probably most famous for the novel Logan's Run *but his stories, varied and pleasing as they are, are what I like best. He's one of those writers whose anthologies I keep close to hand for needed injections of inspiration and just pure pleasure.*

First published in 1988

The thing is, thought Stoner, I shouldn't have gone into this lousy wax museum, that's for damsure. Plenty to see here in Frisco without me buying a ticket and going into this frigging museum of corpses.

I mean, said Stoner to Stoner, that's what they *look* like, right? Like dead people standing there staring at you with those glassy dead eyes of theirs.

It was a rainy Tuesday, late in the afternoon, and Stoner was alone in the place. The heavy-lidded ticket-taker hardly blinked when he took Stoner's money. Looked like a big fat frog to Stoner. Ought to be out on some pond sitting on a lily pod or whatever the hell frogs sat on in ponds.

Stoner was crazy and it bothered him, being crazy, but then a lot of things about Stoner bothered Stoner. Always had, ever since he'd been a kid. Fought with himself a lot.

When he was walking along the street Stoner would argue violently with himself in a loud voice. Some people would turn and look at him but most people ignored Stoner. Most of his life, except when he did really crazy things, Stoner had been ignored. Stoner was used to people moving away from him when he walked toward them while he was scowling and swearing at Stoner.

Stoner didn't like dead people. They reminded him he'd maybe be dead someday and Stoner hated the whole idea of being dead. He swore to himself he wouldn't be. I'll never be dead, said Stoner, and that's for damsure.

The museum entrance was at the bottom of a long flight of stairs and Stoner smelled the rubber matting on the stairs. It smelled like ether in a hospital. Or in a morgue.

The guard who was supposed to watch people in the museum was snoozing on his high wooden stool, tipped back against the puke-colored wall at the foot of the stairs. Maybe he was dead, too. Frigging dead guard!

"How are things?" a voice asked him as Stoner walked into the museum. It was Stoner's voice.

"Not so damn good," said Stoner.

"You should maybe have killed that guy today, the one who gave you the ride up from San Diego," said Stoner. "He probably had some cash on him and a watch or a ring you could've hocked."

"I don't kill people," said Stoner. "You're nuts."

"Hey, we're both nuts," said Stoner. "So what else is new?"

"Why don't you just shut yer gob?" asked Stoner. "Give me some frigging peace."

"Smoke?" And a dark hand, very tan with a lot of hair at the wrist, held out a cigarette. The hand looked like Stoner's. Sometimes, though, it was hard to tell.

"Obliged," said Stoner, taking the cigarette. The hand lit it. Stoner inhaled deeply.

"Sign says no smoking in here," said Stoner.

"Frig the sign."

Stoner was walking along a kind of aisle with ropes at both sides. Old velvet ropes smelling of dead cats. Behind the ropes were the wax people, staring out at Stoner.

He walked up to a buxom young woman. Redhead. She had on one of those long, flouncy *Gone With the Wind* kind of dresses, with a low-cut front. Stoner liked the low-cut front. He put his hand inside the dress.

"Sign says don't touch them," said Stoner.

"So what? So who's to see what I do in here? We're all alone, right?"

"Yeah, I guess so."

Stoner kept walking. He stopped in front of a bearded guy in a tall stovepipe hat who was standing with his hand on the shoulder of a little black kid in tattered overalls and a checkered shirt. He was Abe Lincoln, the guy with the beard.

Stoner reached across the rope and knocked his hat off.

"Why'd you do that?" asked Stoner.

" 'Cuz I think it's a friggin' dumb hat is all," said Stoner.

"I wouldn't have done it," said Stoner. "You got no respect for the President."

"I got no respect for nobody," said Stoner.

Stoner kept going and turned a corner into another room. This one spooked Stoner. It was a room where the French Revolution cut people's heads off. There was a young girl with her hands tied behind her kneeling at the guillotine with her head already off and in a basket.

Stoner reached in and picked up the head.

"I wouldn't do that," said Stoner.

Stoner didn't answer. He tossed the girl's severed head into the air and caught it by its long golden hair. Then he put the head inside his shirt. It made him look pregnant.

"They'll never let you take that out of the museum," said Stoner.

"Frig what they won't let me do."

And he walked into a room full of pirates who were in the middle of a big fight on the deck of a ship. There was a painted ocean around the deck with the paint peeling off the waves.

Stoner stepped over the rope and went up to one of the fighting pirates with a patch over his eye and took the guy's sword.

"It's probably fake," said Stoner.

It wasn't.

It was real. And it was sharp. He cut the pirate's head off with it.

"Fake, my ass," said Stoner.

"You're acting crazy again."

"That's what crazy people do, right? Act crazy?"

And Stoner snorted out a laugh. Sometimes he got a laugh out of things.

He walked through the museum, cutting off heads. Every wax figure he came to he cut the head off. Zip-zap. Zip-zap. Zip-zap.

Stoner was having fun. Maybe coming here into this museum wasn't such a lousy idea after all.

Which was when the guard showed up. The one who'd been snoozing at the bottom of the stairs.

"What the hell's goin' on?" he yelled at Stoner.

"I'm cutting off heads," said Stoner.

"You're under arrest, man," said the guard, reaching for the bright gun at his belt.

"Frig you!" said Stoner. And cut off his head. Zip-zap.

"I thought you said you don't kill people," said Stoner.

"Up to now, I didn't," Stoner replied. "But he was going to arrest me and put me in a cell and you *know* how much we hate being put in cells."

"Yeah," nodded Stoner.

"Boy, oh, boy," said Stoner, sitting on the floor. "I probably made a big mistake cutting off this guy's head." He put down the sword and lit another cigarette. The smoke made his mother's face in the air. He didn't like that.

"What you gonna do now?" asked Stoner.

"I have to think. To plan and figure and work things out."

"Hey, you!" It was the froggy ticket-taker and he was walking down the aisle toward Stoner. "Closin' time," he said. "We're closin' up."

When he got to Stoner he stopped and looked down at the dead guard and then he looked at Stoner.

"Jeez," the ticket-taker said softly. And he began to back away, his face all green. Stoner had to laugh, because now he really *did* look like a frog.

"Where you going off to?" asked Stoner.

But the froggy little man didn't answer. He turned to run.

Stoner finished him.

Zip-zap.

"Okay, boy, you've had it now," said Stoner. "The cops will come and put you in the gas chamber or hang you or put you in the electric chair or inject you with some kind of killer drug."

"I don't think so," said Stoner.

"You gonna plead self-defense?" And Stoner chuckled.

"I'm insane, right? Just like you are. Insane people do insane things. That's logic."

Stoner shook his head. "You never should of bought a ticket to a place like this," he said.

"I won't argue with you on that one," nodded Stoner. "I guess I really screwed up, buying a ticket to this lousy place."

He took the girl's head out of his shirt and looked at it. She was very pretty. He smoothed the long blonde hair and put the head down, gently, next to the dead guard's head.

Then he walked back to the French Revolution room and

stopped in front of the guillotine. He looked up at the suspended blade. A release cord was hanging down from it.

Stoner pushed aside the body of the girl with her hands tied and took her place, kneeling down to put his neck into the wooden groove underneath the blade. Then he jerked the cord.

"It's probably fake," said Stoner.

It wasn't.

Introduction to
Anatomy of
a Killer

by Ed Gorman and Bill Crider

Peter Rabe was a major figure in the Gold Medal movement of the fifties. At his recent death, Mystery Scene *magazine ran the following tributes.*

I n the spring, he would come to Cedar Rapids on a train from California. He would stay for three or four days and then he'd head east.

I'm not sure how long we planned this trip. Two years maybe. He talked about it long before he got sick; and with a certain sad desperation once he knew he had lung cancer.

Peter Rabe is not much remembered now, not in America anyway. In Europe he's still regarded as one of the seminal crime writers of his generation, and deservedly so. Along with John D. MacDonald and Charles Williams, he was one of Gold Medal's Holy Trinity. When he was rolling, crime fiction just didn't get much better.

He was equally good as a friend, shy, wry and always just a bit mysterious. I didn't know much about his background until after he died—Russian Jewish father; German mother; raised in both Europe and the United States—or even about his publishing history. He was that most remarkable of creatures, a good listener. He took pains to understand what you were talking about

—the nuances, the implications—and then he would give you his somewhat halting but always considered (and considerate) opinion. He almost never laughed but when he did, you felt as if you'd just won over the toughest room you'd ever played.

The night he got copies of his Black Lizard reprints, he called me. He took an almost child-like pride in seeing three of his best books in print once more, even though he spent most of his time telling you how much he wished he could rewrite them. At one point that evening, I told him how much he meant to my generation of crime writers and for the first time ever, I heard tears in his voice.

He died quickly. I hadn't spoken to him for a month and suddenly I learned that he was in the hospital; and then, American doctors giving up on him, he was on his way to a Laetrile clinic in Mexico. We talked several times; he was optimistic; and in fact Mexico seemed to cheer him up. He sounded much better.

But not many days later, I phoned the California hospital where he now resided, and a nurse hesitated when I asked about his condition and said I'd have to speak to another department, and when she said, "Are you a relative of Mr. Rabe's?" I knew, of course, he was dead.

Goodbye, my friend. Your books stand as testimony to the sad and rueful way you saw life, and yet—like you—they shine with hard humor and forgiveness.

I drove pass the train depot the other night and imagined you stepping off an Amtrak at midnight, ghostly in the darkness.

I wish it could have been, Peter. I really do.

—Ed Gorman

Peter Rabe is dead. I suspect that the majority of *Mystery Scene* readers are asking themselves right now, "Who's Peter Rabe?" That's too bad.

Peter Rabe was a damned fine writer of paperback original fiction who began his career in the 1950s. He wrote mostly for Gold Medal, but he didn't have the success of a John D. MacDonald, whose books continue to sell in the millions, or even an Edward S. Aarons, whose Sam Durrell series was so popular that it was continued by another writer after his death. He never even achieved the sort of cult following attained by Jim Thompson. And that's a shame, because many of Rabe's novels rank with the best paperback originals ever published, back in the days when writers like MacDonald and Thompson and Charles Williams were all doing books better and more daring than anything the hardback houses were publishing then. Or now. This isn't to imply that Rabe was "like" any of those other writers. He was no more like them than they are like each other. He was an original.

Rabe wasn't a mystery writer, for the most part. He wrote crime stories that were tough, bitter, real, and powerful. What's more, he wrote them with economy, understatement, and cool precision. Anthony Boucher recognized Rabe's talent early and reviewed many of his books favorably in his "Criminals at Large" column. Gold Medal, publisher of most of Rabe's work, gave him a big push at the beginning and plugged his books hard. Yet with all these things going for them, Rabe's books never really took off. By the mid-sixties he was down to doing a spy-spoof series that ran for three books; in the early seventies, he did a couple of mafia books when GM was trying to capitalize on the success of *The Godfather* in any way that it could. Hardly anyone cared about or remembered the fine books that Rabe had been doing only ten years before, books like *The Box, Kill the Boss Good-by, Benny Muscles In,* or the books in the Daniel Port series.

When he was at his best, Rabe brought to his books an intensity that you could feel in your gut as you read, and he wrote stories that were unlike anything else on the racks. In *Kill the Boss Good-by,* for example, Fell, a crime boss is under treatment for a manic psychosis. He leaves the sanitarium in order to fight off a threat to his organization, and in the course of the book he degenerates into genuine madness—while retaining the sympathy of the reader. It's an incredible book. Pick it up, read the first couple of chapters, and then put it down. Just try. The ending is a kick in the kidneys. Power? Intensity? Rabe's got it all going here. Or read *The Box.* Hell, you won't be able to put this one down after the first page or two. It's the north African town of Okar, and a box is unloaded from a ship. The box stinks, and there are funny noises inside. Let the blurb writer take from there: "Out of the box comes Quinn, a screaming, filthy madman who'd been packed alive in his coffin as punishment for losing out in a gangland feud halfway around the world in New York." What happens after that? Read it and see.

Rabe could be funny, too. In fact, some of his toughest books have moments of off-the-wall humor that are doubly amusing because they're so unexpected. And *Murder Me for Nickels* is a crazy-funny mystery with a first-person narrator, so different from *The Box* that you'd think a different man wrote it, but it's equally fine in its own way.

Peter Rabe's writing career ended fifteen years ago, though

the sad fact is that it was effectively over ten or twelve years before that. The fact that for thirty-five years now Rabe's work has been shamefully neglected by readers and students of crime fiction is sadder still. And Peter Rabe's death in 1990 is a tremendous loss to all of us who cared about the man and his work and to those readers who will come to know that work in the future.
—Bill Crider

Anatomy of a Killer

by Peter Rabe

First published in 1960

Chapter 1

When he was done in the room he stepped away quickly because the other man was falling his way. He moved fast and well and when he was out in the corridor he pulled the door shut behind him. Sam Jordan's speed had nothing to do with haste but came from perfection.

The door went so far and then held back with a slight give. It did not close. On the floor, between the door and the frame, was the arm.

He relaxed immediately but his motion was interrupted because he had to turn toward the end of the hall. The old woman had not stepped all the way out of her room. She was stretching her neck past the door jamb and looking at him. "Did you hear a noise just now?"

"Yes." He walked toward her, which was natural, because the stair well was that way. "On the street," he said. "One of those hotrods."

"Did you just come from Mister Vendo's room?"

"Yes."

"Was he in? I mean, I wonder if he heard it."

"Yes. He's in, and he heard it."

Jordan walked by the old woman and started down the stairs. She shook her head and said, "That racket. They're just like wild animals, the way they're driving," and went back into her room.

He turned when her door shut and walked back down the hallway. This was necessary and therefore automatic. He did not feel like a wild animal. He did his job with all the job habits smooth. When he was back at the door he looked down at the arm, but then did nothing else. He stood with his hand on the door knob and did nothing.

He stood still and looked down at the fingernails and thought they were changing color. And the sleeve was too long at the wrist. He was not worried about the job being done, because it was done and he knew it. He felt the muscles around the mouth and then the rest of the face, stiff like bone. He did not want to touch the arm.

Somebody came up the stairs and whistled. Jordan listened to the steps and he listened to the melody. After he had not looked at the arm for a while, he kicked at it and it flayed out of the way. He closed the door without slamming it and walked away. A few hours later he got on the night train for the nine-hour trip back to New York.

There was a three-minute delay at the station, a matter of signals and switches. Jordan sat in a carriage close to the front and listened to the sharp knock of the diesels. There was a natural amount of caution and care in his manner of watching the platform, but for the rest he listened to the diesels. In a while the clacks all roared into each other and the train left.

Jordan never slept on a train. He did not like his jaw to sag down without knowing that it happened or to wake with the sweat of sleep on his face. He sat and folded his arms, crossed his legs. But the tedium of the long ride did not come. He felt the thick odor of clothes and felt the dim light in the carriage like a film over everything, but the nine-hour dullness he wanted did not come. I've got to unwind, he thought. This is like the shakes. After all this time with all the habits always more sure and perfect, this.

He sat still, so that nothing showed, but the irritation was eating at him. Everything should get better, doing it time after time, and not worse. Then it struck him that he had never before had to touch a man when the job was done. Naturally. Here was a good reason. He now knew this in his head but nothing else changed. The hook wasn't out and the night-ride dullness did not come. He set his tie closer and then worried it down again. This changed nothing. He saw himself in the black window, his face black and white and much sharper than any live face so that he looked away as if shocked because he did not recognize what he saw. The shock now was that this had happened. The thing with the arm had happened and he had never known that there was such a problem. Like a change, he thought. A small step-by-step or a slip-by-slip change following along all the time I was going, following like a shadow behind me. But it does not have my shape. The shock of seeing my shadow that does not have my shape . . .

He wiped his hands together but they were smooth and made no sound. He rubbed them on his pants, hard.

It was so bad now, he went over everything, the job, the parts of it, but there was nothing. All smooth with habit, or blind with it, he thought. So much so that only the first time, far back, seemed clear and real. Or as if it had been the best.

The small truck rode stiff on the springs and everything rattled. The older man drove and the younger one, behind in the dark, kept his hands tucked under his arms. The noise wouldn't be this hard a sound, thought Jordan, if it were not so early in the morning and if it were not so cold.

The truck turned through an empty crossing and went down an empty street.

Gray is empty, thought Jordan. He was thin and pale and felt like it.

"I'm coming up front," he said. "The draft is cutting right through me back here."

"What about the antenna? I don't want that antenna to be knocking around back there."

They had a spiky aerial lying in back and Jordan pushed it around, back and forth, so that it would lie steady without being held. The whitish aluminum felt glassy with cold. He crawled forward and sat next to the driver.

"How are you feeling?"

"Fine. Just cold."

"You should have worn more under those overalls. What you wearing under those overalls?"

"I'm dressed all right. I'm just cold."

"Jeesis Christ, Jordan, if you're dressed right . . ."

"My hands are cold. I can't have them get too cold."

The driver didn't say anything to that. He started to look at the younger man but didn't turn his head all the way. He caught the white skin on Jordan's nose and then looked straight ahead again. Why look at him?

"I just hope that antenna's all right back there. Is it jumping around there?"

"It's all right. The tool box is holding it."

"If that tool box starts moving though, I don't want none of them things on the antenna to get bent."

"It's all right."

The driver sucked on his teeth as if he were spitting inward. He looked straight and drove straight, sucking his teeth every so often. He would have liked it better if Jordan had talked back. But Jordan never did.

In a while the driver said, "I hope your hands are warm. We're here," and he rolled to a stop.

The driver got out toward the street and Jordan got out on the sidewalk. They closed their doors without slamming them, and Jordan looked down the length of the empty street, everything gray, except for the fire escapes which angled back and forth across the faces of all the apartment houses. The fire escapes were black and spidery, and the houses looked narrow and very busy with too many windows. But that didn't give life to the view either. It just made it look messy.

"You gonna give me a hand with this thing?" said the driver.

He had the back open and was edging the aerial out. The only thing that doesn't fit in all this, thought Jordan, is the sky. Everything's gray and the sky is blue. It's clean and far.

"You gonna . . ."

"You take the aerial," said Jordan. "You carry it and when you've got it out of the back, I take the tool box."

The driver didn't answer and they did it that way. They went into the third house looking like they belonged. They went up all the stairs, and then up the ladder which went from the landing to the roof. The driver climbed up first while the younger one held the prop antenna for him. When the driver pushed the trap door open the wind caught it and slammed it back on the roof. Jordan held a dead cigarette in his teeth and bit hard on the filter.

In a while the driver looked back through the sky door and said, "Okay down there?"

"Yes." Jordan looked up to where the driver's head was against the sky. "Is it very windy?"

"Some. Pass me up that aerial. But careful now, feller."

He got the aerial and then he helped lift the tool box through, because it was large and awkward. It was not very heavy.

They crossed the roof, which was quite blowy, and the driver had to hold the aerial with both hands. They crossed from one roof to the next, stepping over the little walls which showed where the next building started. Then came the high one and they had to climb iron steps. A draft blew down at them and they could smell warm soot.

When they were up on the building the wind leaped at them as if it had been waiting. All the aerials on the roof and the one which the driver was carrying were whistling a little. The roof looked like a set with a very strange forest, thin trees after something terrible had happened to them.

"There's too much wind," said Jordan. "Christ, that wind."

The driver didn't answer anything. They passed a pigeon coop which was built there on the roof, and now the driver let Jordan walk ahead of him. He saw him look at the pigeons. Jordan was moving his head back and forth. All the pigeons were bluish gray, except one, which was speckled. All the pigeons sat in neat, fluffy rows.

Jordan walked to the parapet and the driver saw how the wind pulled the coveralls around his legs. The driver looked at that and the way Jordan humped over a little, holding the box; and he thought—this hotshot, this expert with specialties, he doesn't look very impressive.

Jordan looked back and told the driver to stand away from the pigeon coop; he did not want the animals to start fluttering around. They should stay as they were, in their rows.

"I'm holding this aerial here and if I step over into the wind . . ."

"Get away from those pigeons because I want them quiet."

The driver moved. He watched Jordan kneel down by the parapet and said nothing. They feed 'em raw meat and pepper, he thought to himself, and this is how they turn out. The raw meat is all those dames, all those dames, and the pepper's the money. All that money. And this is how they turn out. Worried about pigeons.

But the driver was just a driver and understood very little of Jordan's work and what went into it.

Jordan opened the tool box and took out three parts. He snapped the barrel into the stock and he clicked the scope on the top of the barrel. Then he cowered at the rim of the roof and looked down into the empty street.

"Six forty-five," said the driver. He stood back on the roof and could not see the street. "Should be about now," he said.

Jordan did not answer.

"Anything yet?"

"Watch the roof," said Jordan. "Watch the roof and that door back there."

The driver did, but what he wanted to see was the street.

"You know it's that time now, and the only reason I'm talking—"

"Shut up."

It was the first job but Jordan already knew it would be better alone. No one along from now on. It was the first job, but already very private.

The driver heard the sound of a car and saw Jordan hunch and saw the rifle move up.

"Boy . . ." said the driver.

The wind leaned the aerial into his hand with a steady push and the aluminum felt glassy with cold. How does he do it, thought the driver. Hold still like that. I bet he was a monster when he was little. That's how he does it . . .

Jordan spat the cigarette out because the filter was coming apart in his mouth. And he could now get his head into a better position. He took a sighting, very fast, so the barrel wouldn't stick over the roof too long.

The cabby was getting out of his cab; he walked around the hood of the car, and went into the building.

Jordan pulled the gun back.

A good sighting. Fine scope. The double-winged door with the etched glass windows pointing up and the black line where the two wings of the door came together. The place that mattered. The hairline on the crack of the door.

For the briefest moment he felt that he would go out of his mind if he had to wait one instant longer because never again would any of this be so simple. Sight, aim, squeeze, check. How those pigeons stink. And the wind raising hell with the aim. Too much distance. It would have been better if they had told him to make a close play of it, planning it so he would be the cabby. But the distance was good. Everything small like a picture inside a scope and not quite real. And you simply sight, aim . . .

Sight now.

But let the cabby get by, let the cabby get by, for Godsake not the cabby. I don't know the cabby. Why squeeze on him . . . But the crappy thoughts that came. I don't know the other man either . . . Good, good, good. Where in hell was . . . Sight, aim . . . blink. The eyeball coming to a point. *Now* . . .

Big fat crack in the door. Sight, aim, *squeeze* . . .

Big fat crack out of the rifle, and *run*.

Not yet. Check it first.

Big fat blob rolling down the steps. Check it with the *scope*.

Tiny little hole in the forehead, and . . . gone. Making tendrils all over the forehead. And at this distance even the mess looks neat . . .

"Jordan . . ."

He looked back at the driver while he took the gun off the parapet. The driver stood in the wind and the antenna was weaving. He stands as if his pants were wet, thought Jordan.

"Okay?" said the driver. "Okay?"

"All done."

Click when the scope came off, click when the stock came off, other noises when the parts plunked into the box. That scope, he thought, won't be worth a damn after this.

Then they ran.

Which was just something in the muscles. Jordan felt the rush nowhere else, no excitement, and he thought, what did I leave out—what else was there?

When he ran past the pigeon coop the wildness stopped him. There were no more fluffy rows of pigeons, but now a mad and impotent beating around and a whirling around inside the wire-mesh coop and their eyes with the stiff bird stare, little bright stones which never moved with the whirl of fright around them. They beat and beat their wings with a whistling sound and with thuds when they hit.

Godalmighty if that wire-mesh breaks . . .

The driver was ahead and when he came to the end of the roof he looked back and saw Jordan standing.

"Come on!"

Sweat itched his skin on the outside and, looking back at Jordan, a sudden hate itched him on the inside. A little thing with a trigger, taking a minute, he thought, and this happens to him, the pale bastard. Standing there in a loving dream about pigeons, that they all should smash their heads on the wire, most likely. A little thing with a trigger and cracked crazy from it . . .

"Jordan. Come on!"

"Stop screaming," said Jordan. He left the coop and they went as planned.

"But if you're gonna . . ."

"Stop screaming. You feel the shakes coming on, hold them till later. Leave the antenna."

"I thought . . ."

"Leave it!"

The driver left it and turned to run.

"Wipe it!"

The driver wiped it. Then they left as planned.

Later Jordan watched himself, waiting for the shakes to catch up. But they never came. It's over, he thought, or it's piling up. Later he thought of the street, roof, scopesight, everything. The shakes never came. . . .

He sat in his seat and sat in his seat and blinked his eyes often because he did not want to go to sleep. I never sleep in a train and the job isn't over. When I get to New York it's over. Like always. Then I sleep. Look up Sandy? No, and why anyway . . . First I sleep, like always. It takes care of one or even two days. A big, thick sleep which always takes care of almost two days. . . .

Chapter 2

The patrolman always stood at the bar where it curved close to the door. He could turn his head and see a lot of the street or could turn the other way and look at the barmaid. There wasn't much to her or anything between them but the whole thing went with the uniform. The patrolman was young and got along well all around.

The place was chrome and plastic, which was uptown style, and in the window sat a pot with geraniums, because the bar was a neighborhood bar. The patrolman looked out on the street from where he was standing and said, "Here comes Sandy."

The barmaid looked at her watch; it said three o'clock. Sandy always came at three o'clock. He came through the door when the barmaid finished putting his beer on the back table.

Sandy was not blond. He had the name because it was simpler than his real one and sounded a little bit like it. The name was all right because it was friendly and quiet sounding. Sandy had very black hair and a very smooth chin. He wore a wide-shouldered overcoat of soft gray flannel. He wore this coat summer and winter. He had a hat on, dark blue, and he never took that off either.

The patrolman said, "Hi, Sandy," and Sandy said, "Hi, Bob."

"Hot even for August, isn't it?" said the patrolman.

"Yes. Hot." Sandy opened his overcoat and sighed.

"But good for business, huh? For indoor sports."

"I haven't noticed," said Sandy. "I don't think bowling is seasonal."

"I never thought of that," said the patrolman.

"Except for the air-conditioning bill," said Sandy. "I don't even like to think of that bill."

"I can imagine. Nine alleys is a big place to keep cool."

"Had your coffee yet?" Sandy asked.

Sandy asked this every day and the patrolman smiled and said the same thing he said every day. "No. I haven't," he said.

"Put Bob's coffee on my bill," Sandy told the barmaid, which also was part of this thing.

Then the two men nodded at each other and the patrolman watched Sandy go to his booth. He drank his coffee and thought that Sandy could not be too worried about his bowling alley or the air-conditioning bill in August. Sandy wears very nice clothes and has a beer every afternoon and never has troubles or raises his voice. Once Sandy looked up and the two men smiled at each other across the room. That's how the patrolman got along all around.

The phone rang at the other end of the bar and the waitress walked over to it. She went slowly because of the heat. She fluffed her blouse in front and did it a few more times when she got to the end of the bar and then picked up the phone. She put it up to her ear and then put it down on the bar. "For you, Sandy," she said, and walked back to the patrolman.

Sandy looked across at the girl but did not move. She said, "For you," again, and then Sandy got up and said, "Crap," but low so that nobody heard it. When he had picked up the phone he said, "Who is it?" and the voice answered, "Meyer."

"What're you calling here for?"

"Don't waste my time, huh?"

Sandy had his bowling alley on the east side of town, and Meyer had a restaurant an hour's drive north where the guests could look down at the Hudson. The two men rarely met because everything was well organized, and phone calls were even more rare. Meyer was the bigger of the two and sometimes he called.

"There's a man in from the Coast," he said. "With a message."

"Why call here? We got a regular way of . . ."

"He's new. His name is Turner, the new errand man, and I told him to meet you at the place where you are."

"That was smart. The way I run . . ."

"It's arranged. I'm just telling . . ."

"You keep interrupting me, dammit."

"You got nothing to say," Meyer told him. "And this is rush."

Sandy moved the phone to his other hand. Then he said, "With that much of a rush, let him handle it from the Coast. And if it's a heavy job, I don't know if I can furnish right now."

"Talk to Turner about it, will you?"

"Listen, Meyer. I don't run a store with shelf goods, you know that?"

"You run what's been set up. What's been set up is for us to furnish the service, anywhere, and stop thinking like a neighbourhood club."

Sandy looked across at the patrolman and the girl working the bar and while he did that Meyer hung up. Sandy hung up too, without any show at all, and went back to his seat.

"In the last booth," he heard the patrolman say. "The gentleman with the hat."

When Sandy looked up he saw the patrolman leave and saw a short man with a round belly come toward him. Turner was suffering from the heat and his suit hung in folds. He looked all folds, except for the belly which came out smooth like an egg.

"I'm Turner," he said. "I was told . . ."

"I know. Sit down."

Turner sat down and sighed.

"You want a beer?" Sandy asked him.

"Yes. I think a beer would be nice."

Turner slid his rear around on the seat and did not look at Sandy. He disliked this kind of booth. The circular table seemed to want to slice into his belly, and the seat was like a curve on a track and gave no feeling of comfort. Then came the beer and Turner watched the girl pour from the bottle. He watched her hand on the bottle, an uninteresting hand but something to look at for the moment.

"You water the geranium today?" Sandy asked the girl and she said, "Yes." And then, "Lou does, in the evening."

After she was gone Sandy waited a moment, waiting for Turner to talk, but Turner did not look up. He was moving his glass up and down on the table, making rings, and then he took a swallow of beer. Sandy did not want to wait any longer.

"So?"

"Yes. Well, we got this job."

"I know. What details?"

Turner picked his beer glass up again but then did not drink. He put it down again and said, "Do I tell you? What I mean is . . ."

"I'm not the headman," said Sandy, "if that's what you mean. But you talk to me."

"Yes. Well, you know I just run the errand."

"I know."

"What I mean is, you're not the one who does the job, are you?"

"No."

Turner looked at his glass again. There were little webs of foam all around the inside. "Do I talk to the man who does the job?" he asked at the glass.

"Just tell me about it, will you?"

Turner did not make clear to himself whether he wanted to see the man whom he would actually send out on this job, but instead stayed uneasy about all this which he blamed on the newness of his work.

"I thought this was rush," said Sandy.

"Yes, well, there's this hit."

Sandy put his face into his hands and rubbed. He said through his fingers, "All right, so there's this hit. Come on, come on."

"Yes. The job is this old guy, name of Kemp. Big once, on the Coast, and . . ."

"I thought he was dead."

"No, no. Just out, you know? But now, we just got this, he's going to move. He's been in touch with a new group, something new in Miami, and with what Kemp knows and with what these new ones have in mind about our organization . . ."

"Where is Kemp?"

"He's in Pennsylvania. The rush is, we know he's going to move, in a week even, the way it's been figured, and the rush is to get this done now, while he's still sitting down and has an every-day routine. And while he's without organization, living retired like with an everyday . . ."

"You said that." Sandy took a cigar out of his pocket but did not light it. He only looked at it and then put it away again. "I don't have anybody," he said.

"What?"

"I said . . ."

"What do you mean you . . ."

"Stop yelling, will you, Turner?"

Turner shut his mouth immediately and then wiped his head. He did not have much hair and suddenly the sweat on his head was tickling him like crazy. And this errand job. He had thought there would be a clear-cut matter of bringing a message, explaining things with the details he had been given, and that would be his work. Perhaps he would also see the man whom he sent out on the job, but he had not thought of any other kind of excitement or anything, really, which would involve him. He did not talk loud again, but with a fast edginess which was almost mean.

"They say now. I just bring the message and the message is now. And you're set up for this thing, is the way I got the picture. Why in hell . . ."

"Now when?" said Sandy.

"Now, like today. Like now!"

Sandy nodded and looked across the bar and out of the window.

"Everybody is that busy?" said Turner. "How can it be that everybody in a big layout like you run here and that Meyer . . ."

"Not everybody is busy," said Sandy. "But I can't send just anybody."

"What is there, for Christ's sake? You get a finger that can bend around a little old trigger . . ."

"Why don't you shut your stupid mouth, Turner, huh?"

Turner said nothing and picked up his glass. There was a little warm beer left at the bottom and he drank that down without liking it.

"Retired or not," said Sandy, "Kemp is a pro. And special."

"Naturally. That's why."

"And there's three kinds for jobs. There's the nuts, there's the dumb ones, and the ones who are special. What you need is special."

"Special? All I . . ."

"They got a lot trained out of them and a lot trained in. That leaves out the nuts, which we never use, and that leaves out the dumb ones, like your finger around a little old trigger."

"They said now, is all I know, and that we got nobody for it on the Coast. They said now and your outfit is the one to furnish."

"I know. I'm trying." Sandy folded his paper up and stuck it into his pocket. "I got just one right now to fill the bill. But I got to ask him first."

"*Ask* him? What you got, prima donnas?"

"No. And not machines, either."

Chapter 3

Jordan did not expect to be met at the train nor was it the order of things to run into each other in public and acknowledge it. He ignored Sandy and the man with him and kept walking. This impressed Turner as exciting.

Turner had a notion that eyes tell a great deal about someone. He was able to read a great deal into somebody's eyes. But it did not work in the case of Jordan. The man just looked. He did not squint, dart, hood, sink his eyes at or into anything, and he seemed to carry his head simply to balance with the least possible strain. The face was tilted up a little; he had the neck and head of a man who is thin. Though Jordan was not thin. He had a slow step, like a thin man, but that might have been because he was tired.

When Jordan walked by, Sandy said, "I got the car outside," and Jordan said, "Okay," and kept walking.

They all walked together or they did not walk together, depending on who was thinking about it. There were a lot of people coming and going. Turner was in a light sweat.

He felt nobody else was sweating. He felt nobody else wore a coat and hat—as did Sandy—and nobody carried a suitcase—as Jordan was doing. And my God if that suitcase should snap open, what might fall out . . .

When they all got in the car Jordan sat in the back seat alone. Sandy turned once and said, "Hi," and Jordan said the same thing. Then Sandy faced front again and drove away from the curb. He drove back and forth through Manhattan waiting for Turner to talk. But Turner did not get to it. He looked out the rear window a few times, and once he saw that Jordan held a dead cigarette and he offered a light. But this did not start anything either. Jordan said no to the light and Turner said nothing else.

"He's from the Coast," said Sandy after a while. "He runs errands."

"How do you do," said Turner. "How are you."

"Thank you, fine," said Jordan.

"His name's Turner," said Sandy. He did not give Jordan's name.

Turner had a moment of sudden panic, now that the man in back knew his name.

"I'm driving around so you can talk," said Sandy.

"Yes. Very good. You went through a yellow light."

"It's a job," Sandy said over his shoulder.

"Yes. Would you like a fresh cigarette?" Turner asked the back.

"What did you want?" said Jordan.

"Well, yes. It's about Kemp. You know Kemp?"

"No."

"No? Well, it's about him. Sort of special."

"What's special?" said Jordan.

This gave Turner a nervous fit of the giggles, as if Jordan had been making a joke. Jordan had not meant anything like that. What was ever special, he had thought. It upset him to be thinking about this at all. He felt nervous and squinted. I'm tired, he thought and rubbed his face. What's special? I'm tired. That's why these crappy thoughts.

"It isn't special like being tricky," said Sandy. "It's nothing like that. Just it has to be done right away."

"I just got back."

"Yes, well, but this is about Kemp," said Turner and when Jordan did not answer, Turner thought he should now explain as much as he could. "Kemp was—I mean, he is the Kemp who organized, when was it . . . I think it was twenty-five years ago, he's the one . . . You know, he's the only one left over from that time, before the new setup shaped up, and the decision I'm talking about was made on the Coast . . . You sure you don't want a light?"

"He means Kemp's got to go," said Sandy.

"Well, yes," said Turner.

"I know you just got back," said Sandy, "but the way he puts it, there's no time."

"He hasn't said anything yet," said Jordan.

Turner giggled again because he could not stand the remark from the back. It was barren and had to be filled with something, and there had been just enough impatience in it for Turner to build that into a terrible threat. He stopped giggling and would now tell the whole thing so he could not be interrupted.

"This Kemp has been all right for a while, since retiring, living around here and there, not much money or anything, but enough to live around here and there, not too open, you understand, because of the type of background . . ."

"I don't need any of that," said Jordan.

On the train, coming back, Jordan had sat with his shock, but then it had gone away. A thing like the arm would not happen again. If something like that should happen again it would not be like the first time, it would be without the surprise, and then there was always the trick he knew, a flip-switch type of thing, where he split himself into something efficient. Put the head over here and the guts into a box and that's how anything can be handled.

He had settled this, and then he had sat for the rest of the time, almost into New York, but the train-ride dullness had not come. He had tried to unwind, until he had found out there was nothing to unwind.

This too had happened without his having known it, like seeing his shadow which was no longer like his own shape.

There was nothing to unwind. What had wormed at him had been something else. He was dreading the nothing, between trips. The job was now simpler than the time in between.

Jordan dropped his cigarette to the floor of the car and said, "All right. I'll do it, if it looks all right."

Sandy took a breath and kept driving. He nodded at Turner to go on.

"Well, yes," said Turner. "That's the job. Watch the light, Sandy."

Sandy pulled the car over to the curb, stopped, looked at his hands. He kept them on the wheel and talked without looking at Turner. "Maybe if there's no red, green and yellow lights, Turner, and happy motorists driving home from the movies and tired cops dreaming of a cool beer, you think maybe you might get to the cottonpicking point if I fixed all that for you?"

He got out of the car and slammed the door before Turner could answer and walked to the corner into a telephone booth.

Turner sat and said nothing. He was afraid Jordan might be as wild and nervous as the other one seemed to be.

After the call, Sandy drove to an address which was not far away. It took only a few minutes, and the apartment was on the sixth floor. Far away from the traffic, thought Sandy, and close enough so there would be no more of this sweaty stuttering in the car.

The man who opened the door looked young, well dressed, and a little worn out. A gold chain clinked on one wrist, a gold watch ticked on the other, and he knew Sandy and Jordan. He did not know Turner but smiled at him. He had a vague smile for almost everybody.

Sandy said, "Thanks, Bob, much obliged," and the young man said, "Nothing, Sandy, anytime," and when Jordan walked by he grinned at him and said, "Sam boy, you're looking good."

He closed the door after everybody and said they should go

right ahead, straight ahead to the door at the end of the hall.
Then he took Sandy's arm and watched the others walk down the
hall.

"You going to be long?"

"No. But listen, Bob, if it's inconvenient . . ."

"No, no, no." He did not talk very loud. "I just meant, I got
these people coming."

"We can be out . . ."

"Just a party, Sandy. Just a party. Besides, you know everybody."

Turner opened the door at the end of the hall and said "This
one?" and the young man said to go right ahead and then talked
to Sandy again. "Who's your friend?"

"Business. He's all right, just business."

"Jordan business?"

"Yes."

"Oh."

"I'll have everybody out in ten, fifteen minutes."

"That's all right. That's all right. Party'll be over there, see?
Three rooms away, so take all the time."

"Okay, Bob."

"When you're done, if you want to join—"

"Fine. Maybe."

"Bring your friend, you know?"

"Fine."

Then Sandy went through the door and the young man closed
it behind him.

The room had a bed with bare mattress, a night table, dresser
and chair. It all looked new but there was much dust. The air in
the room smelled of dust.

Turner sat down on the bed, Sandy took the chair, and Jordan
stood with his back to the window. He did not look at Sandy and
he talked to Turner, so they would get into the business.

"Are you the spotter?"

"Huh?"

"He wants to know," Sandy told him, "if you did the leg work
on this thing. Where Kemp lives, where he goes, what time he
gets up, that kind of thing."

"Oh! Oh no. I just run errands. I always just run the errands,"
he said to Jordan. "Sandy knows that."

"All right," said Jordan.

"I always just . . ."

"All right."

But then Jordan was sorry to have interrupted because Turner, he thought, might take a long time now. Why do they send a creep, he thought. Why does he sit there and think I'm a ghoul?

"Tell me the next thing," said Jordan. "What have you got from your spotter?"

"Got?"

"I don't think there was time," said Sandy. "Is that right, Turner?"

"Yes. There wasn't any—"

"Let me get this," said Jordan. He took his hands off the window sill and wiped his palms. "You mean this thing hasn't been cased?"

"Well, yes. I mean, it hasn't been. I was trying to explain before, in the bar, you remember? I was going to tell how this came up sudden, about Kemp getting into it again, and ready to cause all kinds—"

"When will I know?"

"When what?" said Turner.

They could hear the front door being opened and people laughing.

"Jordan can't work," Sandy explained, "unless he's got something to work on."

"Yes. Of course." The sounds from the corridor distracted Turner. He now wanted to be done. He had seen this man now, Jordan, he had felt various strange sensations, and he now wanted to be done. Somebody in the hall said, "There's no ice in the bucket."

"Kemp's got to go within a week, at the outside," said Turner. "And nobody's done any casing."

Jordan took a new cigarette out and put it into his mouth.

"So we thought," said Turner, "you would do your own casing."

There was barely a pause and Jordan said, "You must be nuts."

On the other side of the door the hall was empty now, and there was no noise any more to cover the silence in the unused room. Turner smelled the dust. He thought he might sneeze. Then he said, "Well?" looking at Sandy. "Well, what is this?"

The problem was, Sandy knew, that Jordan had just come back from a trip. He was not sure what Jordan did after coming back from a trip nor had he bothered to think about it because Jordan was worked in well and no point thinking about anything beside that—unless there were signs. But there were no signs about Jordan. But the thing now was, he was asked to go right back out which was not usual. Always watch it when it wasn't usual.

"Sam?" he said.

"What?"

Jordan had a match in his hand, playing with it. I think he does sometimes play with a match in his hand, thought Sandy, which means nothing. And he's tired. The thing now, talk personal. We have known each other some time. Make it personal and I know how you feel.

"Put it this way, Sam. Here's a job, four-five days at the outside, in a place with no special angles—medium-size town, nobody knows you, nobody's looking. And there's Kemp with an everyday routine, same place for breakfast, same place where he takes a walk every day. There he is, not expecting, with no organization—and you go in there. I know you're getting rushed out close to the last job, but when you come back you'll get extra time, extra dough. I've mentioned that, Turner, and that's all there's to it. Okay, Sam?"

Jordan struck the match. "The same man," he said, "who goes out to do a job, doesn't also go out there and do his own casing."

"Why?" said Turner.

"When he noses around," said Sandy, "talks to people, he gets seen. That is what he means. That's what you mean, isn't it, Sammy?"

It was so plain, Jordan did not even bother to think about it. It kept him from thinking about something else: that he had never —very carefully never—been in any touch whatsoever with the man who was a job. Except for yesterday's accident. And that, of course, he had thought about quite long enough.

"How big is Penderburg?" Sandy asked.

"You know San Bernadino?" said Turner.

"Jordan," said Sandy, "you know San Bernadino?"

"No."

"Give another example."

"Well, I don't know any other example. It's small, what I mean is, not any too big. What I mean is, you wouldn't stick out right way, just walking down the street. But the way I get it, small enough to get a line on a man who lives there and does the same thing every day. What I mean is, that's how I got the picture. You see it?"

"Talk to Jordan, not me," Sandy told him.

"You see what I mean, Mister Jordan?"

Jordan nodded. He had lit the match and let it burn out, and he had put it down on the window sill. He nodded and played with the matchbook.

Say no to all of it. First, an impossible job, after that, the long stretch of nothing. Say no to all of it. I can't do it.

"It stinks," he said.

Sandy looked down at his shoes and then he got up. He got up with a quick snap in his movement and then walked to the window and back to his chair. Naturally, he thought. Naturally when he does his trick he thinks about nothing except how to set his mark and then blow. He doesn't know if the guy is important or anything. A hell of a lot of these worries don't touch him and "it stinks" is all he knows. No time for a beer is all he knows.

"All right, Jordan. What is it?"

"What?"

"I said what is it, is something bugging you?"

"Maybe," said Turner, "he means he can't handle it."

Sandy gave the fat man a brief look and said, "That kind of talk don't cut any ice with him," and then he looked back at Jordan. "So answer me."

Jordan, of course, had nothing to answer. He did not like Sandy's tone, which was enough reason for him to shut off the topic, and the topic—aside from that—was not a talking matter at any time.

"So why did you say it stinks and you won't take the job?" Sandy asked.

"You know it stinks, that kind of setup."

"That's why I picked you and not some fluttergut jerk."

"That kind of talk," said Jordan, "doesn't cut any ice with me either."

"Maybe there's more cut to it, if I tell you this looks like you maybe got the shakes?"

"You can stop talking crap," said Jordan. "You hear me, Sandy?"

I've got him, thought Sandy. Like everybody he's got to be perfect and don't-mention-the-shakes-to-me. Nice. I've got him. And then Sandy pushed his point.

"If it isn't the shakes, then why get prickly about it?"

Jordan shrugged this time. What had made him sensitive was the word and everything it implied. The shakes themselves were not bothering him, though Sandy could think so, if he wanted.

"Or is it something else?" Sandy said, and while he did not know it, he had Jordan again.

"No. Nothing else."

"What then? I want to hear this."

"You can stop riding me, Sandy."

"I'm not riding you, I'm asking a question. I want to know why missing your in-between break shakes you up enough so you can't take on the next job."

"Nothing like that shakes me up."

"Then what does?" Sandy kept at it.

"Nothing does."

"So why is it no?"

"Don't take that tone with me," said Jordan.

It meant different things to everyone in the room. Turner thought the next thing might be a shot. Jordan thought, this will change the subject. It better change the subject, because some things are nobody's business. And Sandy thought nothing. He carefully dropped every thought because Jordan talking this way was not usual.

"You going on this job or not?" he said quietly, the way Jordan had talked.

Before he asks again, thought Jordan. Before he stirs up what I just found out myself. About the change having crept in.

"I'm going," Jordan said.

This means no change, Jordan thought. This means there was nothing important, and he struck another match and this time lit the cigarette he had in his mouth.

After that it was cut-and-dry business and Sandy stayed out of it. He felt there was nothing else that he needed to do.

"And bring two more glasses," somebody said in the hall, and a door slammed. Jordan took the cigarette out of his mouth, knocked the coal out of it on the window sill, put the dead butt back in his mouth. "So whatever you've got," he said to Turner, "let's have it."

"And the beer," somebody said in the hall, and the door slammed.

Turner made the bed squeak and smiled. "My," he said. "A beer would be nice now, huh?" Then he pulled folded papers out of the inside of his jacket. "Well now," he said, and put the sheets down on his knees.

Jordan sniffed, smelling dust.

"First of all," said Turner, "the name. You got the name, right? Do you want a piece of paper and my ballpoint to write all this down?"

"No."

"Yes. Now. Thomas Kemp. Same name he uses now. And the

town is Penderburg. Address—" and he looked at his papers, "505 Third Avenue. He-he, they got avenues."

"What does he look like?"

"What does he look like? Here you are. I brought this shot. This picture, I mean," and he held it out.

Jordan took the small photo and looked at the old man in it. The old man sat in a chair in the sun, garden hedge behind him, and smiled. He had all his hair, Jordan saw. Maybe kinky.

"Is he gray?"

"Gray? Just a minute. . . . Yes. Sort of streaky."

The sun was bright, and Jordan could not tell much about the man's eyes because of the black shadows. Small eyes perhaps, but then Kemp was smiling. Lines in his face. From smiling? He looked fit, and built chunky.

"When was this picture taken?"

"When was this—let me think. Let me think what they said . . . This year. It happens he's got a daughter in L.A., and the way we got this picture, knowing he was going to visit her, we went . . ."

"I don't need to know that."

"Oh. That's right."

Jordan gave the picture back and then leaned on the window sill again. "Tell me more about where he is now. What he does."

"Yes. And I better mention this," said Turner. "Kemp's got a bodyguard."

Sandy exhaled with a sound which he covered by tweaking his nose, as if something itched him there. He sounded busy, very preoccupied.

Jordan did nothing. He had a matchbook in his hand and was playing with that but he had been doing that anyway. The body-guard thing was a technical matter. He had no reaction to it, except technical interest. "What kind of bodyguard is he?"

"What kind? What do you mean what kind?"

Jordan looked at Sandy and Sandy explained it. "Is he just a punk or has he got training, Turner?"

"Well, he carries a gun. He hangs around all the time and, you know, watches."

"You didn't answer," said Jordan, and Turner, who very much wished all this were over because he had nothing else to say and what else was there anyway, having met Jordan and seen all there was to see, started to giggle again.

"I mean, he carries a gun all the time. *You* know. That kind."

Sandy sighed a slow sigh. Then he said, "In Pennsylvania.

Where they dig coal. And he's got a gun all the time. *That* kind."
Suddenly he slapped his hands on his thighs and started yelling.
"Are you making this up as you go along, Turner, like maybe
working up some kind of a comedy routine, or is this supposed to
be the report that'll lay out this Kemp or whatever?"

"I—what I mean . . ."

"Shut up!" Then Sandy sighed again. He stretched back in his
chair and said to the ceiling, "Of all the jinxed-up, screwed-up
deals that I've ever seen."

Turner squeaked the bed.

"Jordan," said Sandy. "You getting anything out of this?"

"Yes. A few things."

He had a name and a place, and there were two men. He was
startled by Sandy's anger, just as Turner was, though for other
reasons. He was impressed that Sandy had spoken up like this,
though he wished he had not used the word jinx. And now,
maybe, they could break up this meeting and Turner would
leave, and perhaps there would be some time to have a beer
somewhere, but without Turner.

Turner said that he was sorry there was nothing else, and why
couldn't Sandy take a reasonable attitude about this the way his
friend there, Mister Jordan, was taking it, and the only thing
about the bodyguard was, he did not seem to be there because of
Kemp's maybe getting active again, but had been there with him
for some time. "You know how those older ones are," said Turner, "those kingpins, always having somebody hanging around.
You know what I mean?"

"No," said Sandy. "I don't."

"He means habit," said Jordan.

There was a knock on the door and the young man stuck his
head in. "Oh," he said, and smiled at Sandy.

"Yeah," said Sandy. "We're almost done."

"I didn't mean . . ."

"That's all right, that's all right," and he got up, stretching.

"Maybe a drink?" asked the young man.

"Now that," said Turner, "would be a fine idea," and he bus-
tled his papers around and stuffed them into his pocket. "As a
matter of fact, there's a drink I know, what you do is . . ."

"Not right now," said Sandy. "Later." Then he looked at Jordan and said, "Finish up."

"I'm done," said Jordan, "unless Turner here . . ."

"No. I got nothing else."

The young man in the door raised his eyebrows at Sandy, and Sandy nodded at him. "Okay," he said. "We're done."

Then the young man opened the door enough to come in and leaned against the door frame. He smiled at everybody and waited.

"You're looking fine," he said to Jordan. "How you been?"

"Fine. Thank you."

"But tired, huh?"

"Yes. Some."

They all stood around while Turner took his papers out again to refold them, and while Sandy put on his overcoat. Jordan was chewing his cigarette. The party sounds were much clearer now, and with music.

"Tell you what I'll do," said the young man. "How about a drink before you go, huh, Jordan?" and he ran off down the hall before Jordan could answer.

The three men in the room stood around while the young man was gone, and Sandy wiped dust off his pants. Turner said how hot it was and wouldn't a drink be the ticket now.

The young man came back with one drink, which he gave to Jordan. "Happiness," he said.

The drink was straight bourbon with ice, and Jordan kept a mouthful of liquor and let it burn. It distracted him while there was nothing to listen to or to say. He heard the young man say, "How about it?" to Sandy, and Sandy answered, "Who's here?" It was, Max is here, you know Max, and his brother, you know him and his bunch, you know, that crowd, nice. And Sandy said that would be nice and Turner started talking about his special drink again.

Then Jordan thought about his own affairs, just briefly, there being time and need to think more about all of it later. Vague job, which was the kind needing thought ahead of time. Bad having to case Kemp himself, almost as bad as having to touch somebody afterwards. But that made sense. No superstition in that. No jinx. Not casing was caution and not touching was hygiene.

Turner had already left the room. Jordan swallowed the liquor and wiped his face. Then he put the glass on the window sill.

"You didn't finish," said the young man.

"That's all right."

"You want my car to drive home?" Sandy asked.

"No. I'll take a cab." Or, no. Maybe I'll stay, he thought. "Who's here?" he asked, and walked to the door where Sandy and the young man were standing.

"Nobody you know. Not well, I mean. There's Max, I don't know if you . . ."

Just vaguely, thought Jordan. I probably know everybody there, just vaguely. Then he said, "That laugh just now. That sounded like Lois."

"Hey, yes," said the young man. "That's right. You know Lois."

"You want her?" said Sandy. He held a cigar in his hand and was licking the end with his tongue.

And the young man was off down the corridor again. There was music and talk buzz when he opened a door down the hall and then just the mumble again when he closed it.

"When are you leaving town on this?" Sandy asked.

"I'll make it tomorrow. Middle of the day."

"Need money?"

"No. We can work it out afterwards."

"You're not dropping over tomorrow, before going out?"

"No."

The buzz getting big and then the mumble and the young man came back.

"Gee, man, I'm sorry. She's with what's-his-name, you know, Fido's brother."

"I don't know his name," said Jordan.

"Well, you know how it is, he brought her." He smiled and went away.

Sandy took Jordan's arm and they walked down the corridor all the way to the end.

"I'll call that Ruth for you," he said. "I'll call her from here."

"That's all right. You don't have to do that."

"What's a phone call?" Sandy opened the front door.

Jordan said good-by and, "In a week or so . . ."

"Yuh," and when Sandy closed the door Jordan thought, who in hell is Fido's brother. . . .

Chapter 4

He took his suitcase out of Sandy's car and walked back to the main drag. There he hailed a taxi and took it to a place three blocks from his building. He walked the three blocks and smoked a whole cigarette.

He had a room for sleeping and for keeping his clothes. He shut the door, walked to the dresser, bending a little when he walked past where the light hung from the ceiling. He took a clean shirt out of the suitcase and some underwear, and put them into a drawer. He had dirty laundry in a little bag, and he dropped that on the floor. Then he closed the suitcase and put it into the closet. He carried a gun and put that away in the place where he always kept it. Then he sat down on the bed and closed his eyes. He sat like that for a while but could not decide whether he was tired.

She came down the hall to his room, and he knew who it was by the steps. Then she knocked on the door the way she was supposed to and he let her in.

"Hi, Sammy. How's business?" and she laughed too loud.

She went past him, to the night stand, bending a little when she passed where the light hung from the ceiling. She put her purse on the night stand and said, "You got the bottle, Sammy?"

"I forgot," he said.

"Now, Sammy!"

He did not want to leave the room again but he did not want her to leave either. "Wait five minutes," he said and she said, "Naturally, Sammy," and laughed again.

He left and went to the liquor store on his block. If she looks around, he thought, she'll find laundry, that's all.

When he came back with the bottle she was standing and dressed as before, holding the purse against her belly. When Jordan had closed the door and put the liquor bottle next to the bed, she was still standing and holding the purse as before. She clicked the catch and the purse jumped open. So did her smile.

Jordan put money into her purse and she snapped it shut again.

He sat down on a chair near the bed and picked up the bottle, holding it in his lap. He worked the cap off the bottle while the woman undressed.

"You been out of town, Sammy?"

"Yes."

"You just come back?"

"Why do you ask?"

"Because I'm flattered," she said and laughed. She sat down on the bed which made metal sounds under the mattress.

"You're sitting on your hat," he told her.

She pulled it out from under her and said, "Damn it to hell. Damn it to hell, will you look at that!"

"I—you want me to buy you a new one?"

"What's the matter? You don't like me to curse?"

"I ask you, if you want me to buy you a new one, I'd buy you a new one."

"Don't talk crap," she said.

He did not answer and watched her roll down her stocking. She rolled down one but not the other. The other one she pulled off, making it look like a skin hanging down.

When she was naked she lay down on the bed and made a long, end-of-the-day sigh. Then she held out her hand.

"So give it here," she said.

He gave her the full bottle, and she put the neck into her mouth. After the first swallow she gave a little shudder, but none after that. She took a rest and then drank more every so often.

"Sammy?"

"Yes?"

"What you looking at?"

He had been looking at the window. He could not see anything there because it was night outside but the position had been easy on his neck.

"Just that way," he said.

"That way? You can't see out, that way."

"You ever ride in trains much, Ruth?"

"No," she said. She said nothing else and drank.

Jordan took out a cigarette and held it in his teeth. He did not know what else to say either.

"What you looking at, Sammy?"

"I was looking at your feet."

"Jeesisgawd." Then she said he should start taking his clothes off.

He held the cigarette in his mouth and watched her drink. The bottle gave a spark every so often, depending on how she moved it in the light. The spark from the glass was the brightest thing in the room. Then she put the bottle on top of the night stand, doing this just with her arm and without moving anything else. Her eyes were closed now and she lay still.

He got up, took his jacket off, pulled the shirt out of his pants. He unbuttoned the shirt. "How you feeling?" he asked her.

"Just fine, Sammy."

"Tell me something."

"What?"

"Why come here?"

"Why not?"

"That's it?" he asked her.

"Huh?"

"Why you come here, is what I asked you."

"Because nobody wants me either." And then she laughed hard again, without opening her eyes.

Chapter 5

He had her the way it had been with others, not much difference anywhere and when she left, it's a shame, he thought, but it's of no particular importance at all. Though he knew that it could be. It could matter that the woman left him, or that she stayed. However, as at other times where he needed to know how he would feel ahead of time, he had the trick. Where he clicked over to knowing where everything was—head over here, guts over there in a box—and kept only what he could manage. It was like looking at himself under glass.

When he had learned the trick is hard to say, but he had known it already when he had come to New York. The point is that he used it.

It was the worst in him, he felt for a while, and then he felt it was the best, for being so useful.

When he came to New York he lived with a relative whom he had never grown to know and who never knew him. The relative was an old woman and Jordan was no longer a child, and if they wanted anything from each other, it would not have been easy. He slept and he ate at her house and on Saturday, if he had money, he gave her some of it. He and the old woman never had any friction, which was the way Jordan managed it.

He worked on the East Side loading boxes in somebody's shipping department, and later he set pins in one of the nine alleys at Bandstand Bowling. Sandy had hired him and was somebody who always wore a hat. And an overcoat, most of the time.

After work, Jordan hung around the way it was done. They did not hang around the candy store, which was the place for younger ones, but outside a bar. As if they might all have come out of the bar or were thinking about going in, though not anxiously. They were six or seven, looking bored, even about Jordan who was new and when it was not clear yet how he fit in.

Jordan seemed no different from the others except the bully thought Jordan might be different. Who's who was important to the bully, because of his constant worry over matters of prestige.

"California, wasn't it?" said the bully.

"Yes."

"But you didn't say why you lammed out of there."

"I didn't lam. I just left."

"You left a long way. Why New York?"

"It was a place to go," said Jordan.

"Always wanted to see the bright lights, huh?"

That was not what Jordan had meant. New York was a place to go and so it just happened that way.

"So how do you like the bright lights?" And the bully spat in the street. As he spat he saw two men coming out of the night club, so he did it again.

"I don't know," said Jordan and looked at all the steps coming down out of the brownstones.

"Not good enough. That what you mean?"

"I wasn't . . ."

"You got uptown habits, huh?"

"Which?"

"You cop a feel or a lay or a candy bar, ain't good enough for you, is what I mean."

It was not good enough for the bully, which was what he had meant, but Jordan was only concerned with having no friction.

"It's all right," he said. "I got no kicks."

"That you don't," said the bully and laughed. "That you don't." They all laughed with him, at Jordan, but it did not lead anywhere because Jordan did not take it up.

This meant to the bully, Jordan was going to be easy, though the puzzlement was that Jordan did not seem to care how he looked. The bully did not understand this. It needed demonstration.

"Except for that job you got," he said. "That's great kicks, isn't it? I mean, you set 'em up and somebody keeps knocking them down."

Jordan did not answer. Maybe he could leave.

"And working right up alongside the boss. Yessir," said the bully and laughed.

"You don't have to act that way," said Jordan.

They saw that he wanted to leave and all of a sudden there was a ring around him.

"You know Sandy, don't you?" said the bully.

"Yes."

"But he don't know you."

"Why should he?" said Jordan, but the evasion made the bully that much more insistent.

"Why? Don't you watch the breaks?"

"All I'm doing there . . ."

"Is working up to setting two alleys instead of one, right? I mean, ambitious."

"Sure," said Jordan. "Sure."

"You know Jay?" asked the bully. "No. He left before you come in. That boy now, there was ambition."

"Listen. I want . . ."

"Shut up," said the bully. "I'm telling this story."

They all waited for Jordan to say something, or do something, but he held still.

"Like, working alongside Sandy is big time, didn't you know that, Jordan? Like, take Jay. He does this and that for Sandy, and that once, he runs an errand. Fifty bucks to run a parcel up to Harlem, that's all. You didn't know Sandy does other things, huh?"

"No," said Jordan, he didn't know anything about what Sandy did.

"Jay takes the fifty, runs the errand, opens up the parcel on the way. Know what was in it? I said, do you know what was in it?"

"No. I don't know what was in it."

"Half a grand, feller. Half a grand in sawbucks and singles."

"All right," said Jordan. "So Sandy is big."

"That's right. And there you are setting up pins and marking time for retirement, is what I'm talking about. But you know what Jay did?"

"All right. What?"

"Jay kept it. I got robbed on the way, he says, but he kept it." Then he said, "Jay was from California too. Looks like some in California aren't so dumb like some others, huh, Jordan?"

"Where's Jay now?" said Jordan.

"I don't know."

Jordan turned away, looking for a way to leave the ring. "It looks to me," he said, "that guy wasn't so smart after all."

They all thought about that for a moment, what might have happened to Jay or if Sandy might have done something to him.

"But smart and scared ain't the same thing," said the bully. "You smart or scared, Jordan, huh?"

"Depends when," said Jordan and tried to leave again.

They would not let him through. Somebody came out of the night club, and somebody stood on the fire escape of the house opposite. Jordan saw this and felt how cut off he was and that it could not be worse.

"But I want to know something," said the bully. He took

Jordan's arm, thumb hooked into a muscle. "And you don't answer me straight."

"Cut it out," said Jordan, and tried to get his arm away.

"You smart or scared, Jordan. Which?"

"Just cut it out," said Jordan, but it came out dull because he felt dull now.

And when Jordan did not give the bully a good opening for the next thing to do, the bully went ahead without the opening. "I'm going to ask you again and you show me . . ."

Jordan walked to the alley in the middle of all of them and then, against a brick wall, he got his beating.

It was painful, and a weird kind of fight, because the bully was running it. He ran it as a demonstration. He was big enough to keep Jordan well checked, but the whole thing was just vanity fodder. That's why it took long, and so gave Jordan time.

Jordan, of course, fought for different reasons and did not even understand the other's delays.

He kicked the other one in the shin, when the time came. He now had five seconds or more to turn the fight his way, to make his demonstration. There were a number of ways, delaying and painful, to keep up what the bully had done so far. The other one was now doubled up and his face free for the moment.

Jordan grabbed his hair, held on; then his knee came up. The bully's jaw made a wooden sound. Jordan let go of the hair, let the head drop, watched till the other one fell flat on the ground. Finished.

Jordan stepped back. He looked at the others standing there, but they did not move. And the one on the ground was done. It felt so right that for one moment Jordan felt almost upset.

The others started to leave, walking sideways and with their hands in their pockets. They kept looking back until Jordan caught on.

At the mouth of the alley, by the wall, was a man. He wore hat and overcoat and he slowly walked up.

"Well," he said, and stopped by the one on the ground. "I've been watching you." Sandy looked up and then at the one on the ground again.

"Broke the jaw, I think."

Jordan wiped one hand across his mouth and said nothing.

"How'd you do it, Sam?"

"Do it? You mean, how did . . ."

"So quick. You were like a heap of clothes up against that wall, and then this."

"I was watching for it," said Jordan.

"How's your eye?" said Sandy.

"I think it's closing."

Sandy nodded and then he took Jordan's arm. They walked out of the alley, past the night club, and into Sandy's bowling place. They had left the one on the ground where he was, and Jordan did not remember about him until now.

"I think that guy back there could use . . ."

"Forget him. He's got buddies."

"I know."

"I got a drink for you, in my office."

"I just thought . . ."

"You got buddies?"

"What?"

"I said, have you got buddies, so after he would have been through with you, they'd come down to that alley and pick you up?"

"I wasn't thinking like that. I don't think it's got anything to do . . ."

"If you want to go, go," and Sandy went into the bowling alley. "But you did that good," he said over his shoulder.

Jordan stood alone on the street and watched Sandy go. The door made a loud hiss and when Sandy turned inside and disappeared, the door slowed pneumatically and the slit got very small.

There's nothing in the alley any more, Jordan thought, and besides, that was finished. And there's nothing on the street this time of night, and even too late for a movie.

Sandy had stopped at the counter with the cigars and the cash register. He was leaning one elbow on the glass top and looking at the door. He gave a brief smile when Jordan came in and then said nothing else till they had walked to the back of the counter and into his office.

"What I wanted to ask you," said Jordan, "was what you meant before when you said that I did that good?"

"Sit down. You must ache all over. Want that drink?"

"No. Thank you." But Jordan sat down.

"What I meant was you finished it neat. Not like that punk there. You did it neat and pared down, just enough for what was needed. I better get you some stuff for that cut . . ."

The reason Jordan stayed was because Sandy was paying attention. Jordan did not get all Sandy had said, except for the point that Sandy was pleased. And when Sandy asked again how he,

Jordan, had done it, Jordan did not know the right answer, though he got close to the point when he said he had been waiting his chance. He had been watching the fight almost like standing next to it.

"That's maybe the only way you could take the beating," said Sandy, and later added, "That's the best way to do almost anything. Keeps you clean."

But the point always was that Sandy kept paying attention, and everything Jordan did in return, was for that. Not for more attention, but as the natural pay for the one lonely favor. Jordan knowing that the other one kept him in mind.

In a while he ran one or two fifty-dollar errands, and a while later he sometimes went out of town. Get a line on where this man goes, and what the house is like where he lives. Sometimes other details. Jordan cased without knowing what for, and when he learned what for, the shock was quite brief. Sandy spent time with him and the shock was brief. And if Jordan let the worst in him get honed to a fine finish, that's how he bought Sandy's concern.

Once he bought a lighter and had it engraved. It was for no special occasion. When he picked it up he left the store for the bowling alley, though he changed his mind about that on the way. Little changes had started. Jordan no longer worked on the alleys, so he should not really hang around the place very much any more. And for other reasons which made sense.

He did not go to the alley but at a quarter past three went the extra block to the place where Sandy had his beer and read the paper. He could see Sandy through the window of the bar, in back with the telephone. When Sandy hung up, Jordan went in.

He sat down in the round booth where Sandy sat. Nice and round, he thought. Like for playing cards or talk with a beer.

"What are you doing here?" said Sandy.

"Nothing. How you been?"

"Fine, I guess." Sandy put his paper down and asked Jordan if he wanted a beer.

"No. Here. Look at this."

He took the small box out of his pocket and when it sat on the table he took off the top.

"Like it?"

"Nice," said Sandy. "Nice."

The lighter was shiny as if it had never been touched and it lay on a very white cotton bed.

"Did you want something special, Sammy? Because I'm waiting for a call any minute."

"It's for you."

"What, this?"

"The lighter. For you."

"Is that right," said Sandy.

He gave Jordan a smile and picked up the lighter. The chrome got a fat fingerprint on it, and while Sandy wiped at it he looked at the phone. "Very nice lighter," he said. "Can you see the time up on that wall?"

"Three-twenty," said Jordan.

"What's this?"

"Three twenty, going on . . ."

"I said this. This here," and he put the lighter down on the table. The sound went clack.

"Inscription," said Jordan. "I had it inscribed."

Sandy did not say anything. He knew his reaction to all of this, but the right words were not ready yet.

"It says," Jordan went on, "from Sam to Sandy."

Sandy gave the lighter a spin and waited till it lay still again. It spun so fast it whirred. Then it lay still. "That's too bad," he said.

"Too bad? Did you say too bad?"

"From Sam to Sandy. What kind of junk is this?"

Jordan, to save himself, had an impulse to laugh and to say yes, junk it was. But he did not say that. He felt rotten to have thought it, to spit on all the effort that had gone into doing this thing. And besides, the thing was for Sandy, and why didn't he know this?

"You got to cut that crap out, Sam." Sandy looked at the telephone.

"Listen," said Jordan. "Listen here. I got that for you. I just thought of it and got you this gift. What are *you* talking about?"

Sandy did not like his tone. It imposed on him. The whole crappy thing did, the lighter and Jordan. He gave a quick look at the phone, no help though, and then he had the words to make good, sharp sense and to get rid of this problem.

"You don't come to the office any more every day. You don't go and sit in just any bar any more when you and me have a beer. You don't do one or two dozen things because I tell you you don't, because there's sense behind it, and because that's part of the deal. The deal is you're special. The deal is . . ."

"Don't try to pat me on the head," said Jordan.

"Shut your mouth and listen. Maybe this way it sinks in: You don't talk about the work you do and you don't breathe a word about the work you're working up to doing. But you think about it. You think about it all the time till you got it stuck in your bones. I'll use the square word, Jordan, like the squares would say it: You're bad, Jordan, and you're building to do the worst thing." Sandy took a breath as if he had been shouting. Then his low voice got pointed and sharp. "So for the good of the company, Jordan, and to keep away trouble, don't you put your name and my name right next to each other!"

"You're making a thing . . ."

"Shut up. You don't engrave it, you don't say it, you don't . . ."

"All I did was bring you a present. I didn't bring it to the precinct station, I brought it to you."

"I'm talking sense and business, Jordan, not personal crap. I'm telling you . . ."

"I don't know why in hell you're so jumpy," said Jordan. He picked up the lighter and started to drop it back into the box.

"Gimme that," and Sandy grabbed for it.

Jordan let him, because the lighter was Sandy's.

"I'll get rid of that thing and don't you ever . . ."

"What did you say just now?"

Sandy did not answer. He watched Jordan's face and with intentional slowness he dropped the lighter into his pocket and folded his arms.

"You going to keep it?" said Jordan. He did not like the sound of his voice.

I know him best, thought Sandy, and from where does he pull this crap all of a sudden. And if it's serious, once and for all . . .

"Get the hell out of here, Jordan. I'm expecting a call."

Then Sandy waited, while he stared at the bar, because he was badly worried for one long, stiff moment, when it struck him that he did not know Jordan very well.

"You going to throw away that lighter?" he heard.

And if he says yes, Jordan thought, what am I going to do . . . ?

"Yes," said Sandy. He rubbed his mouth.

Jordan tried his trick but it did not work. He was hating Sandy's guts. He tried his trick again but what interrupted was a tired feeling and a tired thought. And if I walk out, then there's nothing either . . .

"You can take it to a jeweler," Jordan said, "and he'll grind the words out for you."

"Yes."

The phone rang and Jordan said, "There's your phone."

Sandy nodded and got up. "Where you going to be tonight?" he said.

"I'll see you tomorrow," said Jordan and walked out.

Nothing else happened, which meant Sandy got his way. And nothing showed with Jordan, because he was special.

Chapter 6

Penderburg looked homey and neat. The houses were red brick with gingerbread porches; there were big elm trees along the streets, and most of the week there was little traffic. Quiet streets and some even pretty. But the town sat in a valley of a most unnatural ugliness. The hills around the small town were geometric. There was a round hill of mining waste north, a long one with camel's hump south, and a third one had a sharp tip and a conveyor going up the side. The conveyor was dribbling rock and shale, and from a distance the long machine was like a stiff-legged insect leaning up the side of the hill. The two older hills were gray and the new ones showed black shimmers. When it rained, they all shimmered.

At nine in the morning, when the sun shone and everything looked like small-town summer, Jordan drove into Penderburg.

The dead hills, he thought, made the sky look out of place. Hot shale hills and little brick houses and only the big sky didn't fit.

Then he looked for everything which was important. He found 505 Third Avenue very quickly, an old apartment house with three stories and the trees in front reaching all the way up. There was an empty lot on the other side of the street, an old empty lot, with trees. Under the trees was a diner, made out of wood. Behind it a gray grass railroad spur, the hill dry in the sun, and also gray grass between the sleepers.

There were no other three-story buildings on the street. One-family bricks, frilly woodwork, a little tower worked into the side, blue shirts and white shirts on the lines in back.

He drove to the shopping square and started from there. It went, hotel, bus depot, church, porched houses, gray hill. Then back again. This time, railroad station, police station, bars, bowling alley, porched houses, the other gray hill. Next, movie house, porched houses, railroad sidings, warehouses, fence along mine, black hill. The highway went around this one. And the last tack not much different, with the other movie, other bars, dance hall Saturdays Only, gas station, gas station, state highway and out.

By late afternoon Jordan knew what was important. He knew streets and distances, how to come and go. He drove out of town and ate in a roadhouse which was five miles away.

He did not eat because he was hungry but because it was a way to spend time. He had to spend time.

He thought, I'll wait till the evening. I never work in the evening, because of the light, rarely in the evening, but what comes now is not the real job yet, the right part, but the wrong part which I have to get out of the way, I never work in the evening, which is always the dead stretch of time waiting to get done, but this time I have this thing to do and it will fill up the evening.

He cajoled himself like that and stroked his jumpiness so it would lie still like a cat. He waited till dark, which came late at that time of year, and drove back to the square in town. He left the car there and walked.

Warm and dark under the trees, he said. Leaf sounds up there, like something swarming. I'm nervous and paying attention to unimportant things.

The apartment house had lighted windows which showed in no special pattern. That one is Kemp's, or that one is Kemp's, or none . . . Jordan stopped at the entrance and looked past the door frame at the mailboxes inside the hall. He did not go in, he just looked in.

T. Kemp, it said. There was a newspaper in the box. Jordan went across to the diner.

There was a waitress behind the counter, and there was a man sitting but Jordan could see only his back. He could see that the waitress had a round face and moved slowly, and the inside of the diner was probably hot. The man wore a cap on his head. But Jordan was not really looking at him, or at the waitress, but now felt the gravel under his shoes. He stood in a tree-dark place outside the diner and heard the leaf sounds and felt the gravel points under his soles. He started to curse but interrupted himself with a quick breath. I've felt gravel before. I've watched before, standing like this, and have spent time before like I did today, laying everything out. And Kemp is in town, I know that; his name is on the box on the other side of the street, I know that; I know everything ahead of time, not counting the details; how it will end, not counting the details; and even that the back sitting there at the counter is not Kemp, and this relief now is fake. Relief is always fake . . . He stopped himself and felt the gravel under his shoes.

The man at the counter got up and was not Kemp. He was too young. When he came out of the diner he was whistling and kept doing it all the way down the street.

Jordan felt no change. He had known that ahead of time, too. Then he went into the diner because he could not stand it to think back and forth any more.

The girl was at the sink and looked up when Jordan came in, but only to say good evening. Then she looked down again and washed dishes.

There was too much paint in the place. The diner was very narrow, with counter, stools, tiny booths, and circus paint everywhere. Red counter, green swivel seats, blue booths, trims and borders and thick colored paint.

"You wait just one second? Or you in a real hurry?"

"No. Go ahead and finish up."

"If you're in a real . . ."

"No. I'm not."

She kept making soap-water sounds and then splashes when she dipped into the rinse, and once she looked over at Jordan but he did not look back. She had started to smile but he had looked away.

It would be easy to say more now, something about take your time, there's no hurry.

She used her forearm to wipe hair away from her face.

Or something about how hot it is.

Her hair was very light brown and her bare arm was very smooth.

I can say nothing about that. There is nothing to say. I will have to talk to her because it is that kind of job, the kind I have never done before and should not be trying. What I do best has nothing to do with people.

"I'm ready now," she said.

He told her coffee with cream and two doughnuts. He had no idea why doughnuts when she bent down at the counter and wrote the order on a pad. He thought two doughnuts are good. I can stay longer.

She wrote slowly and, bending over, her head was close to Jordan. He thought he could feel the skin-warmth coming from her, especially from her hair. The hair fell forward again, the way it had done at the sink, and she was so close, if she doesn't brush the hair back again at the sides . . . Jordan put his hands in his lap and worked his fingers together. They felt thick with heat and stiff with it. She has almost an empty face, he thought, and that's good.

"You want plain or powdered?" she said.

Jordan felt the draft on the back of his neck when the door opened, and if that's Kemp I won't have to talk to the girl at all . . .

"Sugar," said the man, "two black and two all the way."

He wasn't Kemp either. He had a shorn head and a big waist which might have been all muscle. He grinned with gold in his teeth and smelled of grease.

"Stop it," said the girl.

The man laughed and straightened up again after having tried who knows what, thought Jordan, because I wasn't looking. I wasn't looking when she put the cup in front of me, because here it is with the brown coffee smell lifting up to my face and I'm sweating. Naturally. It's hot in here. Naturally.

The girl put the four containers on the counter and said, "That all you want, Davy?"

"Well, mam, if you really want to know, chicken, I could think . . ."

"Don't talk like that, Davy." Her face didn't change at all when she said it, and it seemed she just looked at the man because he was there. Then she said, "You want plain or powdered?" and looked at Jordan.

"If you really want to know, chicken . . ."

"Stop talking like that, Davy."

"Plain," said Jordan.

"And yours is forty-eight cents," she said to the trucker.

"How you been, chicken?" He worked change out of his pocket and grinned at her.

She put two doughnuts in front of Jordan and said, "Fine, Davy."

The trucker put half a dollar on the counter and said because she was such a sweet chicken all around she could keep the change. He felt that was very funny, allowing two cents for a tip, and left it that way till she had picked up all the cups. Then he reached over, when it looked as if he was going to leave, and poked a quarter into the kerchief pocket on her uniform. This, he felt, was even funnier, and the only thing spoiling it for him a little bit was that she didn't slap his hand away or move back or say anything he could use for a comeback.

"Thank you," she said. He went out with his cups balanced on top of each other and laughing, to make the exit fit the rest of the act.

The girl leaned against the service board behind her and folded her arms. "Him and his manners," she said.

Jordan moved his face to show he was listening but the girl wasn't looking. She was stooping down a little to catch her reflection in the black window opposite, and with one hand she patted a wave in her hair. Then she fluffed it up again because of the heat. She could have been alone there. She sighed and folded her arms again. Where her uniform went over the round of her breast she had written Betty on the white cotton. She must have written it looking down at herself, thought Jordan. The script was that uneven.

"He must come in often," said Jordan.

"What?"

"Your friend."

"Him. Huh," she said.

Then he did not know how to go on. He put his head down over the coffee and drank some. Do you have many steady customers coming in here? Like Tom, maybe, my friend old Tom Kemp . . . The questions felt wrong and stiff. He would say them stiff. Even hello and good-by if he had to say it now.

"I never seen you here before," said the girl. "You just coming through?"

"Yes."

He watched the light make patterns on top of the coffee. The light slid. He watched it and hated not having said anything else.

"Most of the time all the same people come in here," she said. "That's why I was remarking."

But Jordan did not pick it up. He thought of the plain matter of fact in this, how much simpler the other part of the job would be . . .

"But they're not all like Davy," she was saying.

"You don't like him?"

"He stinks."

Jordan had no idea how to react to that, so he said nothing. He had not expected she could be this definite.

"You know the kind that thinks they own everything? Well, he's like that. And I don't like it."

"I don't like that either," said Jordan.

"Like there was no other way to get along, you know? Well, there's lots of ways to get along."

"Of course."

"Like being friendly." She looked at the opposite window and frowned at the dark glass. "I'd like that to happen sometime."

She was talking too much and Jordan felt bothered that he was letting her. What she said did not bother him, he felt, just the waste of time.

"Do all your customers live around here?"

"I'd like to know what's wrong with being friendly, you know that?"

She's dull, he thought. One thing at a time. I can ask her about Kemp and not worry too much how she will take it.

"I don't think anything is wrong with that," he told her. "I often think the same way." He said it easily because he did not think about what he said. He felt it was small talk.

"Some do," she said. "Some live around here but some just work down that end a ways. The yard and the depot."

One thing at a time and one after the other. He was not worried about her. He also envied her.

Jordan felt the draft again and then saw dirty pants. The man sat down two seats away, and when he hit the seat he gave a great sigh. Jordan could smell the liquor.

"Without anything," he said.

"They drive a truck," said the girl, "and right away they think they got to be like a truck theirselves, you ever notice that?"

"Black and hot," said the drunk and the girl got the coffee.

The best thing, now that this drunk is here, I pick her up later, thought Jordan. He felt some ease and smiled at her when she turned. It was easy and she smiled back.

Some miners came in and ordered things off the grill and a kid came in to take something out to the car. There was talk and the girl was busy, and Jordan bent over to finish his coffee and doughnuts in peace. After a while he said, "How much is the bill?" and after that, when she would pay attention and look at him when he gave her the money, then he would ask her when the diner closed for the night.

"Onion like always?" she said, and the man next to Jordan said, "Same way, Betty. Don't rush."

She slid dirty dishes under the counter, which made a great crash; she put coffee on the counter, two cups, and turned back to the grill right away and put a raw hamburger patty on top. The raw meat hissed and steamed.

"Pass me the sugar, would you?"

Jordan thought he might smoke one more cigarette and drink one more cup of coffee.

"Would you reach me that sugar bowl over, please?" and this time Jordan knew that the man was talking to him, because his hand was on Jordan's shoulder and he pointed across at the sugar bowl.

"Yes," said Jordan. "I'm sorry."

He picked up the sugar bowl and watched the girl turn around with the plate of onions and hamburger. She said, "I already put sugar in your coffee, Mister Kemp," and she put the hamburger down on the counter. Jordan put the sugar bowl down again.

Everything shrank.

The man in the next seat said something else. "Thanks just the same," he said, and put his hand on Jordan's back once more, heavy and forever, but Jordan sat it out by not moving or breathing, though in the middle of that, from somewhere, he said, "That's all right," and then the hand was gone.

"Thirty-five," said the girl.

Kemp, next to Jordan, was eating his hamburger.

"Did you want to pay?" said the girl. "I thought you said you wanted to pay."

Jordan did not want to talk because he did not know what would come out. He picked his cup off the saucer and smelled the tar smell of the cold coffee.

"Another cup?" she said.

She took the cup and Jordan held the small piece of doughnut he had left. He bit into it, moved the piece back and forth over his teeth, felt the dryness of it and how it lay in his mouth like something which did not belong there. It stayed dry. He would never be able to swallow it. He put his hand up, slowly like everything else, and let the piece drop out of his mouth and into his palm. He put the doughnut into his pocket and left his hand there, too. The doughnut was still dry like a stone but the inside of his hand was wet, and his face.

"It's awful hot here," said the girl and put the fresh coffee down in front of him.

Jordan's shoulder and arm hurt and he would soon have to take his hand out of the pocket.

"Here," she said. "Here's a napkin."

"What?"

"Here's a napkin. Wipe your face."

She put it next to his cup and left. Jordan felt upset with

gratefulness for the napkin she had offered, and for leaving him. He got weak, which relaxed him.

Then he took a deep breath. It was not good and deep but better than before, sitting with his hand in his pocket. It was much better now and in a moment I'll look at the man in the next seat and then leave.

The man next to him lit a cigarette and sighed the smoke out of his lungs. When he had chewed up the hamburger he had sighed the same way, to show how good it was. Jordan leaned away a little and looked.

This was Kemp. Same man as in the photo. Jordan looked at him as if he were a photo. The hair was coarse and tight-curled, one wire hair over the next wire hair. The temples were gray and white, but nothing distinguished. Creases ran out from Kemp's eyes, as if he were squinting into the sun, or were laughing. Jordan did not look at anything else. Kemp was too close.

"Does Paul want anything?" asked the girl.

Kemp turned on his stool and his face swung past Jordan. "Anything for you?" said Kemp.

There was a man in the booth behind and he answered, "No. I'm fine."

Somebody went by and out the door, and Jordan used that to turn and let his eyes go past the man in the booth.

The one in the booth looked at Jordan as if he had been looking at him all the time. Jordan swiveled back and stared into his coffee.

That was Kemp's man. Jordan knew this without any thought, wasted no questions on it. And that blank look had been intentional. He looks that way to cover, or because he is waiting to be provoked . . .

"You aren't sick, are you?" said the girl. "The way your face is wet."

"No," he said. "I'm not sick."

"Maybe it's the coffee. You been drinking a lot of coffee today?"

"Yes. A lot," said Jordan.

"Listen," said Kemp. He leaned closer so that his elbow touched Jordan. "There's no hangover that's been took care of with coffee yet," and he looked into Jordan's face and smiled.

"I just drank too much coffee," said Jordan. He put his hand into his pocket to pay.

"Or you might have something coming on," said Kemp. "All those things feel the same, when they first come on."

"Nothing," said Jordan. "I'm all right."

"But like that doughnut," Kemp kept at it. "Something does ail you, I figured. You spat it out, didn't you?"

When I kill him, thought Jordan, I'll kill him for this.

Just the drunk was left now, and Kemp with his man in the booth.

"You been driving all day?" asked Kemp.

"Yes."

"I thought so. I thought you looked like it. Salesman?"

"Yes. Traveling salesman."

"What you selling?"

"I have various lines," said Jordan.

"Like what?"

"Buttons."

The drunk down the counter laughed. "I couldn't help hearing that," he said. "Did I hear buttons?"

"Yeah, he said buttons," said Kemp across Jordan's face. "You got something against buttons?"

The drunk just laughed.

"You know something?" Kemp said to Jordan. "If there's anything I can't abide it's a bastard like that laughing like that."

"Now you hush up," said the girl to the drunk.

"I don't care what a man's doing," said Kemp, "long as he does his job right and is good at it. That's how I feel."

The drunk laughed again."

"Listen," said Kemp close to Jordan's face. "Go over there and clip him one."

"No," said Jordan. "I don't care if he laughs."

"Go ahead. If there's anything I can't abide . . ."

"No," said Jordan. "Besides, he's drunk."

"Maybe that's why you should hit him now. While he's drunk."

Paul said this from the booth, where Jordan could not see him. But he's looking straight at my neck, thought Jordan. He's sitting very still, waiting, the punk talking, waiting for a fight that won't cost him any effort.

"Harry's leaving right now," said the girl. She walked over to the drunk and said, "He's leaving right now. You hear me, Harry?"

"Well, mam, I was done anyhow, Betty, but if the button gentleman over there . . ."

"Please, Harry. I don't want trouble. Why does there always have to be trouble—"

The drunk got up and gave Betty's arm a pat. He laughed again when he walked past Jordan and then he went out the door. Nobody said anything after that and Jordan got up and put a bill on the counter. He could hear the sound the bill made when the girl picked it up and behind him was a sound from the booth, Paul scratching. Kemp sighed and watched Jordan stand at the counter.

"Good rest tonight," he said, "and you'll be all right."

If he doesn't stop talking to me, thought Jordan, if he doesn't—

"You got a place yet?"

"No."

"Listen. Don't go to the hotel. That hotel . . ."

"There's two," said Paul.

"Don't go to any of them."

The girl said thank you when Jordan gave her a tip.

"You want a nice room?" said Kemp. "How long you going to be here?"

"Couple of days," said Jordan. He thought about it and said, "Week, at the most."

"I tell you about a nice room," said Kemp. "Now this here, this is Third."

"Yes."

"Next block that way is Fourth. You go to Fourth and the up-and-down sort of catticorner from where I live—I live right there, see the building?"

"Yes," said Jordan. "Right there."

"Well, catticorner from there on the Fourth block is this up-and-down with a sign says Rooms. You go there and ask for Mrs. Holzer and tell her I sent you. My name's Kemp."

"Kemp," said Jordan. "Yes."

Kemp held out his hand and Jordan had to take it. He had to shake the hand and then had to give a name. He said his name was Smith. He wanted to give a better name than Smith but shaking the other man's hand was making him stiff and dull.

"You go tell her I sent you, Smith," and then Kemp and his man got up and walked out of the diner.

When the diner was empty Jordan stood there and wished nothing had happened and he could start now. The girl was at the sink and her back was turned; she wore a white dress but with skin tone showing through where it lay close on her skin. Jordan watched the stretch folds move in the cloth and then he turned away. Jinx job, he thought. I met him and nothing gained.

When Jordan opened the door, the girl looked up and said good night. Face empty, he thought. Doesn't want anything.

Chapter 7

There was always a half-hour slump that time of night when she would sit down for a moment and do nothing. If I smoked, she thought, I would now smoke a cigarette. She drank a glass of water and listened to the neon sign hiss in the window. The red, which was a beer-bottle shape, flickered. Then she finished her water, cleared the counter, washed the dishes. Next she swept the alley between booth row and stools which was always the time when Mr. Wexler came in.

He came in without saying hello because he was the owner. He looked wrinkled under the light of the ceiling and all his joints looked like big knots of bone. This showed on his hands, wrists, down the bumpy bend of his back.

The first thing he did was to walk by the girl too close. The side of his hip, like a shovel, pressed along her buttocks. He always did this and she said nothing. He went around to the back of the counter and drew black coffee for himself. He sat down and watched the girl sweep.

"You got crap on your uniform."

She looked down at herself and there was a coffee stain near her belly. She nodded and swept again.

"I want this place clean. That includes you."

"Yes, Mister Wexler."

He watched her belly and sucked coffee over his gums.

"You working here, girl, I don't want those Rabbit Town habits to show."

Wexler was born in Penderburg and so was the girl. An outsider would say the girl was born in Penderburg, but Wexler, and more like him, said she was from Rabbit Town—where the families had nine children, where the chickens lived under the porch, where the coal truck never went in the wintertime because the shale hill ran down to the backyards. In Rabbit Town they used pickings from among the shale.

I hope he burns his gums, she thought. He knows I don't live there any more.

"You call the man about the neon sign?"

"Yes. He wasn't in, Mister Wexler."

"He wasn't in." Wexler held his cup as if he were drinking, and watched. He could see her back and wished she would turn around. "I thought you know him personal," he said.

There was nothing for her to answer. He thinks Rabbit Town when he looks at me and that means one thing to him. He tries it out every night.

"You see him around, don't you? Next time, tell him about the sign." Wexler slurped. "Or ain't there absolutely no time at all for talk?"

"I don't want you to talk like that, Mister Wexler, please," she said.

Wexler laughed. She had turned around now and he just sat for a while.

"How's your sister?"

She wanted to say, which one, stalling him, but that had never worked before and only helped him along.

"The one in Pittsburgh," he said. "She still doing all right?"

"Yes. I guess so."

"I mean she's getting on, I mean older than you. That's a point in her business, no?"

She hit the broom on the edge of a booth and on the next sweep caught it again. She felt awkward; she felt she could do nothing, and she felt in her throat that she wanted to cry. He was old and filthy and worse than any of the other things he always talked about.

"You didn't clean the grill," said Wexler. "When you're done sweeping, do the grill before rushing out of here."

She worked the sweepings into the dustpan, and after she had gotten rid of that came around to the back of the counter to clean the grill.

"Where you going to rush to when you rush out of here, Betty?"

"I'm going home to sleep," she said. "I'm tired." She worked the pumice stone back and forth on the grill and the scrape covered just some of Wexler's laugh. His laugh and the scrape went into each other as if they were the same thing.

She heard him cough and get up. Every night.

"You got to turn the gas off when you pumice the grill," he said.

Other times it was: You're leaning into the gas cocks and pushing them open, or, You're leaning into them and pushing them shut. Every night.

Then he came over where she worked on the grill and put his

hand on the gas cocks and left it there. He left it there, waiting for her to get close to his hand.

"I'm going to get a bigger fan put into that flu here," he said. He stood and looked up into the hood over the grill and let his hand wait. The girl saw little sweat dots on Wexler's scalp.

"That's enough with the stone," he said. "You can wipe it now."

When she reached for the rag she felt his hand, the bones in it, on her thigh.

"Mister Wexler, please—"

"What please, what?"

That was his mouth talking and his face looking smily but the hand was something else, was a secret between him and her, and she should respect the rule of that game.

She moved back with his hand staying on, clamping a little.

"This don't get you pregnant," he said.

Then he always let go at that point and laughed a chicken sound.

She moved back to finish the grill and kept her head down and away so she could not see him. That, she thought, is a horrible thing to say to me. A horrible thing, period. And I'm not going to listen to that much longer. I won't have to listen to that once I leave and it won't be much longer.

The thought was nothing angry, nothing with threat tone in it, because she thought this often and it was really a plan. It was where this side of the horizon and the mythology on the other side ran into each other. She would leave Penderburg sometime, which would leave Wexler and so forth behind. This made sense and absorbed her.

There was more, of course, but vaguely. To get married. To stop working in a while and then just husband and home. But this part was certain and ordained and did not need hoping.

"When you open up tomorrow," said Wexler, leaving, "call the dairy and cancel the sherbet order. Nobody around here eats sherbet."

She said, yes, Mister Wexler, and went to the closet where the bucket was, and the brooms and her dress. She squeezed in there to take off her uniform. And when I leave I can say I wasn't just a waitress but had other responsibilities. Orders, and so on. So that part doesn't worry me, but I first got to leave.

She changed and looked forward to the walk home. Slow, because tired, slow, to make a nice walk. Outside, the night hung warm. She liked that.

When he walked away from the diner he thought the air might change and feel lighter the farther he went. He walked fast, walked by his car at the curb, towards the square with the closed stores. Nothing changed. It's like glue sticking to me. Jinx job. I'll start over. Tomorrow . . . But the thought of waiting that long gave him no comfort and there had to be something he could do so it would not be as if he were delaying the job. I'll walk back and look at the building. Then I check the mailbox position in the hall or maybe the number on the box in the hall and what have I done today then—I've found out where Kemp lives in that building. And nothing else happened today. Let's say that.

But if I had walked out with them when they left the diner, walked across with them and up to Kemp's room . . . He dropped that thought with a great deal of satisfaction, reminding himself he had not been carrying a gun. He didn't work that way. He only carried a gun by plan, not by habit.

Jordan walked back, away from the square. It got darker down the street and he noticed there were no longer the leaf sounds overhead. Unimportant. Where does Kemp sleep? He looked at the building on the other side of the street and the same, and as bad, as sitting with him again, and what was he like? Nice. Tepid word which left out a great deal, but Kemp, sitting and talking, you might say was nice. Not if he knew who I was. Or worse yet: not if I were working for him, did this work for him, not then either. Would he say, go to that rooming house and mention my name to Mrs. Holzer?

Jordan looked at the building on the other side of the street and imagined nothing. Building with Kemp inside, Kemp-target.

"I think he'll be in bed by now," he heard.

Jordan held very still, waiting for more. Or, if I moved now, it would be so wild I could tell nothing ahead of time about what might come next . . .

When he did not turn, the girl Betty stepped around so that she could see him better. "I mean Mister Kemp," she said.

"Ah," he said. "I guess so."

The girl did not know what to say next. He talked so little. Or when he talked, he said nothing to invite a reply.

"I just meant," she said, "you were standing here, I saw you standing here, looking, and I thought you were looking for him because of that room. I thought maybe you had forgotten where Mrs. Holzer lives."

She made it very easy for him. I don't have to open my mouth and she helps, he thought.

"You want me to show you?" she asked.

"That's all right," he said. "No. I'll wait till tomorrow."

"Oh. You were just walking."

"Yes, back and forth."

"Ah," she said. "Yes. It's nice out. Better than daytime even."

He looked at her and her face struck him the way it had done once before. It holds still, he thought. The way a view out of a window holds still for you. There is a landscape and you look away and when you look back again, it is still there.

"I myself like it very much," she said. "Walking. This time of year."

The most harmless thing he did that day, he started to walk, knowing she would walk along. They went down the street.

"I just want to tell you," she said. "I think you were very nice before."

"What?"

"When you didn't take it up with that drunk, that Harry I'm talking about. I noticed that."

"Oh," he said. "What else was there to do."

"No, you were nice about it, not making trouble. I noticed that and I think you were very decent."

He did not react to this but instead thought quickly of a very good reason for this walk with the girl. Ask about Kemp and his habits. End of the jinx day, starting over like this. She's easy and I feel no effort. She is effortless like a view from a window. And I'm Smith, which leaves no problem between us.

Jordan felt invisible, a very fine, powerful feeling, invisible except to the girl next to him, and there was no harm in that.

"Your name's Betty?"

"Yes. Elizabeth. But that's too long, to write on the pocket."

"Yes." He looked at her, at the front where the name had been, and when she noticed it she put her hand up for a moment, feeling self-conscious.

"You got far to go?" he asked her.

"No. Just that way, past the square, maybe ten, fifteen minutes. Of course, I walk slow. I like it, in this kind of weather. You like it?"

"Yes. I do."

They walked past his car but he did not want to say anything about it. He took a cigarette out and put it into his mouth. He said, "You have to walk fifteen minutes?"

"But I don't mind it. I just mind it when I'm very tired or when the weather is bad and then I just wish I had a car. Why don't you light that cigarette?"

"I don't smoke much. Just hold it like this sometimes. You want one?"

"But then, if I had a car, I wouldn't go home, I mean straight home either, you know? I'd take a drive. I don't smoke, thank you."

"I have a car," said Jordan. "Back there."

"You do?" and she looked back where he had pointed. Then she said, "Of course you would. You're a traveling salesman, I forgot."

"Yes," he said. "That's right."

"You must be sick of driving."

He took the cigarette out of his mouth and then put it back in and gave a little bite on the filter. "Would you like a ride, a short ride?"

She nodded and said yes, she'd like that. She didn't want to go home yet but ride with the window open, and did he have any idea what it's like working in that diner and none of the windows open ever. They got into the car and she told him which way to drive out of town where the country was the nicest. He knew the way because he had checked it so carefully during the day though he did not remember about the country being so nice.

He leaned across her, pushing at her a little, and rolled the window down for her and then straightened up again. She smiled at him and thought, if I knew him better now I would like to say something to him but I would hate to be wrong, saying something nice, and would not want to hear him answer with something clever. She knew about one kind of clever talk, having heard it often, and what it meant, a time-killer before the hands on her and then sex. As if she were stupid and did not know what came next and needed leading around by the nose first, with the sex work suddenly upon her like an accident or a total surprise. And that was stupid too and added a false haste to everything, something she did not like.

When it seemed Jordan had forgotten about the window already and was driving out of town, she said, "That was very nice of you, thank you, about the window."

"What?"

"About remembering I like the window open, a ride with the window open," and felt awkward after saying it.

There was a roadhouse ahead on the highway and Jordan slowed.

"You want to go in there?" she said.

"No. But I thought some beer—I'd bring out some cans and we can have it in the car. Driving."

"Yes," she said, "that would be nice." She thought it was fine of him to remember that she liked to ride but said nothing this time.

He got a six-pack and a key and, when he came back into the car, put all of it in her lap. Then he drove again.

"If it were always like this it would be all right, you know that?" she said.

"How do you mean?"

"Here's your can. Watch the foam."

"Thank you."

"Warm like this, I mean. Like this evening. You know where it's warm like this all the time?"

"Where?"

"In Florida. My girl friend in Florida she's been writing me. And she mentions it too. You ever been in Florida?"

"Yes," he said. "Once."

"You mean on business?"

"Yes. That."

"What's your name?" she said. "I don't mean Smith, I mean the other one."

He held the can awkwardly and spilled beer on his pants. "Sam," he said after a while.

"What a Bible name you have. You know, I can't picture any-one buying buttons in Palm Beach, can you?"

"I never was in Palm Beach, I was in Miami Beach."

"That's where my girl friend is! Make a turn here, Sam. This road."

He turned where she showed him onto a country lane. It went up a little. It was hard to tell anything else because of the dark-ness.

"She lives in Miami Beach?"

"If you go slow now I can find the spot. Little slower."

He drove more slowly and looked at her leaning out of her window.

"She works in a stand where they sell juices. You know those juice bars they have in Florida all over? She works in one of those, squeezing juices. Here it is."

"Here?"

"Stop a minute."

They were on the top of a rise where the lane got wide enough for the car to pull off to one side, then the rise dropped off again and Jordan could see nothing but the night there. He stopped the car for the girl and she leaned on the window sill and looked out.

"This, I bet, is a lot like Florida," she said.

"Where?"

"Turn the lights off."

He turned off the lights and after a while he saw a little better in the darkness.

"That's the beach," she said. "You see the lights?"

Somewhere down below he saw a curve of light and perhaps it looked the way a beach might look at nighttime.

"Penderburg is over that way and this is the Number Three Conveyor. We just call it that, the Number Three Conveyor. It goes up that new shale hill. Did you ever see tile roofs?"

"See what?"

"Like in Florida, you know? Those tile roofs with the round-looking tile."

"Spanish tile roofs."

"Spanish tile. That's what my girl friend calls them. There. You can just see them there."

He moved closer and when he put his head next to hers he could see the work sheds by the mine. They were made out of corrugated tin. The overhead light in the yard showed the geometry of the tin and from the distance it might have been what she wanted it to be.

The girl had a soft odor, something like soapy water.

"And when I've saved enough," she said, "I'm going down there. To Florida."

Not from soap, he thought, because it isn't an odor of chemistry. It's skin. He remembered the look of her arm with fair skin, showing no texture. He did not touch her arm or look at it now but only thought about the way it had looked.

"I've never been there," he said, "except on business."

It struck her that he had said the same thing before, and talking as little as he did, that he had repeated himself. She turned her head to look at him. She did it slowly because he was close and she did not want to bump into him, bumping noses, perhaps, which would be terrible. She leaned her head against the post of the door and she could see mostly his eyes.

"It must be terrible," she said, "seeing all those places and it's always on business."

She saw his eyes move so they no longer looked at her and then he looked back at her. "It's the first time I've thought of it," he said.

She wished she were not holding her can of beer. She could do nothing with it, he being so close.

"And now I don't want to think of the places at all," he said.

She wished she did not have the beer because her fingers would be cold and perhaps wet, and she wanted to touch the side of his face. He looked down so that she could see only his forehead and could not tell what he was looking at. She sat still and heard herself breathe.

"I want to go someplace sometime," she said, "because I don't have to. You feel like that, Sam?"

The worst times are between jobs, he remembered.

"I'd even like to come to Penderburg sometime. After I've left, I mean, and am living elsewhere. Come here and just walk through the streets and have nothing to do and look at things."

She saw him reach over to the window and drop his beer can out. It made a thunk on the ground because it wasn't empty.

"Is that how it is when you get to a new town?" she asked him. "When you go to a new town on business?"

"When I go to a new town on business," he said, "I don't even see the new town. It could be the place where I was before. It's all the same. The job is always the same."

He then did a strange thing, lifted his hand and put his fingers over her mouth. It was a quick motion but did not startle the girl because he moved smoothly.

"Though why this is not the same," he said, "I don't know."

He felt her mouth under his fingertips and that she slowly kissed them.

It's different, he thought, because I'm not yet on a job. This is like the time in between, dead time usually. He did not know that it was much more different than that. He put his head down and his face into the side of her neck and his hand on her. The girl dropped her can of beer and held still for him. He did not wonder about the difference now, that he was not really with her because he was between jobs, but that he was with her because he had run from one.

Chapter 8

He took the girl home very late at night, and then he drove out of town again and slept in the back of his car. It was part of the original plan. Nothing else had been part of the original plan, and he felt disturbed and superstitious for the rest of the night. In the morning he drove into town and stopped at the bus station. He shaved and washed some in the rest room and after that had breakfast at the counter which was in the station. It did not occur to him to go back to the diner because that was something else entirely and this was a different day. The sun shone early, and Jordan walked across the square where the old men already sat under the trees and where a farmer unloaded produce in front of a store. Jordan went to the end of the square where he could see the length of Third Avenue.

He did not feel uneasy until he saw someone come out of Kemp's building. He was doing the part of the job which he did not want, the part which showed him who the other one was. But the man at the building was not Kemp. Jordan turned back to the square but did not know where to go. He did not want to lose sight of Kemp's building.

There was a store window with bolts of cloth and two dummies wearing flower print dresses in it. This store might buy buttons, he thought. One dummy had a foot off the ground because the limb had not been screwed in all the way. Jordan turned away, not liking the sight. That was when he saw Paul. The man stood by the curb, watching Jordan.

"Don't go away," he said.

He had his hands in his pockets and one foot up on the curb and his head was tilted because of the sun. Paul looked easy and very uncomplicated. Once he ran his tongue over his teeth.

"Been selling any buttons today?"

Jordan put his hands into his pockets but it did not feel relaxed. He took his hands out again and let them hang. This was more natural for him. He stood like that and gave Paul a slight smile. Paul was a familiar thing. He was nothing new, he was nothing important; and if he should become part of the job, it would be a side issue.

"No," said Jordan. "I haven't sold any yet."

"How come?"

"I'm still casing."

"Casing? Button salesmen do casing?"

"I learned the word in the movies. I go a lot. Do you go a lot?"

Jordan took a cigarette out and turned it back and forth in his fingers. Paul was watching that. Then he said, "What?"

"Do you go to the movies a lot?"

Paul did not know how to take that, because everything of course had an angle. And he did not remember Jordan this way. He had a fixed notion of what a man might be like who sells buttons and who backs out of a fight. Paul came up with a formula and said, "What's it to you?"

"Nothing. Where's your friend Mister Kemp?"

"Kemp? Why?"

"I see you, I think of Mister Kemp. You know, that's how I met both of you."

But the answer did not please Paul. It did not relax him because it was his job not to be relaxed, and for a long time this rule had been the only reminder that he did have a job and was important.

"For a button salesman you ask an awful lot of questions that don't have a damn thing to do with buttons, you know that . . . What's your name?"

"Smith."

"Smith. That's right. I never knew there were any real Smiths."

Jordan did not take it up and the tone did not bother him. He had his tack now and was working.

"I wanted to see him. That's why I asked. Where is he now?"

"He's busy."

"I wouldn't want to bother him."

"Then why see him?"

"I haven't found the house he was talking about last night. To rent a room."

"*I* remember where he said it was. I got it all clear in my head because Kemp knocked himself out explaining it straight. How come you don't remember a simple—"

"I was thinking about something else."

For a button man, Paul thought, this one is mean. He's untrimmed mean, the thin-nosed bastard, but before Paul was ready with his answer for that, Jordan turned, walked away.

Now, Jordan thought, he's got to follow.

"Hey—" and when Jordan did not answer, "Fourth is that way," said Paul. "There's nobody going to rent you a place here on Third." Then he was next to Jordan, keeping pace. "And the diner's run by an old man this time of morning."

"I'm going to see Kemp," said Jordan.

Paul prickled with irritation and could not think of a good thing to say. *"Mister* Kemp to you, button man." It did not come up to the mark. "And he ain't up," said Paul.

"Good. Then he'll be home."

"Button man—" The bastard is walking too fast. "Not up for you, button man."

"You his nurse?"

"Yeah. I'm his nurse."

But Jordan kept walking without giving an answer, and Paul kept on walking and did not talk any more either. Jordan felt he had learned what he had to know. Kemp's muscle took his job seriously. He was through bantering and was coming along. Whether or not he knew that it was serious made little difference, because unless he, Jordan, could shake the man later, it would come to the same thing. The little fat man from the Coast might have bought himself double service.

In the hallway of the building Paul would not say where Kemp was living. This one, thought Jordan, might be worse than he looks, because he is stupid and trying to make up for that with his stubbornness. Jordan looked at the mailboxes and then went to the third floor. Window at end of hall, runner on floor, fire escape to the back, card on door, *Thomas Kemp.* Jordan knocked.

He had to knock because Paul was standing there with him and it would not look innocent to walk away now. He knocked again which would seal it that he had to stay.

Kemp was up. He opened the door looking rumpled, and half of his face had lather on it. This made him look different from Kemp in the photo and Kemp last night in the diner, almost like somebody Jordan did not know.

"Well, lookee here," said Kemp. His smile looked clownish because of the foam. "Smith, wasn't it?"

There was one room, and a door to another one. Bed, sink, other things, lived-in clutter.

"Come in."

Jordan came in and Paul closed the door. Kemp kept smiling. There was a foam glob on his upper lip and he blew up at it. There was now a large nose hole. "Been working this early in the morning?" said Kemp.

Then he went back to the sink and Jordan did not have to say anything, except no, he hadn't been working yet. Kemp shaved and looked into the mirror and said Jordan should wait just a minute and find a seat.

There was just one chair and Paul sat in it. He had his legs crossed and dipped one foot. Every time Kemp scraped, Paul dipped his foot.

"He was real anxious to see you," said Paul.

"Oh?" Kemp grinned into the mirror. He worked the razor around the grin. "What for, Smith?"

"I couldn't find that room last night," said Jordan. "You remember telling me . . ."

Kemp splashed and rubbed water all over his face and made a blowing sound into his hands. Then he used a towel. When Jordan looked up it was again Kemp's face with the squint lines by the eyes, the gray hair, young man's grin. Jordan rubbed his nose and looked out of the window. "I can come back when you've had your breakfast," he said. "Or if you'll tell me when you're free, when you don't have anything to do during the day . . ."

"I'll take you now," said Kemp. "How's that?"

It wasn't any good. Jordan nodded, but it probably would be no good going with Kemp because it would not help Jordan to find out how Kemp spent his day. He knew when Kemp got up and had an idea when he went to bed. And that Paul hung around all the time. It might have to be enough. Or he would have to go with Kemp and talk more.

"I can take him," said Paul. "Why should you bother?"

"No bother," said Kemp. He put a jacket on and pulled up his tie. Then he grinned into the mirror again, from very close, to see what his teeth were like. "I take a walk anyway," he said. "Before breakfast. Ready?"

They walked down the street with Paul following the two men. Jordan watched a garbage truck creep down the street. Because there were trees all along, the truck was in and out of the light.

"Business any good in town?" Kemp asked.

"I don't know yet. I haven't tried yet."

"Kind of slow, aren't you?"

"Yes."

"You know something? I've never seen anyone have a cigarette habit the way you do. Holding it that way, unlit."

Jordan threw the cigarette away and Paul, in back, laughed.

Kemp said, "Where you buy your merchandise, Smith?"

"In New York."

"Good profit?"

"It's a job, Mister Kemp."

"But the investment is low, isn't it?"

"I don't know," said Jordan. "Over the years, it isn't low."

This time Kemp laughed and they walked a while without talking. Then Paul said, "You're going the long way."

"I know," said Kemp. "You mind, Smith?"

"No. I don't mind."

"It's a nice day," said Kemp. "That's why."

Jordan looked at the mountain of shale which started on the other side of the railway tracks. "There aren't many places to walk here, if you like to walk."

"It's okay. I just walk on the streets. Like this way, and then around to Fourth street."

"You take this walk every morning?"

"Yes. I'd walk more, except Paul isn't much for it."

"He always comes along?"

"We're kind of together," said Paul.

"Yes," said Kemp. "Except we part ways on the movies. Christ, him and those movies."

Jordan waited for more but nothing came. "You don't see the same movies?" he said.

"I don't see any. Just Paul goes."

"This burg can drive you nuts," said Paul.

"Won't be long now," said Kemp. He sighed and looked up at the trees.

There was more talk but it meant nothing. There were niceties with the landlady who said she favored young men who came to town on business and Jordan paid for a room, one week in advance. Then the two men stayed with him while Jordan walked to the square for his car, and then they passed him again on their walk back, while Jordan was taking a suitcase into the rooming house. Kemp just nodded and walked by but Paul stopped and watched.

"That's damn little luggage for a salesman," he said.

"What I use for business," said Jordan, "is in the trunk of the car. I don't need that in my room," and then he went inside.

Upstairs, he sat in his room for a while. He sat near the window which opened on the house next to him, a yard with a chicken coop, and in the distance, the back of Kemp's apartment. It was ten in the morning and Jordan did some of the routine things.

He laid out toilet stuff, but not all of it. He laid out enough to make an impression, but he did not leave his hairbrush out or his razor. They were things which carried traces of him and which he would not want to leave behind. The toothpaste was new, the toothbrush was new, and the razor blades. He left those out but he wiped them. He put some shirts on a chair and they were new too. They had no laundry marks and they were not his size.

He had a twenty-five caliber target pistol and a thirty-eight Magnum. For the Magnum, because of the racket, he also had a silencer. He looked at the guns for a moment and thought that the smaller gun would be all he'd need. There would be time to aim and no need for a big slam. The target pistol would still make less sound, even counting the silencer on the Magnum, though he worried a while about the pitch. The report of the target gun had a high pitch, where the Magnum didn't. The Magnum was louder, but with the silencer it did not sound like a gun shot so much. Jordan could not decide and locked up the suitcase. He would think about it and decide later. This did not make him nervous. This was part of the craft.

He put the suitcase into the closet, locked the closet. He left the room and locked it. He drove partway out of town where all the filling stations lined the road. He filled the tank at one, got oil and air at another. In a garage one street over he had all the spark plugs changed because he did not like the sound of the motor in idle. He had the points cleaned and asked for a battery check. The battery was new but the check was routine. One cell needed water.

He drove out of town a short way and ate lunch on the road. He did not want to run into Kemp or Kemp's man any more. After lunch he smoked a cigarette and looked out of the window. There was a potato field and some cows behind a fence to one side. The sun was high and bright now.

He went back to his room and slept for two hours. When he got up he washed his face and then sat by the window. He clipped his fingernails and he chewed on a cigarette. After he had looked out of the window a while, he noticed that the coop down below was not for chickens. There were pigeons inside.

He lay down on the bed again, got up a short time later. He looked at the new tube of toothpaste, at the shirts, and once at the suitcase in the closet. He sat down again, by the sink this time. He had the window in back of him and watched a drop from the faucet. It was mid-afternoon and the waiting was worse than the job.

He made tiny turns on the head of the faucet and tried for a rate of drip which was just before the point where the drops slid together to make a thin stream. Between that time and evening he managed this twice.

"Those were lousy french fries," said Kemp.

He lay down on the bed and put his shoes up on the baseboard.

"I said those were lousy french fries."

"Yeah. Yeah, they were," said Paul.

There was an evening wind and the curtain moved. Paul hitched around in his chair so that the curtain would not reach him.

"You read that magazine yesterday," said Kemp. In a while he said, "Paul."

"Yeah?"

"You read that magazine yesterday. How often you read the same thing before you get it?"

Paul put the magazine down and pulled a cigarette out of his pocket. He did not take the pack out of his pocket but just one cigarette.

"I was looking at the pictures is all."

He lit the cigarette and picked up the magazine again.

"It's quarter to seven," said Kemp.

"Huh?"

"What in hell's the matter with you, Paul?"

"Nothing." He sighed and looked at his cigarette. "Those were lousy french fries," he said.

Kemp pulled his legs up and pushed the shoes off his feet. Then he dropped them on the floor. "It's quarter to seven. You'll be late for the movie."

"Yeah. The movie." Paul stretched in the chair and said, "I don't think I'll go. I wanna read this magazine."

"Ohforchristsakes," said Kemp.

Paul looked at Kemp, waiting for more, but nothing came.

"What's the matter with you," he said. "Why you riding me?"

"What's the matter with *me?*"

"Yeah. If I wanna sit here and read a magazine . . ."

"You can't read."

"Now listen, Kemp—"

"You listen. You go to the movies. You go to the movies and just figure it's going to be maybe one more week like this and no more. So go to the movies."

"What are you gonna do?"

"I'm going to think about you sitting in the movie, for God's sake! Now beat it!"

"Listen, Kemp—"

Kemp groaned. Then he said Paul shouldn't put on so and how much worse it would be if he, Paul, had to make a living selling buttons, for instance, instead of resting his butt in a movie and being able to look forward to a very bright future in no more than a week or so.

"You know what I think of that guy, don't you?" said Paul.

"He's not your type is what you want to say."

"He's a creep."

"Leave him alone. Rest yourself."

"Did you ever see any of the buttons he's selling?"

"No. Buttons are very small."

"Now listen, Kemp. I been trying to tell . . ."

"You're going stir crazy," said Kemp. "Go talk to Betty."

"Listen, Kemp. You ever see a salesman before what never brags about his loot or the territories or what in hell they brag about all the time?"

"We're no customers is the reason."

"I been trying to tell you . . ."

"Go to the movies."

"You know something, Kemp? *I* wouldn't buy nothing from him, you know that? He—what in hell is the word—he don't come out. You know what I mean?"

"Shy?"

"Shy? He ain't shy, man. I don't know what but he ain't that way."

"No," said Kemp. "He isn't really shy."

"So? Like I been telling you!"

"Go to the movies, Paul."

Paul gave up. He did not want to talk any more about something which he wasn't certain about, and he had no way of dealing with Kemp when he took the tone of the older man.

"I'm going to the movies," Paul said.

"Why, how you think of those things?"

"What are you gonna do?"

"Spend the evening, Paul. I'm going to just waste it away."

"You staying here?"

"Yeah, I'm staying here and I want to stay here alone!"

"All right," said Paul. "I'm going."

He left. He felt less sure about everything than before, and for a moment he stood in front of the house on the street. He looked up the street and down the street but not as if looking for something but like one who did not know what to look for and feeling sullen about it. His good will had been insulted. He could not tell Kemp about it but he would make somebody feel this. Go sit in the diner? He looked across and saw the girl Betty through the windows in front. To hell with her, he said. Go to the movies and to hell with all this. I'll go to the diner with Kemp afterwards. Like always. And the button man might even be there. Go to the movies now and then the button man. That's the ticket. The evening all planned and no problems about any of it. Sit in the dark in the movie, that's no problem, and later the button man, in the diner, that'll be just as good.

Paul walked down the street, toward the square, and he even felt something like interest. He did not think he had seen this movie before and that would mean almost two hours of entertainment. The street was dark and the square up ahead was lit up. Maybe the movie would be something funny. Maybe a cops and robbers thing and he'd laugh while the yokels sat there with the kiss of drama all over them. Or a big, bad syndicate thing, he'd laugh.

He was late for the movie but he stood near the ticket booth for a moment and looked at the girl behind the glass. She thinks she's a movie star. She looks at everybody like they're a scout and treats everybody like they aren't. She's going to rot here. She's going to have a white-eyed miner for a husband and ten slug-coloured babies. He said nothing to her when he bought his ticket because ignoring her hairdo and make-up would be even worse. Yessir, he thought, this is the life I'm getting away from.

"I give you enough for two tickets, honey. Where's my two tickets?"

"Oh—I thought—I didn't see anybody . . ."

"Gimme two tickets, honey. One seat's for my feet."

He bought two tickets and laughed. Then he saw Jordan.

Paul walked a ways into the movie because he hadn't quite realized anything yet but then he stopped and looked out again.

The button man. The creep son of a bitch on the side of the square, standing there with that wet butt in his mouth. And no sample case either. Going home? Not going home. He's thinking about going into the movie to beef up his life for the evening. Not the movie.

Walking. Who's the button man? Nobody knows the button man, not even Kemp. What I don't like I don't like and the button man fits into that dandy.

Why Third. Who does the son of a bitch know on Third? Betty. Everybody loves Betty.

And me with two tickets paid for in my pocket and creeping after the button man loving Betty. Who'd love a thing with a wet butt in his face. . . .

Son of a bitch, he's cagey. If he don't act like a stranger in town. If he don't act like he didn't know Betty from nothing, with his back to the diner and looking the other way. Who does he know?

Kemp.

To sell Kemp buttons, and he don't carry a sample case. To ask about renting that room and he's got it rented already. To hang around and be a pain in the neck because who in hell is anybody with a name like Smith. . . .

Not Kemp? Just a walk, then, which is worse yet. The button man takes a walk where he knows people on the same street and he doesn't stop to see either of them. He doesn't stop to see either of them because he doesn't like to be followed. Just for that . . .

Then Paul kept his distance and stayed in the dark to see what the other one would do. He watched Jordan go to the end of the block and turn down the street which joined Fourth. Paul didn't follow. He crossed by the apartment building, through the back, past the pigeon coop and he stood in the dark drive where he could see Jordan come down the street.

Have a word with him now? He's thin and a button salesman but like Kemp said, not really shy. Not really a button salesman, maybe. . . .

He watched Jordan open the trunk of his car and take out a suitcase which he took into the house.

Time to go through his samples? That is the same suitcase he took into the room that same afternoon . . . Leaving, then, staying. . . .

Jordan came out again very soon and got into his car. What a sweet-sounding motor, thought Paul. What a weird thing to watch somebody move, not know what the man does, and to dislike the son of a bitch right from the start and then more so the less he made sense. With a sweet-sounding motor like that he drives like a funeral. . . .

Slow enough to walk, thought Paul, and he walked. He rounded the corner to Third when Jordan's car crept up to the apartment building. There it stopped.

Paul started to run.

And this time the bastard saw me for sure, thought Paul, because why should he take off like that. A type like that and he takes off with the tires squealing. That don't fit, Smith don't fit, the buttons don't fit. . . . He ran to the lot where the diner stood and where his car was parked. He jumped in and then he thought that son of a bitch should hear this—the kind of noise he, Paul, was making; how the motor let out a scream and the gravel shot out and the whine when the car hauled over and into the street. And that's all for you, button man. . . .

And now he's running and he's driving as if he knew the road and the countryside well. He's running from me hell-bent-for-leather.

When Paul realized this he stopped wondering who Smith was; he stopped turning it back and forth in his mind if he was salesman, or grifter, or a man who had come down to wheedle a deal, or had come casing even, because now the other one ran and Paul after him with never a doubt he would make it. And if I can't talk to him, he said to himself, then you will, Anna-Lee, and he squeezed his left arm into his side so he could feel the holster.

The car up ahead didn't cut speed at all when it turned. It leaned so heavily into the turn that Paul held his breath for a moment. Then he braked very sharply because he didn't know the road which the one up ahead was taking.

Black top and two lanes and plenty of bumps. The two tail lights up ahead bounded up and down. Break a spring, you bastard, but nothing else. I'll break the rest for you, button man. . . .

Then the car was gone.

Paul gunned and had to fight the wheel when he came into the bend of the road and what pulled him through, so it seemed, was the sight of the red lights up ahead again. Steady as . . . He had stopped, that's why! Slammed into the side of the road with one door hanging open, with the lights still on, with one front wheel almost hanging over where the embankment dropped off and the bridge railing started. Why the door open? He fell out that way. Why had he been running? Because I was after him.

Paul grinned and stopped his car so that it slammed down on the frame.

"Smith?"

He could look down the embankment but at the bottom he saw only dark.

"Smith? Hey, button man!"

"Yes?"

He thought he could see him now, down by the culvert which went under the bridge.

"Come on out!"

He could see Smith standing there and that man would have

looked the same had he stood on a street. Smith looks weird standing in weeds up to his knees.

"Don't be scared, boy. I come to buy buttons. Smith?"

"Yes?"

"Where are you?"

"Here."

"I got all night, Smith. You hear me?" and he moved toward the bridge so that his shadow stretched out ahead of him.

Smith doesn't move. No sir, but now he does. Back, he does, and afraid of my shadow. Yessir, that one scares . . .

"Smith, little buddy, can you see me clear?"

"Yes."

"Oh my God, you sound all choked up."

This time no answer. Oh my God, how I hate the bastard.

"Little button buddy, here I am. For a sample—"

Then it spat so fast, Paul barely heard all the sound that went with it.

Oh my God, oh my God, how I hate, he thought, and was finished.

Chapter 9

High angle shot, thought Jordan. Chest or head? Hard telling, with the headlight glare making false borders around his shape, and the foreshortened angle.

He put the gun in his pocket and climbed up the bank, through the dry weeds.

With the kind of jerk he had given, I think it was chest.

Paul, on his back, was dead, of course, and the jacket had slid up into bunches and the pants had pushed up to his calves. How that always happens. Chest. Like I thought. . . .

First, Jordan moved the cars. He moved Paul's car to the other side of the bridge and well onto the soft shoulder. He turned the lights off and left the key in the ignition. Then he walked back and moved his own car to the other end of the bridge, also well off the road. This way, the cars would not alarm any motorist.

Jordan got out of his car and after he had closed the door, leaned against it for a moment. Dark and hot and I'll lean here for a moment and then go back. The rest can be as simple as it's been so far, because it needs no planning, because all I have to do is grab him by the back of the jacket and drag him down to the culvert. Done.

Jordan walked away from the car and back to the bridge.

But he's lying on his back and can't be grabbed by the back of the jacket.

Jordan held out his hand for the railing and when he touched it —he knew he would touch it—gave a start.

He's dead, so don't worry. This almost made Jordan giggle, though he did not let himself. It stayed a sharp, fluttery tickle in his throat.

Jordan slowed on the bridge because he could now see the body on the soft shoulder.

Though this is not a job as jobs go. None of it fitting the habits. Everything I do now is with the props gone. That new.

He worked his hand along the railing and walked like a blind man. He could see well enough now, but did not want to.

And even the job as jobs go hadn't been all that good. It had gone easily, because of the habits, but the habits had not been quite good enough for all that was needed. For instance, he thought, and then, for instance, again. I'm calmer already, he thought. But I got him at the right time for the best light but not at the right time for the best drop. He should have stood closer to the edge so he'd drop down the incline all by himself.

Jordan stopped. He could see it lying there, crabbed out with arms and legs the way they always do.

He would now have to touch it.

His scalp moved on his skull, and he thought he could feel his skull tight and hard over the inside of his head. He had an upsetting image—all of him curled soft into the inside of the skull. But it's the second time. This is not the first. . . . He started to sweat, thin and quick, when he saw that it was worse now and not easier.

Then he moved because it became impossible to do nothing.

Jordan bent down and touched. He thought about the time after this time, all done with this, never again this, and so registered very little of what he was doing or what the body was doing, but the worst moments came through.

He touched the jacket high up and yanked. A dead arm swung around and hit Jordan's ankle. After his gasp the breath came out of Jordan's throat, shocking him with the sound because it was like a giggle. But his throat felt all right after that, without the strain in it.

I won't drag him down, I'll roll him down. I'll do that and between now and the moment when I touch it again a headlight will swing around the far bend, and I'll have to let all this go and just run, just run.

But he only thought this and suddenly scratched his head where sweat tickled him and for a moment he was just scratching —nothing else—and after that he had his feelingless calm again, out of nowhere, but the way he was used to it. He only worried for one split second about the quick switches that went on inside him, but that thought never got anywhere because then he touched again.

He dragged like a dog worrying a bone. When the body was over the edge Jordan let go with a quick jerk of his hand and kept jerking his hand like that, through the air, a little bit like a conductor with temperament. Because the body wasn't rolling. But the quick pizzicato beat kept up Jordan's speed. The dead arms and legs made contrary motions; Jordan kept worrying the thing like a bone, down the bank, through the weeds, feeling intent and all right about it because all the worry was in his hands. What he touched, how much he touched, where. And when he pushed it into the culvert, which took perhaps two minutes, he counted time by the number of times he pushed against bone instead of flesh.

Done, back through the weeds which were pulling at him. He kept wiping his hands and then wiped them with the weeds. They were not wet but brittle and dry and Jordan, wiping over and over, cut himself. Up the bank, job over. And how quick and clever the whole thing. It had probably been spite to start with— Paul following him by the movie—but then it was the plan working. It was good to know about plans working. Going down Third, drawing Paul after. Stopping at Kemp's place, getting Paul all riled up. Then the fast walk around to Fourth—Paul already there, having cut through a lot; then moving the suitcase to give him time and to mystify him, then the slow stunt with the car so he could follow on foot, and then driving off fast when Paul showed up again near Kemp's building.

Jordan worked up the incline to the highway, rehashing things this way, something he had never done. Job over.

Though this was not yet the important one.

Before the haste went out of him and left just nervous splinters, he rushed all the rest. He drove the dead one's car a little ways down the next lane and from there up a path which went to a spent quarry. Jordan knew it was there, drove Paul's car there, and left it. Jordan was not concerned with eliminating all trails but only with working for time. They would find the dead one and they would find the car. He worked for one day's leeway, and the trail would lead nowhere.

He ran back to the highway and his haste didn't change into something else until he sat in his car and knew what he would do next. There was all this momentum but it now turned sharp and clean. Clean like routine. Kemp was next.

Jordan drove back to town, sitting neat and still. He sat with his head on top of his neck like a stopper on top of a bottle. Fine. Everything fine now. Finish it. . . .

He went through Third and saw a light where Kemp's room was. He drove past and turned through the square, doubling back to Fourth. To pick up his suitcase in the room and then finish. He parked and when he went across the street he went fast and kept his hand on his pocket. The Magnum was heavy and Jordan did not want it to swing. Then would come Magnum in suitcase, target pistol for job, suitcase in trunk, drive to Third, check target pistol in front seat, car on street pointed the right way, up Kemp's building, finish it.

Jordan opened the door to his room where the light was on and then everything became very slow. The brain, the movement of the door closing, the door *thunk* when it closed, even Kemp. He sat in Jordan's chair, looking slow, and he held Jordan's other gun.

"Ever use one of these?" he asked.

Jordan stayed by the door and the weight of the Magnum in his pocket was so great that he felt his right shoulder ache and thought Kemp must notice any moment.

"You don't look well, Smith. Why don't you sit on the bed?"

Jordan walked to the bed and wasn't aware of any muscles moving in him. He was only aware of Kemp telling him to sit down.

And this is the payoff for Paul, he thought. This is the payoff. Not for the job he had done, but for having done the job wrong. He had touched him afterwards.

"Jeesis," said Kemp. "You can smell pigeons all the way up here. You mind if I close the window?"

"There's a chicken coop down there," said Jordan.

"No. It's a pigeon coop. Hear 'em fluttering?"

"I thought it was a chicken coop."

"No. Mind if I close the window?"

"Go ahead," said Jordan.

Kemp smiled and closed the window behind without changing position. With one hand.

"That's better. Come on, Smith, relax, huh?"

"I can't," said Jordan.

"You're no salesman, are you?"

Jordan did not answer. He shifted a little on the bed and sighed. It was a natural sigh.

"And Smith yet. What a handle to pick. Don't you know about Smiths?"

"No."

"There aren't any." Kemp laughed.

The Magnum wasn't so heavy now because it was resting on the bed.

"Make it easy on yourself, Smith, why don't you."

Jordan nodded and put both hands down on the bed. It did not relax him but it would be more efficient.

"I'm not saying you're dumb all the way, or *that* obvious, and maybe I just spotted you, Smith, because I got some background. That surprise you?"

"I am surprised. Yes."

"Take your coat off, why don't you?"

"Thanks. No."

"Okay."

Kemp looked at the target pistol in his hand and didn't say anything for a moment. Jordan crossed his legs for position so he could lean on one elbow.

"And loaded yet," said Kemp. "This," and he nodded the gun.

Jordan finished leaning down on one elbow.

"You like this type?" Kemp asked.

"What?"

"This kind of gun," said Kemp, "means one or the other to me. Either hobby, or business."

"What do you want from me?" said Jordan.

" 'Fess up, I guess. Instead of me getting it out of you."

Jordan shrugged, which brought his right hand where he wanted it for the moment.

"I think I'd like this kind myself," said Kemp. "Very accurate, isn't it?"

"If it's balanced good."

"Is it?"

"For my hand."

"I noticed it's top heavy for me. You got a long thumb?"

"Yes."

"Figures." Then Kemp sighed. "Look," he said, "I'm just talking around to make you feel relaxed. Honest, Smith."

Jordan put his right hand on his hip and when there was no objection, he did relax. He relaxed into a balance which was like a steel spring balance.

"I mean it, Smith. Put it away."

He leaned forward and held the gun out. Jordan was not prepared. He was so set that he felt the Magnum might go off if he moved even a little.

"You won't say it, I'll say it, Smith. You're on the lam, aren't you?"

It took almost as long to get back to normal, thought Jordan, as it had taken him to get set. He straightened up with a pain in his back and he reached out for the target gun so that it felt like slow motion.

"Well?" said Kemp.

"Yes. You're right."

Jordan took the gun and turned it to look at the clip. The butt was empty and he held a cold gun.

"I took it out," said Kemp, "because I'm afraid of guns. Imagine that thing goes off in here. Bad for both of us." He pointed and said, "I left the clip in your suitcase."

Jordan tapped his knees with the long barrel and then he tossed the gun on the bed. He felt exhausted and didn't want to try figuring moves any more. Not for the moment. Not after all this.

And the Magnum was out. The silencer was in the suitcase and the racket would be too much. After that, even if the gun went off like a normal gun, after that he would have to run with half his things left in the room because all he would have time to grab would be the new tube of toothpaste on the dresser, a shirt of the wrong size, meaningless things like that.

Nothing now. He just wished Kemp would leave.

"So tell me, Smith. Who do you know?"

"Nobody. I don't know anybody who makes any difference," said Jordan.

"You know me."

"Kemp. That's all I know. Just the name."

"Well, let me tell you a little."

"Listen. I just as soon you wouldn't. I mean it, Kemp."

Kemp raised his eyebrows and watched Jordan sit on the bed. He thought the other man looked suddenly tired.

"I just meant for an introduction. Just a talk, Smith . . ."

"I don't want to talk."

". . . to see if there was something for you and me in it."

"What?"

"Maybe there's a job. Maybe I can use you."

"Ohmygawd—" said Jordan, and rubbed one hand over his face.

"Well, maybe not," said Kemp. He got up and scratched under one arm. "I didn't mean in this town, if that's what you meant." He walked to the door and stopped there. "Just think about it, huh, Smith? Before you blow town, come over and see me. Okay?"

"Yes," said Jordan. "I will."

Chapter 10

After Kemp was gone Jordan locked his door from the inside. He took his jacket off, so as not to feel the weight of the Magnum. At the closed window he looked at the black glass.

I'm not built for this and I'm not trained for this. It comes to the same thing. I know so much and no more and it isn't enough. Or there is always something worse. It comes to the same thing.

Then he turned away from the window because he was beginning to notice his reflection. He packed, the way he had planned it, and he started all over the way he had planned it, because he really did not know anything else.

On Third he parked in the lot next to the diner, heading the car the way he wanted. He thought about leaving the motor running but decided against it. There was light in the diner. There were two other cars in the lot, and somebody friendly might turn off his key, take it out, bring it into the diner for safekeeping maybe. He turned off the motor, put the key in his pocket, stuck the target gun into his belt and buttoned his jacket. If the silencer would only fit the pistol he would have liked that. It was a margin of safety. This was now a job for margins of safety.

He crossed behind the diner where the garbage cans stood, and a cat ran away. The cat made a potato roll over the ground and he picked it up. It was a big, raw potato and he took it along.

At Kemp's door he knocked.

"Paul?"

"No. Smith."

"The door's open. Come on in."

Jordan went in and closed the door behind him. Kemp was on

his bed, dressed, shoes off, a paper across his middle. The paper went up and down with his breathing. Kemp was lying down and stayed that way. This is a bad angle, thought Jordan. The radio next to Kemp was playing mood music.

"Well now. You're looking better." Kemp turned the radio down to a mumble and smiled from his pillow. "You come for the job?"

"I got a job."

"Christ—"

Jordan had the gun out and he worked the potato over the end of the barrel.

"Smith . . . Wait a minute. Let's talk . . ."

Jordan didn't talk. In the movies there is talk, for the drama. Jordan worked without drama. Or there is talk because there is a grudge. There was no grudge.

"Smith, just lemme . . ."

"Sit up."

"Yes, I was gonna say, lemme sit up—"

"Go ahead."

While Kemp sat up Jordan took a stance. He never fired from the hip because when he fired he was never on the run. He aimed straight-arm and only the potato bothered his aim.

"For God's sake—"

The voice was hoarse as if it had the worst kind of cold and after that type of sound there was often a scream. Jordan did not want that and would have been ready if the potato did not interfere with balance and sighting.

"Smith . . . I ask . . . I beg—"

Dull sound, slightest recoil, potato spraying all over. Kemp's head snapped back and went *thunk* on the headboard. Mood music mumble. The hole was high and the blood was just filling it. Black in the light.

A drawn-up knee collapsed and the leg dangled a little and Jordan was going down the stairs.

When he got out on the street he stood for a moment and took a deep breath. He thought that the air was just right. He himself felt right and he felt finished with the job he had come to do.

A young couple came down the dark street and Jordan turned his head away out of habit. He crossed the street to his car and noticed that the diner was dark. He got into his car, feeling right and finished. When he put the key into the ignition he noticed that his hand was shaking.

He did not know why it was shaking because everything felt right now and he was done. He took the gun out of his belt, wiped the end of the barrel across his pants because the metal was wet from the raw potato. He wiped and wiped and then he put the gun under the seat. He started the motor, got into gear almost immediately so that the car jumped and the motor died.

It was not his habit to drive this way. He had a routine with the car where he started the motor, nursed it in idle, then got into gear and took off, smooth and gentle-footed.

While he started over again he thought about everything, thinking too much. At first, way in the beginning, the work had been hard, with everything effort. When that became better, a job was achievement. After that, a job was smooth habit. That had been most of the time now and had felt like the final thing.

He took off the way he was used to it, except faster. There was a man by the letterboxes inside the vestibule. He had a lunch bucket under his arm and was getting his mail.

But this time, thought Jordan, there was this. He was done but his hand was shaking. He was done but he drove too fast. If more of me were shaking, he thought, I would know why I'm feeling this way. Just my hands are shaking, so it's nothing. A fine job up in that room.

What upset him now was that he was thinking about it at all.

He drove through the square and took the street at the other end which went out of town.

Maybe eight minutes since, he thought. That's three more than planned.

What upset him again was not the loss of three minutes but the thoughts he had about a job which was really well done. This felt indecent.

On the other side of the street someone was walking and then turned up to a house with no lights in the windows. The porch light went on and Jordan saw the girl from the diner. She still had her uniform on and was carrying a purse over her arm. She went into the house while Jordan passed.

He kept driving because he was now nine minutes off. Yes, yes, yes, and such a fine finish after that godawful thing on the bridge and then under the bridge. I would hate, he suddenly said aloud, to leave here without such a neat thing done like the Kemp job.

The voice shocked him and the thought—that there had to be thought about any of this—shocked him so that he held the wheel hard, rocking on it. The wheel gave with the rocking, the springiness keeping the rocking motion going. Jordan kept nodding back and forth. What now, what now, he kept thinking, what more, what more now. It's done, it's done—double everything, because it went with the rocking. All the props gone out from under, he thought, all the props I never knew had been there, like don't talk to him, don't touch him, don't know him too well. But they *don't* mean a thing, and his thinking got loud again, because I *did* finish . . .

But he did not recognize himself. He stopped rocking because it made him sick, and he stopped thinking, because that made him sick. He was able to stop thinking because it was easier just to feel the confusion.

She wouldn't think anything like that about me. Her dumb face knows everything and I'm Smith and sell buttons. Her dumb face doesn't care if I'm Smith or sell buttons. She never once mentioned anything like it. She mentioned that I am a gentleman. Jeesis. She mentioned that she likes a quiet man. "You want me, Sam? You want me, Sam, and you don't talk around it. I like that."

She can't be all wrong, he thought. She must know something. She's dumb which just means there's no confusion, and if she says now, Sam, you look fine and not shivery like one day ago— she can't be all wrong. He swung the car into a U-turn and drove back toward town.

He knocked on her door, and she said, "Who is it?"

"Smith."

"Who?"

"Sam. You remember me?" he said through the door.

"Oh, Sam! Come in!"

Jordan went in and closed the door behind him. Betty was on the bed. She had a housecoat on, her shoes were off, and there was a magazine lying across her middle. The magazine went up and down with her breathing. The radio next to her bed was playing mood music.

She said, "Hi, Sam," and, "You know, you're looking ever so much better." She smiled from her pillow and turned the radio down to a mumble.

Jordan let go of the door knob behind him and felt his hand tremble. He did not move away from the door but leaned against it. He began to tremble all over. He did not move, not his eyes or anything, except for his trembling.

Her smile faded a little and then just went away. She raised herself up on one arm and stared at him. "Sam," she said, and then, "Sam?"

She got off the bed slowly and then she walked toward him and came all the way over. She did not say anything else or walk faster but when she was up to him, she slowly put up her hand and laid it on the side of his face. "What is it, Sammy?" she said.

He leaned his face into her hand and closed his eyes. He had to explain nothing, do nothing, and could just stand this way while the girl came closer and put her face next to his. "Come sit down, Sammy," she said. "You'll be all right."

He sat down in the chair she had and was not trembling any more. She brushed at his lapel and said, "How did you ever get raw potato on there. It's just like raw potato," but Jordan was not trembling any more and what she said and did had nothing to do with before any more, with the use of a raw potato. The girl was concerned over his suit and she was concerned that he should sit and rest. It meant that.

"You're not used to the heat," she said and opened his tie and collar a little. "Or is it something else?"

"It's that," he said, "and also something else. But you don't have to worry about it, Betty. It's nothing for you to worry about."

She sat on the arm of his chair and looked down at him. "Are you sick?"

"No. It's something hanging on, but I'm not sick. Really, Betty."

She thought he does not look sick. A little worn, perhaps, needing sleep, but he's all right. He said so and he smiles.

"What do you need, Sammy? Can I do something?"

He took a cigarette out and asked for a match. He puffed on the flame and then he sat back in the chair and looked at the girl and the room.

"I'd like to stay a moment," he said.

"Of course, Sam. You mean, you're leaving?"

"Yes. I'm done here."

"Ah," she said. "You've done your business. Was it good?"

"I'm done," he said. "Yes."

She got up and went to the bed. He watched her lean over the bed and straighten the cover on it. He liked watching her do this. When she straightened up she brushed some hair back and he thought it was a beautiful gesture.

"I'm sorry," she said, because he was looking at her and she felt that her housecoat looked old. She looked down at herself and straightened the front.

"I like you in that," he said. "Really. I like you better in a housecoat than in anything else."

She felt it was nice of him to say this and she made no other remarks about it.

"Can I give you something?" she said, "I don't have a real kitchen, but iced tea, something like that. I can give you something simple like that."

He said that he liked iced tea and then when she said there was a can of sardines and some crackers, he said he liked that, too. He watched her in her housecoat, opening and closing the icebox she had, making the iced tea and getting the sardines out on a plate and the crackers. He would not have stopped for any of this somewhere else but he felt calm and well watching her bring all those things and sitting with him afterwards, eating.

"I'm glad you came over before leaving," she said. "That was very nice of you."

"I like seeing you, Betty."

"I think you were very nice, I mean, the times I've seen you."

"I have to go," he said. "It's a shame."

She nodded a little, nothing serious, and put the plate and crackers away. "Maybe, if you come through here again . . ." she said.

"Yes. I would look you up."

"Or maybe if you ever get to Miami. You know, I expect to be in Miami sometime. I told you."

"Yes."

"It's warm like this all the time, isn't it?"

"The sun shines and there's a breeze from the ocean and nights it's warm. If there's something blooming," he said, "you can smell it, nighttimes."

He knew nothing like this about Miami, having been there on business only and having finished in a very short time, but he thought all this might be true and he knew that she liked hearing it.

Then she gave him the address of her girl friend in Miami and said if he ever got there and if she herself got there sometime soon . . .

He went to the door and she stood with him for a moment and brushed at his lapel.

"Well," she said, and smiled.

"Thank you," he said, just so.

He kissed her on the side of her mouth and stroked her back.
"I've liked you," she said. "Good-by, Sammy."

"Good-by," he said, because this was a short daydream, and he
did not want to do anything to change it or to see it become
impossible. He stroked her back and felt her hands on his arms.

"If you want me," she said next to his face, "I mean, before you
go. Before you have to go, Sammy . . ."

They went back to the bed and she turned off the lights and the
radio. Then she helped him with his tie and shirt buttons. Then
he undressed her, moving as slowly as she.

Chapter 11

Everything being different, Jordan did not drive back the way he
had planned. He left town going south, instead of taking the
north way; he doubled around on new roads, replanning the
routine, and when morning came he was still in the country and
not going straight back on the turnpike as he would have done
had all this been the old schedule. None of this was upsetting to
him because the job was done and the rest, afterward, had been a
matter apart from the job. In the morning he stopped at a hotel,
went to bed, slept for twelve hours. It was a deep, dull sleep, with
only a moment of thinking just before he dropped off. Her one-
room place, with a bed and a corner for cooking on a hotplate.
Frill curtains, which had looked new and cheap. Housecoat, and
the girl moving around him. Had been reading a magazine on
her bed. It had been like coming from work, resting, watching
her do housework, then sleeping together.

Having been trained to a very special point, pathetically ordinary things had become Jordan's peace.
Sandy leaned on the glass counter and looked down at the cigar.
He reached into the case and watched his hand take a panatela
and when he had it in his mouth he looked across the bowling
alley. He especially watched alley six and seven where the
Kantovitz Kats and the Burns Machine Company were playing
tournament. A man with the white and purple shirt of the Kats
came to the counter and asked for three cigars.

"You got any money on this, Sandy?" and he nodded back at
the alleys.

"No. I don't gamble."

"Too risky for you?" and the man laughed.

"That's right," said Sandy and gave the man his cigars. "Who's winning?"

"They are."

The phone rang under the counter and Sandy reached down without looking. He put the receiver to his ear and said, "Yeah?" After that he listened for a short while, then said, "No," and hung up.

"They're winning," said the man in the shirt, "but not because of any superior ability. It's the balls. They got tournament balls and we got all kinds. I think it makes a difference."

"I told you I'd get you the new ones. You could have ordered . . ."

"Sandy, we don't got that kind of dough."

"I can't go any lower. I'm giving them to you for what it costs me anyways."

"Sandy, with your kind of connections you can get 'em for less than they cost. You know that."

"I got no connections like that. I don't make anything on them as it is. Honest."

"I believe you." The man lit his cigar and said, "Business is tough."

"That's right."

The phone rang again and Sandy picked it up as before. He said, "Yeah," and then "Yeah," and hung up. He wouldn't have minded standing at the counter some more and talking, but he pushed himself away and said, "Gotta run. I hope you guys make it."

"We won't. But think about those balls, will you, Sandy?"

"I will. I'll check around," and then he went to the back for his hat and overcoat.

Sandy had to drive for about fifteen minutes. He tried to go faster, because in the heat the draft helped, but there was a great deal of traffic. He drove with one arm on the window and let the draft run up his sleeve.

Maybe Venuto can help, he thought. He owes several favors and knows Dryer Supply. Maybe he can get the balls at manufacturer's price, and why not. He owes several favors.

Sandy turned off the thoroughfare and went through the wholesale district. Drygoods, then papergoods. There were trucks and semis parked on the street and angled into alleys.

Because I hate to see somebody lose all the time, thought Sandy. Nice, strong outfit like the Kats, why should they lose all the time, just because of no-good equipment.

He parked with two wheels on the sidewalk and two in the gutter, which was the only way traffic was able to pass him on the street.

He went into a store with the windows painted black half way up and inside nothing but storage space. The place had the dry smell of a great deal of paper. There were tall stacks of it all around, wrapped in brown packages. Sandy went past one side of a shelf which divided the long place in two. The other side of the store was the same as the first, except that there was a desk and a bulb hanging over it. The desk and the bulb were surrounded by paper packets so that the space looked like the inside of a box.

"Hello, Bass," said Sandy.

"Sit down."

Sandy took a chair next to the desk and said, "Christ, how can you work in this place?"

The other man didn't answer. He was bald and squat and the suit he wore didn't fit the place. It was dark flannel, cut up to date, and his shirt was a fashion pink. His bald head was very smooth and his face had heavy lines.

"Well?" said Bass.

"Nothing. I would have called you."

"He ever been late before?"

"No. Not unless he calls. He hasn't called though."

Bass took his ballpoint and made zigzags on an order blank.

"I want you to send somebody down there."

"That's no good. I never do that, at this kind of time, and especially with a burg like this Pender—what was it?"

"You just said it. Penderburg."

"Yes. For all I know the whole place is popping. You should get a paper. I'm sure they got a local paper."

"You just said it, that it's a burg. Where'm I going to get a paper from there?"

Sandy shrugged and looked at the stacks all around. "Maybe the car broke down," he said.

"His car ever break down before, on a job?"

"No."

"Maybe something else broke down." Bass looked up and asked, "How long you had him?"

"He's all right. I see him all the time."

Bass looked at his ballpoint and then at Sandy. Sandy shook his head.

"No. He's been fine. He's quiet, kind of, but that's all."

Bass shrugged and got up. He stretched his back and said,

"How quiet is fine?" Then he looked at a crack of light between the stacked paper packets, where a window was on the other side. "Meyer is on pins and needles and says I should call you over and get you to explain this thing. And what you're going to do about it."

"Frig him," said Sandy and he got up. "I got things to do."

Bass turned around and watched Sandy go. Bass was just the man in the middle and the less he had to do with this the better.

"I meant to ask you," said Sandy and he stopped by the door. "You know Venuto?"

"Who?"

"Never mind," said Sandy and then he left.

He stood by his car for a moment and watched a semi snake up to a loading platform. And if Venuto can't do anything, maybe I'll ask Schultz. I hate to see those Kats lose all the time.

"Hey! Sandy!"

He turned and saw Bass in the door to the paper place.

"He just called your place."

"From where?"

"He's in town."

"Where in town?"

"He left word you should call him at the number you got. You'd know where."

"Okay. I know," and Sandy got into his car.

"Wait a minute. Call him up and tell him to show at Meyer's place."

"When?"

"Now, damn it. What are we running here, anyways?"

"A business. What else?" and Sandy drove off.

Meyer's place had terraces and glass walls in the dining rooms, so that the weekend trade from the city could look at the hills in comfort or out at the river. This was not a weekend and the big dining room was locked up. Meyer walked back and forth on the dance floor, and when he looked up he did not see the rolling view outside the large windows but all the empty chairs and tables.

Meyer did not look like a restaurant owner but perhaps like a man who sold houses. He was small and his clothes looked untidy, the kind of untidyness which says there are things more important than clothes. Meyer had a face like a hawk.

The first car which drove into the lot brought Bass. He parked in line with the other cars; he went into the bar and had a drink next to the other guests. There were not very many. They were mostly women having an afternoon drink, and they talked about maid and gardener problems.

Bass went through the door which said *Gentlemen* and from there out through another door which said *Gentlemen.* That way he got into the dining room.

Meyer nodded at him and Bass nodded back. Then Bass sat down at a table and looked out of the windows.

Sandy and Jordan came in by a different way. Not even Meyer had noticed when they had driven up. They came in through the empty terrace and only Sandy said hello.

They all sat down at the empty tables and since there were so many tables, everyone sat at a table by himself. A bug was beating itself to death on the sunny side of the terrace; for a moment there was no other sound.

Meyer looked at Jordan but all Jordan did was look back. The two men did not know each other well. Then Meyer drummed his table a few times and twitched his nose. "All right," he said. "Done?"

Jordan nodded.

"How come you're late?"

"There were two of them."

"The guard too?"

"Had to," said Jordan.

"How come we didn't hear sooner?"

"Because I just got back."

Jordan took a cigarette out of his pocket and put the filter between his teeth. He held it like that, looking almost as if he were grinning.

"All right," Meyer said again. "I want to know more. Something here isn't regular."

"What more?" said Jordan. "You want his head on a platter?"

Bass looked at Sandy and Sandy looked down at his fingernails. Meyer looked shocked. Then he said, "All right. Jokes. All right. But you never been late before. What kept you?"

"I never had to do my own casing," said Jordan.

Bass had thought Jordan would say something else. He thought the natural answer would have been, I never had to kill two on one job. But Jordan said nothing else. He had closed his eyes, sighing, but kept holding the cigarette in his teeth like before, teeth showing, as if in a grin.

"I want to know more about it," said Meyer.

This is as bad as doing the thing, thought Jordan. And screw Meyer. Hold that talk. Better not say "screw you" to Meyer.

"More?" said Jordan. "What are you, a pervert?"

After that Jordan lit his cigarette, and everyone watched him doing it because it was the only thing that was happening. When Meyer talked again, he sounded carefully slow, almost uninterested.

"Something ailing you, Jordan?"

"I'm fine."

"You sound like you need a rest maybe."

"I don't want a rest."

"Oh."

"There's a point," said Bass, "when a man doesn't necessarily know that he needs a rest. Like when I get to the point—"

"Not the same thing," said Jordan. "I don't sell paper, you know that?"

Jordan smoked and looked at Bass because Bass happened to be most in line. Then he looked away from Bass and watched Sandy. Sandy was getting up and walked to the table where Jordan was sitting. He bent sideways a little and looked down at Jordan's suit.

"How come it's all buttoned, Sam?" he asked. "With this heat and all, Sam?"

"How come you wear an overcoat all the time, Sandy?"

Sandy said, "Because I'm a little bit nuts," and then he reached over and patted Jordan on the front where his stomach was.

He did it with the back of his hand and his big signet ring made a hard sound when it tapped.

It took less than a second, Jordan slapping the hand out of the way, and he looked immediately the way he had looked before, but all the others—shocked with the suddenness—did something. They sat up more, touched tie, shifted seat.

"Since when," said Sandy, "are you carrying a gun, Sammy, while not working?"

Jordan said something filthy, which was almost as much of a shock as the other thing, his sudden slap.

The bug on the terrace had changed his sound. He wasn't bumping any more but just buzzed. He was on his back, the way it sounded, buzzing. And they could all hear the phone ringing. It was someplace far away and somebody picked it up almost immediately. Meyer looked away, at a door in the back, and everyone waited. Then he got up and left the big room.

Jordan had worked the coal out of the end of his cigarette and watched it smoke itself out in the tray on his table. The dead stub was in his mouth. Sandy asked Bass if he knew Schultz and when Bass answered no, he didn't know any Schultz, Sandy explained he was interested in buying some bowling balls. This sounded like nonsense to Bass, coming from Sandy, but Bass didn't feel detached enough to make anything of it. Then Meyer came back.

He had a newspaper in his hand and sat down where he had sat before.

"Business call?" said Bass.

"That was Sherman." Meyer put the paper on top of his table. He looked down at it, and talked that way. "I don't think you know Sherman. Just somebody runs errands for me."

"How about it," said Jordan. "We done?"

"He just called," said Meyer, "I should look at the afternoon paper."

He leafed through it and said, "Only page nineteen."

Jordan got up and dropped his butt in the ashtray.

"I haven't slept much," he said.

"Sleep on this," said Meyer. "Kemp's alive."

Chapter 12

"For a minute there," said Bass, "I thought he was going to pass out."

All three of them stood by their tables and looked out at the parking lot where Jordan was driving by and out to the highway.

"He just got pale," said Sandy.

"But *that* pale."

"You know, professional pride."

"Let's go to my office," said Meyer and he took the paper along.

They still had the view like before but the room was smaller and Jordan was no longer there. It changed the mood between them—nothing to do with feeling better or worse—but a change from a big room to a small room, a change from four people to three, a change of sitting closer together now, all to one side of Meyer's big desk. If there had been a stove, they might all have sat closely around it.

"What do you think?" said Bass and looked at Sandy.

"I want to hear what's in that paper."

Meyer nodded and looked at it again. "He's alive, in a hospital. Duncaster County Hospital, says the article."

"Is that the county where that burg-something is located?"

"Sherman's finding out. What it says here, somebody downstairs got riled by the radio blaring—Kemp somehow upset his radio maybe, when he wasn't dead, and that radio kept blaring there on the floor."

"Maybe Jordan had turned it up on account of the shot," said Bass.

"No. He doesn't do that," said Sandy.

"I was saying," and Meyer rattled his paper, "the guy from downstairs says he went up to Kemp's door, after midnight sometime, and after knocking and knocking he tried the door and went in."

"And?" said Bass.

"And what? He found Kemp there. What else?"

"How'd they know it was Kemp?"

"Yeah. That's a nice one. Gunshot, so naturally cops. Just a minute," and Meyer looked for a paragraph. "Here: *A search of the victim and his room offered no identifying information, and beyond the landlord's contribution of his tenant's name, nothing else could be learned about the victim. Only on the basis of a fingerprint check was the victim's full identity established several hours . . .*"

"He wouldn't talk?" asked Bass.

"It says here he's out. It says here—just a minute—it says he's in critical condition and in a coma. And partial paralysis, one side."

"Can he talk that way?"

They didn't know. They thought maybe he would die and if he did not die, maybe he would still not be able to talk. They knew nothing else. Only that Jordan had missed.

"Anything about the other one?" Sandy wanted to know.

"No. Just that there must have been another occupant in the apartment. They're looking for him."

"I hope Jordan did him right."

"He said two."

"He also said Kemp was done and he isn't."

They sat and smoked. Meyer folded the paper and looked at the two others. Then he looked only at Sandy.

"What's he been like?"

"Like?" Sandy looked from one to the other and didn't know how to say it. "You know . . . Just, I guess, normal."

"What I mean is . . ."

"He's never missed before, if that's what you mean."

"He shoots good, is that right?"

"Sure."

"Then why not this time?"

Sandy did not know what to answer.

"Here Kemp was lying in bed. The article says, he fell out of bed. Here he's in bed. Jordan walks in with his gun. No distance to worry about, nothing. He does a job and misses."

"Maybe somebody walked by in the hall outside," said Bass.

Sandy shook his head. "First of all, that wouldn't throw him. Second of all, he wouldn't fire."

"Does he use a silencer?"

"So what? He can hold the gun in his foot and not miss."

"All right," said Meyer. "So it's nothing like that." He sucked air through his nose and then coughed it out. "So let me ask you this. The way he was acting before."

"Getting pale?"

"No. That's normal. Before that."

"Professional pride."

"Whatever. I mean before that. The way he talked all of a sudden."

"He was tired. Like he said."

"He ever been like that before?"

"No."

"He ever been tired before?"

Sandy shrugged. He crossed one leg over the other and shrugged again.

"Ask him."

"That's what I'm talking about. I did and you heard how he got with me. Nasty."

"And the gun in his belt, remember?" said Bass.

Sandy got out of his chair and went to the window. He looked at the view, put his hands in his pockets, took them out again. Then he turned around.

"Look. He's an investment, you know? Think of it that way."

"I'm thinking he's maybe a liability."

"Just give it a little time, will you?"

"Maybe Kemp will die," said Bass, as if that made any difference.

Meyer didn't bother to answer. He looked at Sandy and then he closed his eyes.

"What I'm saying is, you're responsible."

Sandy got annoyed and put his hands back into his pockets. He pushed them deep as if looking for a coin.

"I never liked the whole thing from the start, Meyer, I told you that. You don't send a gun out doing his own casing and you don't send 'em out an hour after they come back from another job. I told you that, Meyer."

"What's so tough about casing?"

"How in hell do I know? All I'm saying is, you don't . . ."

"He gets paid good, don't he?"

"Yeah. He gets paid good," said Sandy and then he did not say anything else because he did not know how.

Meyer got up, walked around the desk, leaned his rear against it.

"I'm sending a man down to check this thing out."

Sandy put on his coat. "I'd leave it lie," he said. "It's too close to the time when they're looking the hardest."

"And give the fuzz all over that Penderburg the time of their lives running a hot trail?"

"Jordan doesn't leave a trail," Sandy said but felt foolish for having said it as soon as it was out. Nothing was quite so sure any more, about Jordan.

Meyer did not take it up. The point was too obvious. But he said, "There's only two things which are the worst with the kind of operation we run. First, if a gun misses. Which has happened. Second, if he leaves a trail. Which I hope hasn't happened. The first is bad enough because it leaves one too many who can talk his head off, and the second is worse because the trail leads to us. They catch one man, that's one less man. They catch wind of an organization, that's everything down the drain." Meyer got up and sighed. "So I'll handle that end. Penderburg. You check out Jordan."

"I'll look him over," said Sandy and went to the door.

"And let me hear tonight."

"What?" said Sandy. "Tonight what?"

"How he is. What you think."

The trouble with Meyer and his kind, they handle things like there are no human beings in it. "He'll sleep all afternoon," said Sandy. "I'll look him over tonight."

"Your Wednesday afternoon routine can wait," said Meyer. "You check Jordan out now and to hell with everything else."

Sandy did not argue. Meyer was being a bastard about this, rushing things because he was nervous, and running it as if there were no human beings in it. Jordan wasn't going to run amuck if unattended this afternoon, and Sandy's own Wednesday routine also would not throw anything out of kilter.

"All right," said Sandy. "Unless he's asleep."

"Check him out," Meyer said again.

"All right."

"Because if Kemp doesn't go on his own, Jordan will have to finish it."

Jordan was not asleep but sat in his room, by the window, and looked at the building opposite. He could see the flat roof line and the flat-line windows under that. On the windows he read Optic Supply Co., Central Dental Supply, and after a skip of one black window, J. S. Mackiewisznitz. What Mackiewisznitz sold Jordan did not know. This was time in between. Jordan sat and looked at the building opposite.

This was not time in between. Jinx job. There's no time between jinx jobs because when the jinx hangs on the job's never over. . . . Maybe Kemp will die by himself?

Jordan took a small pair of scissors from the shelf over his sink and cut his nails. Then he put the scissors back, gave a twist to the faucet by the sink, sat down again.

This was clearly not time in between like the other times. I'm waiting too much for what will come next, he thought. It feels lousy. Talk to Sandy? No. He says less than I do. Jordan thought about Penderburg, then the girl, and could not keep the two apart. It made him feel irritable. He sat and looked at the building opposite and his mood jumped back and forth, from screamy to dull. He got up and twisted the faucet again, which hurt his hand. The two have nothing to do with each other. She, one thing that happened, finished and clean. The job, one thing that happened, not finished—

When the knock came on the door Jordan asked who it was and when he heard Sandy's voice he opened the door. He had a brief moment when he knew that he did not want to see Sandy now but when that made no immediate sense, Jordan acted like always; quiet, wait what he says, and what might he like.

"Not sleeping, I see. How you feel, Sammy?"

"Why?"

That was not acting like always. Jordan knew it, but not till it had happened, and Sandy knew it, but did not want to give it weight. He laughed and said, "Was a stupid question. You're not sleeping because you're not tired and that's how you feel."

Jordan nodded and closed the door. Screamy and dull, back and forth. But I slept good last night. . . .

"Leave the door open," said Sandy. "First off, we get your dough, okay?"

"First off?"

"Sure. You just got back and we'll have a beer, huh?"

"Oh," said Jordan. "Yes."

"We'll drive down to my place and you wait in the bar down the block and I run over and get the money."

Jordan thought, yes, there it is again, and I almost forgot. There's so much for you, Sam fellow, and no more. You don't show your face here, and we don't talk to you there, and with all the money you're making, why kick?

In the meantime Jordan did not answer, though he always answered when Sandy said the usual things. That's conversation. But he did not answer, this time, which was the first sign, and one which Sandy missed.

They drove to Sandy's neighborhood and stopped at a corner. Sandy pointed and said, "You wait in the bar there while I run over and get the money."

"That's all right," said Jordan and did not get out of the car.

"That one," said Sandy. "Don't you want a drink?"

"You got a bar in your alley," said Jordan. "I'll have a drink there."

"You mean, go along?"

"And to get my money."

"Sammy, I think . . ."

"You think what?"

Now, of course, it was clear. The boy should be asleep, thought Sandy. Natural, to get irritated. And if I push this fast and he goes home to sleep, it won't ruin the afternoon's routine. Meanwhile, better keep him in harness.

Sandy stopped in front of his bowling alley and said, "You're not going in with me. That's just sense."

"Nobody knows me here any more," Jordan said. "That's just sense," and he got out of the car and walked into the building.

Sandy watched Jordan go in and did nothing. He was not sure if there might not be a scene. But after this, starting right now in private, I'll have to show that son of a bitch how to get back in harness. He went after Jordan who was waiting for him at the counter with the cigars.

"The office," said Sandy, and went to the back of the counter.

There was a man doing paper work in the office and Sandy told him to get out for a minute. Jordan closed the door after the man and Sandy went to the small safe. He didn't open it but turned around.

"Give me that gun, Sam."

"I'm not carrying a gun," said Jordan.

He looked at Sandy and Sandy looked Jordan up and down. He walked up to him when Jordan took one step back. The desk touched him from behind and Jordan sat down on it.

"I'm not carrying a gun," he said again and then he smiled. "And if I were, Sandy, do you think you could frisk me?"

He's playing games. The bastard is playing games with me, as if he and I didn't know each other!

"Sandy," said Jordan. He wasn't smiling any more and his voice was low. "I don't want to act like you and I don't know each other. I'm just, it's just that kind of time. Coming back like this, the deal sour . . ." and he opened his coat so that Sandy could see there was no gun anywhere. "Okay, Sandy?" he said. "Okay?"

But Sandy missed it. The switch was too fast for him, and the afternoon ruined for him, and Jordan better get back into harness.

"Don't pull a trick like that on me again," he said and turned away. "Come over here and get your dough."

He kneeled by the safe, opened it, took out a green box which he put on the floor. He hadn't heard Jordan's steps but then he saw his shoes next to the box. He didn't see Jordan's face and didn't know that Jordan had almost said, I don't want the money, and when he did hear Jordan talk it was games again.

"Are you in a great hurry?" Jordan said.

Sandy missed the tone because he was tense. "Yeh," he said. "That guy outside is my auditor and I pay him by the hour." Then he opened the green box.

Jordan went down on one knee and Sandy counted out fifties and hundreds. He put them on the floor next to the box and snapped the box shut again.

"Pick it up," he said. "Come on."

"That was four," said Jordan. "I get eight."

And if he's edgy there's one way to remind him what this is all about. "Kemp isn't dead yet," he said.

"One of them is."

"He doesn't count. You know that."

"Kemp's almost dead," said Jordan. "Or as good as dead."

"Don't argue with me. Take the four gee."

But Jordan was not interested in the money. He was interested in arguing.

"It was eight."

Sandy hitched himself around and leaned on one hand. "He

isn't dead yet. But he will be. Like you said. Now listen. If he doesn't go by himself," Sandy watched Jordan and thought his face tightened up, "then you go back there and get done with the job."

At first Jordan did not answer. He looked down and watched his hands fold the bills double and then he put the bills into his pocket. He rubbed his left eye with one finger.

"Who said that?"

"Meyer."

"And you?"

"Me too."

"And all that brings the other four gee?"

"Right. Like I said."

Sandy locked the box back into the safe and the two men got up. "Clear now?" said Sandy.

Jordan brushed at his knees.

"You got all of this clear the way it's going to be?"

"We'll see," said Jordan.

Sandy said nothing. He had heard Jordan give wrong answers, or no answers at all, but he had not seen Jordan be cagey before. The pressure gets all of them different. This one argues. Nasty talk. Bound to happen with an unfinished job. Best thing will be, he goes back to that Penderplace, gets it done, puts some vinegar in it. Did the job cold and not liking it, that was the trouble. Sandy sighed.

"Well, what are you going to do with all that dough, Sam?"

"I think I'll spend it. Wouldn't you?"

Now it's glib. Whole afternoon shot and it's talk on top of that. I'm a grease monkey and this bastard is engine trouble. Overheated engine trouble.

"Let's go and have this beer," said Sandy.

"That won't cost much."

"You want the beer or don't you want the beer?"

"Aren't you worried?"

"Huh?"

"Worried. Who might see you with me, and in the daytime."

"Jeesis Christ, Sam, will you lay off that idiot talk?"

Jordan laughed. Sandy did not like that either, not that sound, the way Jordan was doing it, but the case was a clear case of nerves and maybe the whole thing would solve itself if Jordan felt he should go home and to bed. But Jordan did not want that. He wanted the beer they had been talking about and to relax in the meantime, talking. That's what it did for him, he said. It relaxed him to be talking.

They left the bowling alley and drove to a place called the Dawdler's Bar. There were several places, like this bar, where Jordan could go, or Jordan and Sandy could go, and there would be no problems about it. They drank beer in a booth and Sandy put coins in the juke box. Jordan faced the other way, toward the street side, and where the sun slanted in he could see dust move in the light. Then he watched the juke box which had colored lights dancing and spiraling, and after he had watched for a while he discovered the system. The flickers and spirals repeated themselves every three-quarters of a minute.

Sandy thought about Jordan's four thousand dollars and what he would do with it if he had just earned it. Sandy had no idea what he would do.

"Another round?" he said.

"No."

"You say no?"

They had not talked, sitting there, and now the talking was not any easier than the mute part before.

"Let's go to Monico's," Jordan said.

There were several places, such as Monico's, where it was not all right for Jordan to go. Sandy might go there, or perhaps someone like Meyer, a different echelon when it came to the social. Jordan was not known there, which was as it should be, and he was not wanted there, which only made sense.

"They're closed," said Sandy. "It's afternoon and the place is still closed."

Sandy said other things, much more to the point, but Jordan did not even get nasty again. He got up and said, "Are you coming?"

"But it's closed, damn it."

"Are you coming?"

"Of course I'm coming."

"Then we'll get in, won't we?"

They got in. A man in shirt sleeves came to the door; when he saw Sandy through the glass of the door he opened up and said, "Hi, Sandy." He did not know Jordan and just nodded at him, a little bit puzzled.

"You see?" Sandy waved at the low room, dark with none of the lamps turned on. "Closed. Get it? Nothing."

Bar, with the bottles shrouded under a long, white sheet, empty tables, empty chairs, empty bandstand in one corner.

Frescoes with goats and minor gods capering, grape garlands, looking dumb and useless with nobody looking at them.

"You're a little early," said the man. "They're still rehearsing."

Sandy did not say anything but Jordan said, "Still rehearsing? Where?"

So they went to the back. They went through a smoking room where you could hear the toilets going off and from there to a room in back with the stage one length of the wall. There were couches, easy chairs, little tables. All the seating equipment faced the same way.

"You want a drink?" asked the man. "Frank isn't here to mix up anything but if you want a bottle . . ."

"Bring the bottle," said Sandy. "Hell yes. I was going to say bring the bottle."

"Bourbon, wasn't it?"

"Hell, yes, bourbon."

The room was dark except for what light came from the stage. The stage wasn't lit for effect, just efficiency. The footlights were off and the two overhead lamps made a dull yellow light on the row of girls who stood on the stage listening to the thin man with the longish, elaborate hairdo. He had black hair, and wore a white shirt, black pants, white socks, black shoes. He explained the dance.

The girls wore almost anything, but very little of it. Jersey striped this way, jersey striped that way, blue shorts, red shorts, leotards, heels. They all wore heels. The piano went thumpety thump and some of the girls did something with one leg and the hip.

"*That's* it," said the man with the hairdo. "Work it *through*. On the thumpety *thump* you got to work it *through*."

"Mary and Jack," said one of them. "It's less work lying down."

"*Pu-leeze!*"

It was not very hard because it was not really dancing. It was mostly display. And they were all built alike and for the same thing.

And maybe this isn't a bad turn at all, Sandy thought, because the place is dark and won't open for hours and by then he'll be out of here. He hasn't slept much and isn't used to much liquor. He didn't like hearing about having muffed the job and less, maybe, having to finish it. This'll tire him out. . . .

"The second one from the left," said Jordan. "That's Lois, isn't it?"

"Yeh, that's Lois."

From the distance she looked like all the other ones. Round rear, smooth thighs, and the standard-size breasts.

"That why you came here?" Sandy asked.

Jordan had not even known that the girl worked in the Monico. "Yes," he said. "That's why I came here."

"Listen, Sam. You remember I told you she and Fido's brother . . ."

"But she works here."

"What's that got to do with it?"

"Nothing," said Jordan. "And that's why I'm looking."

Jordan got up before Sandy could stop him and walked to the stage. He stood at one end of it and watched.

"Who's he looking at?" said the girl next to Lois. "You?"

"Legs," said Lois and when the piano went thumpety *thump* she was late with the thing she was supposed to do.

"Pu-leeze!"

They all started over.

"You know him?" asked the girl.

"Once."

"Who is he?"

"You don't want him. He's with Sandy."

"Gee—"

"Pu-leeze! You are not coming *through!"* The man with the hairdo glared and then he yelled, "Like *this!"* and did the coming through thing better than the line-up had done it.

"I'm sure he's looking at you."

"He can go to hell."

"Stop!"

The piano stopped and all the girls stopped. All the bosoms went up and down, because of the exertion and all the girls stood on their long standard legs, one straight and one cocked.

"What did you say about me?" asked the man with the hairdo.

"I said you did that *well,"* said Lois.

"Because I *practice."*

"Dry-run Charley," somebody said, and there might have been envy in it.

But the man with the hairdo did not take it that way and got venomous. He said how more vertical dancing and less horizontal dancing might get them much farther than they thought because a good dancer might even get married some day and last a lifetime.

Jordan stood to one side of the stage and looked at the cigarette in his hand. He felt no interest in the Monico any more and wished he were somewhere else.

"And now, *positions.*"

They all complained and did very badly on the thumpety *thump,* and in a while the man with the hairdo gave up and said rehearsal was over. All the girls walked off the stage and some of them looked down at Jordan and a few of them looked farther back into the room. Sandy must be up, thought Jordan, and walking this way.

"All over," said Sandy behind him. "Let's go."

Jordan caught the relief in the voice, and he caught how Sandy looked at the stage and how Lois looked back. What a keen, idle memory, Jordan thought, remembering that pitiful time, that once in her apartment.

"There's a back to this place, isn't there?" he said. "For more business."

"Sam, I've told you and you got eyes to see this place isn't open for . . ."

"How's Lois?"

"Lois."

"Yes. How's Lois. She like the work?"

Sandy looked away and held his breath for a moment. The problem was now that the matter was partly personal, a much harder matter than just dealing with Jordan, important property. But think of it that way: he was property, and because of a wrong job and no time yet for relaxing, in a funk. A matter of discipline. Nothing personal.

"That why you came here? Lois?"

"You asked that before," said Jordan. "You remember asking me?"

"All right, Sammy. All right." He told Jordan to wait for a minute and went to the back part of the place, the part Jordan had talked about.

Behind the door next to the stage was a corridor with a long line of doors. There was faint, artificial light, and a faint, artificial odor. Powder, perfume. Behind the first door Sandy could hear the girls talking, a chatter without any words and as uniform as their looks when they worked on the stage.

Sandy knocked on the door and when somebody asked, who is it, he said his name and then the door opened. The room was full of tables with naked bulbs; the girls were sitting around putting on faces, taking off faces, and some were changing clothes.

"I'll be right out," called Lois.

Sandy waited in the door and when Lois came she smiled at him. She still had her jersey on, and the shorts, but was barefoot. "You got rid of him?" she asked.

"No."

"No? You can't stay?"

"Close the door."

She came out into the corridor and closed the door.

"He wants you," said Sandy.

"Crap," she said. "Oh crap." Then she noticed how angry Sandy was, how he had one eye squinted smaller than the other and how he kept pulling one cuff of his shirt. "Is the bouncer here yet?"

"I don't know. But if it's Benny's day, he comes early. He might be here now."

"That would be nice," said Sandy. "If it's Benny, that would be just right."

Then he told Lois he would look for the bouncer and she should go down to room three in a while and not worry about it, and how she should behave. Then he went to look for the bouncer.

Benny was in the linen closet where he hung up his clothes and changed into his tux. He also had a mirror there, to check how the cummerbund looked and how his hair was arranged.

"Don't you knock?" he said. When he saw it was Sandy he wished he had said something stronger.

"I got a job for you," said Sandy.

"I'm working for you? Since when am I . . ."

"You know Jordan? Guy works for me?"

Benny put his hands on his hips and then let them hang again. Then he put them back on his hips. "So?"

Then Sandy told him. Benny did not like Sandy any better now than at any time, but he said, "Sure, feller. Anything to keep the club clean and for decent folk."

Then Sandy went back to the room with the stage, where Jordan was waiting. He stood by the footlights, on the wrong side of them, and the room was much darker now. More lights were turned off and nobody else was there.

He looks like somebody asking for a job, thought Sandy. The way he stands there and waits. The picture was neither quite true nor did it satisfy Sandy. For the first time that he could remember his picture of Jordan was mixed up. It used to be Jordan, shy and quiet, then less shy and much more quiet. Now this. Now this ill-fitting, sharp-sitting way of his, where nothing matched, where the meanness came from nowhere, and it showed that Jordan did not know what to do with it.

"Well? You want her?"

Jordan turned and sucked breath through his nose. "Yes," he said. "Why not?" and they walked to the door in the back.

It had sounded like a real question. It would have surprised Jordan had he gotten an answer, but he would have been grateful for an answer. He felt so little at the moment, he wished somebody would say something to him.

The room was number three, with big drapes over a window and a big pillow pile in one corner. There was no bed, just the vast pillow pile with two low seats next to it and a small table. There was a radio and Jordan sat down by the table and played with the knobs. He got a sudden loud blare of music and turned it down too far so that it only murmured. What a lousy sound, he thought. There's no sound as lousy as that mumble, and he clicked it off.

The girl said, "Hi, Sam," behind him and closed the door. She still wore the same things as before, the little shorts and the jersey with stripes stretching around her. She went to the pile of pillows and sat down on it.

"You see that cabinet back there?" she said. "There's liquor in there. And fixings."

"Oh. You want some?"

He acts like a hick, she thought. She crossed her legs and looked at him without smiling. She did not remember him being so slow.

He got a bottle, two glasses, and poured.

"No," she said. "Not for me. For you."

Jordan sat down on his seat and watched the liquor make a commotion inside the glass. He swirled the glass and then took a small sip, as a gesture.

"I watched you dance," he said.

"How'd you get in?"

He looked up, but not for long. He watched the liquor in the glass. "How've you been, Lois?"

"Fine."

"Ah. That's good." He looked up once and saw her scratching behind an ear. He looked away again, because she had not smiled.

"Well," he said, "you like it here?"

"Huh?"

"You like it? What you do."

"What kind of a question . . ."

"When did you get up today?" he said.

"What kind of a question is that?"

"Just, I just wondered," he said. He gave a small, interrupted shrug. "Just in general. How you spend a day."

"I work and I sleep. Like everybody."

"And it's like that all day, full with it?"

"Jesus, Sam, what are you talking about?"

"Just a question. Normal question. Not everybody does the same work and has the same day?"

"That's right," she said. "And how's yours?"

He took a drink and then blew air through his lips. "I don't work all the time. I don't think I work as often as you do."

"Why, you creepy son of a bitch!"

He looked at her, blinked a few times. Then he took a cigarette out and lit it. "We're just talking," he said. "Spending time. Why get sore with me?"

"Because you asked for it?"

He looked at the smoke make a spiral at the end of the cigarette and then he shook his head. He smiled and shook his head.

"What you come here for?" she asked.

"I know. You don't want me and how do I take it. That what you asked?"

This time he looked up and smiled at her and she hated his face. She could say nothing.

"And how do you take it, sitting here with me?" he asked this time.

She felt vicious but had a rule against that, so it sounded prim. "If you're going to do a thing well you got to perfect the right habits. Good work habits. And that's how I can sit here with you."

He took a hot drag on his cigarette and talked the smoke out. "There aren't that many habits," he said. "There comes a point and no habit will do."

It was getting too serious for her and nothing was getting done. For a moment she wondered why he had come but she had work habits and thought she knew. But so far, nothing accomplished. . . .

"Why don't you forget about work," she said and made a smile.

He looked up too late for the smile but he saw her lean back on the pile of pillows and stretch out. She did it well. When she did this, it said, when I lie down you want to lie down.

"Sit here," she said. "I can't see you."

"That's all right," said Jordan. "I'm fine."

Her work habits won't do her now, he thought. It's a painful sight . . . He was done and he wanted to leave. The professional part which would come next did not interest him and he did not want to watch the girl become more forced and he himself awkward.

"Sam?"

"Yes."

"Come on." He did not answer right away and she lay on her back, listening for something else. It's time, she thought. Goddamn all of them. "Come on, Sammy," she said again.

This time she sat up and pulled off her jersey.

Like peeling a fruit, he thought, a smooth-skinned fruit.

She sat in a small, white brassière, the red shorts, and then she arched to unhook herself.

"You still have your shoes on," he said.

She held still for a moment, letting it grow that she was being used, misused and insulted. Then she yanked one shoe off and threw it at him.

"You lousy son of a bitch!"

Jordan leaned out of the way and got up. He felt depressed and felt wrong for having stayed this long. He got up and went toward the door but the girl was in the way. She was loud and foul, very loud, and would not let him pass. She screamed insults at him with a high timbre as if calling for help.

Jordan put his hands on her arms to move her out of the way. He felt wrong and depressed. "We just talked," he said. "And it wasn't any good."

"Damn you," she yelled, "damn you, you bastard creep," and the door jumped open.

There was the bouncer, small-hipped with cummerbund and farther back in the dark hall, Sandy was there, and talk, talk, talk, sharp and fast to fit all this. And why, thought Jordan, why . . .

He got in one good punch; it felt like a good one, in his arm and shoulder, but suddenly the girl was silent, they all were, and it killed all of Jordan's intent. Sandy back in the hall, looking, the girl back by the wall, looking, Benny as close as he needed to be, looking, looking, concentrated and cold . . . Is that what they see—like Paul, or like Kemp—is that what they see, when I step up to them? No. The bouncer does this for love—I've *never*. I never knew they disliked me this much. . . .

Jordan got beaten badly. He had doubled over and had started

to cry though nobody saw this because of all the smear on his face
and the method in general. Sandy was dim in the hall but was the
only one Jordan saw in the end. This was perhaps due to the
angle. Then Sandy walked away with the girl. Benny—as a fact—
hardly mattered.

Chapter 13

"Can you make it?"

He could make it. He got up and stood. Sandy let go of his arm
and held out a wet rag. "Wipe yourself."

Jordan wiped and gave the rag back.

"Can you make it?"

"Why? Why was this—"

"Rule of the house. The bouncer thought . . ."

Jordan did not hear the rest because he was not listening. I did
not know they disliked me this much.

"Can you make it?"

"Sure."

"Can you drive?"

"Sure."

"Here. Here's the keys. Take my car."

"Sure."

"Maybe I should drive you home?"

"Sure. I mean, no. I'm sure no."

"I got something else to . . ."

"Sure."

When Jordan was in his room he sat on the bed for a while and
felt the pain start. He went to the sink and had a very hard time
opening the faucet because he had shut it so tight earlier. He
washed and it started to hurt more.

He saw that it was fairly dark outside and that soon he would
go to sleep. He felt strangely comfortable with his pain because it
was strong and concrete. That way, he did not think. But he did a
few things, step by step and uncomplicated by thinking, even
without any clear, urgent feeling.

He walked along the wall, down the stairs, to the drugstore at
the counter where he bought a styptic stick. At the adjoining
counter he bought one envelope and a stamp. In the back, on the
shelf for the telephone books, he wrote on the envelope, putting
down as much as he knew: *Betty. Diner on Third Avenue. Penderburg,*

Pa. He took a bill out of his pocket and put it inside the envelope. He stamped, sealed, and dropped the letter into the mailbox outside. Was it five C? I think it was five C. He walked home. He worried about the money, and why five C instead of one. Who was she? Why not more. A grand. He went to his room and, on his bed, fell asleep almost immediately.

One week later Kemp was still alive. And they had found Paul under the bridge, in the culvert, because of the smell. It was now a gang killing with solution imminent and the guard around Kemp in the hospital was heavy. Kemp stayed in a coma but breathed inside his oxygen tent.

Jordan stayed in his room, on the bed, and sometimes he loosened the faucet a little so that he could watch, by turning his head, how the drops came slowly. He cleaned his guns a few times, in order to concentrate. He knew how to make a proper job of this, a good craftsman's job, though it meant more than that. And I'm going to tilt right out of my mind if I don't hold on to the few things I know.

But it did not help. What he knew felt jinxed. What he knew for these days were things he had never paid attention to before: the bedsheet wrinkled under his back, the stain on his towel from washing his face, the morning noise, noon noise, and evening noise three stories down on the street. He liked the noon noise best because it was one car, two cars, one laugh, two voices, all distinct from each other. He never looked at his ceiling, because it made him feel flattened and small. Once or twice, it seemed, he had a fever.

He called Sandy from the drugstore, for information. There wasn't any. There had been no change.

"How's your head?"

"Much better. Thank you."

"Where you calling from?"

"The drugstore, here at my corner."

"When you called yesterday, you called from the same place?"

"Yes."

"Now listen to me, Sam. Stop making these lousy calls from the same place all the time if you know what I'm talking about. There is . . . Stop interrupting. There isn't a thing gained by these calls you keep making except maybe you get spotted once or twice too often. First news, I get word to you."

"Sandy, I can't just . . ."

"You loused it up. Not me. And stop calling."

"It's been over a week. There's got to be some . . ."

"When Meyer decides what next, you'll hear about it. Listen, I got a tournament on."

"How's Lois?"

"What you say?"

"Good-by," and Jordan hung up.

He stayed in the booth for a while, turned to the blank wall. A line of sweat moved down his cheek, and he stuck out his tongue to lick. He would not call Sandy again. The upsetting thing was how it came over him, how a faint sting happened and next he would say something which he had not thought up ahead of time. Stupid things, without feeling to them. How's Lois . . .

He called Bass. He had no difficulties with Bass but also learned nothing. Bass did not like to be called by Jordan, he had no information, and he said all that. He said, "If you call here again I'm going to do something about it."

"How are you?" said Jordan. "Are you all right?"

"What?"

"I won't call you again," said Jordan, and hung up.

Next day he called Meyer. Jordan ordered a hamburger at the drugstore counter and while it was on the grill went to the booth and called Meyer. Meyer was not easy. Jordan had to call three numbers and with the third one he had to wait a while till the girl went to see if the call was wanted. Jordan ran his tongue around the inside of his cheek, where a cut wasn't healed and it tasted like metal. He spat on the floor and put his foot over it.

If he says Kemp is dead, that will change everything. It will mean time in between like always. No. It'll be Sam Smith this time, Sam Smith doing between-time vacationing. The thought pleased him though he had no idea where he might go.

"Hullo?"

"Meyer?"

"Yes, who . . ."

"This is Smith. I . . ."

"What?"

"Jordan. I meant Jordan. I said Smith because . . ."

"Who in hell gave you leave to call here? Don't you got any better sense than . . ."

"The reason I said Smith . . ."

"Shut up!"

Jordan did, feeling patient. The dullness of patience was something new he had learned. He had not needed patience before.

". . . be sure you'll know before long what's what, if anything

happens. Meanwhile, there's nothing. And meanwhile I want
nothing from you!"

"I mean, is there no plan?"

"Didn't you hear what I said just a minute ago? And we don't
do this kind of business on the phone, damn your crazy head!"

"I've got to know . . ."

"You sit tight and wait like the rest of us!" and Meyer hung up.

Jordan forgot to stop for his hamburger and walked out on the
street. The sun shone and he thought he might get a new room,
with a new view, and more sun perhaps. I might spend more time
there. Sam Smith unemployed. He watched himself walking past
a store window and thought he looked like anybody. But if no
one believes me, how can I be somebody else? Paul thinks I'm
Smith and he's dead. Kemp thinks I'm Smith and doesn't count. I
mean, how can you talk to Kemp, down under in the oxygen tent.
What's Betty's last name . . . ?

Chapter 14

"When I think of it," said Jane, "when I imagine I have over four
hundred smackers—you know what I'd do?"

"There's a customer," said Betty.

"Where?"

"The short one there. The little boy," and she pointed to
where the head stuck up over the counter.

"And I bet he wants orange juice."

"Orange juice," said the boy. "A small one."

Jane got the orange juice and Betty looked out the stand to the
other side of the street. There were planted palms, there were
convertibles moving, and some of the buildings across the way
had Spanish tile roofs. There was sun over everything and the
beach was behind the next block.

"I was saying . . ." said Jane.

"But I told you, honey; I told you right when I came when I
told you all about it. I said, Jane, some of this is for you."

"Let me finish," and Jane folded her arms, leaned against the
cooler, and looked up at the coconuts which hung on strings and
had faces on them. "If I had that money," she said, "you know
what I'd do?"

"No," said Betty, very patient.

"I'd go to Oregon, is what I would do, for the apples. I want to
see nothing but apples and forget all about oranges."

Betty had heard that several times before but she smiled. "It's nice here."

The other girl didn't answer that and then they had customers.

After a while they sat down on their stools and Jane smoked a cigarette. Betty drank orange juice.

"You know what really kills me about this?"

"About what?" said Betty.

"About all this," and she swept her arm over everything: stand, juicers, street, traffic, palms, sunshine. "The sticky fingers," she said. "I got these constantly sticky fingers."

"Oh. From the orange juice."

"Just say juice, Betty. The other goes without saying."

They had customers and didn't talk for a while. Betty had a small pain in her back, from bending down into the cooler.

"It's four o'clock, honey," said Jane. "Don't forget your doctor's appointment."

"It's only fifteen minutes. The last time I walked it, I got there . . ."

"You know what I'd do if I had a doctor's appointment, let's say an appointment at eight in the evening? You know what I'd do at, let's say seven in the *morning?*"

"You'd worry about it all day."

"Ha. At seven in the morning I'd call the boss, and I'd tell him—"

"You got a customer, Jane."

She got to the office in time but then had a long wait. After the doctor she took a long walk and when she took the bus into Miami she got off at the wrong stop. It was almost dark when she got to the rooming house and she walked slowly. There was a palm tree next to the house and she could hear the leaves scraping.

"Honey?"

She stopped on the porch steps and saw Jane on the swing. The swing clattered when the girl got up and Betty saw Jane dressed to go out.

"He's here," said Jane.

"What?"

"The one, you know. The one you been telling about."

All Betty said was, "Gee—"

"He don't look rich."

"What's he look like?"

It sounded one way to Jane and was meant another way by

Betty. It had slipped out that way because she could not remember his face too well.

"I don't know. Pale, I guess."

"Oh."

"You better go in now. He's been there an hour." Jane put the strap of her bag over her shoulder. "I won't be back before two."

"You don't have to do that, Jane."

"Are you kiddin'? 'Bye now," and she started down the steps. "Wait a minute, I almost forgot!"

Betty stopped in the door and waited. Jane came close and then, "What did the doctor say, honey?"

"Three months."

"Three? Was it him?"

"How could it be?" Betty went into the house.

She could not tell whether he seemed especially pale because the light was almost gone in the room. She saw him get up from a chair and come toward her. When he was close she saw he was smiling.

"Remember me?" he said.

She had the feeling, for a moment, that she did not.

"What a question, Sam! Why, what a question!"

She thought he would want to kiss her but he did nothing. He stood there smiling and she was still struck by that. His smile was a stretch of his face, though this did not make a false smile but only an awkward one. He was embarrassed, she felt, and it embarrassed her. She stepped up quickly and gave him a kiss. He gave her a kiss and straightened up again. He deserves more, she thought, and knows it, but he is a gentleman.

"I guess you got the money," he said, "didn't you?"

"It was you, wasn't it, Sam?"

"Surprised you, huh?"

He was still smiling, as if trying very hard. The girl reached up with a small gesture and stroked his face. Then she turned away. She went to the couch and sat down there. "Sam," she said, "come and sit with me, Sam."

She looked down into her lap when he sat down next to her and so could not see him at all. "I don't know what to say, Sam." She smiled, but did not show him her face.

"I don't either," he said.

She leaned over to the side of the couch and turned on the radio. "Have you eaten yet?" she asked him. "What I mean is, did you just come to town, Sam?"

He did not answer because the radio was coming alive and he

leaned across her and snapped it off. When he sat up again and saw her face, he quickly smiled again. "I don't like it," he said. "I'd rather talk to you,' and after that, after there was more silence, he said, "even if we have nothing to say."

Then he took her arm in his hand and held it. "I've just come to town," he said. "Yes."

"I think it's wonderful that your business . . ."

"I came just to see you."

She pressed her arm against her side, to give his hand a squeeze. He could smell the slight acid odor of orange peel.

"What's your last name?" he asked her.

She was very startled and laughed.

"Mine's Smith," he said. "I've come to see you."

"Evans. Elizabeth Evans."

"Mine's Smith," he said again, and then he took out a cigarette which both seemed to end this conversation and also to make it a point of importance.

How nutty, she thought. We both should have laughed about this name thing because actually, it could be funny.

"Now we'll eat," he said.

She was glad he had brought that up because it was a topic and something to do, and she said since coming to Miami she had not been out yet at all and so didn't know where they might go.

"I'd like us to eat here," he said. "I don't mind waiting. I'll sit and watch."

She did not mind that either though she was sorry she had nothing special. Peas from a can, and there were hot dogs, there was . . .

"It's all right," he said. "Whatever. Put your housecoat on."

"What?"

"Put your housecoat on. You're home."

She laughed and he smiled back and in a way, she thought, what he says just sounds strange at first but then really isn't.

He sat on the couch and by turning his head he could see the head of the palm outside the window, the one which kept rattling its fronds. The window had the same curtains which he had seen before in the girl's Penderburg room. Jordan, as he knew he would, felt well now. He sat, looking at everything the room with the curtains and the used furniture, the girl moving back and forth in the kitchen alcove, and while he saw mostly her back he also felt that much more at ease because of that. As if they had known each other a long time and had no need for the special. He saw nothing cheap, common, crummy, or little, nothing of the pathetically small in his choice of an evening; he saw none of that because it was not there. It was not there, because the pressure and effort which had brought him this far had been so sharp and tremendous.

She put ice-water in glasses next to the plates, which was a restaurant habit, and she served him first and kept watching his plate, which was no habit at all but was natural. After eating they had instant coffee, and they talked about how quickly she had left —two days after he had sent the money—and about how long he could stay this time. He would tell her, he said, he would tell her soon.

She pressed no point, though she asked personal questions. Why shouldn't she, was Jordan's feeling. I'm Smith. I am out of town a lot, because I travel on business; I come home here between times, because I have time in between.

The evening was dull, slow, warm, and harmless. That way, it lasted and lasted.

It gave Betty time to think of a number of things. Four hundred, she thought, maybe four hundred is enough. If I knew him better, I might ask him about it, tell him about it. He might even help. He's a gentleman, really. He's gentle.

When Jane knocked on the door it was not two yet. But there had been nothing for Jane to do after the movie was over and she'd thought: It's my room as much as hers and who is Smith anyway. She knocked, with a lot of purpose, and then she called through the door.

"That's all right," Betty called back. "Come on in." And when she's in, Betty thought, she's going to say something like, how are you two lovebirds, or something.

"Well, well, well," said Jane. "How are you two bugs in a rug?"

Jane was the only one who laughed, though Jordan got up from the couch and said something about Jane might want to sit there, and Betty said, wouldn't it be nice to have some iced tea.

She made iced tea, and Jane sat down on the couch and told Jordan to sit down next to her. Then she talked a lot, touching her hair, hiking a strap, peeling the lacquer off one of her nails. But she watched Jordan all the time and tried budging him in various ways. It's a good thing, thought Betty, that he's calm and a gentleman, or I would feel badly embarrassed for Jane.

"So, how you doing?" said Jane. "I mean, in your business." Her voice had a splash sound and was too loud.

"Fine," said Jordan. "Nothing special."

"You down on business, Mister Smith?"

"No. Just a visit."

"Oh. You salesmen. I bet everybody else thinks you're down on business, huh?" and when he did not answer, "Buttons, isn't that what you told me, Betty?"

"Yes," said Betty from the sink.

"Is it a good business, Mister Smith?"

"No. Not very."

"Oh, I bet you're just saying that, Mister Smith, aren't you?"

Jordan got up and went over to the sink. He gave the faucet a twist and then went back to sit down again.

"Well, I do beg to differ," said Jane, "about the way you interpret your business, because I do happen to know about that generous gift you sent Betty. It made Betty very happy, didn't it, Betty?"

"Yes, very. You want me to put lemon on the table?"

"You know what I'd do, Mister Smith, if I got a gift like that from an admirer? I'm not saying I got an admirer, you understand, but . . ."

"You'd go to Oregon to see the apples," said Betty.

"Well, that was very funny. You haven't got the tea strong enough, I don't think. Tell me, Mister Smith, are you married?"

"No."

"Ah! But divorced."

"I've never been married."

"A woman hater!" and she laughed with a clickety sound. "Is he a woman hater, Betty?"

What had been there for Jordan was thinning out. It was thinning out into an embarrassing daydream. A time in a hot room with a view of a dusty palm in the next lot, and the girl by the sink talking flat and about something hard to remember. He would remember everything Jane was saying.

"Tell me, Mister Smith, what's the name of your company?"

"Don't you want your iced tea, Jane?"

"Betty, you keep interrupting. Tell me, Mister Smith, will you come often? Is it one yet?"

"Yes, it's one," said Jordan.

"You must hear this program! The Two Sleepy People, and it's the swooniest . . ."

"Leave it off."

"What?"

She had the radio on and Jordan got up and clicked it off again.

"You mean you don't like music, Mister Smith? And I thought, right from the start when I saw you, Mister Smith, a sweet, quiet gentleman like . . ."

"Leave."

"What did you say?"

"Leave. Come back tomorrow."

"Why, you must be out of . . ."

"Here's ten dollars. Go to a hotel for the night."

Jane got up and when she stood up she started to laugh, loud and straight into Jordan's face. *"That's* a switch! What do you take me for giving me money and telling . . ." She stopped talking because she did not really feel brazen any more, watching Jordan. He was somebody else now . . .

"Boy," she said. "These button men—" and gagged on it with a sudden jolt when Jordan hit her in her face.

It hurt, but above all she was frightened. He said, "Get out," again and she ran. She heard him say, "Don't you ever say that to me," and she nodded her head, nodded her head, while trying to get the door to the hallway open. He grabbed her arm to make it hurt and took her out to the porch where he turned her around, toward him. "Git," he said. "Git and don't mess what I've got."

He snapped her around toward the steps and she almost stumbled. Then she ran.

Jordan did not watch her but went inside. He went to the table and picked up a glass of iced tea, and while he drank it he looked all around. All like before now. Only Betty is frightened. He put his glass down and went up to her and put his hands on her face. "I want you here," he said. "Not her."

"But, but you hit—"

"I've never done that before." Then his face changed, and before she could see what it meant he moved very close, put his head next to hers. "Don't be frightened. Please. Don't be frightened . . ."

She suddenly knew herself to be very important, that nothing else mattered between them, except what he felt about her. She took him into the next room, left the light on in the front room, left the light off in the bedroom, stood still when he took off her clothes. She waited next to the bed while he got undressed, and when they lay down together they lay still for a long time. They made love once and then lay together because he did not let her go.

Chapter 15

He sat in the plane and sometimes moved his head so he could feel the cool blow of air from the vent overhead and sometimes he looked out of the window, at the clouds below, though with not much interest. A commuter does not look out of the window with much interest. Smith, leaving Miami for New York, where Jordan worked. It would be all right. The apartment, the pieces of furniture, pots and pans, and the girl there, happy with it. It would be all right. Jordan is a good provider.

In New York it was too warm and the sky slate-colored with rain hanging there. By the time Jordan got out of the taxi in town he felt wet under his shirt and his palms were wet. He also felt a stiffness in his neck. He watched the taxi drive down the street and hated the sight of the street and the car leaving.

He went into the drugstore but stopped on the way to the telephone booths to sit down at the counter. He looked at the booths every so often and drank a large glass of orange juice. Then he went to the back and placed his call.

His neck hurt with a slight stiffness and the phone was slippery in his palms. Maybe he isn't in. No. He'll be in. This isn't Wednesday afternoon. Tomorrow is Wednesday. He listened for the ring and felt nervous thinking about things that did not matter. Was Kemp dead by now? That mattered.

"Bandstand Bowling."

"Is Sandy there?"

"Just a minute." It took a little time and then Sandy said, "Yuh?"

"This is Jordan."

Sandy did not answer right away and Jordan could hear the hollow sound when the pins get hit.

"Where in hell you been, you sonofabitch?"

Jordan moved the phone to his other hand, wiped his free one on his pants. "I was out of town."

"Ah. You were out of town."

"Yes. Time out. Between time."

"Between time. You didn't know, maybe, this thing wasn't over, this thing was hanging fire and you were supposed to hang around?"

"I got to relax sometime. You know?"

But Sandy cut Jordan off. He thought there might be explanations next and that did not interest him.

"You know the trailer place," he said. "Meet me there. And leave right now."

"Listen, Sandy. What's developed? You know."

"Get off the phone and get over to where I said I . . ."

"Just tell me."

"I will," and Sandy hung up.

What it means, thought Jordan, what it means . . . He got out of the booth and pushed the folding door shut behind him. Kemp is alive.

The jinx hangs on. But Jordan, you're a good provider and who else is going to keep Smith alive? Think of it this way: The first time in Penderburg was a job on Paul. Done. And the second time in Penderburg will be a job on Kemp. How do you shoot a man in an oxygen tent? Won't that cause an explosion?

Jordan walked four blocks to the place where he kept his car. He carried his overnight bag, since he had not yet been home, or as if on a job. Jordan the good provider and how else am I going to keep Smith alive . . .

On the Jersey side, before Newark started, was a house trailer lot on the side of the highway. There were two or three lots like it, and secondhand car places in between. And garages and gas stations. Like everybody is going to take off, thought Jordan. Like everybody organized to kill their time in between. Jordan pulled into the lot which said Trailways in neon, a big neon sign which showed green-fluorescent against the gray daytime sky.

The man at the office shack bent down to look and then he straightened up again and looked out at the highway. Jordan drove to the back where the two-axle house trailer stood with the sign in the picture window, *Another Trailways-Safari-Leisure-time-Home Sold to a Happy Customer.* Sandy was in the open door. When he saw Jordan he stepped away from the door.

The inside smelled of linoleum and plywood. There was a rubber-blade fan on the kitchen sink blowing air to the living-room area. All the windows had drawn, flower print curtains. The couch under the picture window was covered with the same curtain print. The formica table was bright red and yellow. A determined cheerfulness everywhere.

Sandy stood away from the fan and was smoking a cigarette. He rarely smoked cigarettes. Meyer sat in the couch. His bald head seemed grimly bald with all the prints and the color around. His sharp bird-face looked hungry. There was a young man in the bedroom passage whom Jordan did not know. The young man rubbed one shoe against the back of his calf and then looked at the shine.

"Where were you?" said Meyer.

"Short vacation."

"Sit there," said Sandy. "Your face is dripping."

Jordan sat down in the chair but the fan draft was like a sheet flapping against his face. He got up again and wiped his hands. And going back to Penderburg isn't going to be the worst thing at all. It's end of jinx time and means Jordan the very good provider, keeping Smith alive . . .

"I got you over here," said Meyer, "so you can catch up on the news."

"What do I do?" said Jordan.

"First you should listen," said Sandy. "Wipe your face."

Meyer said, "Kemp is dead."

Jordan wiped his face. "Kemp is dead?"

Nobody said anything to that except the young man in the bedroom passage. The silence embarrassed him and he snickered. "Jeesis," he said, "the man of steel."

"Well," said Jordan. "Well, well, well," and then he coughed to cover the squeak in his voice which he was sure would come any moment. "Jinx time to jig time," he said. "What do you know . . ." Then he laughed. It was not a funny sound and he stopped it very soon.

He did not know how to be just glad. And he did not think that the men in the trailer would understand if he laughed. He allowed, "Well, well, well," again and, "I must say, yes sir, that is something."

"Will you shut up a minute and listen?" said Meyer.

Jordan took a deep breath and took a cigarette out of his pocket. He rolled it back and forth between two fingers and said, "Certainly. What else is there?"

At that point he squeezed the cigarette too hard and the paper split open. It annoyed him that his fingers should do something which he knew nothing about ahead of time.

"So listen close," said Meyer. He leaned his arms on his knees and talked straight at Jordan. His voice sounded somewhat like a cough. He was not sure he was reaching the other man and was straining. "Kemp's dead and never said a word."

"Good. Fine."

"Just listen, Sam. Will you?" said Sandy. Then Meyer went on again, the rasp in his voice sounding close to anger.

"Dead without a word, like I said. Fine. And the bodyguard,

when he started to smell, he didn't lead anywhere either. Fine. Standard. They talked to the landlady where you stayed and she has an idea you got black hair and look dangerous. Like it should be. And now, if you please, they're still not done."

Jordan put a cigarette into his mouth and held onto the filter with his teeth.

"Since when," Meyer yelled suddenly, "since when you been whoring around on a job, Jordan?"

"You say whoring around?"

"Because they're looking for that bitch!"

Jordan sat still and did not worry very much. He knew much more about this girl than the men in the trailer and what was true above everything was that the girl Betty did not fit or belong into any of this and therefore Jordan could not get excited.

"Sherman," said Meyer. "Get on that phone again."

The young man in the bedroom passage pushed away from the wall and went out of the trailer. Sandy and Meyer watched him leave but Jordan was looking down at his hands. They were quite dry now, he noticed. His face felt dry too.

"They find her," said Meyer when Sherman was gone, "they find her, Jordan, and what do you think's going to happen?"

"I don't know," said Jordan.

Sandy gave a quick look over, then turned away again. He did not like the tone Jordan had used, and the dumb words. He knew Jordan was not dumb and he had never seen him act sullen.

"You don't know!" said Meyer, and he looked back and forth between Sandy and Jordan. "You come back and don't know if the hit took or not. You don't know any better than to go out and make time with some lay while you're out on a job. And you don't know what's going to happen to you once they find that woman and tell her who's been laying her between business assignments! What *do* you know?"

"She doesn't know my name," said Jordan. He said this because it was the most important thing at the moment. That the girl knew Smith and nobody else knew him. That was important.

"Who else in Penderburg paid any attention to you, Jordan?"

"They're dead."

"And she's alive."

"But they haven't found her," said Jordan. "Isn't that what you said?"

"But I'll tell you what they know. She left town. She took off for

Florida. She'd been talking about that for a long time and she bought a bus ticket that way."

"Where in Florida?" said Jordan. He was not too keenly interested because nobody here knew anything that was important.

"She's got a girl friend in Miami Beach and they're looking for her."

"Have they found her?" and Jordan looked across at the dry faucet.

"Sherman's checking again."

"They won't find her."

"What? What do you know about this?"

"Nothing," said Jordan. "I just mentioned my feelings."

Meyer jumped up with his bald head turning red. "Feelings? What in hell has any of this got to do with feelings? What's a cut-and-dry job got to do with your lousy feelings? Now you listen . . ."

Sherman came back into the trailer and Meyer yelled at him. "Well? What?"

"About the same," said Sherman. "What they got new is she's seen this guy before leaving, this button salesman by the name of Smith. They think maybe . . ."

"*Smith?*"

"Yes. Smith."

"You gave the name *Smith?*" said Meyer and leaned toward Jordan. "Will you explain to me sometime, sometime when there's peace and quiet, how you came to pick such a clever, such a damn clever name like the name Smith?"

"It wouldn't mean anything to you," said Jordan.

Meyer had no time or patience to get this answer straight and besides it was crazy impertinence anyway. If they didn't need the son of a bitch so much . . . "What else," he said to Sherman. "Come on, come on."

"And they think maybe Smith is it, or at least worth looking at, seeing he shows in town, is buddies with Kemp, Kemp gets his, and . . ."

"We got all that. What *else?*"

"And now they got that this girl friend in Miami, in Miami Beach, works in a juice bar. One of those orange . . ."

"All right, all right. Orange juice bar. What else?"

"They're looking. They got the Miami cops on this thing, but of course there's a hell of a lot of those juice bars all over Miami and Miami Beach."

"All right." Meyer got up and pushed the yellow and red table out of the way so he could walk straight to the door of the trailer. "You take it from here," he said to Sandy. "You talk to the wunderkind." Then he snapped around at the door and looked at Jordan. "You remember her name?"

"Yes."

"You remember her face?"

"Yes."

"Like she's going to remember yours, Jordan. So get her quick, Smith." Then he meant to get out. He made a disgusted face and meant to get out of the door.

How Jordan got to the door so quickly was not clear to Meyer, but Jordan was there, very close, holding the door so it would not open and his face with a clamped look . . . But the strangeness of his face could just be, Meyer thought, because I've never seen him this close. And then all Jordan said was, "I've never done a job on a woman."

After that Jordan let go of the door and stepped back and perhaps none of this had really happened, thought Meyer, and just everything about the son of a bitch is a surprise to me. How Sandy gets along with this creep is beyond me. . . .

"Come outside a minute," he said to Sandy. Meyer frowned and left the trailer.

Sandy went out after Meyer and Sherman and when he looked up at the sky he thought it might rain any minute. Meyer had his hands in his pockets and stood away from the trailer a ways. Sandy went over there.

"You saw that just now?" said Meyer.

"What?"

"When he held the door shut."

"I saw that. He held the door shut."

Meyer did not know how to put it. And what Jordan had actually said had not been anything special.

"You mean the nerves," said Sandy. "The way he's jumpy."

"Maybe you call it jumpy," said Meyer. "I don't know."

Sandy, when it came to his handiwork, felt a certain loyalty, or at least felt something like that, because of the effort he had put out over the time. Jordan, because of strain and an unorthodox job, had been fairly jumpy, but now with the end of it soon, with the girl out of the way, there would soon be no more of this. Besides, Meyer should stay away and keep his browbeating tactics for his office help.

"I keep wondering," said Meyer, "if we're making a mistake."

"Jordan goes out on this! He's the only one who knows the girl by sight."

"Sure. That's reasonable. Is *he?*"

"Damn it, Meyer, you keep riding this thing. You keep riding it without knowing the first thing about it. I've spent enough time . . ."

"You've never seen him crack up before."

Sandy lost his temper because Meyer was interfering where he had done none of the work. He kept his voice as low as he could and anger made him sound hoarse. "When he cracks I know it. When he gets quiet and doesn't say a thing, then I start worrying. When he goes under, believe me, I know how his type turns out: he'll fold, crawl in a corner, and he'll shiver there."

Meyer waited a moment and looked up to the sky. Might rain any minute, he thought. Then he said, "So let us all give thanks that he's prickly and offensive. And that he's all yours." Then Meyer turned and walked away.

Chapter 16

When Sandy came into the trailer Jordan was at the kitchen counter. He was leaning there and his hand was on the faucet.

"There's no water in there," said Sandy.

"You never know."

Sandy closed the door and then he asked Jordan if he could bum a cigarette. Jordan said, "Sure," and gave him one. Then Sandy smoked.

"Well. You heard the man."

"Who's idea was it?" asked Jordan.

"Idea?"

"That I should go after her."

"It just came up."

"It was yours," said Jordan. "I think it was yours."

"All right. So it was mine."

"Sandy, it's not a good idea."

Sandy inhaled too deep and felt it burn way down. "You can relax," he said. "After this one, you can relax."

"You could send another man down and I'll give him a hand. I got an idea how to get to this girl, to this Betty, and the other man can do it as fast."

"That doesn't make any sense," said Sandy.

It made a great deal of sense to Jordan, how he would handle that kind of arrangement, and what he would save. Jordan felt weak, suddenly, when he thought about all he would save. . . .

"Sandy. I'm asking you," he said.

Sandy did not like the tone, since it confused him. He said, "All this over a lay?" and thought it would change the mood. It changed nothing.

"Please," said Jordan. "Please, Sandy. I'm asking you this."

The silence was too thick after that and the face Jordan showed —Sandy squinted, blew smoke, threw his cigarette into the dry sink. Mushy! If his goddamn face doesn't look soft and gone.

Sandy got mad. He had one thing in mind, had one picture about this, and there had never been cause before to change what he thought and for sure this wasn't the time for any changes on his part. Soft and hard was the scale here. You go soft; how to fix it? Go hard. He talked fast and spitty with his excitement and with no time to watch how Jordan reacted.

"Soft and hard," he said. "That's what I'm talking about. You go soft, you fix that one way, fellow; you fix that and go hard. You been mushing apart at the seams piece by piece, Jordan; piece by piece, the way I've been seeing it. Over not getting your break when you came back from the last trip, over going out on a job with a little switch in the routine, over getting a lay which was maybe the nuts, just compared to the last one, and so help me, Jordan, if I ever seen a punier set of bad reasons, a more laughable, crappier little bunch of bad reasons, so help me I don't know when that might have been. Jordan!"

"Yes."

"You follow me, Jordan?"

"Yes."

"You don't follow through on this thing, I don't know what's going to be with you. I don't know how you're going to make it and I don't know if you're going to make it at all. But I know one thing, you son of a bitch, and so do you! Once I don't know any more how you're panning out, that's that, feller! That's that!" His throat hurt and he took a deep breath. He talked low now, and relaxed after the shouting. "That would be that, Sam Jordan, and you'd never make it again."

He sat down. He wiped his mouth, feeling wetness, and added what this was all about. "What happens to your type when they're through, we don't have to discuss that."

"Of course," said Jordan.

What Sandy had listened for had finally happened. "Of course," Jordan had said with his voice and the shortness like always. He's come around, finally, thought Sandy. It was so much what Sandy expected, he missed out on the way it had happened.

Jordan, at some point, had stopped listening to Sandy. He was done listening.

Then they left the trailer. "Why in hell doesn't it rain," said Sandy when they walked over the lot.

Chapter 17

They saw each other once more that day, when Jordan was packing in his room and Sandy dropped in. He stood around and watched Jordan pack and was satisfied how he did it.

"You're taking three guns?"

"Sure."

"I didn't know you always took three guns."

"I take one when everything's certain. I take two when there's a choice but it isn't all clear. The third one is nothing. It's just a twenty-two automatic."

"So why . . ."

"Cats have nine lives. I have three guns."

Sandy grunted something but did not say any more. He wants three guns? Let him have them. Or nine lives, if he felt that was an advantage.

"I got your four gees for the Penderburg job," he said. "You want it now?"

"Drop it in the suitcase."

Sandy dropped it in the suitcase and watched Jordan take things out of drawers. "Where do you keep your dough, in a bank?"

"No. I got a place."

"Oh. Smart."

"Oh yes."

Then Sandy sat on the bed a while longer and watched how Jordan packed his suitcase so neatly.

"You're taking the plane, aren't you?"

"Eight-ten, National, flight two-seven-one."

"I know that one. I never liked it because it gets you there in the middle of the night."

"I like that."

"Yes. I see where it makes sense. You starting in on this right tonight?"

"Yes."

"So maybe I'll hear from you tomorrow."

"That's right. Wednesday."

Sandy felt relief hearing all the concrete parts of the planning and seeing the right, sensible way in which Jordan packed. He felt there was no more for him to do, which was true enough, and he left. Jordan closed the door after him and went back to his suitcase.

He took garters out and snapped them around his calves. He took the twenty-two back out of the suitcase and hooked it under one of the garters where the elastic had a gimmick sewed on for the purpose. In the beginning, some time back, Jordan had worn the small gun this way, because he had felt like a beginner. It had served no other purpose and in a while he had stopped. Quite a while back.

He took the roll of hundreds and fifties and opened the bills up. Then he climbed on a chair and took the end cap off a curtain rod and pulled out a very tight roll of bills which he had kept there. He combined all the bills and tucked them into a place inside his suitcase.

When he left his room there were some shirts left in one drawer, new shirts and not his size. There were also unused razors in a sealed cellophane wrapper and a full can of shaving lather. He himself always used cream.

At nine that evening Jordan left the plane at the Washington airport. Washington, D.C., was even hotter than New York and it was not raining there either.

Benny liked the job and he even came to work early. He walked into Monico's ten after four when he knew that rehearsals were over, and the first thing he did was to go to his cubicle where he changed into the black pants, dress shirt, and cummerbund. He liked what the cummerbund did to his shape and for that reason always left the tux jacket off. he left it on the hook until later and walked out into the corridor.

It went one way to the stage and the other way to an exit door with a red light. That was required by law. The door led to a walled yard and the wall had an alley on the other side. Like the weekly ice, this door was for protection, though the weekly ice went regularly and was enough. Nobody used that door. Benny passed numbers five, six and seven. The next door went to the dressing room. It was open and all the girls were inside. They sat at their tables with the lit-up mirrors and some were farther back where the shower room was. When Benny stopped at the door he smelled the creams and the lotions.

Like a court eunuch, Benny had a number of privileges. He had the run of the corridor and the rooms all along there, and after rehearsals he liked to walk into the dressing room.

He took a cigar out of his shirt pocket, walked through the door, and watched himself coming in on one of the mirrors. "Hi, girls, hi, girls," he said.

They answered or didn't answer, depending on where he was looking.

"You're getting fat," he said to one of them.

And she said, "You keep looking at it while I'm sitting down, so naturally."

Lois came in from the shower room and had a big towel over her shoulder. She wore that and the shorts and had washed her hair. Her head was down and her hair hanging over her face. "What a whoozy masculine odor," she said. "I bet Benny has brought his cigar."

Some laughed and Benny laughed and he had in mind to say something clever. Lois said, "Hold the dryer for me, Benny?" and sat down at her table.

He pulled up a chair, close to hers, and plugged in the dryer. "Cut it shorter," he said. "It'll dry faster and show more." He looked at her bent head and her hands fluffing her hair. When she made the right movement he could see her bare front.

"She can't," someone said two tables down. "It's got to, after all, be longer than Evelyn's."

She pronounced it Eve-lyn, with a long *e,* and they all laughed about the dancing instructor.

"What a name for a guy," said Benny. "I can't get over it."

"It's British. Over there they got this same name for the men and women."

"A lisp don't make him British."

"But his father's a lord."

"Eve-lyn's no lord, he's a lady," and they laughed again.

Benny watched Lois fluttering her hair and he watched her elbows. He had an idea elbows showed true age when nothing else might in a woman, especially with the ones here. He bent down a little, trying to see the girl's forehead. That was another revealing part. Forehead, and sometimes the eyes.

"Benny?"

He straightened up and said, "Yes."

"I feel a draft," said Lois.

"Naturally. I got this dryer trained straight at you."

She threw her hair back and kept her face turned to the ceiling. Benny turned off the dryer and the room was quiet.

"On my legs, Benny. I mean a draft on my legs."

"Maybe it's the hall door being open."

Lois picked up a brush and went through her hair. She dragged it and whipped it through and Benny watched. She had put the towel down on the table.

"You want me to blush, Benny?"

"Blush? I'm just looking."

"I don't like eyeballs touching me, Benny. Be a sweet and close that door?"

"Sure," he said, and got up. He went to the door and looked out in the hall. He saw no doors open there and felt no draft. "I don't feel nothing," he said.

"I don't feel it any more either," said Lois, but when Benny came back, she thought of something else. "Get me my robe, be a dear, on the bathroom door?"

He looked behind the door and told her it wasn't there.

"I left it in back last night," she said. "I think I left it in number three."

"Okay," he said. "Okay."

He walked down the corridor which had dim little sconces along the two walls. They made a gray, spotty light in the passage, meant as thoughtfulness for the customers. Benny had to go almost as far as the exit door because three was in the rear.

Inside he switched on a light because the curtains were always drawn, and then he switched on the light in the small bathroom where he found Lois's blue robe. Like a telephone booth, he thought, and looked at the tiled cubicle. When he switched off the light there he heard the door in the hallway open.

"You want to catch a cold?" he said and watched Lois come in.

"My compact," she said. "Did you see it in there?"

She had the towel around her shoulders again but took it off when she came toward him. She turned and held her arms back and Benny helped her on with the robe.

"It's in this pocket," she said. "Never mind."

"Oh good," he said. "Then I don't have to leave right off."

"Never mind, Benny."

But he stayed where he was and left his hands on her. He slipped them around her, to the front.

"Benny, please," she said and tied the cord at her waist.

"Huh?" he said next to her ear. "What do you say, Losy, huh?"

"Benny, let go. I feel like something in a window, in a store window, I mean."

"You don't feel like it to me."

"For heaven's sake, let go, Benny. You're like a baby."

"Listen, if you think I'm like . . ."

"No."

"How about it, Lois?"

"I can't. You know he's coming any minute."

"That's all I need. A minute."

"Ask Sue. You know he's coming any minute."

"To hell with Sue and to hell with him. You know what I think of him."

He let go of her and she fixed her robe. "What did he ever do to you?"

"Nothing. And he never will. There's just some I like and some I don't like is all. How about it, Lois?" and he stepped up again.

"Please, Benny. Not now."

"Later?"

"All right. Later."

"Before showtime."

"All right. Then."

They were done with the topic and thought of other things. "You going to use number three?" Benny asked.

"Might as well. Turn the radio on, will you, Benny? I'm going back for a minute to get my mules."

She left number three and Benny stayed in it. The next thing Lois ran into Sandy, he coming one way in the hall and she going the other.

"Hi, sweets," she said. "Go on back. I'll be just a moment."

"Number three?"

"Sure. Three," which was the part Jordan heard.

Sure, three, he thought, and I don't see a one of them. One across the way in the room where everything happens, one down the hall, and one just a ways beyond that one. Jinx job. Here he comes. What a shadowless corridor with those nasty, dim lights. Here he . . . Now. Poor, shadowless Sandy and wouldn't he jump with fright if I reached out now and touched him. . . . Touched him? Nobody touches that one. Poor Sandy. The cigar though, I could drill that cigar straight out of his face or straight into his face and he'd know that, of course, he'd know that and would worry about it. Jeesis Christ, what happened to my cigar, that kind of thing. . . . Turn. Nice big back going into that door. Number three, where I got it, number three, where the

. . . Now? But the girl might still be down the hall and the noise she'd make would be too much to bear. They scream so with that ten-mouse scream piercing straight out of their gullet. . . . Good. That's a good light in that number three workroom over there. Christ. They got the radio going. Jinx job. Easy, Jordan. You're the provider, Jordan, and how else keep Smith alive? What else but this, Jordan, what else did he teach you and what else is there now but to do the best thing you know how, Jordan, to keep Smith alive? Can't have Jordan walking around trailing a corpse behind him, some dead Smith corpse hanging down and getting tangled with what Jordan might call a clean job of providing . . . Goddamn that radio mumbling. Door closed. Now. Corridor empty. Now. *Now!* Ohmygod how—what is it? How whatever it is hurts. But it's going to be clean. Very clean when it's over. Smith there, Jordan here, dead jinx, clean all over . . . Now, provider . . .

As soon as he pushed the door open to number three Jordan, clean, was the professional. He didn't even hate anybody or want anybody. He was fast and barely visible and never lost his head once though he saw the jinx job setup with the first glance through the door. Two of them and the radio going and a drip faucet sound from farther back.

But he did not have to touch a thing, just look, do it, be done, end of jinx job. There was Benny's big back, there was Sandy by the opposite wall, there he was pouring liquor into the glass on the table and the radio behind, that mumbling mood music over everything.

Sandy straightened up, looked up, and smiled. He's never smiled at me this way, and the last thing he'll do is smile at me just that way. Now. And he fired.

He felt clear and good as soon as he had done it and before Benny could turn Jordan was no longer there. Jordan had had his glimpse, which was all the touching he needed, the smile looking at him, the smile gone absolutely, then Sandy leaning, and the mess on the wall behind Sandy's head.

Clean job, good provider, dead jinx, Smith breathing a sigh. Jordan closed the exit door without slamming it and ran.

Chapter 18

He ran because he was in a rational hurry. There was this much time and this much to do and to make all of it fit it meant fast now. No haste, but fast. Fast was clean and haste was messy and now, of course, everything was finally clean. And this for the final touch, a present for Smith.

Jordan stopped walking when the Forty-second Street library was exactly opposite. He stopped to give himself time to calm down.

Not a present for Smith, but like a present for Betty. It would be: I give you this absolute Smith, this absolutely real Smith, Betty; look at me in black and white, Betty, so absolutely clear cut and right; hell, we could even get married. Jordan laughed and walked into the library.

He sat down in the newspaper room and held a paper. At seven, as always happened, Caughlin walked in. Jordan let the old man sit down and then waited another few minutes.

Caughlin, like his habits, was always the same. He had a brown overcoat on, long and large, which had one button high up in front. The button was closed so that the shirt would not show. The shirt was an undershirt. Caughlin took his glasses out, brushed white hairs back over his skull, started reading. He never looked right or left when he read, which made him seem stiff-necked or stolid.

"Evening, Caughlin," said Jordan.

Caughlin waited till the other was sitting. Then he looked sideways and back at his paper again.

"Good evening, Jordan," he said. "Why me?" and his Adam's apple started bobbing. There was no sound when Caughlin laughed, just the Adam's apple bobbing. "Am I a job or do you want one?"

"I need one."

"Murder in the Reading Room," said Caughlin, and seemed to be laughing again. "Corny, isn't it?"

"Stop the crap, Caughlin."

"And start the music."

Jordan said nothing because everybody knew the old man was crazy, though this was to say nothing about his work. His work was expensive and could not be touched.

"I need everything from the bottom up," said Jordan, "and I need some of it right away."

"What name?"

"Smith."

This time Caughlin laughed with a sound. A man at the next seat looked up from his paper but Caughlin, who rarely turned his head, kept on laughing and paid no attention. When he was done he looked down at his paper and talked again.

"I'd be ashamed to sell you something with the name of Smith, Jordan."

"But it *is* Smith. I'm saying, it has to be Smith. Birth certificate, car registration, insurance, driver's license, social security. Samuel Smith."

"Too many esses."

"What?"

"Sounds like a superior job."

"It is."

"And who's paying for it?"

"I am."

"I thought you said it was a job, Jordan."

"Damn you, stop digging," he said. He was glad that the old man did not look up and would not see the mistake show in Jordan's face. "I get reimbursed for it," said Jordan, "which is the new way we got of handling things."

"Ah. There've been changes."

"You seem the same."

"Permanent, superior quality. When do you need this?"

"Jinx time."

"What was that, Jordan?"

"Jig time, jig time. I mean now."

"I can't get it for you all in one day. What do you need first?"

"The birth certificate."

"Ask the impossible, and it costs extra."

"Caughlin, come on. This is rush."

"Easiest way, Jordan," and Caughlin never changed his face, "is for you to go out and do a job on a Smith and then bring me the papers so I can fix them up."

"You going to keep horsing around here with that nut talk, Caughlin, or do I get this job done?"

"Murder in the Reading Room."

It's part of the price. You buy from Caughlin and part of the price is the digging and squirming he does like a worm and you better take it.

"What do you need the things for, Jordan?"

"I'd only lie to you."

"All my customers do. But they all say something."

Jordan said nothing.

"Need it that bad?"

He needed it so badly, Jordan felt suddenly on the point of

tears or a scream, he did not know which, both Smith and Jordan screaming why all this . . .

Because a wife can't testify against her husband, it struck him. That's why. I'm Smith and I marry her, for that good reason. The scream went and Jordan felt right again, admiring the quick lie he had made. He knew full well he was lying, the same as he knew there was no Smith and no Jordan, but it worked well that way.

"Smith is an easy name," he said. "You've got to have something on file that I can use."

"I do," said Caughlin. "Needs a little work, but is a good birth certificate."

"You son of a bitch, why didn't you say so in the beginning?"

"I like to talk," said Caughlin.

"I want it tonight," said Jordan. "Get on it now so I can have it tonight."

"Too expensive."

"Come on!"

"Four thousand, counting your hurry."

The price for Kemp.

"And the driver's license," said Caughlin, "that's for nothing."

The price for Sandy. I mean, speaking of money, thought Jordan. He said, "I got five hundred with me. You get the rest when you're done."

They went outside and stood on the street. It was still light but the street lights went on. Caughlin said something poetic about that and then he said he wanted the five hundred.

"At your place. I want to see the merchandise."

"I got to fix it a little."

"I know. I want to see what you're going to fix."

They walked through a small park where the bums sat in the warm evening air and from there down a street with tall office buildings which were all shut for the day. The street was quiet and empty because of the hour.

"This one," said Caughlin, and they went into an alley between two buildings and from there through a steel door into the furnace room. There was a dry heat in the basement room and just one bulb burning, near the panel which had to do with the heating and the air-conditioning system.

Caughlin lived behind that room. He lived in an enclosure with a good door, but the room behind turned out to be no room at all. It was like a bin. There was no window, but there was one diagonal wall with a hatch on top where the coal used to come through when they had heated with coal.

The floor was covered with newspaper and the walls were glued over with newspaper.

"I'm in the news," said Caughlin. He said this to everyone who came in there and it sounded automatic. Some of the papers on the floor lifted gently at the edges when Caughlin closed the door.

There was a cot, a table, a closet—nothing else would fit into the place. In the closet were a great number of things, dirty laundry at first sight. Caughlin rummaged around in the darkness and came up with a sheet of paper.

"This one," he said.

It looked all right. It made Jordan forty-five years old but aside from that it was a good document.

"Make me younger," said Jordan, "and for the first name, make it Samuel."

"That's your name."

"Yes."

"All amateurs do that. Like they're afraid to let go altogether."

Jordan laughed. He could let go Jordan and fall into Smith and he could let go Smith and fall back into Jordan. It was that kind of forever situation and he felt there was nothing neater.

"When?" he said.

"I can change the name easier than the age . . ."

"Naturally," said Jordan.

"Age," Caughlin finished off but did not seem to feel interrupted. "But to do both of them . . ."

"Just the name. Leave the age. When?"

"Tomorrow. Early."

"Tonight."

"I'll work all night."

"Do it faster."

Caughlin shrugged and took the five one-hundred-dollar bills Jordan held out. "Between twelve and one tonight," he said. "Come back here."

Jordan nodded and went to the door.

"I admire the calmness of a worker like you," Caughlin said behind him.

Jordan stopped, and turning to look at the old man, he tore some of the sheets on the floor.

"In the face of loss and disaster," said Caughlin.

"Like what, Caughlin?"

Caughlin sat down on his cot and made the springs squeak a

few times, to fill the silence. Then he said, "I see where Sandy is dead."

He did not creak the springs again and the only sound was Jordan lifting his feet carefully, so as not to tear paper again. Then he leaned against the door. "You know that?" said Jordan.

"Don't you?"

"How come you know that?"

"You think all I do is read the papers?"

"No," said Jordan. "I know you don't."

It would, of course, not be in the papers because what went on in the back of Monico's rarely ever got beyond a known circle. But a shadow man like Caughlin, of course he might know.

"I know you knew Sandy," said Caughlin, "but did you know Benny?"

"No."

"The one who did it. The one who does bouncing at Monico's."

"Who did it?"

"Benny. The one who does bouncing at Monico's."

"Well, well, well," said Jordan, or his voice said it while he listened to it. "Why?"

"For the hoor what fingered him. I don't know her name."

Jordan did not say Lois or anything for a moment. Then he said, "That's no reason."

"Of course not," and Caughlin laughed. Then he said, "You sound like the one who did it," and laughed some more. "Like what Benny said."

"Like what Benny said?"

"He said, 'That's no reason. Even a guy I don't like I wouldn't do in for a hooker.'"

"He said that, did he?"

"But they got him."

"They?"

"Who else, the cops?" Caughlin laughed again.

The way this is handled, Jordan knew, was by the private justice department. He knew about that part. He put his hand on the knob of the door, wanting to leave.

"They done with him?" he said.

"I thought you might know about that," said Caughlin. "Considering your line of work."

"Stop digging," said Jordan. "Would I need to be Smith for a routine like that?"

"When they're done with him, will you let me know?"

"I don't even know where they're keeping him."

"Shor's Landing," said Caughlin. "Will you let me know?"

"Why?"

"I'm morbid," said Caughlin. "Why else know anything?"

"I'll be back midnight," said Jordan. "You be here and be done with the job."

He left that way, saying no more than he always did, Jordan all harnessed and held neat with his habits, avoiding the busy streets because that made sense, but done thinking about problems because they had all been settled. Even Caughlin the talker didn't worry him. While I'm in town he'll be busy; when I'm in Miami, let him talk. Oh the sense of it, Jordan thought, and even with Meyer with a nose like a pointed question, oh the ease of the answers, if he should ever ask. I thought you were in Miami? I needed the stuff from Caughlin. I thought you had a job on this what's-her-name? Her name is Mrs. Smith and a wife cannot testify against her husband. And besides, she won't. She won't. No, she won't. How come, Jordan? Because Smith takes care of that.

He walked, neat, clean, and all settled, and had time for the other thing.

He thought, what a beautiful, warm evening with nothing to do. With Jordan having time in between and Smith, getting shaped up to perfection. Jinx dead, he began, hours late, but completely, to appreciate the right thing he had done.

The first job ever that had not been a job, and the beauty of it, he kept thinking. Done like a job, that Sandy thing, but with a first-time feeling of ripe satisfaction. Well, of course, it had been necessary, but it was beautiful too. Sandy, had he lived to know it, would agree and would say, Sammy, I'll pay you double. Not that he didn't pay, of course, for Sandy always meant money. Dear Sandy, yes how well he paid, always and from start to finish.

Nine o'clock and more time to go.

And, for instance, Lois now, I even wouldn't mind her. A true time-in-between girl if I'd only known it sooner.

But while Jordan felt free now, he did not feel foolish. He did not go to the Monico or even waste time on the notion. Maybe next time I'm back in town and between Jordan and Smith time. This is between Jordan and Smith time, but that does not mean I should be foolish.

Ten o'clock and more time to go and Jordan, very sensible,

agreed with his thoughts that he might spend the time out of town.

He stole a car and drove to the Jersey side. He took his first ride through a warm night and with no need to go anywhere. He even whistled.

Eleven o'clock and below the dip was Shor's Landing.

This shows, he said, how perfect everything can be, because it is.

Shor's Landing was a line of docks on a little lake, a line of lights hanging between tall posts, and a restaurant—more lights —where woods started again, and cabins—few lights—where woods came from the other side.

The pine needles breathed out a nighttime smell and the band at Shor's Landing made nighttime music. Everybody dancing, thought Jordan. It's not bedtime, just nighttime.

These must be lovers, thought Jordan. This cabin is dark like the others but with two sleepless voices.

This one? Empty. Shor is not renting too well.

And in this one a fisherman, with ear plug and nembutal to make certain he'll be up fresh at five in the morning. And he has a belly, as I can tell by the snore.

Ah yes. This one by the door with a cigarette. Glow and fade, glow and fade, nervous in the night and wishing he were some-where else. Who wants to sit by the door of a cabin with the music someplace else and the bed taken up and the holster making a heavy patch of black sweat. . . . What did Sandy used to pay for that type of job, ten fins?

Jordan walked up to the cabin and asked the man for a light. Before getting the light he kicked the man under the chin, be-cause the man sat low on the stoop and the method was sound-less.

The screen door creaked and Jordan thought, I bet Benny thinks this is it.

He was on the bed, as expected, tied up, as expected, gagged and sweated. Jordan knew this ahead of time because the method was standard.

After that, standards having nothing to do with it; Jordan turned on the light by the bed and smiled down at the man.

"I bet you think I'm it," he said.

Benny could not talk but he got it across with his eyes and the worm-bunched wrinkles on his forehead. And he wetted his pants, though Jordan did not know this.

"I'm not," said Jordan. "This is me, in between time."

He took the pillow out from under Benny's head and put it over his head, on his face.

God, I don't want him to suffocate, Jordan thought, and pressed the twenty-two into the pillow and fired.

Then he picked up the pillow to see if the shot had been all right, but because of the feathers glued down all over he was not too sure. He put the pillow back, and the gun, and did it again. Soft, muffled thud, and this time Benny did not jerk. Jordan went by that.

Almost twelve and I better hurry. He turned off the lamp and left the way he had come.

And even though he was in a hurry there was no jumpy tension in the way he felt. All was new, all was fine, Smith being done up to perfection back in town, and this, Jordan knew, was the first time ever, the first in-between-time job, only done out of idleness.

Chapter 19

Meyer, because of all that had happened, was still at his desk in the middle of the night. Then he got two phone calls one after the other.

"Mister Meyer, how are you?"

"Who in hell . . ."

"Not well, I notice, not too well."

"Do I know you?"

"Not directly, but just the same. This is Caughlin."

The nut. And how did that forger get this number?

"Would you buy a birth certificate with the name of Smith?"

"Listen! My name's Meyer which is bad enough, but if I should want your merch . . ."

"Not you. I meant that just for an example. For a fact though, this is for somebody else."

I'll wait. For a minute I'll wait, thought Meyer. Caughlin is a talker but with his prices he is not all nut.

"For who?" said Meyer.

"Whom. You mean, whom."

"Goddamn your crazy . . ."

"Please, Mister Meyer. You know I always end up serious."

Meyer said he was sorry and would Caughlin hold the phone for a minute. He put his hand over the receiver and said, Smith,

Smith. Then he yelled at the door, "Come in here a minute," and Sherman came in.

"That Penderburg dame," Meyer said, "who did she say was her button salesman?"

"Smith. That's the name Jordan gave."

Meyer nodded and bit his lip. "When did Sandy say Jordan left for Miami?"

"Sandy's dead."

"I know that! Preserve me—" Meyer said to nobody and then he screamed again. "When? I asked you, *when?*"

"Last night sometime. I think he said . . ."

"Call National and Capital and whoever else flies the Florida run and check out on his flight. Jordan or Smith. Where he got on and got off."

Then Meyer talked to Caughlin again. "You still there?"

"Mister Meyer, the price just went up."

"Yeh. Sure. Listen. Your Smith customer, when is he picking up?"

"That isn't free information either."

"But he isn't picking up in the next half-hour."

"Mister Meyer, the way I earn pin money . . ."

"I know. The price just went up. My point is, Caughlin, I want to call you back."

"Why?"

"Half an hour."

"You don't think it's important?"

"That's why I want to call back in half an hour."

"The customer is paying four thousand dollars. You still think it isn't important?"

"You gave that away for free, didn't you, Caughlin?" and Meyer hung up.

If he needed Caughlin, and Meyer thought that he did not, then he would call back for sure. And at that moment the phone rang again.

"Caughlin," said Meyer, "when I say half an hour . . ."

"Hey—is this Meyer? Let me talk to Meyer."

"Yes?" said Meyer, because the voice sounded sick.

"Benny's dead."

"What?"

"This is Ferra, you know, Ferra. I got hit on the head, I mean got jumped here at the Landing, and then Benny is dead."

Meyer groaned through the whole story, through the whole thought that the Sandy thing made no sense now, not that the

Benny thing made any sense either, except haywire sense, if there was such a thing. He hung up and went into the next room.

"I got this," said Sherman, "there's no Jordan anywheres, but a Smith took the eight-ten National flight out as far as Washington."

"D.C.?"

"Yes. That."

"So?"

"But his ticket was paid into the International at Miami."

Meyer nodded and went back to his desk. He picked at some papers there and then walked to the dark window.

He thought, Sandy once said if that one goes he'll be crawling into a corner and whimpering . . .

Then Meyer walked back to the other room and laid it out to Sherman what he wanted done.

When Jordan turned into the street with the office buildings, there was one lighted place, right at the corner, and after that came the dark street. He walked past the hamburger place with its bright, steamy windows, and when he passed the door somebody said, "Psst—"

Jordan did not stop or look around because the sound made no sense to him.

"Mister Smith."

This time he stopped and the hate in his sudden movement was automatic.

"If you'll just turn around slowly, Mister Smith, you'll feel ever so much better."

Caughlin stepped out from the crack between buildings and walked with his stiff head held straight, facing front. He walked to the hamburger place and said, "You should follow me."

Run. Put the scream of fear into a very fast run. . . . That was how much everything broke in on Jordan, as if nothing good had ever happened before and nothing good was hoped for in any future. . . .

"Wait," he said and grabbed for Caughlin's arm.

Caughlin stopped immediately and tried to smile Jordan's motion away.

"You son of a bitch," said Jordan. "What? What happened?"

"We should go into the restaurant so that . . ."

"I'm going to kill you bone by bone, old man, bone by bone if you're double-crossing me—"

"Jordan, please. It's more complicated than that."

"We're going to your basement, old man."

"That is precisely, Jordan, precisely why I am here. To tell you about that. And you must get off the street."

Jordan let go of the arm and when he looked down the dark street he realized that he himself stood in a bright shaft of light. He pulled Caughlin again, away from the door and into the shadow. Caughlin talked now without being pressed any more.

"They're in the street," he said, "and I think it's for you."

Jordan looked and saw nothing. Then he saw a car pull away from the curb at the end of the block, pull away slowly, and the lights going on only later. But the car was going away, not coming closer.

"You don't mind being seen," said Caughlin, "but they do."

"More," said Jordan. "Tell me more."

"It's very complicated. You can let go my arm." But Jordan did not and Caughlin tried again. "It has to do with raising the ante."

"You said four thousand. If you . . ."

"I know. It didn't work."

"We're going to the basement."

"No. I'm trying to tell you, by way of help, if you can believe that . . ."

"I want the paper, old man, I must have the paper!"

"The double-cross is," Caughlin tried again, "that by way of double-crossing me in a matter of business, there's a stake-out for you which I am trying to counteract, counter-cross if you wish, as a pure matter of ethics and because you're my only true paying customer, though that isn't the whole . . ."

"Who? Who is there?"

"How redundant . . ."

"They're all dead, except you."

"Meyer knows," said Caughlin, and Jordan, with a great, sudden tiredness thought how wrong he had been that last time.

The between-time idleness job. What a strange, wrong thing to have done. Like a—like a killer. Jordan felt ill and leaned by the wall.

"Now, the point I was delicately trying . . ."

"The paper," said Jordan. "Come on."

Or Jordan the provider, even he would not be worth anything any more, without the paper to make Smith. This has got to be, got to be; he kept going on, and pulled the old man down the street.

"This one," said Caughlin and stopped by the big door which

showed the bulb in back over the elevator and the narrow hall leading there.

"The basement door you showed me is down the alley."

"I should want to check first, Jordan. For heaven's sake, if I were you . . ."

"All right, all right—"

Caughlin kept knocking on the glass door for a while till a man came out of the lighted elevator. He limped and kept craning his neck to wake up. When he stopped by the door and saw Caughlin, he kept craning a while and then opened up. "I thought you was downstairs. Ain't you supposed to be watching the furnace?"

"It's summer time," said Caughlin and went in.

"I meant was, ain't you supposed to be watching the blowers because of that air-conditioning trouble up on the third?"

"Yes, yes, yes."

"And why ain't you using the back way, like you're supposed to?"

"Door slammed shut."

They all went down the hall, to the lighted elevator.

"And who's this here? You know you ain't supposed . . ."

"Air-conditioning expert." Caughlin looked at Jordan and said, "Good, huh?"

"You mean you gonna take the elevator? Why don't you . . ."

"How I hate a whiny old man," and Caughlin took Jordan past the elevator to the back stairs. "Sometime when you have nothing to do, Jordan, why don't you, just between times . . ."

"Damn you, shut up!"

The door to the staircase hissed a little when it swung back and Caughlin took Jordan one flight up. "While I go and check," he said, "I'll leave you . . ."

"Wait a minute."

"Jordan. Please. You're worth four thousand dollars."

"Three-five, Caughlin."

"Why, of course, three-five. And as a token of my you-know-what," he put his hand into his pocket and took out a card. "A beauty, isn't it?"

It was a bona-fide driver's license, state of New York, for Samuel Smith with a local address.

"Take it."

Jordan took it. "I need that other paper," he said.

"Now you admire this while I go and check," and Caughlin left Jordan in the dark, first-floor corridor where a firm had fixed easy chairs, scenic photos, and its advertising in a restful manner.

Jordan watched the door hush shut and sat in the dark with his hand on his belt. In a while, because of the long wait, he pulled the Magnum out and held it.

Caughlin did not go all the way down to the basement. He stopped on the ground-floor landing where the pay phone hung on the wall and dialed his number again. Meyer, he felt, should have his one more chance.

Meyer, said Sherman, had gone to bed, and when that and some questions did not stir the old man into any worthwhile talking, Sherman said, go to hell, the deal's off, and he should go to bed too.

Caughlin drew his resigned conclusion, looked down the wall to the basement door, and then sighed. I'm a coward, he said, and why change now? He went to get Jordan then, so that they could go to the basement.

"There's nobody down there," he said. "Come along."

"How do you know? Just by walking in?"

"The truth is, I didn't even walk in. I called my informant and got the all clear."

"You're scared."

"I know. Are you?"

"Yes," said Jordan, and though it shook Caughlin and made him gape it was now too late for anything else because they were down at the door. "I want the paper," Jordan said again, and Caughlin pulled open the metal door.

One of the air-conditioning motors was humming.

"Usually," said Caughlin, "the light by the furnace . . ."

At that point, he got shot.

Caughlin spun and pitched into the railing which ran down the cellar stairs and Jordan tossed himself flat on the floor. He heard, "Got the wrong one—" and then, "but I think both of them—" He did not listen to all of it because he spun on the floor where he lay halfway through the basement door and with a hip shot blew out the bulb back of him in the stair well.

Now both sides were in the dark.

The motor hummed and it took him a while to hear anything else. And then I'm going to get the paper . . . He then heard a short scuffle which was way in the basement and while that went on Jordan got off the floor. He stood up on the cellar landing and let the door hiss shut behind him.

There was a useless shot, because Jordan was no longer in line with the door. While the shot still twanged back and forth on the concrete, Jordan bumped into the fire extinguisher next to the door. He yanked it off the hook.

"Hey—" someone said in the basement. "Hey, you think he's still here?"

Jordan spun the wheel on the extinguisher and tossed the cylinder off the landing. When it bounced into the basement the sound was a fright.

Two quick shots, useless.

Then the thing lay there in the dark and just hissed.

Jordan said nothing, the two down in the basement said nothing.

"Hey—" and then, "Jeesis in heaven what *is it?*"

"I don't know. Just shut up, I don't know—"

After that Jordan told them, "It takes about one minute. If you think you got the guts, put out that fuse."

The thing lay there in the dark and hissed.

"—Fuse?"

"Shut up," said the other one. "Shut up, shut up—"

"Forty seconds maybe," said Jordan.

It hissed.

"Hey . . . Hey, you up there!"

"Thirty maybe."

"Hey you up there, you're Jordan, ain't you Jordan?"

"What good will it do you?" said Jordan. He licked his lips in the dark and wiped his free hand.

The hiss changed then, because the pressure was going down.

"For godssake answer up there, will you please?"

"Turn the light on," said Jordan, "and I'll stop the fuse."

"Okay. Now hold . . ."

"You shut up you shut up," said the other one.

"Fifteen and Geronimo," said Jordan.

"Wait!"

"Toss your guns where I can hear them clatter," said Jordan.

One clattered, by the foot of the basement stairs, the other one didn't. The other one fell on top of the dead Caughlin, but Jordan knew it was there.

"Okay, you got them. Now just hold it, Jordan, do you hear?"

Jordan got ready to see in the sudden light, and the bulb went on.

There was a big, foamy puddle of white on the floor and the fire extinguisher in it, still burbling a little. The two men in the light were just staring. It gave Jordan good time to come down the short stairs, and as soon as he was there he shot first one and then the other. They both got identical holes in the forehead and were dead when they hit the floor. And then the rush was on Jordan again and he jumped over the men and ran to the back of the furnace. Back there. Caughlin's door was locked.

Reason had nothing to do with it, just a wish strong as his will. He pulled, wrenched, rattled the door and said hoarse things. He lost his senses, found them, lost everything he had ever learned, got it all back at the wrong moment, lost one hope after another, turned into worm, rat, idiot, rage, hate splinters, baby panic, a gasp in no air. . . .

But he would not go back up the short flight of stairs to where the Caughlin corpse lay, and turn it over and touch it for the key. . . .

And then the footsteps came down the other side of the basement door, they went limpedy-limp, and the easiest thing in the world, Jordan thought, when he shows in the door now . . . The old man from the elevator pulled open the door and came in, gaping, standing a split second away from being dead. He made one more limpedy-limp—That's an idleness standing there, said Jordan, and I *know* better. . . .

One more sick tired drag on the door and Jordan ran. He gave up and ran with mouth open, voiceless, because the wail in him got all used up in the running.

Chapter 20

She said, "My God, Sam! What happened to you?"

He sat down in a chair in the room she had furnished and was ready to tell her what he had meant to do, what he had done instead, how confused it had left him, that she, Betty, was the only thing in all this that had never confused him, and that he thought this is what he had wanted all the time.

Later, he thought, after a breath. What he said was, "Nothing. It's all right."

"But—but honey, you looked like you *ran* all the way."

"I rented a car," he said.

She laughed and said she liked his sense of humor. She came over to him and ran her hand through his hair. "You have an accident, Sam?"

"Yes. A real one."

"Bad, honey?"

"I don't know yet. But it shook me."

"Well, you just tell me later," and she went to the front window where she pulled up the blind. "I didn't know you were coming, Sammy, or I would have fixed up something. Did you notice the new couch I bought?"

"Close the blind, Betty."

"Close it?"

"No. Leave it open. So I can look out." He got up and looked out. He looked across the porch of the bungalow he had rented for her and up and down the street full of late sunshine. No palms here, but there was Spanish tile on the house across and Betty had liked that.

"You don't want to eat now, do you, Sam? You don't look . . ."

"No."

She came over and wanted to lean against him but he changed it into something else, holding her, so she would not lean into the gun.

"You look," she said, "you look almost a little older, or something."

"No sleep," he said. "It's been very hard sleeping."

Then she took him into the bedroom and wanted to help him off with his coat. "No," he said. "I'll do it," and she laughed again and said that was just like him, not to accept a little consideration.

"No," he said, "it's not that."

"Not that?"

"I will, in a while," he said. "But right now I'm not yet done running."

She did not understand that and laughed this time for that reason. "Sam," she said. "Look what I bought in the meantime."

While she went to the chest of drawers, he put the gun in the closet and hung up his jacket there.

"Look. And just today. Just as if I knew you were coming." She held the fine spun nightgown up and moved it back and forth in the air. "Like it?"

"Yes," he said. "I like you *very* much."

He sat down on the bed and she said, "Oh, Sammy. You're so tired you don't know what you're saying."

He did not correct her, because he was tired.

"You going to stay a while this time, Sam?"

"Yes. Really."

"How nice that will be, Sam. How nice."

"Yes," he said, and stretched out on the bed.

"You want a nap before eating, don't you, Sammy."

"Stay here."

"If you want me to."

"Yes. Stay here."

She sat down on the bed and he laid his hand on her thigh. She put her hand on his and gave it a small push.

"You're not wearing a housecoat," he said.

"Well, I wasn't, I mean . . ."

"No. Stay here."

She stayed and then he said she should put on the new night-dress she had bought.

The sun was going outside and part of the time while she undressed he closed his eyes and just heard the sounds she made with cloth against skin. Once a car got louder down the long block, but Jordan was so worn he did not tense till the car had gone by and then he relaxed again.

"I'll lie down next to you," she said.

They lay like that and Jordan almost went to sleep. But he did not want to lose knowing that she was there, and the darker it got the more he listened for other things.

She moved against him and he stayed awake. He moved his hand over her and felt her skin in the places where he liked to feel it especially. They lay like that and touched only in a few places and she thought, should I tell him before or should I tell him after. He is so friendly now. . . .

"Sam?"

"Don't move away."

"I wasn't going to."

"Stay like this, Betty, and I'll talk to you."

We'll talk, she thought, and this is a good time to tell him.

"I tried and I tried," he said, "but not all of it really came off. It's mistakes that happened, wrong things along the line, but what I did wrong, Betty, my faults, I mean, they—I don't know, Betty, I don't know how to say it . . ."

He said more, with the worry pushing him, the worry about not being able to keep Smith and Jordan apart, the new awful thing which he had never imagined, but the girl wasn't listening then. She felt a quick panic.

"Are you trying to tell me you're married?"

"Married? Hell no," and he sat up, trying to focus.

She had heard how shrill she had sounded and how it must have struck him. She thought before I lose my courage I must speak. "I remember you said no once before, Sam, but you were acting so strangely, and here I have this important thing, this worry on my mind, and if you say so, Sam, of course I . . ."

"What?"

"I'm going to have a baby."

He said nothing but she felt his quick move and she panicked again. "I mean, you got to take that into consideration, Sam. You got to remember I sit here all alone and only you know where and I got this worry . . ."

"Baby?"

"Yes."

"Who says?"

"The doctor said so when I . . ."

"When?"

"Three months now."

He jumped off the bed and wiped his mouth, staring at her. Dark now in the room. He had talked and asked all the last things from sheer confusion but that was done. Clear now.

"Three months? From *me?*"

"Sam, Sammy. I didn't mean—what I meant was, was something else. What . . ."

"Shut up." I'm rattled, he thought, and then said it, "I'm rattled. Shut up for a minute—"

She lay still and confused and he thought that face there, I have never seen anything emptier. What is there . . . Except for the lie she tried, the lie with the baby . . . One lie in back, that was Sandy; one lie in front, staring empty. . . . Easy, try it easy like Jordan does this, and he stepped back almost into the closet. Smith gone now, he thought, but don't give up Jordan. And no between-time kick, on-the-run kick any more. And my God, he thought—and there was a sound in his throat—what is left now . . .

The light snapped on.

The man nodded his head and nodded the gun at Jordan.

"Wasn't she supposed to be dead?"

"Sam! He's got . . ."

She stopped when the killer walked farther into the room, and when Jordan moved over where the killer wanted him.

"Where's your gun?"

Jordan nodded at the closet.

"Ah," said the killer, and left it to lie there when he saw it on the shelf. Then he turned all the way back to the room.

"A shame," he said. "She could have stayed in one piece if I could have gotten you elsewhere. But now she's going to see this."

Jordan sank into the chair behind him and his breath came with a paper sound.

"I think I'll do her first. Real shame," and he lifted the gun the way Jordan would do it. Outside a motor raced loud. He took a stance the way Jordan did when he was not on the run.

The girl gagged when she saw the gun come up to level, and she understood nothing when all that stopped.

Jordan, the way he hardly ever did, squeezed from way low and the killer seemed to draw up his shoulders. When he fell, Jordan was over him, looking hard for the little hole which did not show clearly because of his clothes. He held out the little twenty-two and made a hole where he wanted it. He felt nothing.

When the girl made a hoarse sound Jordan looked up. He felt rattled and confused, Smith-Jordan confused. He looked at her drawn up on the bed and said, "Don't be afraid, Betty. He's dead."

Then he ran out. He saw the car by the curb, motor revving, but when he ran out on the porch he thought better of it and pulled back. So the car took off.

He stood on the porch and watched the car go. He was not so confused that he did not know what came next. Next would come the same thing, the same thing again, with only one finish to it. He knew the routine. He felt heavy and still. One more run, he said, one more run. Not for long now, but for just a little . . .

He ran back into the house and into the bedroom.

"Betty . . ."

"Please!"

"Quiet, Betty, quiet quiet. Here now, get this on."

"What are you—who are—"

"Nonono. Forget that. Sam Smith. Remember? And the buttons." He held the coat to her but she stepped back into a corner.

"Betty, please," he said, "Betty, please. One more run is all, Betty sweet, one more and it's over. When you're gone and it's over, they won't want you any more."

"What are you—"

"He said so, remember? Before he was dead. Here, the coat."

She put it on, so he would go away. When she had it on he pulled money out of his pocket. "Now this, Betty. Stick it here, in the pocket," and he held the thick roll out with two hands.

"No. I won't touch . . ."

"Betty."

"You're some filthy kind of . . ."

"Please," he said, talking slower now. "Please don't quarrel."

He put the money into her pocket and she held still with fright.

"You come now," he said. "Here, shoes. Then we go. Run, I mean."

She put the shoes on and he rushed her. He left his jacket where it was, but was not so confused that he did not take the Magnum. He put it in the place under his belt but moved it into the pocket when he saw how she looked at it.

"Please," he said again. "Don't quarrel," and he ran her out to the street.

He ran her to the car at the corner and when they were inside he drove fast and skilled. For a while they sat next to each other like that without talking, he not talking because of all he was thinking. What there was of him and the things he had done, so that she would know the bad and the good of him, and what he had wished would have happened. But he did not know enough about any of it and the confusion kept him from talking. She sat still too, so he felt that she felt the same kind of things, and was kept from talking. Once he reached over and made a light stroke on her arm. Her fright kept her silent and stiffened.

Her fright made her keep step with him when they ran into the airport; and when he found a ticket for a plane which left in five minutes; and when he rushed her last through the gate and said something she did not understand. . . .

He latched the chain across the empty gate and watched the plane swivel slowly and then move slowly with a big roar. It moved out of the light and in a while it will fly off, he said to himself.

He felt no need to watch that. And he did not remember where her ticket went. Just that the girl had been.

They picked him up again in town and they had him when he went into the bus station. He had gone into the station because there were people. Then he saw the three men and knew immediately.

They shot him against a wall with a summer schedule behind him, and that got torn too.

It felt to him as if he sat on the floor a long time, and for one very bad moment a sudden, great wildness almost tore him open, like pigeons beating around inside a wire-mesh cage and even their eyes with the stiff bird-stare turned wild with glitter.

But he made that all go quiet again. He could not see any more and wished he had said more to the girl, had told her some things he had done, so that she would know the bad and the good of him and he would not be just a blank.

He had a great deal of pain and then died.

When the policeman turned him over, he found one driver's license which said Smith and another one which said Jordan.

"Must be Jordan," he said. "There aren't any Smiths."

Night-Walker

by Robert J. Randisi

Robert J. Randisi is just now starting to be appreciated for the lean, stripped-down approach he's brought back to the private-eye novel. Last Exit from Brooklyn *was a notable novel in a notable year, and he's got two more just as good waiting publication.*

First published in 1978

He sits at the dimly lit bar and listens to the conversations going on around him. He does not concentrate on any one conversation, but strains to catch at least a piece of each separate one within earshot. With a wave of his hand he orders a second drink and continues to listen. He is listening for a certain phrase to be spoken, at which time he will make his plans and act upon them.

The words, however, when spoken, do not come from any of the conversations going on around him, but from the bartender as he brings him his third drink.

"So, what do you think?" the bartender asks.

Glancing at the heavily built man behind the bar, he asks, "About what?"

Pointing to the far end of the bar the bartender says, "We was having an argument, about Ali and this new guy. I think the challenger is gonna get hurt pretty good, but those guys figure Ali is taking the guy too light. Me, I know Ali can beat a nobody like this bum. I mean, who is he, you know? He's a nobody!"

He stares at the overweight bartender for a few moments before telling the man, "Go back to your friends."

Frowning, the bartender starts to say something else, but thinks better of it and moves off . . .

Finishing his drink, he rises to leave, stopping only to ask the hatcheck girl, "What time does the bartender work until?"

"Midnight," she answers and, batting heavily made-up eyes at him, adds, "Why? Won't I do?"

Without answering, he leaves the bar and picks a spot outside.

The bartender leaves at five minutes past midnight. He turns right and proceeds towards an alley. As he passes the alley he is grabbed by the neck from behind and dragged in. Although the attacker is smaller and thinner, his strength is sufficient to hold the bigger man until he chooses to release him, deeper into the alley. There he pushes the bartender against the building.

"What do you want?" the heavier man cries, eyes wide with fright. "I ain't got no money! What do you want?"

Slowly the smaller man takes a switchblade from his pocket and allows the four-and-a-half-inch blade to spring from the six-inch handle. Although at its widest the blade is a mere three-eighths of an inch it is a very effective weapon.

Rotating the knife slowly, he catches the frightened man's eyes with his own, then he plunges it swiftly into his belly. The man screams. He falls to the ground whimpering. The last words he hears before dying are "Everybody is somebody."

He rides the subway, listening to the conversations. Not to any one conversation, but to at least a part of every one he can.

He listens for a certain phrase.

From behind him he hears, "I wouldn't go out with Arnold on a bet. He's so short—a little fat nobody."

He turns to see who is speaking. The girl is young, not yet twenty, with blond hair and smooth skin. He watches closely to see where she gets off, and follows when she does.

It is late and he and the girl are the only two to leave the train. The girl gives him a brief and suspicious look, satisfying herself as to who got off with her and what he looks like. Apparently what she sees does not frighten her and she begins to walk towards the stairway to the street. He notices that there is no clerk in the change booth. He follows the girl closely and calls to her as she approaches the stairs. She turns, but does not see the blade in his hand. She does see his intense eyes when they catch hers and hold them.

"What is it? What do you—" she begins, her voice tinged now with fear. He steps in and, in one swift motion, plunges the thin blade into the girl. She falls to the floor clutching herself. The last words she hears before dying are "Everybody is somebody."

It is almost morning, almost daylight. He cannot function correctly in daylight. Somehow the sunlight inhibits him, makes him a different person. At night it's different. In the daytime, as a janitor in a high school, he is a nobody. He cleans floors, walls, the yard and locker rooms, the lunch room—everyone believing that, as a janitor, he is subject to their commands.

"Clean that up, Woodley."

"I dropped some milk, Woodley, mop it up, would you, please?"

"Who's that? Oh, just Woodley."

In the daytime he is Woodley the nobody.

But everybody is somebody, so at night when darkness falls, he is somebody.

Dust to Dust

by Marcia Muller

Marcia Muller is one of the major voices of modern crime fiction. She writes mainstream novels that just happen to have a mystery in them, and she writes in a practiced, careful style that gets better each time out. She is rapidly becoming without peer in the private-eye genre.

First published in 1982

The dust was particularly bad on Monday, July sixth. It rose from the second floor where the demolition was going on and hung in the dry air of the photo lab. The trouble was, it didn't stay suspended. It settled on the Formica counter tops, in the stainless-steel sink, on the plastic I'd covered the enlarger with. And worst of all, it settled on the negatives drying in the supposedly airtight cabinet.

The second time I checked the negatives I gave up. They'd have to be soaked for hours to get the dust out of the emulsion. And when I rehung them they'd only be coated with the stuff again.

I turned off the orange safelight and went into the studio. A thick film of powder covered everything there, too. I'd had the foresight to put my cameras away, but somehow the dust crept into the cupboards, through the leather cases, and onto the lenses themselves. The restoration project was turning into a nightmare, and it had barely begun.

I crossed the studio to the Victorian's big front windows. The city of Phoenix sprawled before me, skyscrapers shimmering in the heat. Camelback Mountain rose out of the flat land to the right, and the oasis of Encanto Park beckoned at the left. I could drive over there and sit under a tree by the water. I could rent a paddlewheel boat. Anything to escape the dry grit-laden heat.

But I had to work on the photos for the book.

And I couldn't work on them because I couldn't get the negatives to come out clear.

I leaned my forehead against the window frame, biting back my frustration.

"Jane!" My name echoed faintly from below. "Jane! Come down here!"

It was Roy, the workman I'd hired to demolish the rabbit warren of cubicles that had been constructed when the Victorian was turned into a rooming house in the thirties. The last time he'd shouted for me like that was because he'd discovered a stained-glass window preserved intact between two false walls. My spirits lifting, I hurried down the winding stairs.

The second floor was a wasteland heaped with debris. Walls leaned at crazy angles. Piles of smashed plaster blocked the hall. Rough beams and lath were exposed. The air was even worse down there—full of powder which caught in my nostrils and covered my clothing whenever I brushed against anything.

I called back to Roy, but his answering shout came from further below, in the front hall.

I descended the stairs into the gloom, keeping to the wall side because the bannister was missing. Roy stood, crowbar in hand, at the rear of the stairway. He was a tall, thin man with a pockmarked face and curly black hair, a drifter who had wandered into town willing to work cheap so long as no questions were asked about his past. Roy, along with his mongrel dog, now lived in his truck in my driveway. In spite of his odd appearance and stealthy comings and goings, I felt safer having him around while living in a half-demolished house.

Now he pushed up the goggles he wore to keep the plaster out of his eyes and waved the crowbar toward the stairs.

"Jane, I've really found something this time." His voice trembled. Roy had a genuine enthusiasm for old houses, and this house in particular.

I hurried down the hall and looked under the stairs. The plaster-and-lath had been partially ripped off and tossed onto the floor. Behind it, I could see only darkness. The odor of dry rot wafted out of the opening.

Dammit, now there was debris in the downstairs hall, too. "I thought I told you to finish the second floor before you started here."

"But take a look."

"I am. I see a mess."

"No, here. Take the flashlight. Look."

I took it and shone it through the hole. It illuminated gold-patterned wallpaper and wood paneling. My irritation vanished. "What is it, do you suppose?"

"I think it's what they call a 'cozy.' A place where they hung coats and ladies left their outside boots when they came calling." He shouldered past me. "Let's get a better look."

I backed off and watched as he tugged at the wall with the crowbar, the muscles in his back and arms straining. In minutes, he had ripped a larger section off. It crashed to the floor, and when the dust cleared I shone the light once more.

It was a paneled nook with a bench and ornate brass hooks on the wall. "I think you're right—it's a cozy."

Roy attacked the wall once more and soon the opening was clear. He stepped inside, the leg of his jeans catching on a nail. "It's big enough for three people." His voice echoed in the empty space.

"Why do you think they sealed it up?" I asked.

"Fire regulations, when they converted to a rooming house. They . . . what's this?"

I leaned forward.

Roy turned, his hand outstretched. I looked at the object resting on his palm and recoiled.

"God!"

"Take it easy." He stepped out of the cozy. "It's only a dead bird."

It was small, probably a sparrow, and like the stained-glass window Roy had found the past week, perfectly preserved.

"Ugh!" I said. "How did it get in there?"

Roy stared at the small body in fascination. "It's probably been there since the wall was constructed. Died of hunger, or lack of air."

I shivered. "But it's not rotted."

"In this dry climate? It's like mummification. You could preserve a body for decades."

"Put it down. It's probably diseased."

He shrugged. "I doubt it." But he stepped back into the cozy and placed it on the bench. Then he motioned for the flashlight. "The wallpaper's in good shape. And the wood looks like golden oak. And . . . hello."

"Now what?"

He bent over and picked something up. "It's a comb, a mother-of-pearl comb like ladies wore in their hair." He held it out. The comb had long teeth to sweep up heavy tresses on a woman's head.

"This place never ceases to amaze me." I took it and brushed off the plaster dust. Plaster . . . "Roy, this wall couldn't have been put up in the thirties."

"Well, the building permit shows the house was converted then."

"But the rest of the false walls are fireproof sheetrock, like regulations required. This one is plaster-and-lath. This cozy has been sealed off longer than that. Maybe since ladies wore this kind of comb."

"Maybe." His eyes lit up. "We've found an eighty-year-old bird mummy."

"I guess so." The comb fascinated me, as the bird had Roy. I stared at it.

"You should get shots of this for your book," Roy said.

"What?"

"Your book."

I shook my head, disoriented. Of course—the book. It was defraying the cost of the renovation, a photo essay on restoring one of Phoenix's grand old ladies.

"You haven't forgotten the book?" Roy's tone was mocking.

I shook my head again. "Roy, why did you break down this wall? When I told you to finish upstairs first?"

"Look, if you're pissed off about the mess . . ."

"No, I'm curious. Why?"

Now he looked confused. "I . . ."

"Yes?"

"I don't know."

"Don't know?"

He frowned, his pockmarked face twisting in concentration. "I really *don't* know. I had gone to the kitchen for a beer and I came through here and . . . I don't know."

I watched him thoughtfully, clutching the mother-of-pearl comb. "Okay," I finally said, "just don't start on a new area again without checking with me."

"Sorry. I'll clean up this mess."

"Not yet. Let me get some photos first." Still holding the comb, I went up to the studio to get a camera.

In the week that followed, Roy attacked the second floor with a vengeance and it began to take on its original floor-plan. He made other discoveries—nothing as spectacular as the cozy, but interesting—old newspapers, coffee cans of a brand not sold in decades, a dirty pair of baby booties. I photographed each faithfully and assured my publisher that the work was going well.

It wasn't, though. As Roy worked, the dust increased and my frustration with the book project—not to mention the commercial jobs that were my bread and butter—deepened. The house, fortunately, was paid for, purchased with a bequest from my aunt, the only member of my family who didn't think it dreadful for a girl from Fairmont, West Virginia, to run off and become a photographer in a big western city. The money from the book, however, was what would make the house habitable, and the first part of the advance had already been eaten up. The only way I was going to squeeze more cash out of the publisher was to show him some progress, and so far I had made none of that.

Friday morning I told Roy to take the day off. Maybe I could get some work done if he wasn't raising clouds of dust. I spent the morning in the lab developing the rolls I'd shot that week, then went into the studio and looked over what prints I had ready to show to the publisher.

The exterior shots, taken before the demolition had begun, were fine. They showed a three-story structure with square bay windows and rough peeling paint. The fanlight over the front door had been broken and replaced with plywood, and much of the gingerbread trim was missing. All in all, she was a bedraggled old lady, but she would again be beautiful—if I could finish the damned book.

The early interior shots were not bad either. In fact, they evoked a nice sense of gloomy neglect. And the renovation of this floor, the attic, into studio and lab was well documented. It was with the second floor that my problems began.

At first the dust had been slight, and I hadn't noticed it on the negatives. As a result the prints were marred with white specks. In a couple of cases the dust had scratched the negatives while I'd handled them and the fine lines showed up in the pictures. Touching them up would be painstaking work, but it could be done.

But now the dust had become more active, taken over. I was forced to soak and resoak the negatives. A few rolls of film had proven unsalvageable after repeated soakings. And, in losing them, I was losing documentation of a very important part of the renovation.

I went to the window and looked down at the driveway where Roy was sunning himself on the grass beside his truck. The mongrel dog lay next to a tire in the shade of the vehicle. Roy reached under there for one of his ever-present beers, swigged at it and set it back down.

How, I wondered, did he stand the heat? He took to it like a native, seemingly oblivious to the sun's glare. But then, maybe Roy *was* a native of the Sun Belt. What did I know of him, really?

Only that he was a tireless worker and his knowledge of old houses was invaluable to me. He unerringly sensed which were the original walls and which were false, what should be torn down and what should remain. He could tell whether a fixture was the real thing or merely a good copy. I could not have managed without him.

I shrugged off thoughts of my handyman and lifted my hair from my shoulders. It was wheat colored, heavy, and, right now, uncomfortable. I pulled it on top of my head, looked around and spotted the mother-of-pearl comb we'd found in the cozy. It was small, designed to be worn as half of a pair on one side of the head. I secured the hair on my left with it, then pinned up the right side with one of the clips I used to hang negatives. Then I went into the darkroom.

The negatives were dry. I took one strip out of the cabinet and held it to the light. It seemed relatively clear. Perhaps, as long as the house wasn't disturbed, the dust ceased its silent takeover. I removed the other strips. Dammit, some were still spotty, especially those of the cozy and the objects we'd discovered in it. Those could be reshot, however. I decided to go ahead and make contact prints of the lot.

I cut the negatives into strips of six frames each, then inserted them in plastic holders. Shutting the door and turning on the safelight, I removed photographic paper from the small refrigerator, placed it and the negative holders under glass in the enlarger, and set my timer. Nine seconds at f/8 would do nicely.

When the first sheet of paper was exposed, I slipped it into the developer tray and watched, fascinated as I had been since the first time I'd done this, for the images to emerge. Yes, nine seconds had been right. I went to the enlarger and exposed the other negatives.

I moved the contact sheets along, developer to stop bath to fixer, then put them into the washing tray. Now I could open the door to the darkroom and let some air in. Even though Roy had insulated up here, it was still hot and close when I was working in the lab. I pinned my hair more securely on my head and took the contact sheets to the print dryer.

I scanned the sheets eagerly as they came off the roller. Most of the negatives had printed clearly and some of the shots were quite good. I should be able to assemble a decent selection for my editor with very little trouble. Relieved, I reached for the final sheet.

There were the pictures I had shot the day we'd discovered the cozy. They were different from the others. And different from past dust-damaged rolls. I picked up my magnifying loupe and took the sheet out into the light.

Somehow the dust had gotten to this set of negatives. Rather than leaving speckles, though, it had drifted like a sandstorm. It clustered in iridescent patches, as if an object had caught the light in a strange way. The effect was eerie; perhaps I could put it to use.

I circled the oddest-looking frames and went back into the darkroom, shutting the door securely. I selected the negative that corresponded to one circled on the sheet, routinely sprayed it with canned air for surface dirt, and inserted it into the holder of the enlarger. Adjusting the height, I shone the light down through the negative, positioning the image within the paper guides.

Yes, I had something extremely odd here.

Quickly I snapped off the light, set the timer, and slipped a piece of unexposed paper into the guides. The light came on again, the timer whirred, and then all was silent and dark. I slid the paper into the developer tray and waited.

The image was of the cozy with the bird mummy resting on the bench. That would have been good enough, but the effect of the dust made it spectacular. Above the dead bird rose a white-gray shape, a second bird in flight, spiraling upward.

Like a ghost. The ghost of a trapped bird, finally freed.

I shivered.

Could I use something like this in the book? It was perfect. But what if my editor asked how I'd done it? Photography was not only art but science. You strove for images that evoked certain emotions. But you had dammed well better know how you got those images.

Don't worry about that now, I told myself. See what else is here.

I replaced the bird negative with another one and exposed it. The image emerged slowly in the developing tray: first the carved arch of the cozy, then the plaster-and-lath heaped on the floor, finally the shimmering figure of a man.

I leaned over the tray. Roy? A double exposure perhaps? It looked like Roy, yet it didn't. And I hadn't taken any pictures of him anyway. No, this was another effect created by the dust, a mere outline of a tall man in what appeared to be an old-fash-ioned frock coat.

The ghost of a man? That was silly. I didn't believe in such things. Not in *my* house.

Still, the photos had a wonderful eeriness. I could include them in the book, as a novelty chapter. I could write a little explanation about the dust.

And while on the subject of dust, wasn't it rising again? Had Roy begun work, even though I'd told him not to?

I crossed the studio to the window and looked down. No, he was still there by the truck, although he was now dappled by the shade of a nearby tree. The sun had moved; it was getting on toward midafternoon.

Back in the darkroom I continued to print from the dust-damaged group of negatives. Maybe I was becoming fanciful, or maybe the chemicals were getting to me after being cooped up in here all day, but I was seeing stranger and stranger images. One looked like a woman in a long, full-skirted dress, standing in the entrance to the cozy. In another the man was reaching out— maybe trying to catch the bird that had invaded his home?

Was it his home? Who were these people? What were they doing in my negatives?

As I worked the heat increased. I became aware of the dust which, with or without Roy's help, had again taken up its stealthy activity. It had a life all its own, as demonstrated by these photos. I began to worry that it would damage the prints before I could put them on the dryer.

The gritty air became suffocating. The clip that held my hair on the right side came loose and a lock hung hot and heavy against my neck. I put one last print on the dryer and went into the studio.

Dust lay on every surface again. What had caused it to rise? I went to the window and looked down. Roy was sitting on the bed of the truck with the mongrel, drinking another beer. Well, if he hadn't done anything, I was truly stumped. Was I going to be plagued by dust throughout the restoration, whether work was going on or not?

I began to pace the studio, repinning my hair and securing the mother-of-pearl comb as I went. The eerie images had me more disturbed than I was willing to admit. And this dust . . . dammit, this *dust!*

Anger flaring, I headed down the stairs. I'd get to the bottom of this. There had to be a perfectly natural cause, and if I had to turn the house upside down I'd find it.

The air on the second floor was choking, but the dust seemed to rise from the first. I charged down the next flight of stairs, unheedful for the first time since I'd lived here of the missing bannister. The dust seemed thickest by the cozy. Maybe opening the wall had created a draft. I hurried back there.

A current of air, cooler than that in the hall, emanated from the cozy. I stepped inside and felt around with my hand. It came from a crack in the bench. A crack? I knelt to examine it. No, it wasn't a crack. It looked like the seat of the bench was designed to be lifted. Of course it was—there were hidden hinges which we'd missed when we first discovered it.

I grasped the edge of the bench and pulled. It was stuck. I tugged harder. Still it didn't give. Feeling along the seat, I found the nails that held it shut.

This called for Roy's strength. I went to the front door and called him. "Bring your crowbar. We're about to make another discovery."

He stood up in the bed of the truck and rummaged through his tools, then came toward me, crowbar in hand. "What now?"

"The cozy. That bench in there has a seat that raises. Some sort of woodbox, maybe."

Roy stopped inside the front door. "Now that you mention it, I think you're right. It's not a woodbox, though. In the old days, ladies would change into house shoes from outdoor shoes when they came calling. The bench was to store them in."

"Well, it's going to be my woodbox. And I think it's what's making the dust move around so much. There's a draft coming from it." I led him back to the cozy. "How come you know so much about old houses anyway?"

He shrugged. "When you've torn up as many as I have, you learn fast. I've always had an affinity for Victorians. What do you want me to do here?"

"It's nailed shut. Pry it open."

"I might wreck the wood."

"Pry gently."

"I'll try."

I stepped back and let him at the bench. He worked carefully, loosening each nail with the point of the bar. It seemed to take a long time. Finally he turned.

"There. All the nails are out."

"Then open it."

"No, it's your discovery. You do it." He stepped back.

The draft was stronger now. I went up to the bench, then hesitated.

"Go on," Roy said. His voice shook with excitement.

My palms were sweaty. Grit stuck to them. I reached out and lifted the seat.

My sight was blurred by a duststorm like those on the negatives. Then it cleared. I leaned forward. Recoiled. A scream rose in my throat, but it came out a croak.

It was the lady of my photographs.

She lay on her back inside the bench. She wore a long, full-skirted dress of some beaded material. Her hands were crossed on her breasts. Like the bird mummy, she was perfectly preserved—even to the heavy wheat-colored hair, with the mother-of-pearl comb holding it up on the left side.

I put my hand to *my* wheat-colored hair. To *my* mother-of-pearl comb. Then, shaken, I turned to Roy.

He had raised the arm that held the crowbar—just like the man had had his hand raised in the last print, the one I'd forgotten to remove from the dryer. Roy's work shirt billowed out, resembling an old-fashioned frock coat. The look in his eyes was eerie.

And the dust was rising again . . .

Faces

by F. Paul Wilson

F. Paul Wilson wrote the best-sellers The Keep *and* Re-Born. *He's a horror-science fiction-adventure writer who is as good a storyteller as you'll find anywhere. He's got a novel called* SIBS *that will, I predict, be nominated for a best-novel Edgar the year it appears. This story, "Faces," is one of the two or three best stories of the entire eighties.*

First published in 1988

Bite her face off.

No pain. Her dead already. Kill her quick like others. Not want make pain. Not her fault.

The boyfriend groan but not move. Face way on ground now. Got from behind. Got quick. Never see. He can live.

Girl look me after the boyfriend go down. Gasp first. When see face start scream. Two claws not cut short rip her throat before sound get loud.

Her sick-scared look just like all others. Hate that look. Hate it terrible.

Sorry, girl. Not your fault.

Chew her face skin. Chew all. Chew hard and swallow. Warm wet redness make sickish but chew and chew. Must eat face. Must get all down. Keep down.

Leave the eyes.

The boyfriend groan again. Move arm. Must leave quick. Take last look blood and teeth and stare-eyes that once pretty girlface.

Sorry, girl. Not your fault.

Got go. Get way hurry. First take money. Girl money. Take the boyfriend wallet, also too. Always take money. Need money.

Go now. Not too far. Climb wall of near building. Find dark spot where can see and not be seen. Where can wait. Soon the Detective Harrison arrive.

In downbelow can see the boyfriend roll over. Get to knees. Sway. See him look the girlfriend.

The boyfriend scream terrible. Bad to hear. Make so sad. Make cry.

Kevin Harrison heard Jacobi's voice on the other end of the line and wanted to be sick.

"Don't say it," he groaned.

"Sorry," said Jacobi. "It's another one."

"Where?"

"West Forty-ninth, right near—"

"I'll find it." All he had to do was look for the flashing red lights. "I'm on my way. Shouldn't take me too long to get in from Monroe at this hour."

"We've got all night, lieutenant." Unsaid but well understood was an admonishing, *You're the one who wants to live on Long Island.*

Beside him in the bed, Martha spoke from deep in her pillow as he hung up.

"Not another one?"

"Yeah."

"Oh, God! When is it going to stop?"

"When I catch the guy."

Her hand touched his arm, gently. "I know all this responsibility's not easy. I'm here when you need me."

"I know." He leaned over and kissed her. "Thanks."

He left the warm bed and skipped the shower. No time for that. A fresh shirt, yesterday's rumpled suit, a tie shoved into his pocket, and he was off into the winter night.

With his secure little ranch house falling away behind him, Harrison felt naked and vulnerable out here in the dark. As he headed south on Glen Cove Road toward the LIE, he realized that Martha and the kids were all that were holding him together these days. His family had become an island of sanity and stability in a world gone mad.

Everything else was in flux. For reasons he still could not comprehend, he had volunteered to head up the search for this killer. Now his whole future in the department had come to hinge on his success in finding him.

The papers had named the maniac "the Facelift Killer." As apt a name as the tabloids could want, but Harrison resented it. The moniker was callous, trivializing the mutilations perpetrated on the victims. But it had caught on with the public and they were stuck with it, especially with all the ink the story was getting.

Six killings, one a week for six weeks in a row, and eight million people in a panic. Then, for almost two weeks, the city had gone without a new slaying.

Until tonight.

Harrison's stomach pitched and rolled at the thought of having to look at one of those corpses again.

"That's enough," Harrison said, averting his eyes from the faceless thing.

The raw, gouged, bloody flesh, the exposed muscle and bone were.

Somewhere in the darkness above, someone was watching him. Probably from the roof. He could sense the piercing scrutiny and it made him a little weak. That was no ghoulish neighborhood voyeur, up there. That was the Facelift Killer.

He had to get to Jacobi, have him seal off the building. But he couldn't act spooked. He had to act calm, casual.

See the Detective Harrison's eyes. See from way up in dark. Tall-thin. Hair brown. Nice eyes. Soft brown eyes. Not hard like many-many eyes. Look here. Even from here see eyes make wide. Him know it me.

Watch the Detective Harrison turn slow. Walk slow. Tell inside him want to run. Must leave here. Leave quick.

Bend low. Run cross roof. Jump to next. And next. Again til most block away. Then down wall. Wrap scarf round head. Hide bad-face. Hunch inside big-big coat. Walk through lighted spots.

Hate light. Hate crowds. Theatres here. Movies and plays. Like them. Some night sneak in and see. See one with man in mask. Hang from wall behind big drapes. Make cry.

Wish there mask for me.

Follow street long way to river. See many lights across river. Far past there is place where grew. Never want go back to there. Never.

Catch back of truck. Ride home.

Home. Bright bulb hang ceiling. Not care. The Old Jessi waiting. The Jessi friend. Only friend. The Jessi's eyes not see. Ever. When the Jessi look me, her face not wear sick-scared look. Hate that look.

Come in kitchen window. The Jessi's face wrinkle-black. Smile when hear me come. TV on. Always on. The Jessi can not watch. Say it company for her.

"You're so late tonight."

"Hard work. Get moneys tonight."

Feel sick. Want cry. Hate kill. Wish stop.

"That's nice. Are you going to put it in the drawer?"

"Doing now."

Empty wallets. Put money in slots. Ones first slot. Fives next slot. Then tens and twenties. So the Jessi can pay when boy bring foods. Sometimes eat stealed foods. Mostly the Jessi call for foods.

The Old Jessi hardly walk. Good. Do not want her go out. Bad peoples round here. Many. Hurt one who not see. One bad man try hurt Jessi once. Push through door. Thought only the blind Old Jessi live here.

Lucky the Jessi not alone that day.

Not lucky bad man. Hit the Jessi. Laugh hard. Then look me. Get sick-scared look. Hate that look. Kill him quick. Put in tub. Bleed there. Bad man friend come soon after. Kill him also too. Late at night take both dead bad men out. Go through window. Carry down wall. Throw in river.

No bad men come again. Ever.

"I've been waiting all night for my bath. Do you think you can help me a little?"

Always help. But the Old Jessi always ask. The Jessi very polite.

Sponge the Old Jessi back in tub. Rinse her hair. Think of the Detective Harrison. His kind eyes. Must talk him. Want stop this. Stop now. Maybe will understand. Will. Can feel.

Seven grisly murders in eight weeks.

Kevin Harrison studied a photo of the latest victim, taken before she was mutilated. A nice eight by ten glossy furnished by her agent. A real beauty. A dancer with Broadway dreams.

He tossed the photo aside and pulled the stack of files toward him. The remnants of six lives in this pile. Somewhere within had to be an answer, the thread that linked each of them to the Facelift Killer.

But what if there was no common link? What if all the killings were at random, linked only by the fact that they were beautiful? Seven deaths, all over the city. All with their faces gnawed off. *Gnawed.*

He flipped through the victims one by one and studied their

photos. He had begun to feel he knew each one of them personally:

Mary Detrick, 20, a junior at N.Y.U., killed in Washington Square Park on January 5. She was the first.

Mia Chandler, 25, a secretary at Merrill Lynch, killed January 13 in Battery Park.

Ellen Beasley, 22, a photographer's assistant, killed in an alley in Chelsea on January 22.

Hazel Hauge, 30, artist agent, killed in her Soho loft on January 27.

Elisabeth Paine, 28, housewife, killed on February 2 while jogging late in Central Park.

Joan Perrin, 25, a model from Brooklyn, pulled from her car while stopped at a light on the Upper East Side on February 8.

He picked up the eight by ten again. And the last: Liza Lee, 21, Dancer. Lived across the river in Jersey City. Ducked into an alley for a toot with her boyfriend tonight and never came out.

Three blondes, three brunettes, one redhead. Some stacked, some on the flat side. All caucs except for Perrin. All lookers. But besides that, how in the world could these women be linked? They came from all over town, and they met their respective ends all over town. What could—

"Well, you sure hit the bullseye about that roof!" Jacobi said as he burst into the office.

Harrison straightened in his chair. "What did you find?"

"Blood."

"Whose?"

"The victim's."

"No prints? No hairs? No fibers?"

"We're working on it. But how'd you figure to check the roof top?"

"Lucky guess."

Harrison didn't want to provide Jacobi with more grist for the departmental gossip mill by mentioning his feeling of being watched from up there.

But the killer *had* been watching, hadn't he?

"Any prelims from pathology?"

Jacobi shrugged and stuffed three sticks of gum into his mouth. Then he tried to talk.

"Same as ever. Money gone, throat ripped open by a pair of sharp pointed instruments, not knives, the bite marks on the face are the usual: the teeth that made them aren't human, but the saliva is."

The "non-human" teeth part—more teeth, bigger and sharper than found in any human mouth—had baffled them all from the start. Early on someone remembered a horror novel or movie where the killer used some weird sort of false teeth to bite his victims. That had sent them off on a wild goose chase to all the dental labs looking for records of bizarre bite prostheses. No dice. No one had seen or even heard of teeth that could gnaw off a person's face.

Harrison shuddered. What could explain wounds like that? What were they dealing with here?

The irritating pops, snaps, and cracks of Jacobi's gum filled the office.

"I liked you better when you smoked."

Jacobi's reply was cut off by the phone. The sergeant picked it up.

"Detective Harrison's office!" he said, listened a moment, then, with his hand over the mouthpiece, passed the receiver to Harrison. "Some fairy wants to shpeak to you," he said with an evil grin.

"Fairy?"

"Hey," he said, getting up and walking toward the door. "I don't mind. I'm a liberal kinda guy, y'know?"

Harrison shook his head with disgust. Jacobi was getting less likeable every day.

"Hello. Harrison here."

"Shorry dishturb you, Detective Harrishon."

The voice was soft, pitched somewhere between a man's and a woman's, and sounded as if the speaker had half a mouthful of saliva. Harrison had never heard anything like it. Who could be—?

And then it struck him: It was three A.M. Only a handful of people knew he was here.

"Do I know you?"

"No. Watch you tonight. You almosht shee me in dark."

That same chill from earlier tonight ran down Harrison's back again.

"Are . . . are you who I think you are?"

There was a pause, then one soft word, more sobbed than spoken:

"Yesh."

If the reply had been cocky, something along the line of *And just who do you think I am?* Harrison would have looked for much more in the way of corroboration. But that single word, and the soul deep heartbreak that propelled it, banished all doubt.

My God! He looked around frantically. No one in sight. Where the fuck was Jacobi now when he needed him? This was the Facelift Killer! He needed a trace!

Got to keep him on the line!

"I have to ask you something to be sure you are who you say you are."

"Yesh?"

"Do you take anything from the victims—I mean, besides their faces?"

"Money. Take money."

This is him! The department had withheld the money part from the papers. Only the real Facelift Killer could know!

"Can I ask you something else?"

"Yesh."

Harrison was asking this one for himself.

"What do you do with the faces?"

He had to know. The question drove him crazy at night. He dreamed about those faces. Did the killer tack them on the wall, or press them in a book, or freeze them, or did he wear them around the house like that Leatherface character from that chain-saw movie?

On the other end of the line he sensed sudden agitation and panic: "No! Can not shay! Can *not!*"

"Okay, okay. Take it easy."

"You will help shtop?"

"Oh, yes! Oh, God, yes, I'll help you stop!" He prayed his genuine heartfelt desire to end this was coming through. "I'll help you any way I can!"

There was a long pause, then:

"You hate? Hate me?"

Harrison didn't trust himself to answer that right away. He searched his feelings quickly, but carefully.

"No," he said finally. "I think you have done some awful, horrible things but, strangely enough, I don't hate you."

And that was true. Why didn't he hate this murdering maniac? Oh, he wanted to stop him more than anything in the world, and wouldn't hesitate to shoot him dead if the situation required it, but there was no personal hatred for the Facelift Killer.

What is it in you that speaks to me? he wondered.

"Shank you," said the voice, couched once more in a sob.

And then the killer hung up.

Harrison shouted into the dead phone, banged it on his desk, but the line was dead.

"What the hell's the matter with you?" Jacobi said from the office door.

"That so-called 'fairy' on the phone was the Facelift Killer, you idiot! We could have had a trace if you'd stuck around!"

"Bullshit!"

"He knew about taking the money!"

"So why'd he talk like that? That's a dumb-ass way to try to disguise your voice."

And then it suddenly hit Harrison like a sucker punch to the gut. He swallowed hard and said:

"Jacobi, how do you think your voice would sound if you had a jaw crammed full of teeth much larger and sharper than the kind found in the typical human mouth?"

Harrison took genuine pleasure in the way Jacobi's face blanched slowly to yellow-white.

He didn't get home again until after seven the following night. The whole department had been in an uproar all day. This was the first break they had had in the case. It wasn't much, but contact had been made. That was the important part. And although Harrison had done nothing he could think of to deserve any credit, he had accepted the commissioner's compliments and encouragement on the phone shortly before he had left the office tonight.

But what was most important to Harrison was the evidence from the call—*Damn!* he wished it had been taped—that the killer wanted to stop. They didn't have one more goddamn clue tonight than they'd had yesterday, but the call offered hope that soon there might be an end to this horror.

Martha had dinner waiting. The kids were scrubbed and pajamaed and waiting for their goodnight kiss. He gave them each a hug and poured himself a stiff scotch while Martha put them in the sack.

"Do you feel as tired as you look?" she said as she returned from the bedroom wing.

She was a big woman with bright blue eyes and natural dark blond hair. Harrison toasted her with his glass.

"The expression 'dead on his feet' has taken on a whole new meaning for me."

She kissed him, then they sat down to eat.

He had spoken to Martha a couple of times since he had left

the house twenty hours ago. She knew about the phone call from the Facelift Killer, about the new hope in the department about the case, but he was glad she didn't bring it up now. He was sick of talking about it. Instead, he sat in front of his cooling meatloaf and wrestled with the images that had been nibbling at the edges of his consciousness all day.

"What are you daydreaming about?" Martha said.

Without thinking, Harrison said, "Annie."

"Annie who?"

"My sister."

Martha put her fork down. "Your sister? Kevin, you don't have a sister."

"Not any more. But I did."

Her expression was alarmed now. "Kevin, are you all right? I've known your family for ten years. Your mother has never once mentioned—"

"We don't talk about Annie, Mar. We try not to even think about her. She died when she was five."

"Oh. I'm sorry."

"Don't be. Annie was . . . deformed. Terribly deformed. She never really had a chance."

Open trunk from inside. Get out. The Detective Harrison's house here. Cold night. Cold feel good. Trunk air make sick, dizzy.

Light here. Hurry round side of house.

Darker here. No one see. Look in window. Dark but see good. Two little ones there. Sleeping. Move away. Not want them cry.

Go more round. The Detective Harrison with lady. Sit table near window. Must be wife. Pretty but not oh-so-beauty. Not have mom-face. Not like ones who die.

Watch behind tree. Hungry. They not eat food. Talk-talk-talk. Can not hear.

The Detective Harrison do most talk. Kind face. Kind eyes. Some terrible sad there. Hides. Him understands. Heard in phone voice. Understands. Him one can stop kills.

Spent day watch the Detective Harrison car. All day watch at police house. Saw him come-go many times. Soon dark, open trunk with claw. Ride with him. Ride long. Wonder what town this?

The Detective Harrison look this way. Stare like last night. Must not see me! Must *not!*

Harrison stopped in mid-sentence and stared out the window as his skin prickled.

That *watched* feeling again.

It was the same as last night. Something was out in the backyard watching them. He strained to see through the wooded darkness outside the window but saw only shadows within shadows.

But something was *there!* He could feel it!

He got up and turned on the outside spotlights, hoping, *praying* that the backyard would be empty.

It was.

He smiled to hide his relief and glanced at Martha.

"Thought that raccoon was back."

He left the spots on and settled back into his place at the table. But the thoughts racing through his mind made eating unthinkable.

What if that maniac had followed him out here? What if the call had been a ploy to get him off-guard so the Facelift Killer could do to Martha what he had done to the other women?

My God . . .

First thing tomorrow morning he was going to call the local alarm boys and put in a security system. Cost be damned, he had to have it. Immediately!

As for tonight . . .

Tonight he'd keep the .38 under the pillow.

Run away. Run low and fast. Get bushes before light come. Must stay way now. Not come back.

The Detective Harrison *feel* me. Know when watched. Him the one, sure.

Walk in dark, in woods. See back many houses. Come park. Feel strange. See this park before. Can not be—

Then know.

Monroe! This Monroe! Born here! Live here! Hate Monroe! Monroe bad place, bad people! House, home, old home near here! There! Cross park! Old home! New color but same house.

Hate house!

Sit on froze park grass. Cry. Why Monroe? Do not want be in Monroe. The Mom gone. The Sissy gone. The Jimmy very gone. House here.

Dry tears. Watch old home long time till light go out. Wait more. Go to windows. See new folks inside. The Mom took the Sissy and go. Where? Don't know.

Go to back. Push cellar window. Crawl in. See good in dark. New folks make nice cellar. Wood on walls. Rug on floor. No chain.

Sit floor. Remember . . .

Remember hanging on wall. Look little window near ceiling. Watch kids play in park cross street. Want go with kids. Want play there with kids. Want have friends.

But the Mom won't let. Never leave basement. Too strong. Break everything. Have TV. Broke it. Have toys. Broke them. Stay in basement. Chain round waist hold to center pole. Can not leave.

Remember terrible bad things happen.

Run. Run way Monroe. Never come back.

Til now.

Now back. Still hate house! Want hurt house. See cigarettes. With matches. Light all. Burn now!

Watch rug burn. Chair burn. So hot. Run back to cold park. Watch house burn. See new folks run out. Trucks come throw water. House burn and burn.

Glad but tears come anyway.

Hate house. Now house gone. Hate Monroe.

Wonder where the Mom and the Sissy live now.

Leave Monroe for new home and the Old Jessi.

The second call came the next day. And this time they were ready for it. The tape recorders were set, the computers were waiting to begin the tracing protocol. As soon as Harrison recognized the voice, he gave the signal. On the other side of the desk, Jacobi put on a headset and people started running in all directions. Off to the races.

"I'm glad you called," Harrison said. "I've been thinking about you."

"You undershtand?" said the soft voice.

"I'm not sure."

"Musht help shtop."

"I will! I will! Tell me how!"

"Not know."

There was a pause. Harrison wasn't sure what to say next. He didn't want to push, but he had to keep him on the line.

"Did you . . . hurt anyone last night."

"No. Shaw houshes. Your houshe. Your wife."

Harrison's blood froze. Last night—in the back yard. That had been the Facelift Killer in the dark. He looked up and saw genuine concern in Jacobi's eyes. He forced himself to speak.

"You were at my house? Why didn't you talk to me?"

"No-no! Can not let shee! Run way your house. Go mine!"

"Yours? You live in Monroe?"

"No! Hate Monroe! Once lived. Gone long! Burn old houshe. Never go back!"

This could be important. Harrison phrased the next question carefully.

"You burned your old house? When was that?"

If he could just get a date, a year . . .

"Lasht night."

"Last night?" Harrison remembered hearing the sirens and fire horns in the early morning darkness.

"Yesh! Hate houshe!"

And then the line went dead.

He looked at Jacobi who had picked up another line.

"Did we get the trace?"

"Waiting to hear. Christ, he sounds retarded, doesn't he?"

Retarded. The word sent ripples across the surface of his brain. Non-human teeth . . . Monroe . . . retarded . . . a picture was forming in the settling sediment, a picture he felt he should avoid.

"Maybe he is."

"You'd think that would make him easy to—"

Jacobi stopped, listened to the receiver, then shook his head disgustedly.

"What?"

"Got as far as the Lower East Side. He was probably calling from somewhere in one of the projects. If we'd had another thirty seconds—"

"We've got something better than a trace to some lousy pay phone," Harrison said. "We've got his old address!" He picked up his suit coat and headed for the door.

"Where we goin'?"

"Not 'we.' Me. I'm going out to Monroe."

Once he reached the town, it took Harrison less than an hour to find the Facelift Killer's last name.

He first checked with the Monroe Fire Department to find the address of last night's house fire. Then he went down to the brick fronted Town Hall and found the lot and block number. After that it was easy to look up its history of ownership. Mr. and Mrs.

Elwood Scott were the current owners of the land and the charred shell of a three-bedroom ranch that sat upon it.

There had only been one other set of owners: Mr. and Mrs. Thomas Baker. He had lived most of his life in Monroe but knew nothing about the Baker family. But he knew where to find out: Captain Jeremy Hall, Chief of Police in the Incorporated Village of Monroe.

Captain Hall hadn't changed much over the years. Still had a big belly, long sideburns, and hair cut bristly short on the sides. That was the "in" look these days, but Hall had been wearing his hair like that for at least thirty years. If not for his Bronx accent, he could have played a redneck sheriff in any one of those southern chain gang movies.

After pleasantries and local-boy-leaves-home-to-become-big-city-cop-and-now-comes-to-question-small-town-cop banter, they got down to business.

"The Bakers from North Park Drive?" Hall said after he had noisily sucked the top layer off his steaming coffee. "Who could forget them? There was the mother, divorced, I believe, and the three kids—two girls and the boy."

Harrison pulled out his note pad. "The boy's name—what was it?"

"Tommy, I believe. Yeah—Tommy. I'm sure of it."

"He's the one I want."

Hall's eyes narrowed. "He is, is he? You're working on that Facelift case aren't you?"

"Right."

"And you think Tommy Baker might be your man?"

"It's a possibility. What do you know about him?"

"I know he's dead."

Harrison froze. "Dead? That can't be!"

"It sure as hell *can* be!" Without rising from his seat, he shouted through his office door. "Murph! Pull out that old file on the Baker case! Nineteen eighty-four, I believe!"

"Eighty-four?" Harrison said. He and Martha had been living in Queens then. They hadn't moved back to Monroe yet.

"Right. A real messy affair. Tommy Baker was thirteen years old when he bought it. And he bought it. *Believe* me, he bought it!"

Harrison sat in glum silence, watching his whole theory go up in smoke.

The Old Jessi sleeps. Stand by mirror near tub. Only mirror have. No like them. The Jessi not need one.

Stare face. Bad face. Teeth, teeth, teeth. And hair. Arms too thin, too long. Claws. None have claws like my. None have face like my.

Face not better. Ate pretty faces but face still same. Still cause sick-scared look. Just like at home.

Remember home. Do not want but thoughts will not go. Faces.

The Sissy get the Mom-face. Beauty face. The Tommy get the Dad-face. Not see the Dad. Never come home anymore. Who my face? Never see where come. Where my face come? My hands come?

Remember home cellar. Hate home! Hate cellar more! Pull on chain round waist. Pull and pull. Want out. Want play. *Please.* No one let.

One day when the Mom and the Sissy go, the Tommy bring friends. Come down cellar. Bunch on stairs. Stare. First time see sick-scared look. Not understand.

Friends! Play! Throw ball them. They run. Come back with rocks and sticks. Still sick-scared look. Throw me, hit me.

Make cry. Make the Tommy laugh.

Whenever the Mom and the Sissy go, the Tommy come with boys and sticks. Poke and hit. Hurt. Little hurt on skin. Big hurt inside. Sick-scared look hurt most of all. Hate look. Hate hurt. Hate them.

Most hate the Tommy.

One night chain breaks. Wait on wall for the Tommy. Hurt him. Hurt the Tommy outside. Hurt the Tommy inside. Know because pull inside outside. The Tommy quiet. Quiet, wet, red. The Mom and the Sissy get sick-scared look and scream.

Hate that look. Run way. Hide. Never come back. Till last night.

Cry more now. Cry quiet. In tub. So the Jessi not hear.

Harrison flipped through the slim file on the Tommy Baker murder.

"This is it?"

"We didn't need to collect much paper," Captain Hall said. "I mean, the mother and sister were witnesses. There's some photos in that manila envelope at the back."

Harrison pulled it free and slipped out some large black and whites. His stomach lurched immediately.

"My *God!*"

"Yeah, he was a mess. Gutted by his older sister."

"His *sister?*"

"Yeah. Apparently she was some sort of freak of nature."

Harrison felt the floor tilt under him, felt as if he were going to slide off the chair.

"Freak?" he said, hoping Hall wouldn't notice the tremor in his voice. "What did she look like?"

"Never saw her. She took off after she killed the brother. No one's seen hide nor hair of her since. But there's a picture of the rest of the family in there."

Harrison shuffled through the file until he came to a large color family portrait. He held it up. Four people: two adults seated in chairs; a boy and a girl, about ten and eight, kneeling on the floor in front of them. A perfectly normal American family. Four smiling faces.

But where's your oldest child. Where's your big sister? Where did you hide that fifth face while posing for this?

"What was her name? The one who's not here?"

"Not sure. Carla, maybe? Look at the front sheet under *Suspect.*"

Harrison did: Carla Baker—called 'Carly,' " he said.

Hall grinned. "Right. Carly. Not bad for a guy getting ready for retirement."

Harrison didn't answer. An ineluctable sadness filled him as he stared at the incomplete family portrait.

Carly Baker . . . poor Carly . . . where did they hide you away? In the cellar? Locked in the attic? How did your brother treat you? Bad enough to deserve killing?

Probably.

"No pictures of Carly, I suppose."

"Not a one."

That figures.

"How about a description?"

"The mother gave us one but it sounded so weird, we threw it out. I mean, the girl sounded like she was half spider or something!" He drained his cup. "Then later on I got into a discussion with Doc Alberts about it. He told me he was doing deliveries back about the time this kid was born. Said they had a whole rash of monsters, all delivered within a few weeks of each other."

The room started to tilt under Harrison again.

"Early December, 1968, by chance?"

"Yeah! How'd you know?"

He felt queasy. "Lucky guess."

"Huh. Anyway, Doc Alberts said they kept it quiet while they looked into a cause, but that little group of freaks—'cluster,' he called them—was all there was. They figured that a bunch of mothers had been exposed to something nine months before, but whatever it had been was long gone. No monsters since. I understand most of them died shortly after birth, anyway."

"Not all of them."

"Not that it matters," Hall said, getting up and pouring himself a refill from the coffee pot. "Someday someone will find her skeleton, probably somewhere out in Haskins' marshes."

"Maybe." *But I wouldn't count on it.* He held up the file. "Can I get a xerox of this?"

"You mean the Facelift Killer is a twenty-year-old girl?"

Martha's face clearly registered her disbelief.

"Not just any girl. A freak. Someone so deformed she really doesn't look human. Completely uneducated and probably mentally retarded to boot."

Harrison hadn't returned to Manhattan. Instead, he'd headed straight for home, less than a mile from Town Hall. He knew the kids were at school and that Martha would be there alone. That was what he had wanted. He needed to talk this out with someone a lot more sensitive than Jacobi.

Besides, what he had learned from Captain Hall and the Baker file had dredged up the most painful memories of his life.

"A monster," Martha said.

"Yeah. Born one on the outside, *made* one on the inside. But there's another child monster I want to talk about. Not Carly Baker. Annie . . . Ann Harrison."

Martha gasped. "That sister you told me about last night?"

Harrison nodded. He knew this was going to hurt, but he had to do it, had to get it out. He was going to explode into a thousand twitching bloody pieces if he didn't.

"I was nine when she was born. December 2, 1968—a week after Carly Baker. Seven pounds, four ounces of horror. She looked more fish than human."

His sister's image was imprinted on the rear wall of his brain. And it should have been after all those hours he had spent studying her loathsome face. Only her eyes looked human. The rest of her was awful. A lipless mouth, flattened nose, sloping forehead, fingers and toes fused so that they looked more like flippers than hands and feet, a bloated body covered with shiny skin that was a dusky gray-blue. The doctors said she was that color because her heart was bad, had a defect that caused mixing of blue blood and red blood.

A repulsed nine-year-old Kevin Harrison had dubbed her The Tuna—but never within earshot of his parents.

"She wasn't supposed to live long. A few months, they said, and she'd be dead. But she didn't die. Annie lived on and on. One year. Two. My father and the doctors tried to get my mother to put her into some sort of institution, but Mom wouldn't hear of it. She kept Annie in the third bedroom and talked to her and cooed over her and cleaned up her shit and just hung over her all the time. *All* the time, Martha!"

Martha gripped his hand and nodded for him to go on.

"After a while, it got so there was nothing else in Mom's life. She wouldn't leave Annie. Family trips became a thing of the past. Christ, if she and Dad went out to a movie, *I* had to stay with Annie. No babysitter was trustworthy enough. Our whole lives seemed to center around that freak in the back bedroom. And me? I was forgotten.

"After a while I began to hate my sister."

"Kevin, you don't have to—"

"Yes, I do! I've got to tell you how it was! By the time I was fourteen—just about Tommy Baker's age when he bought it—I thought I was going to go crazy. I was getting all B's in school but did that matter? Hell, no! 'Annie rolled halfway over today. Isn't that wonderful?' Big deal! She was five years old, for Christ sake! I was starting point guard on the high school junior varsity basketball team as a goddamn freshman, but did anyone come to my games? Hell no!

"I tell you, Martha, after five years of caring for Annie, our house was a powderkeg. Looking back now I can see it was my mother's fault for becoming so obsessed. But back then, at age fourteen, I blamed it all on Annie. I really hated her for being born a freak."

He paused before going on. This was the really hard part.

"One night, when my dad had managed to drag my mother out to some company banquet that he had to attend, I was left alone to babysit Annie. On those rare occasions, my mother would always tell me to keep Annie company—you know, read her stories and such. But I never did. I'd let her lie back there alone with our old black and white TV while I sat in the living room watching the family set. This time, however, I went into her room."

He remembered the sight of her, lying there with the covers half way up her fat little tuna body that couldn't have been much more than a yard in length. It was winter, like now, and his mother had dressed her in a flannel nightshirt. The coarse hair that grew off the back of her head had been wound into two braids and fastened with pink bows.

"Annie's eyes brightened as I came into the room. She had never spoken. Couldn't, it seemed. Her face could do virtually nothing in the way of expression, and her flipper-like arms weren't good for much, either. You had to read her eyes, and that wasn't easy. None of us knew how much of a brain Annie had, or how much she understood of what was going on around her. My mother said she was bright, but I think Mom was a little whacko on the subject of Annie.

"Anyway, I stood over her crib and started shouting at her. She quivered at the sound. I called her every dirty name in the book. And as I said each one, I poked her with my fingers—not enough to leave a bruise, but enough to let out some of the violence in me. I called her a lousy goddamn tunafish with feet. I told her how much I hated her and how I wished she had never been born. I told her everybody hated her and the only thing she was good for was a freak show. Then I said, 'I wish you were dead! Why don't you die? You were supposed to die years ago! Why don't you do everyone a favor and do it now!'

"When I ran out of breath, she looked at me with those big eyes of hers and I could see the tears in them and I knew she had understood me. She rolled over and faced the wall. I ran from the room.

"I cried myself to sleep that night. I'd thought I'd feel good telling her off, but all I kept seeing in my mind's eye was this fourteen-year-old bully shouting at a helpless five-year-old. I felt awful. I promised myself that the first opportunity I had to be alone with her the next day I'd apologize, tell her I really didn't mean the hateful things I'd said, promise to read to her and be her best friend, anything to make it up to her.

"I awoke the next morning to the sound of my mother scream-ing. Annie was dead."

"Oh, my God!" Martha said, her fingers digging into his arm.

"Naturally, I blamed myself."

"But you said she had a heart defect!"

"Yeah. I know. And the autopsy showed that's what killed her —her heart finally gave out. But I've never been able to get it out of my head that my words were what made her heart give up.

Sounds sappy and melodramatic, I know, but I've always felt that she was just hanging on to life by the slimmest margin and that I pushed her over the edge.''

"Kevin, you shouldn't have to carry that around with you! Nobody should!''

The old grief and guilt were like a slowly expanding balloon in his chest. It was getting hard to breathe.

"In my coolest, calmest, most dispassionate moments I convince myself that it was all a terrible coincidence, that she would have died that night anyway and that I had nothing to do with it.''

"That's probably true, so—''

"But that doesn't change the fact that the last memory of her life was of her big brother—the guy she probably thought was the neatest kid on earth, who could run and play basketball, one of the three human beings who made up her whole world, who should have been her champion, her defender against a world that could only greet her with revulsion and rejection—standing over her crib telling her how much he hated her and how he wished she was dead!''

He felt the sobs begin to quake in his chest. He hadn't cried in over a dozen years and he had no intention of allowing himself to start now, but there didn't seem to be any stopping it. It was like running down hill at top speed—if he tried to stop before he reached bottom, he'd go head over heels and break his neck.

"Kevin, you were only fourteen," Martha said soothingly.

"Yeah, I know. But if I could go back in time for just a few seconds, I'd go back to that night and rap that rotten hateful fourteen-year-old in the mouth before he got a chance to say a single word. But I can't. I can't even say I'm sorry to Annie! I never got a chance to take it back, Martha! I never got a chance to make it up to her!''

And then he was blubbering like a goddamn wimp, letting loose half a lifetime's worth of grief and guilt, and Martha's arms were around him and she was telling him everything would be all right, all right, all right . . .

The Detective Harrison understand. Can tell. Want to go kill another face now. Must not. The Detective Harrison not like. Must stop. The Detective Harrison help stop.

Stop for good.

Best way. Only one way stop for good. Not jail. No chain, no little window. Not ever again. Never!

Only one way stop for good. The Detective Harrison will know. Will understand. Will do.

Must call. Call now. Before dark. Before pretty faces come out in night.

Harrison had pulled himself together by the time the kids came home from school. He felt strangely buoyant inside, like he'd been purged in some way. Maybe all those shrinks were right after all: sharing old hurts did help.

He played with the kids for a while, then went into the kitchen to see if Martha needed any help with slicing and dicing. He felt as close to her now as he ever had.

"You okay?" she said with a smile.

"Fine."

She had just started slicing a red pepper for the salad. He took over for her.

"Have you decided what to do?" she asked.

He had been thinking about it a lot, and had come to a decision.

"Well, I've got to inform the department about Carly Baker, but I'm going to keep her out of the papers for a while."

"Why? I'd think if she's that freakish looking, the publicity might turn up someone who's seen her."

"Possibly it will come to that. But this case is sensational enough without tabloids like the *Post* and *The Light* turning it into a circus. Besides, I'm afraid of panic leading to some poor deformed innocent getting lynched. I think I can bring her in. She *wants* to come in."

"You're sure of that?"

"She so much as told me so. Besides, I can sense it in her." He saw Martha giving him a dubious look. "I'm serious. We're somehow connected, like there's an invisible wire between us. Maybe it's because the same thing that deformed her and those other kids deformed Annie, too. And Annie was my sister. Maybe that link is why I volunteered for this case in the first place."

He finished slicing the pepper, then moved on to the mushrooms.

"And after I bring her in, I'm going to track down her mother and start prying into what went on in Monroe in February and March of sixty-eight to cause that so-called 'cluster' of freaks nine months later."

He would do that for Annie. It would be his way of saying goodbye and I'm sorry to his sister.

"But why does she take their faces?" Martha said.

"I don't know. Maybe because theirs were beautiful and hers is no doubt hideous."

"But what does she *do* with them?"

"Who knows? I'm not all that sure I *want* to know. But right now—"

The phone rang. Even before he picked it up, he had an inkling of who it was. The first sibilant syllable left no doubt.

"Ish thish the Detective Harrishon?"

"Yes."

Harrison stretched the coiled cord around the corner from the kitchen into the dining room, out of Martha's hearing.

"Will you shtop me tonight?"

"You want to give yourself up?"

"Yesh. Pleashe, yesh."

"Can you meet me at the precinct house?"

"No!"

"Okay! Okay!" God, he didn't want to spook her now. "Where? Anywhere you say."

"Jusht you."

"All right."

"Midnight. Plashe where lasht fashe took. Bring gun but not more cop."

"All right."

He was automatically agreeing to everything. He'd work out the details later.

"You undershtand, Detective Harrishon?"

"Oh, Carly, Carly, I understand more than you know!"

There was a sharp intake of breath and then silence at the other end of the line. Finally:

"You know Carly?"

"Yes, Carly. I know you." The sadness welled up in him again and it was all he could do to keep his voice from breaking. "I had a sister like you once. And you . . . you had a brother like me."

"Yesh," said that soft, breathy voice. "You undershtand. Come tonight, Detective Harrishon."

The line went dead.

Wait in shadows. The Detective Harrison will come. Will bring lots cop. Always see on TV show. Always bring lots. Protect him. Many guns.

No need. Only one gun. The Detective Harrison's gun. Him's will shoot. Stop kills. Stop forever.

The Detective Harrison must do. No one else. The Carly can not. Must be the Detective Harrison. Smart. Know the Carly. Understand.

After stop, no more ugly Carly. No more sick-scared look. Bad face will go away. Forever and ever.

Harrison had decided to go it alone.

Not completely alone. He had a van waiting a block and a half away on Seventh Avenue and a walkie-talkie clipped to his belt, but he hadn't told anyone who he was meeting or why. He knew if he did, they'd swarm all over the area and scare Carly off completely. So he had told Jacobi he was meeting an informant and that the van was just a safety measure.

He was on his own here and wanted it that way. Carly Baker wanted to surrender to him and him alone. He understood that. It was part of that strange tenuous bond between them. No one else would do. After he had cuffed her, he would call in the wagon.

After that he would be a hero for a while. He didn't want to be a hero. All he wanted was to end this thing, end the nightmare for the city and for poor Carly Baker. She'd get help, the kind she needed, and he'd use the publicity to springboard an investigation into what had made Annie and Carly and the others in their 'cluster' what they were.

It's all going to work out fine, he told himself as he entered the alley.

He walked half its length and stood in the darkness. The brick walls of the buildings on either side soared up into the night. The ceaseless roar of the city echoed dimly behind him. The alley itself was quiet—no sound, no movement. He took out his flashlight and flicked it on.

"Carly?"

No answer.

"Carly Baker—are you here?"

More silence, then, ahead to his left, the sound of a garbage can scraping along the stony floor of the alley. He swung the light that way, and gasped.

A looming figure stood a dozen feet in front of him. It could only be Carly Baker. She stood easily as tall as he—a good six foot two—and looked like a homeless street person, one of those animated rag-piles that live on subway grates in the winter. Her head was wrapped in a dirty scarf, leaving only her glittery dark eyes showing. The rest of her was muffled in a huge, shapeless overcoat, baggy old polyester slacks with dragging cuffs, and torn sneakers.

"Where the Detective Harrishon's gun?" said the voice.

Harrison's mouth was dry but he managed to get his tongue working.

"In its holster."

"Take out. Pleashe."

Harrison didn't argue with her. The grip of his heavy Chief Special felt damn good in his hand.

The figure spread its arms; within the folds of her coat those arms seem to bend the wrong way. And were those black hooked claws protruding from the cuffs of the sleeves?

She said, "Shoot."

Harrison gaped in shock.

The Detective Harrison not shoot. Eyes wide. Hands with gun and light shake.

Say again: "Shoot!"

"Carly, no! I'm not here to kill you. I'm here to take you in, just as we agreed."

"No!"

Wrong! The Detective Harrison not understand! Must shoot the Carly! Kill the Carly!

"Not jail! Shoot! Shtop the kills! Shtop the Carly!"

"No! I can get you help, Carly. Really, I can! You'll go to a place where no one will hurt you. You'll get medicine to make you feel better!"

Thought him understand! Not understand! Move closer. Put claw out. Him back way. Back to wall.

"Shoot! Kill! Now!"

"No, Annie, please!"

"Not Annie! Carly! Carly!"

"Right. Carly! Don't make me do this!"

Only inches way now. Still not shoot. Other cops hiding not shoot. Why not protect?

"Shoot!" Pull scarf off face. Point claw at face. "End! End! *Pleashe!"*

The Detective Harrison face go white. Mouth hang open. Say, "Oh, my *God!"*

Get sick-scared look. Hate that look! Thought him understand! Say he know the Carly! Not! Stop look! *Stop!*

Not think. Claw go out. Rip throat of the Detective Harrison. Blood fly just like others.

No-No-No! Not want hurt!

The Detective Harrison gurgle. Drop gun and light. Fall. Stare. Wait other cops shoot. Please kill the Carly. Wait.

No shoot. Then know. No cops. Only the poor Detective Harrison. Cry for the Detective Harrison. Then run. Run and climb. Up and down. Back to new home with the Old Jessi.

The Jessi glad hear Carly come. The Jessi try talk. Carly go sit tub. Close door. Cry for the Detective Harrison. Cry long time. Break mirror million piece. Not see face again. Not ever. Never.

The Jessi say, "Carly, I want my bath. Will you scrub my back?" Stop cry. Do the Old Jessi's black back. Comb the Jessi's hair. Feel very sad. None ever comb the Carly's hair. Ever.